SECRET DREAMS IN ISTANBUL

T0150970

SECRET DREAMS IN ISTANBUL

NERMIN YILDIRIM

TRANSLATED BY
ÜMIT HUSSEIN

ANTHEM PRESS

Anthem Press
An imprint of Wimbledon Publishing Company
www.anthempress.com

This edition first published in UK and USA 2021
by ANTHEM PRESS
75–76 Blackfriars Road, London SE1 8HA, UK
or PO Box 9779, London SW19 7ZG, UK
and
244 Madison Ave #116, New York, NY 10016, USA

Original title: *Rüyalar Anlatılmaz*

Copyright © Nermin Yıldırım 2012
Originally published by Doğan Kitap
English translation copyright © Ümit Hussein 2021

British Library Cataloguing-in-Publication Data
A catalogue record for this book is available from the British Library.

Library of Congress Control Number: 2020950142

ISBN-13: 978-1-78527-582-1 (Pbk)
ISBN-10: 1-78527-582-8 (Pbk)

Cover image: Mucize Copsey

This title is also available as an e-book.

To Joan

Contents

1

Pilar

Those inside stayed inside
And those outside stayed outside.

Ece Ayhan, "Keys"

It was 3:00 a.m. when Pilar called the police to report her husband missing. She had held on until then in case he appeared, tried several people he may have been with, left seven messages, each more frantic than the last, on his mobile phone that had been switched off for hours, been to his studio and called every hospital in the phone directory asking if her husband was there. Left to her own devices she would have called the police earlier, but, on Isabel's advice, administered by phone all the way from Madrid, she had tried to stay calm and contained the urge. In actual fact she didn't see the point in waiting so long. Her husband wouldn't just up and vanish on a whim. He was responsible; he always called, even if he was going to be just a few minutes late. If it was this time of night and he still hadn't phoned or come home, and she couldn't even reach him on his mobile phone, then, without a doubt, it was ominous.

Breathlessly she had explained the matter to the policeman on the other end of the line. But alas, the young man on that shift didn't seem to have grasped the importance of the situation. He asked her irrelevant questions in a tone that sounded half asleep and insisted on misunderstanding the answers, clearly considering everything she was telling him so mundane he couldn't possibly take them seriously. Who knows how often he had heard the same story. Who knows how often the missing person had shown up, oblivious of the time, only hours after he had been reported missing by his frantic family, key in hand, and been met at the door by his entire household as he fumbled to insert it.

But Eyüp never overdid the drink. He never showed up blind drunk in the middle of the night. He was nothing like any of this apathetic policeman's other cases. That's why Pilar was so anxious and apprehensive. She wished they would snap into action right away and dig her husband out of whichever hole he was hiding in. But the policeman was taking his time; never mind summoning the police corps to race off in pursuit of Eyüp, he was grudging about even allowing her to report him missing.

"But madam, as I told you, we can't start the process of searching for a missing person until twenty-four hours have passed."

"What if something happens to him before that? What if something is happening to him right now? Will you accept responsibility for that?"

"But madam, if every—"

"Look, I can't wait any longer. If I have to, I'll call back and tell whoever answers the phone that I haven't heard from my husband for twenty-four hours, but I can't wait any more. Kindly assist me."

"Well, in fact ... All right, I'll take down the details and we'll look into it," said the officer, appearing to have relented at last. "What did you say your husband's name was?"

When another policeman called her at 7:00 the following morning, her eyes, bloodshot from not having slept a wink all night, lit up with hope.

"Well? Do you have any news?"

"Madam, your husband left Barcelona at 14:30 yesterday."

Pilar didn't know what to say. She wasn't sure whether to be surprised, relieved or seriously worried.

"Ho ... How?"

"With Iberia Airlines."

Was this policeman making fun of her? Obviously she wasn't enquiring about her husband's preferred airline. She was confused, that was all, her mind wasn't registering what her ears were hearing.

"No, I mean ... Where did he go?"

"We've confirmed that your husband boarded the 14:30 flight to Istanbul."

"What! Istanbul?"

"Yes, madam."

Pilar couldn't say "Why didn't I know about this?" She had to make do with suppressing all the thoughts racing through her mind and mumbling her thanks to the policeman who had informed her. When she ended the conversation there were dozens of loose ends in her head and she felt a heavy weight on her heart.

No sooner had she hung up than the phone started ringing again. This time the person on the other end was her sister Isabel, who, from the moment she had heard what had happened, had been phoning every hour on the hour to see if there was any news. She had waited up all this time, ignoring her husband Paco's entreaties to get some sleep, staying up all night, just like her sister, when in fact what she needed to do was take care of her health and get a proper night's sleep. She was in the final stages of pregnancy.

She was amazed to hear what the policeman had said. Knowing full well it was futile, she attempted to console her sister with, "At least nothing terrible has happened to him. He hasn't had an accident or anything." Then she hazarded, "Maybe something has happened to someone in his family." What if the poor man had jumped straight onto a plane the moment he heard the news and, in the pandemonium, had forgotten all about calling his wife? If she could have believed that the purpose of this sudden visit was to bid farewell to some departed relative Pilar would have been relieved, insensitive though it would have been to the feelings of the hapless deceased. But unfortunately, knowing as she did that her husband wasn't all that keen on even the living members of his family, she couldn't contemplate that as a serious possibility. Furthermore, she wasn't interested in consolation but in getting to the bottom of what had happened. And she kept repeating to herself: Eyüp isn't dead. He hadn't been involved in a terrible car accident. He had simply left. Merely taken himself off, just like that, without a murmur, without a single word . . . But why?

Try as she might to lie down and close her eyes, it did no good. They were two dark holes that only the apparition of Eyüp could light up. Two dark, sleepless, unhappy, anxious holes . . .

The last time she had seen her husband, he was fast asleep in bed. She had considered waking him up as she was leaving but decided against it in case he had had another sleepless night. Because his sleep was constantly interrupted by the nightmares that had been afflicting him of late, his concept of time was all messed up and his days and nights had become blurred. But days and nights should always stay separate; once they merged there was only night.

Pilar kept casting her mind back to the previous night. Nothing untoward or out of the ordinary had occurred. Eyüp had come home a bit late again because he had worked overtime to finish a job. As they hadn't felt like cooking, they had heated up a pre-packaged Mercadona tortilla. If Vicky (everyone in the family called her mother, Victoria, Vicky) had found out, she would have teased her saying, "I would have run away too if you'd fed me that for dinner." No no, she would never have teased her; she would have imagined the worst and gone out of her mind with worry. Which was why Pilar had no intention of telling her anything for now.

After dinner they had idled in front of the television in the living room for a bit. Pilar had told him about her work at the office; he had said little and listened intently. Then he had gone into the study to read and had come to bed just as his wife was dozing off. There wasn't much about his manner to suggest he was planning to run away from home the next day. True, he was a bit distracted and a bit listless, but Pilar had put that down to fatigue. All the spark had gone out of the poor man since these sleepless nights had started. And when you added the pressure of work . . . For the past week he had been working even harder than usual, on a panel he had been commissioned to complete in record time for a shopping centre that was due to open in the city centre, and he had been coming home completely worn out. Wrack her brains as she might, Pilar could come up with nothing to distinguish the previous night from the one before that, or any sensible reason why her husband would suddenly take off in such haste.

Had she been a different woman, she may have jumped to any number of conclusions, or envisioned scenes of torrid adultery. For example, if Ramon vanished suddenly and it then transpired he had flown to another country without saying a word, Paz would have immediately assumed he had a mistress. She would have sifted through all the women in her husband's office, gone through every one of his old school friends and ex-lovers with a fine-toothed comb, settled on one and sat her down in the window seat of the plane in her head. And then, wholeheartedly convinced it was all true, she would have gone into mourning.

But Pilar wasn't like that. And as for her relationship with Eyüp . . . She could sense that the man she loved was in danger, and could do nothing except worry. They had known each other for 11 years, and to this day neither of them had ever done anything behind the other's back. And now, like it or not, this sneaking off to Istanbul without a single word was an open invitation to all the malevolent thoughts she had kept at bay all these years. Might something, like that business with the baby, for example, have driven him away from her? Like the raindrops that beat against the roof and, slowly, imperceptibly, eroded it over the years . . . perhaps he had felt stifled and oppressed and longed for freedom, for liberation from her dreams of a future that would force him to shoulder new responsibilities. He hadn't had the courage to tell her to her face and had just upped and left . . . The mere thought of such a possibility crushed Pilar's heart. To lighten her burden she reminded herself of the good times she and Eyüp had shared. The day they had met in Paris, their first holiday together, the fados they had listened to in Lisbon as the unruly waves crashed onto the shore ... How exciting those early days had been. Love transported them to a different planet, a tiny planet comprised of two people. To a brand new universe in which they inhaled one another's breath for air. They no longer needed the things they used to consider vital. They felt neither hungry nor thirsty, nor needed to sleep. They made love as though drinking, as though eating, and rested on each other's breasts as though sleeping. Given the chance, each would have ripped their heart open so the other could step inside. And inevitably, just as this delirium had a beginning, it also had an end. Unfortunately, or perhaps fortunately ... Being in love lasted as long as it took for the lover to start feeling hunger. As long as it took to come back down to earth from the planet comprised of two people ... And Eyüp and Pilar had both been on earth for a long time now. An Amália Rodrigues song echoed in Pilar's ears from their Lisbon holiday. The weight on her heart did not lift. She crossed the threshold of that mournful song and drifted into a restless sleep.

When the telephone woke her up it was eleven o'clock. She raced to the living room and seized the receiver in the hope it might be news of Eyüp.

"Pilar, where are you?"

"Ah Vicky, it's you." For a moment Pilar wondered whether Isabel had spilled the beans and scared the poor woman out of her wits. Ever since she was a child her sister had never been able to keep a secret. But she soon realised that Vicky knew nothing. She had called her at the office for their customary morning chat, and when they told her she wasn't in, had dialled her home number. It was only when her mother mentioned it that Pilar remembered she worked in an office. Of course, once she had got sucked into Eyüp's disappearance everything else had gone clear out of her mind; it hadn't entered her head to call the office to say she wouldn't be in. Then again, no one but her mother, who had made it her mission to know everything, checked what time she arrived and left, but still, it was only courtesy to call when she was going to be late, or when she was going to work from home. Especially these days, with such a big project on her hands . . .

Oblivious of her daughter's turmoil, Vicky launched into an enthusiastic report of that day's gossip. The opposite neighbour's house had been repossessed. They had nothing to show for themselves now but that was too bad; they could have considered that when they were pocketing all that credit from the bank. Then she started grumbling that her husband was insisting on driving to the beach. He had a craving for La Pepica's paella and had been going on about it like a 3-year-old from the moment he had opened his eyes. But Vicky wasn't taking any chances, either with the August heat or with her husband's blood pressure. So they were staying at home.

"You're right," said Pilar, because her mother loved being right. Then, claiming she had several work calls to make, she deftly extricated herself from the line. Once she had replaced the receiver she was amazed by her own cool-headedness. Although she felt slightly guilty for hiding her troubles from Vicky, there was no doubt that divulging the details of this drama, which even she had not yet grasped, would only serve to worry the poor woman. Just let her get to grips with it first, and then, when the time was ripe, she would let Vicky in on it too. Her mother was 60 years old, her father 72. People of that age needed protecting from stress and excitement. Furthermore, Vicky's solicitude and imperious advice were the last things she needed right now. Sorting this out with as little fuss as possible was the best thing for everyone concerned.

Although a little voice inside her whispered that it was pointless, she decided she needed to call Eyüp's family. As Isabel observed, her husband's sudden flight to Istanbul may have had something to do with them. Granted, his ties with his family were so weak as to be practically non-existent. He hadn't seen his brother and sister for years; even when they got married he had informed them only after their honeymoon, with a brief telephone call. With time Pilar had grown accustomed to the situation that had at first seemed so strange. She knew from her own uncle Ander that every family could have its fugitive. And that every fugitive could suddenly show up one day. So she decided to give it a try and phone them.

Eyüp had an old telephone book containing all his Istanbul contacts. This practically unused directory was kept in the bookcase drawer in the study. Pilar raced inside to find it. No sooner had she opened the door of the study than she was assailed by the loud bang of the balcony door. As though lying in wait for this opportunity, the open window of the study tensed and blew all its breath inside. This breath, causing the white net curtains concealed behind the blinds to billow out like sails, blasted all the large sheets and tiny scraps of paper on the desk skywards, transforming the study into a battlefield. The gust was tremendous. With everyone gasping for a bit of breeze in this extreme heat, I must be the only lucky soul whose windows are blown out of their frames by a tempest, she mused, picking up the papers scattered by the wind and replacing them on the desk.

She opened the tiny drawer in the bookcase in the study. She foraged amongst notebooks crammed on top of each other, crumpled sheets of used notepaper and newspaper cuttings, conserved for some unknown purpose. She was annoyed when she failed to find the trusty telephone book she had always assumed Eyüp kept there. This time she tried the desk drawer. That too was packed with piles of scrawled-on notepaper and used sketch pads. As bending down to examine them hurt her neck, she took out the whole lot and made a heap on the desk. Yes, the telephone book was there. She wondered briefly on which page she would find the number she was seeking, then, like a gambler taking a chance, she opened the book at the letter H. She raised her finger that had sallied forth like a diminutive detective and let it fall on the number under "home" on the first line of the page.

Pilar went into the living room and threw herself onto the three-seater sofa that Eyüp had always disliked. When they had gone out to buy it her husband had condemned the sofa as cumbersome and ugly and had carried on by criticising its colour and shape. And after they had bought it anyway, at Pilar's insistence, he had barely sat on that lovely sofa, preferring instead those sunken, tatty, wing-back chairs. He seemed so quiet, calm and compliant on the outside, but God he was stubborn!

Now as she sat on the sofa, Pilar felt a pang of regret as she recalled the day they had gone out shopping. Why had she been so obstinate about getting her own way? Weren't they going to live in this house together, and weren't they both going to use the furniture? She chased away the thoughts that set upon her as she reached across to the coffee table for the telephone. There was no point in obsessing over such things and upsetting herself. And besides, she doubted the reason why her husband had upped and left was because he didn't like the furniture!

As she was keying in the numbers on the telephone, she realised her hands were trembling. She had never spoken to anyone from Eyüp's family before. How strange that her first phone call to them should be to say, "My husband's disappeared, is he at yours by any chance?" But this was no time to consider what was strange and what was normal. She held her breath and waited. It was ringing.

"Hell-o?" said a young woman's voice.

Swiftly she structured the sentences in her head.

"Hello. I'm calling from Barcelona. My name is Pilar.
"..."

"I'm Eyüp's wife."

"Who? Who?"

"My name's Pilar. I'm Eyüp Bahriyeli's wife."

An exclamation of surprise that under any other circumstances would have been funny came from the other end.

"Ohhhhh!"

The owner of the voice held the phone away from her mouth and called out to someone:

"It's a woman, she's foreign. I think she's Eyüp's wife."

For some time, the only sound was a rustling. Then the telephone changed hands. The voice of the receiver's new proprietor was shaking:

"Hello . . ."

"Hello. My name's Pilar. Who am I speaking to?"

"Müesser. I'm Eyüp's sister."

There then followed a tangible, palpable, frosty silence, so intense it was audible. While Pilar considered how best she could broach the subject, the woman, striving to melt the silence that had been moulded with ice, started talking:

"How are you?"

Pilar restricted her response to a brief, "Thank you." No, she wasn't going to lie and say, "I'm well." Furthermore, she had no time to waste on chit-chat.

"I'm sorry to bother you. I want to . . . ask about Eyüp. I'm calling to ask if you've heard from him."

"From Eyüp? Er . . . I haven't seen my brother for a long time. We assumed the two of you were together."

And she added timidly:

"Are you not?"

Pilar, persuaded the best thing to do was simply spit it out, and feeling uneasy about the mild shock she had inflicted on the person on the other end of the line, had no idea how to proceed. They didn't know then. That meant her husband hadn't gone home. Continuing the conversation would achieve nothing other than worrying the woman she was speaking to, but she realised she had left it a little late to lie or to hang up.

"Apparently Eyüp went to Istanbul yesterday. I wondered whether he might have gone home, to see you I mean."

"No he hasn't. Does that mean he's here now?"

"I believe so."

Nervously, the voice on the other end enquired:

"Erm . . . Are you in some sort of trouble?"

Pilar suddenly felt as defenceless and in need of affection as a child. She wanted to unravel her feelings and pour out her heart to Eyüp's sister, whom she had never met.

"He didn't tell me he was leaving. I found out he had taken the plane to Istanbul when I telephoned the police to report him missing. I don't know why he went. I'll calm down if I find him, but right now I'm a bit anxious. I'm worried about him."

"I understand," whispered the voice on the other end of the line. "No, he hasn't been here. For a long, long time . . ."

"I don't know what to do to find him. If you hear anything will you let me know?"

"Yes of course."

"Do you have our home telephone number?"

"No."

Pilar gave her the number. She had to repeat it once, and then once more before the woman finally managed to write it down. After Müesser had read out the number she had noted, Pilar said "Okay. If you hear anything, please let me know. I'm frantic with worry."

"If he comes . . ." sighed the woman, "of course I'll call you."

Time dragged by. First she telephoned the office and told them she would be working from home; then, attempting some semblance of normality, she set out a simple breakfast on the table. She drank her coffee but, after picking at the croissant in front of her for 10 minutes, she got up and tossed it in the bin. She sat at her computer and clicked on the lighting plans for the gallery she was working on. She made an effort to look over the layout of the fittings, but gave up when her thoughts kept drifting. Then she flicked from one television channel to another, searching for something to distract her. Eventually, weary of watching and crestfallen, she pressed the "off" button on the remote control. Nothing she did helped; nothing could loosen the knot lodged in her throat or lighten the weight on her heart. Her anxiety was so overwhelming that nothing could divert her mind, or raise her spirits. Searching and waiting for someone made one impervious to everything except that person's existence. It made one deaf to every sound except the voice of the person one was awaiting, blind to every shape except that of the one being sought. Regardless of the closeness of the person awaited to the person awaiting, with time, he was transformed into the third-person singular and, the more distant he grew, the deeper one descended into the swamp he had become. When that happened, whether there or not, he became "him." "Him" if he was there, and no one if he wasn't!

Given that she couldn't go out in case she missed a call regarding Eyüp, she opted for quenching her need for fresh air beside the open window. She watched the couples walking in the street. Some strolled hand in hand, arm in arm, while others walked as though they weren't talking, with a gap the size of two people between them. She and Eyüp disliked walking without touching. Even if they didn't hold hands, they required contact between some part of their bodies. This man, who won't walk without touching my arm, can't have abandoned me, can't have just run off, thought Pilar. Without a doubt there was something fishy in this business. She sensed that her husband needed her, and feared that every moment spent dilly-dallying at home would drive the man she loved further away from her. All at once her face lit up as though she had suddenly woken up to a fact just waiting to be noticed. Of course, what she had to do had come to her in the end!

"What are you going to do in Istanbul?" said Isabel, with a mixture of amazement and annoyance. "You just sit tight, Eyüp will call any day now, you'll see."

But she was wasting her time. Pilar had already bought her ticket; she had even telephoned her husband's family to tell them she was going. And there was someone else in Istanbul too, a friend of Eyüp's. They had met in the past. He might be able to help. Doing something would make her feel much better than sitting around waiting passively. She told her sister not to worry about her. As soon as she was settled in a hotel she'd give her the number of the place where she was staying. Besides, her mobile would most likely work there too. Okay, to be on the safe side, she'd give her Eyüp's family's home number too. No, she didn't know her return date yet. She had bought an open ticket but wasn't planning to stay forever; she'd return right after she found Eyüp. All she asked was for her to keep it secret from Vicky. Pilar had said a customer was causing last-minute problems about something and that she had to go to the site in Seville to sort it out.

Having hung up, she realised that sharing her problems with Isabel had exhausted her. Divulging difficulties could at times be more draining than enduring them.

The next morning, as she ran to answer the ringing phone, it struck her that waking up to this sound had become a habit these past few days. Each time she would seize the receiver eagerly, entreating it to bring news of Eyüp. She repeated the ritual.

"Good morning Pilar."

It was Paz. Like everyone whose hopes have been dashed, Pilar was dismayed.

"Did I wake you up?"

Reluctantly she looked at the clock on the wall; it was nearly 9:00. The alarm she had set when going to bed would soon go off too.

"No no, I was up." Somehow, whenever the telephone curtailed her sleep she couldn't bring herself to confess as much to the caller. It was as though sleeping were somehow shameful or awaking to the sound of a telephone more unforgivable than waking someone up.

It was no surprise to discover that Ramon was the reason behind her friend's calling at this unsociable hour. And she began to listen to Paz's hoarse voice telling the sorrowful story that was the first news of the day, frequently dissolving into tears. Last night Paz had found a message in her husband's phone. It was from someone listed as "Marc," who, for some reason, was arranging a date for today in room 312 of the Majestic Hotel. Paz asked what her friend thought of the message, which ended with "I miss you madly." But Pilar couldn't come up with a single sensible comment. Try as she might to say something comforting, her brain refused to collaborate. She was so overwhelmed by her own troubles she was powerless to console anyone else.

As for Paz, while at any other time she would have squabbled all night over the slightest perceived betrayal, she was now struck dumb with horror at having her heretofore unfounded suspicion confirmed. She knew that any investigation would uncover painful, unwelcome evidence and was thus at a loss as to how to proceed. She wondered whether to go to the hotel at the appointed time, but couldn't make up her mind. She obviously wanted to be reassured. But the last thing Pilar needed right now was to find herself embroiled in an intrigue of this nature, which is why she opted for the fugitive's solution. Knowing full well that coming clean about Eyüp would mean enduring the grief of Paz's incriminating conclusions, she repeated the lie she had fed her mother and said it was a real shame she couldn't see her that day but she had to go to the site in Seville. Then she counselled her to keep calm and hung up, having assured her she would call soon. She hadn't succeeded in putting on a show of flawless friendship but, given the circumstances, this was the best she could do.

Pilar poured herself a cup of coffee and started her preparations. She threw a few things into a tiny bag and opened the drawer of the bedside table to take her passport, but couldn't find it. Strange, all her identity papers were usually here. It occurred to her that she may have placed her passport with Eyüp's after last month's trip to Toulouse. Eyüp's identity card was in the drawer of the bedside cabinet on his side of the bed. When she eased the drawer open, her passport appeared as though she had placed it there with her own hands. But naturally, her husband's was not. She was just about to close the drawer when she noticed a black notebook. It was the notebook in which Eyüp wrote down his dreams so he could show his doctor. Some nights he would get up, put on the bedside lamp, pen the dream he had just had, then plunge back to sleep. He didn't discuss his dreams with his wife very often. Whenever she asked him he would brush her off with a vague, "Oh, they're just senseless, bitty, fragments of dreams." Even then it had never once entered Pilar's head to sneak a peek at his notebook. Besides, she wasn't in the habit of poking her nose in her husband's writings behind his back. But of course, this was different. She needed everything and everyone who might possibly provide even the tiniest clue to Eyüp's departure. Family members, friends, dreams, fantasies, realities ... When her curiosity conquered her coyness, she extracted the notebook from the drawer, where it lay, as docile as a lamb. One by one, two by two, she started skimming the pages. The writing became confused with sketches, and concise notes became confused with long-winded lettering that continued for several pages. She smiled sadly upon seeing that her husband had recorded his dreams in his mother tongue. Eyüp always said the best way of telling whether someone had adapted to a foreign country was from the language of their dreams. If he had dreamt in the language he had written them in, then maybe he hadn't adapted to being here, even after all these years. Perhaps, subjugated by nostalgia, he had upped and returned to the country he behaved as though he didn't miss in the slightest. No no, that was impossible. Because it was hard to accept, first, that her husband, who had severed all ties with his country through his own choice, could feel such longing in the first place, and, second, that a craving for his country could suffice to explain his abandoning her without a word, leaving her frantic. For a while she gazed at her husband's notes written in scrawling letters that he seemed to have borrowed from a child just learning to write. She would read them. But, because she had things she needed to finish first, she tossed the notebook into her bag, together with her passport.

She called her office before she left. Many architects' offices in Barcelona shut up shop in August, and all the staff took their holidays at the same time. But not this summer. Although most of the team members were on holiday, the office was open and the staff working tirelessly to complete assignments. Because she had told them months ago that she wouldn't be taking her annual leave in August, they had entrusted her with the deadline for the completion of the gallery. But her requesting leave out of the blue like this had complicated matters, particularly for Nina. Having explained once again over the phone the application plan that she had already sent by email, she said to her long-suffering friend, "I'm so sorry to land these inspections on you at such short notice Nina. I'll do everything I can to be back as soon as possible."

"Don't rush. Of course you have to be with Eyüp at a time like this. Don't worry about work, we'll deal with it."

She had no intention of worrying. In fact, she couldn't care less about the gallery. She couldn't care less about anything except Eyüp, but she could hardly confess as much to her selfless colleague. Besides, lately she had completely relinquished her habit of telling the truth. For the past couple of days, she had been performing a juggling act to present each person with a different lie. She had told the office Eyüp had lost his elder brother and they had to travel to Istanbul for the funeral. Because her colleagues were not acquainted with the particulars of Eyüp's relationship with his family, this sudden trip did not strike anyone as strange. Naturally it gave her no pleasure to lie so promiscuously to everyone who crossed her path, but neither had she been able to bring herself to declare, "Excuse me but my husband has left home, I'm just off to find him." She reached for her bag with a sigh. She was all set to leave.

Indescribable tension assailed her as the plane took off. Added to her apprehension that she may not find Eyüp was the anxiety of meeting his family. What would she say to them? Where, how was she going to look for Eyüp? She gazed hopefully at the aeroplane's tiny window, as though the answer were waiting there. She spied honey-coloured beams of light sparkling on the blue atlas adorned with soft cotton fields. The plane was a white sailing ship advancing smoothly on a sea of warm milk. She was proceeding somewhere in between the ground and the sky, her foreboding more the result of fear of the pirate ships she may meet on the way than of the unknown nature of her destination. Given the impossibility of stopping the plane and disembarking, Pilar sought solace by clinging to the notion that she would return from this adventure with Eyüp in tow. She closed her eyes, but sleep evaded her. As she fretted over how she would cope with the journey, she recalled the black notebook she had cast into her bag and wondered how it could have slipped her mind. Eyüp's dream diary ... She extracted it from her bag and opened the first page with a mixture of deference and trepidation, as though she were touching a sacred text. Eyüp's terrible handwriting, which at times looked like the work of a child, and her inexperience in reading in Turkish would doubtless slow her down, but she didn't let it distress her; after all she had plenty of time. In fact, until she found her husband, all she had left was time. Now time was creeping painfully, at a slower than usual pace. Like a patient in quest of a cure, she held the notebook close up to her face. And slowly started reading ...

★ ★ ★

My doctor, whom I consulted because of irregular sleep and unsettling dreams, believes it will be useful to investigate my nocturnal life, which, in his opinion, must be very convoluted. For that reason, he counselled me to record my dreams, which trouble me, as much when they are manifest as when they're not, in writing. So I, convinced the best way of freeing myself of them completely is by bringing them out into the open, reserved this notebook, which I got from the stationery shelves of Mercadona, for my dreams.

My dreams ... their mere existence disturbs me because, ever since they have been coming to visit me, my nights have become confused with my days and reality has become confused with fantasy. No sooner does my body embrace sleep than they too seep in slyly through the memory of the past, the dregs of recollections, the mist of fantasies and every fine fissure they can find, crowding into the shadows of my mind. They weigh me down with such oppression, such a burden, that I can barely make it to morning.

They distress me with their absence because, no matter how much they exhaust my mind and soul during the night, I can't recall them the following day. I feel only the weight of the intense unease they inflict. Not satisfied with sabotaging my nights, they destroy my days too. If I knew exactly what it is that blackens my nights, I might be able to take some kind of precaution, or find some way of calming myself. But, with the exception of one, that makes it to morning as a vague apparition, leaving my mind in tatters, I don't remember any of them. I awake in the mornings with a sour taste in my mouth from the night before, a pain in my heart and a heaviness in my soul.

Left to my own devices, I think I would prefer putting up with that purgatory to petitioning a stranger for help. But I couldn't keep refusing my wife's delicate, carefully phrased requests on the subject of "professional support." And so, eventually, I knocked on the doctor's door.

My doctor, Jordi Carcel, recommended I put my dreams down in writing to make our sessions more productive.

I answered with a smile that if, at the same time as being incapable of deciphering my post-dream anxiety, I could be certain of having dreamt at all and, by any chance, remember a sufficient proportion of what I dream to enable me to put it into writing, I would have no need to share either my money or my time with him. When I made this comment he must have understood that I wasn't undermining either his person or his profession, that I only intended to capitalise on this chance to bemoan my inability to recall my dreams, because he didn't seem in the least offended. I trust he was trained to be tolerant of everything he hears. That's why, by way of an answer, he limited himself to divulging a few facts about dreams.

According to him, everyone has dreams. Even those who insist they never dream. People aren't divided into those who do and don't dream, but into those who do and don't recall their dreams. Right at the start of the conversation I felt indebted to my doctor for consoling me by sparing me from feeling like I am the only desperate wretch in the world smitten with such a tragic destiny. Yes, when I realise that, like everyone else, I too am sharing my troubles with others, I selfishly feel reassured. When all is said and done, the worst afflictions are those that befall no one but us.

According to my doctor, we can dream endless dreams in one night, but usually the ones we remember are the last ones, or the ones we have in the phase immediately prior to waking up. In other words, it isn't for nothing that nightmares are the dreams we remember the most. Someone who wakes up with a start in the throes of a nightmare is more disposed to remember their dream, as they were still having it when they woke up. In the same way as those who wake up to the sound of the alarm clock are likely to remember the dream they were forced to discard midway. The moments that pass after waking up work against the memory, effacing all traces of the dream, one by one. But there are techniques that can counteract that.

Doctor Carcel started off by informing me that the recipe for remembering my dreams was establishing regular sleeping and waking patterns and clearing my head of all clutter before going to bed. Dreams could easily go missing in murky minds. Before falling asleep I was to tirelessly instil into myself the notion that I would remember my dream in the morning. I was not to consume rich food before bed, nor drink alcohol or take medication. I was none too pleased about that last part, because my dear doctor was begrudging me the medicines I had hoped he would prescribe to stabilise my sleep, ripped to shreds by dreams. He asserted that sleeping pills would construct solid walls over the already obstructed paths of my memory. He did not intend to restore first my sleep, then my dreams, but first my dreams, then my sleep. My doctor, who reserved practically the same distant timbre to refer to my dreams as he would have used had he been referring to my intestines, recommended I kept the notebook I was going to record them in by my bed, somewhere I could reach it effortlessly the moment I stirred. He advised me to take it easy when I woke up, open my eyes a little at a time and try to linger around the borders of the dream I had just had, rather than leaping out of bed. He added that, being sluggish with sleep at that time of day, I may well be tempted to postpone writing down what I remembered until some other time, but that succumbing to that desire would be a mistake. Because, there was no doubt about it, even if I remembered them in minute detail at that moment, I was guaranteed to forget any dreams I put off writing. Therefore, I was to carefully record everything that was in my head, even the particulars that seemed basic and meaningless. At that stage, instead of wasting time trying to ascertain what my dreams meant, I should aim to write them down as quickly as I could and be as specific as possible.

"Write down the people you see in your dreams, the places you go, the sounds you hear, the lot. Even colours, sounds and tastes, anything that comes into your mind . . ."

"How shall I write it?" I asked my doctor, who was starting to speak like the residents of Elm Street. Because, naturally, I had never kept a dream diary before. If such things came with a prescribed format or method, I needed to know what it was.

"As I said, the most important thing is to write down the dream straight after you have had it. If you wake up in the dead of night after a dream, don't delay writing it down until morning; write it immediately. You should describe your dream in as much detail as possible. Sometimes you may find it difficult to transcribe what you see into words. In that case, if it simplifies matters for you, you can try describing what you see by means of a sketch, however basic. What's more, once you have written down as much of the dream as you have retained, I will also request that you record how you felt when you woke up, and what that dream evoked in your mind. In other words, if you perceive similarities or parallels between your dreams and real incidents in your life, or if they remind you of actual occurrences, you should note that down too."

"Perhaps I should have asked before, but there's something very basic that's bothering me. Before I start waking up in the middle of the night to bury my nose in notebooks, I want to know for certain why I'm doing it. Do you mind my asking?"

"So that you can remember your dreams."

"Even I, your humble servant whose savviness in the field of medicine is restricted to the names of a few painkillers, know that much. But what puzzles me is how exactly my remembering these dreams is supposed to help me. You said people are divided into those who remember their dreams and those who don't. Apart from moving me into the other category, how else will clarifying my nights impact on my life?"

"Once we decipher your dreams we'll discover many other facts about you. That way we'll be able to define the problem we're trying to tackle."

I asked, not to be facetious, but because I was genuinely flummoxed.

"Don't you feel that using dreams as a starting point for getting acquainted with people is somewhat similar to using horoscopes as a starting point for forming an opinion of them? For example, do you reach the same conclusions about everyone who dreams they are falling quickly from a considerable height? Once you have accessed my dreams, will you subject me to the same interpretations you've given patients who have related similar dreams to you in the past? To be honest, I'm mistrustful of the scientific value of an approach which is as generalised as believing that all people born under the sign of Pisces will spend next summer in a state of anxiety."

My doctor was clearly accustomed to sceptical clients – bless him, he preferred this term to "patients" – who thought they were clever. He seemed to respond with the same humane calm, both to those who sought reassurance about what they were letting themselves in for and to those seizing the opportunity to show off their intelligence.

"I'll answer you this way: we are going to use your dreams as a tool for descending into your subconscious, for discovering the reasons for your anxieties and concerns. During this process we will of course start off from a number of studies of the symbols of dream imagery and make use of certain generalisations. But on the other hand, I must also tell you that, as a method, before we hazard any interpretations about someone who dreams they are falling from a great height, we examine that person's past and appraise their dream in the light of what it might mean in relation to that past. Which is to say that two separate people who have lived very different lives and who subsequently dream one night that they are falling from a great height are subject to very different interpretations."

To be subject to interpretations … It was a tiresome way of seeing things. Particularly given that the surname of the man purporting to be the guardian of my dreams means prison … This was doubtless an ironic twist of fate. Doctor Carcel continued as though he could read my mind:

"Keeping a dream diary is actually a lot of fun, don't think of it as a duty. It may be that eventually you'll forget about me and keep writing it just for yourself. Particularly once you see how much your night life reveals about your days …"

I enquired whether he too kept a dream diary, but instead of replying, he just smiled. It would have changed nothing if he'd said no; I was a child who had been raised to emulate what the teachers said, not what they did.

As a child, whenever I had a new notebook I could never sit still until I had filled the first page. Exactly the same as now ... Presently I'm going to place my notebook in the drawer of the bedside table right next to my head. Let's see if my dear doctor's suggestions will serve any purpose. Will I, I wonder, soon have a dream I will remember well enough to write down here?

2

Müesser

You'll find it as easily as if you'd put it there with your
own hand,
I've remained rooted in the place where I was born.
                    Faruk Nafiz Çamlıbel, "The Chalk Statue"

Müesser's heart missed a beat as her brother swerved from lane
to lane to overtake the white Opel in front of him. Fearing the
worst-case scenario, she first of all tugged at her earlobe with
her forefinger and thumb, then tapped twice on the car door.

"I beg you, please slow down, we still have time."

She dreaded getting into Veysel's car. Because her brother's
foul temper grew much worse when he was behind a wheel.
How many times had he leapt out of the car and picked a fight
with people right before her eyes! Once, he and a man he had
hurled the filthiest curses at just because he hadn't given way to
him had got into such a punch up that passers-by had had a job
pulling them apart. Müesser inevitably remained silent in these
situations. Even if she ventured to plead with the man beside
her to calm down, to please stop it, her whispers were too weak
for anyone to hear. Whenever she was afraid, her voice would
withdraw inwards and hide somewhere deep inside her.

This time, along with his usual fractiousness, there was
Veysel's unwillingness to contend with. It had taken all her
powers of persuasion to make him consent to this journey. And
now he seemed to be wreaking revenge for being forced to
drive, by racing with unnecessary rage and frightening the life
out of his sister.

"She can jump into a taxi. What business have we got in Yeşilköy?" he had said yesterday.

Perihan had fanned the flames, as though set on touching her husband's tetchy spot, "Yes, why don't we bring out the drums and trumpets and hail her with a fanfare while we're at it! After all these years she honours us with a visit, and the crafty wench wangles it so she has a private taxi at her beck and call. Isn't that just great," she had whinged. Veysel tended to do the exact opposite of anything Perihan said. Perhaps that was why he had turned to his sister and said, "Okay, okay, we'll pick her up. But all I'm doing is bringing her home, that's it. Don't go hassling me with take her here, pick her up from there. I'm not ferrying any damn infidel all over the place; I've got things to do," he had spat.

Müesser hadn't dared say, "The person you refer to as 'any damn infidel' is your sister-in-law." On the one hand, she hadn't wanted to prolong the argument, but on the other hand, because she too was aware of the oddness of the situation, she couldn't see the point of proclaiming the extent of their kinship. What was uppermost in her mind, and for some reason didn't seem to interest the others at all, was Eyüp's presence in Istanbul. Perihan's indifference to that was understandable; after all, they had never met. But Müesser was offended by Veysel's lack of interest in his brother's fortunes. She had telephoned her brother immediately after the first call from Spain and informed him that Eyüp's wife had called. The woman claimed their brother had come to Istanbul.

"So, what's it to me?" was all Veysel had to say.

"His wife says Eyüp has gone missing."

"Am I supposed to seize a lantern and go out searching for him? And he's not missing; how can a grown man go missing?"

"His wife thought he was with us."

"God grant her sense and wisdom," Veysel had said and, using the arrival of a customer as an excuse, had hung up. His anger towards the brother who didn't want anything to do with them was logical, but his total lack of concern for him, his resolve to dissolve the bonds of blood and let them bleed was unforgivable. At that point Müesser couldn't help wondering whether he knew something she didn't. Or did Veysel already know Eyüp was coming? Why hadn't he been in the least bit surprised? But she hadn't dwelled on that remote likelihood for long. And anyway, why would Veysel hide something like that from her? There was no need to delve any deeper into that futile doubt. Whenever those issues arose, her brother was so quick to flare up that, never mind demanding explanations, she didn't even dare ask him any questions.

After the second telephone call, when he discovered that Eyüp's wife was coming, Veysel had flown into a rage and yelled, "That's all we need! What's she coming here for? Do we have to be lumped with her now!" Seizing her chance, Perihan had spitefully added, without wasting any time:

"Huh, the man's obviously left her and fled all the way here to Istanbul. What's she doing chasing after him? Abla, couldn't you have said we'll call her if we hear anything and told her not to bother making a wasted journey?"

Müesser ventured to say, "I could hardly say don't come. That's so rude," but was cut short by Perihan's icy response.

"Oh, don't let's offend her, whatever we do! It's not rude not to call or care if we're dead or alive all these years, but this is rude, is it? Her husband has completely washed his hands of his whole family; he couldn't even be bothered to come to his brother's wedding or his nephew's birth. How many years have I been married, I've got a son who's nearly as tall as I am and I've yet to see my brother-in-law's face! What's got into this woman to make her travel all the way here all by herself?"

"The poor woman's worried about her husband."

"She's coming to spy on us more like. Some people have no pride! Go ahead and make yourself miserable chasing after your husband who's left you, and then, with no shame whatsoever, come knocking on the door you've never once set foot in all these years . . . It's not on, I'm telling you."

Because Müesser trusted neither Perihan's tactlessness nor Veysel's gratuitous rages, she had felt the need to warn them both gently before closing the matter:

"No matter what, she's our guest. Not only is she our brother's wife, but she's also a foreigner; she's coming all that way. Let's do our duty and be hospitable to her . . . Who knows, thanks to her, we may even get to see Eyüp."

She voiced the last sentence in a near whisper, as though making a wish and fearing she would break the spell. Directed inwardly, to herself . . .

When, with a violent whack, Veysel silenced the radio that had started to crackle, Müesser started speaking, both to make conversation and in an attempt to soothe her brother, however slightly:

"I wonder what kind of person she'll be."

"What are you so curious about? Judging from the way she's just upped and come, she's off her head. Sane people aren't for the likes of us anyway."

Müesser pretended she hadn't heard that last sentence.

"Well, she is a foreigner. I don't know."

" . . . "

"But you should hear her, she speaks such good Turkish. At first I could hardly understand what she was saying, because she sounds different. But when I listened carefully I realised that, Mashallah, there's not a single word she doesn't know, she can say everything, and pronounce it. She's worked hard at learning it, I liked that."

" . . . "

"No, but she didn't have to learn. There's nothing forcing her to learn when she's so far away, is there? But look, she obviously set her heart on doing it and she's made a real effort, that's comforting to know."

"Who's to say she's not some Turk who's turned her back on her faith and her nation like our dear brother. And there's you all innocent, getting all excited because our sister-in-law has bothered to learn Turkish."

"Bite your tongue! Who's forgotten their faith and their nation? Don't go wronging people. No, it's obvious she's Spanish. And that's what Eyüp said when he phoned as well."

"Abla!"Veysel raised his voice. Don't keep droning on about when he phoned, or I'll really fly off the handle! Anyone who hears you will think he's on the phone day and night asking after you. He got married and honoured us with a phone call announcing it! No introducing her to us, no wedding, no invitation. You're swept off your feet with gratitude if he phones once a year, yet you never stop talking about your darling little brother! For all you know he might have worked his way through five different wives since he first announced he was married; he could have kept dumping them one after the other. And maybe this latest wife's Turkish, how would you know? It's not as if his highness bothers to keep in touch and let us know what the hell he's up to. And, I don't know about his faith, but he's definitely shunned his nation. The bugger is how old now, and he still hasn't fulfilled his duty to his motherland! God knows what new passport he's gone and got himself over there, who knows who he's applied to and what country's citizen he is now. But oh no, you still won't hear a word against your precious little brother. You just go on, but you haven't got a clue!"

Concluding it would be futile to continue, Müesser bowed her head. She didn't try and remind him that the guest's name was the same name Eyüp had told them over the telephone when he had called years ago to say he was married, or set out to defend her younger brother. Because conquering Veysel's mulish obstinacy was harder than convincing a camel to leap over a ravine. Besides, staying silent was her only strategy for coping with stressful situations.

They followed the sign to international terminals. Veysel spouted venom about needing to leave his car in the car park because it was too risky to park on the kerb, seeing as he couldn't tell how long he would have to wait. They went into the airport together. Müesser managed to pass the security gates without any problems, but her brother set off the alarm and had to be searched.

"I'll tell you what you can do with your stupid X-rays and your sodding security ..." he muttered to himself as he threaded the belt he had just had to remove back through the belt loops of his trousers. This scene, which would instantly strike any outside observer as distasteful, made Müesser smile. She reached over and relieved her brother of the fistful of loose change he had removed from his pocket when passing through the security gates and that was now preventing him from putting on his belt. Then, his snarl still intact, Veysel murmured, "Thanks." Her affectionate gaze effaced the scowl from her brother's face. She believed her brother wasn't the way he seemed; he just didn't know any different, and the only reason he was so volatile was because he was embarrassed to show his feelings. The years had played with every last line on his face and transformed him into someone totally different. His eyes alone remained unchanged; they were still the eyes of a child. Müesser recognised those eyes, even when they clouded over with his enraged glares that were so obsessed with cursing and fighting. Whenever she gazed at her brother's eyes, the taste of the mints passed around in paper hats at mevlits during their childhood filled her mouth.

"There's still another ten minutes before the plane lands," said Veysel. "Let's sit down over here." They settled themselves on the metal bench immediately behind the mass concentrated opposite the arrivals gate. For a while they waited in silence, surveying the scene. Then Veysel asked, as though the thought had only just occurred to him:

"How the hell are we meant to recognise her?"

Instead of answering, Müesser swallowed. So he had finally become aware of this slight problem that had been preying on her mind for several days but that she hadn't dared state for fear of sparking her brother's fury. It had all happened so quickly that Müesser hadn't thought to ask the woman on the telephone. The second time she had called, her first concern was whether there was any news of Eyüp. When Müesser had said there wasn't, the woman had blurted out, without beating about the bush, "I've bought my ticket, I'm coming to Istanbul tomorrow." It must be so simple for these foreigners to just up and flit from one country to another.

"You're very welcome," Müesser had stammered. The news had both dumbfounded and delighted her. If his wife came, Eyüp was bound to join them too. For a fleeting moment she forgot that the motive for this visit was the fact that her brother had vanished. It was as though she were arranging a big family get together. As though they were going to roll out pasta dough, wrap vine leaves for dolma, fry flour for helva and boil sherbet, so the whole family could congregate around a big table and eat and drink and make merry. Engrossed in that romantic reverie, she had enquired only about the woman's arrival time in Istanbul. "We'll come and meet you," she had said. And, much as the voice on the other end had murmured and mumbled that it really wasn't necessary, she acted as though she hadn't heard. And she had been equally deaf to her sister-in-law's claims that she could stay in a hotel. In fact, she had made no mention of the hotel to her family for fear they might say yes, excellent idea, let her go. She had noted down the guest's flight details on a scrap of paper and hung up, with a bitter sweet sensation on her tongue. When the issue of how she would recognise Pilar dawned on her shortly afterwards, she had somehow shied away from calling the number her sister-in-law had given her the previous day and asking. Concluding that if it wasn't such a major source of concern for the person who was coming, then it couldn't be such a big deal, she had preferred to do what she knew best – to wait with resignation. But now Veysel was quite rightly enquiring. "I'm sure she'll recognise us," she improvised, surmising that seeking solace in silence would incense her impatient brother.

"How?"

"She must have seen pictures of us."

"Where would she have seen pictures of us?"

"Eyüp will have shown them to her, of course."

"Abla, have you gone off your head? Where would Eyüp have got a picture of us from? Even imagining he did show her a photo, it would have been from 20 years ago. Didn't you ask her anything? I don't know, like what does she look like, what colour clothes will she be wearing, that kind of thing."

Müesser's tail instantly disappeared between her legs. Like a guilty child, she merely bowed her head.

"You lot are enough to drive a man mad. But it's all my fault. This is what I get for going along with you!"

The woman ignored the disgruntled muttering next to her. Besides, she had had plenty of practice in sacrificing her own peace of mind to save getting into an argument, listening instead of speaking and, when necessary, turning a blind eye and a deaf ear to the events she witnessed. Acquiescing to her brother's torrent of wrath raining down on her head, she trained her eye on the door of the arrivals lounge. She attempted to picture the guest who was about to arrive. As her younger brother was now 37 years old, his wife must be in her thirties or thereabouts. Someone walking alone, constantly looking around her, searching for someone waiting for her, someone a little anxious maybe, maybe someone a little sad . . .

Veysel, who was keeping an eye on the flight information on the overhead electronic panel, said, "The plane has landed. She'll be reclaiming her baggage and stuff now. She'll be out any minute. Let's get up and slowly start making a move towards the door." She was just about to attribute this mellowing to remorse, but her brother couldn't pass up the chance to add:

"That is, if we ever manage to work out who she is . . . oh for God's sake!"

This made Müesser heave a silent sigh. "Ah my Veysel," she thought. "You won't give your soul a breathing space. You tussle with everyone and attack everything. You think it makes you feel better, but look, rage presses down heaviest on the person bearing it, look at how you're crushed under its weight." Naturally her brother didn't hear the troubled voice speaking inside her. If he had, he would have definitely flared up and ranted with rage, as though masking a wound, or barking at an enemy. But Müesser was well aware that people were not as big as what they said, but as what they refrained from saying. Postponing her sighing for the moment, she moved towards the door.

There were two kinds of passengers coming out of the exit. Those who were being met, and those who were not.

Those that strode out looking straight ahead had no one to meet them. They seemed to be putting up a brave front to conceal their insignificance. They quickened their pace, hastening to make it to some mystery destination on time. It was as though they wished to conceal their embarrassment at being so inconsequential from the people standing around them by trying to look as though they were here on urgent business. By way of an excuse for the humiliation of having no arms to fall into after having traversed the seas, passengers marched at full speed, looking not from left to right, but at a secret target on the horizon. Those in the second group, the ones being met, were snug in the secure harbour of those being awaited. They stepped out of the door with smiles and excitement all over their faces. No sooner were they standing outside than their eyes started seeking the person awaiting them, shining like fireflies once they located them. Müesser anticipated that the person she was expecting would not arrive in such jolly spirits. That's why she sought someone anxious, someone searching for something familiar in the faces of the strangers surrounding her in this huge crowd.

Her eyes pursued two separate women whom she suspected of being the person she was expecting. One was a willowy, swarthy, slender woman. She was wearing a white dress with straps. Her face bore an expression of the utmost gravity. The moment she stepped out of the door she glanced around rapidly, then, as though she were in the wrong place, or had regretted coming after the very first step, she strode off with a downhearted demeanour. Müesser was on the verge of nudging her brother to announce that their guest had arrived, when the woman shook hands with a suited man who was standing amongst the people waiting outside the arrivals door. The second suspect was a stoutish blonde woman. After coming out of the door she walked a short distance, as though sure of where she was headed, then halted and scrutinised the faces of the people waiting. Just as Müesser was preparing to attack, another woman appeared through the arrivals door and, quickening her pace, caught up with her friend, and the two of them continued on their way, talking and laughing. Throughout all of this, Veysel took no notice of anyone. He made do with tugging at his moustache drooping from either side of his lips.

Just then the door slid open again. This time a lot of people sallied forth simultaneously. An elderly Japanese husband and wife, a very blonde couple with a large family in tow, tousled youths with rucksacks, women, men ... A tired-looking, thin woman caught Müesser's eye. Her apprehensive face, adorned with auburn, wavy hair, and the purple rings under her hazel eyes were evidence of several sleepless nights. Despite all the sorrow and weariness, it was still an attractive face. Striking, with its full lips, prominent cheekbones, straight nose, sprinkled with barely perceptible freckles ...

The woman walked out of the door at a calm pace. She was wearing a black T-shirt with straps and a pair of cream-coloured linen slacks. She was carrying a bag too tiny to qualify as a case. As she walked she looked at the section where the people awaiting passengers were standing. She was gazing either at everyone at once, or at no one in particular; that wasn't very clear. Her eyes were dazed, as though unsure of whom she was seeking. She seemed to be waiting to be discovered rather than actively searching for anyone herself. Nudging her brother, Müesser signalled the woman she had singled out with her eyes. By some strange coincidence, just at that moment the woman she was pointing out realised she was under scrutiny. They stared at each other in silence for a while. They seemed to be asking with their gaze and blinking in response.

"Is that her?" said Veysel.

"I don't know; she's looking at us too. Should we go and ask?"

Instead of replying, Veysel pursued his distrustful scrutiny of the woman. He considered it brainless to take everything he saw and heard at face value, priding himself on his flair for constantly doubting all things, however trifling, as though he were liable to fall into someone's trap, as though people might trick him at any moment. In his view everyone was guilty until proven otherwise. So unshakeable was this conviction that, because he dreaded being duped, he would never make the first move, regardless of the matter at hand. If anyone had asked him, he would have claimed this trait was wiliness rather than cowardice. Because he was so certain it was better to be safe than sorry, he approached even the new day with caution. And he always carried something reminiscent of fear in his eyes, something others mistook for indignation ...

Once she realised he was resolved to stand there until he received a sign from her, Müesser walked towards the woman without waiting for Veysel. It wasn't that she wasn't shy, but perhaps it was the excitement of following a path that might lead her to her younger brother that made her think there was no harm in being a bit more forthright than usual. Once she was level with the woman, she opened her mouth to speak. But somehow no sound would come out of her mouth. The fact that the woman before her was foreign made her feel intensely self-conscious. They had understood each other well enough on the telephone, but she had no idea how they would communicate once they were face to face. She had never had any need to speak to someone from a different country before. She was already embarrassed by the possibility of her utterances being incomprehensible, or of not being able to understand the guest's speech. Fortunately, the woman took the initiative and asked:

"Are you Eyüp's sister?"

Taking a deep breath, she replied happily:

"Yes, yes, I'm Müesser."

She was overcome with a childlike embarrassment as she pronounced her name. She felt like apologising for having it. She didn't like her name and assumed that anyone who heard it wouldn't like her either. It wasn't that she aspired to a more modern or showier name; it was just that she was convinced names taken on loan from others influenced fate ... Knowing as she did that people were imprisoned in their fate and that fates were imprisoned in their names ... she didn't like her name.

She gazed fondly at the woman who said, "Pilar" as she held out her hand. She didn't feel as though the person in front of her was a stranger she was meeting for the first time, but as though it were her younger brother Eyüp, for whom she had been aching for years. A part of him, a keepsake, or a coded message waiting to be deciphered ... These thoughts gave her a warm glow inside. Tossing her embarrassment aside, she touched the woman's shoulders and, disregarding the distant handshake on offer, timidly hugged her.

"Welcome!"

She then pointed out Veysel, dragging his feet as he slowly followed behind.

"This is my brother Veysel. Our middle child."

Pilar, unsure of how much warmth she was expected to show after just being hugged, limited herself to shaking the grave hand held out to her. "Come on," said Veysel, "let's not hang around here. Let's go to the car." Although he attempted to take the guest's bag, her unexpected resistance made him withdraw pensively.

When Müesser insisted, saying, "You're tired out after travelling. Don't be embarrassed, give it to him," Pilar shyly and hesitantly handed it over. Only after taking her bag did Veysel say, as though it had just dawned on him that she was the guest they had been awaiting, "Welcome Pilar Hanım." With the awkwardness of someone unaccustomed to such gestures, his lips curved in an imperceptible smile.

"Thank you."

At that point, unable to contain herself, Müesser exclaimed, with childlike excitement:

"Mashallah! She speaks such excellent Turkish!"

As soon as they got into the car Veysel asked the guest if she had ever visited Istanbul before. When the woman replied that she had not, he visibly relaxed. So, obviously, like his sister, he too was uncomfortable when he contemplated the possibility that Eyüp may have come to Istanbul without seeing them. The notion that he had shunned and rejected his home, his nation and everything about it after leaving was less painful than thinking he had remembered his nation and shunned only them. Those left behind preferred the idea that he who had left had entirely renounced his whole lifetime rather than that he had renounced only them. Being left behind was a solitary stone eagerly awaiting the chance to trip up the person it was pining for. Although the pain of the one who had fallen flat on his face would sear the stone's heart much more than it would the victim's, it would at least allow the stone to live out the dilapidated fantasy of throwing its arms around the beloved with whom it was finally reunited.

Veysel, who had complained on the way there about being coerced into picking Pilar up, launched into a guided tour on the way back, briefing her about each of the areas they passed. Müesser observed the sulky child concealed under her brother's tough exterior and sighed. He could feign as much indifference as he liked, but clearly Veysel too was pleased at the prospect of making some kind of connection with Eyüp after all these years. Steering with one hand, he eagerly pointed out buildings with the other, relating anecdotes about each neighbourhood, although their sister-in-law didn't seem overly concerned by what he was saying. But, in all fairness, she was refined; every so often she would nod and smile and at least pretend to be interested. Müesser contemplated the cruelty of the woman's predicament. Her husband had suddenly disappeared off the face of the earth and she, consumed by anxiety, had set off in search of him. Having never married, Müesser had no idea how it felt to wake up one morning and find she had no husband, but she had sampled becoming abruptly bereft of a brother. Why had Eyüp become that way, she wondered. Why did he persist in forsaking his family and remaining missing? She had never known why he had abandoned them. For years she had puzzled over the possibility that she may have committed an offence that had upset and affronted her brother. Ever since he was a child Eyüp had never been very tame. He was irritable with the whole household, not just with one or two of them. He kept himself aloof from everyone. He was always anxious to be alone. Müesser attempted to attribute it to his having lived away from home from a young age. After primary school her brother had gone to boarding school. True, he was hardly what you would call lovey-dovey with any of them before that. He would shut himself in his room and immerse himself in his picture books, feeling no need to come out and talk to anyone in the house unless it was really necessary. When he was a bit older, the only way Müesser could persuade him to spend any time with her was by taking him to the cinema. The only activity they could engage in together was watching films.

Even though she received no eager reciprocation, she loved her brother with real maternal devotion. She was 9 years old when Eyüp was born. The 9-year-olds then were nothing like the 9-year-olds today. She considered Bülent, who, despite being 12, still had the mind-set of a child, whereas at his age she had long been a little woman, bearing the burden of the whole household on her frail shoulders.

She had been horrified that morning, a few months before Eyüp was born, when she had got out of bed and been faced with the sight of blood-stained sheets. At first she had assumed she had been smitten with some fatal illness. She had no idea what to do or whom to turn to. She couldn't even say anything to her mother for fear she would be so grief stricken something would happen to the baby. She at least had lived 9 years; she had seen the world. But that wasn't true for the baby; it wasn't even born yet. Fearing the anguish that would afflict her mother would jeopardise the baby's life, she resolved to keep quiet, to breathe her last in the clutches of the horrific illness if need be. In floods of tears, but at the same time swollen with the secret pride of having sacrificed herself for an elevated end, she dragged her legs, numbed with terror, to the toilet. When she returned she found her mother waiting for her at her bedside, with one hand on her stomach. In great distress, little Müesser looked at her mother's stomach, at her brother or sister. She wished to ensure that everything was in order. Because her mother had seen what she should not have seen. She had discovered what she should not have discovered. She stared, first at the sheets, then at her daughter's face. Suddenly her hand, which she raised from her swollen stomach, ascended into the air. Müesser followed the single, swift sortie of that hand with anxious eyes. Following previously designated coordinates, the hand, having hovered in the air briefly, brought down a hard, resounding slap on her cheek, with the jubilation of a hunter who has spotted the prey he has been seeking. This unexpected smack was administered with such force that the small girl lost her balance and crashed to the ground at her mother's feet. Overcome by pain, fear and bewilderment, she was unable to contain the tears pricking at her eyes and finally released them. She couldn't work out whether her mother was punishing her for being ill, or because the sorrow her illness had occasioned was going to make the unborn baby ill too.

It was only afterwards that Müesser realised what it was all about. Like all the women on her mother's side, she too had taken her first step into womanhood prematurely and been punished in advance for the dishonour that would bring her. From that day her mother, who had announced the end of her childhood with a slap, started cautioning and scolding her daughter for no reason and was much stricter with her than before. And although once she was safely out of sight she secretly continued to play with her old dolls, which she had made from her mother's old scraps of material, in the presence of others she started to behave like a little adult. She had helped out with the housework before, but after that first important step towards womanhood, she shouldered a greater share of the household chores. On the day he was born, her mother placed Eyüp into her arms before anyone else's.

"Look," she said. "Do you see how tiny he is? If I'm this baby's mother, you're his second mother."

At that moment Müesser's feelings for all the dolls she had been forced to turn into orphans abandoned in a corner evaporated. She had a real baby now. She was going to be a mother! She hugged her brother affectionately. She loved him more than anyone else.

She would wake up in the dead of night, jump out of bed and rush to his cradle to check if he was still breathing. Afraid of waking him, she would tiptoe to his bedside. She would press her ear against his chest and listen to his breathing, inhaling his infant's fragrance. She would not be easy until she had witnessed the peaceful rise and fall of his tiny chest. She was not certain if it was her love of babies that had made her take charge of her brother so readily, or if her love of babies originated from her taking charge of her brother. What was certain was that from that tender age, Müesser had doted on Eyüp as though he were her own child; determined to be a miniature mother, she had devoted her days and nights to him. Veysel was her brother as well, she loved him too of course, but not like she loved Eyüp. As far as she was concerned, Eyüp was the most important thing in the world. So thoroughly had Müesser thrown herself into this job of motherhood that her mother had no qualms about delegating all responsibility for the baby to her daughter and had sampled the peace of mind of having her burden reduced, however slightly.

But the older he got, the more Eyüp distanced himself from everyone, including his sister. He turned into an isolated, aloof, unlovable child. Hafize pinned the blame on her daughter, saying, "You petted him so much when he was a baby, you stifled him." Naturally she too was upset by her son's unfriendliness, but what was unmistakeable was that no one was as distressed by the situation as Müesser. As though she had predicted way back then that the only child she would ever love and be loved by and through whom she would taste motherhood was her brother, the end of her playing at being mummy hit her particularly hard. For years she would ask herself which sin, whose sin she was being punished for. For which sin was she paying the price by not being able to bear a baby of her own when she wanted one so badly? She had never done anything to hurt anyone in this life, never inflicted the slightest harm on anyone. But still, she had been denied her dearest wish, the bliss of motherhood . . .

Startled by Pilar's timid voice, Müesser came back to the car from the distant destination she had drifted to.

"Where are we going?"

"Where do you think, home of course."

It was Veysel who answered. Underlying that sentence, which, on the surface, almost sounded as though he was snapping, was a tentative attempt to be hospitable. Müesser realised that and felt secretly pleased. She knew her brother couldn't remain indifferent to the guest; she understood that actually he too was excited by the prospect of news of Eyüp, and it made her happy.

Pilar started saying, "I can go to a hot—" But Müesser cut her short immediately:

"Absolutely not. We won't hear of it."

"But I don't want to bother—"

"Nonsense, it's no bother at all. There's plenty of room for you in that huge house. Besides, we've already got your room ready."

The guest looked uncomfortable. Müesser attributed it to her feeling anxious about staying with people she hadn't met. They may well be her husband's family, but, given that they had never met before, it was understandable she should feel that way. Never mind anything else, the poor woman might feel out of place just because she was in a strange country. Particularly when you considered the reason that had brought her here in the first place . . .

"Do you have any more news of Eyüp?" she asked shyly. She had wanted to ask the moment she had seen Pilar, but, not wanting to rub salt into the woman's wounds by being over hasty, she had decided to give her a short breathing space.

"No," replied Pilar. "I imagine you haven't either."

"No, we haven't. There's been no word from anyone."

Veysel cleared his throat, as though preparing to declare something extremely important

"Now look here Pilar Hanım, don't get me wrong, you're very welcome in our house, but just let me tell you, you're searching for your husband in the wrong place. The man hasn't set foot in Istanbul for years; I doubt you know that. Or, if he has, we certainly didn't get to see him. Why should a man who's never once shown any concern for his family, or come to visit them in all these years, suddenly turn up now? Don't be offended, but your husband couldn't care less. Yesterday he upped and left us, who knows, today he may have upped and left you. If I were you I wouldn't go fretting about it too much."

Müesser's back broke out in a cold sweat. She had feared this would happen and it had; Veysel was off on his hobby horse. He obviously wasn't going to rest until he had stirred up some trouble. Please God let the woman not be the oversensitive type, she thought.

"Veysel, don't," she half pleaded.

"I'm not doing anything. I'm just telling her what's what."

"I don't know where he's disappeared to. But I don't think it's like you say it is either. All I know is that he's in Istanbul. And that I'm going to do everything I can to find him," replied Pilar. Her voice was frosty. Her gaze had become defiant, her lips tense.

To change the subject Müesser broke in abruptly, asking, "Are you hungry? Veysel's wife, Perihan, is bound to have had the table ready for ages. We'll be home soon, then we can eat."

"I had something to eat on the plane."

How prickly the woman's voice sounded. Of course, I don't blame her, thought Müesser. Veysel was never happy until he'd made some comment that would get people's backs up. But at the same time she realised it was the resentment he harboured against his brother that was provoking his rage. Veysel had never been able to come to terms with being abandoned, shrugged off. He had always been envious of Eyüp, even as a child. Because Eyüp was brighter, got brilliant marks at school and always achieved anything he set out to do, whereas Veysel was lazy. He had grudgingly stuck it out until the end of secondary school, and then, instead of having the discipline to go and get an education that would have secured him a decent job, he had preferred to loaf about in the streets enjoying himself. They weren't short of money; one by one, two by two they had sold off the plots of land their father had left them and, heedless of the truth that every fortune will run dry in the end, they lived like royalty. All that abundance made Veysel complacent. He was in no rush to shoulder any responsibilities. Once he had completed his military service he opened a grocery store, and that was all the success he aspired to in life. But Eyüp wasn't like his older brother. Ever since he was a child he had had a passion for books. Whether it be a schoolbook or an illustrated novel, he always had his nose in a book. He had even learned how to read, all by himself, at the age of 5. Seeing the child was very keen, they had started him at school early. Although he was younger than his classmates, he was an outstanding student and his reports were full of straight As. Then he got a scholarship for that French school and left home. Using her brother's sleepwalking habit (as a child he had woken up several times in places other than the bed he slept in) as an excuse, Müesser had battled against the idea of boarding school, but, despite all her valiant efforts, she lost the fight. Looking at her unsociable son, who insisted on going, Hafize decided that, under the influence of his peers, he might become a bit more extroverted if he studied as a boarder, and consented to his departure. With no husband and three children at home … Who knows, that may have been the solution that best suited her. Thus Eyüp left home for the first time. And he never again thought of that house as his home.

He would return reluctantly at weekends and during the summer holidays and sit around with a long face.

It went without saying that Veysel had also been jealous about his brother leaving home. Although at the start he had felt satisfaction at the prospect of getting to rule the roost, he soon realised it was more difficult to compete with Eyüp's absence than with his presence. Absolutely everything about him, from his performance at school to his loafing around in the streets, was compared with the clever, sublime child who was away from home. And then of course there was the matter of his looks. Eyüp was like his mother. He had large, deep-green eyes, and long eyelashes … His face, framed with curly hair, and his tall, lithe body gave him the appearance of a young man who was getting more handsome by the day. Veysel, on the other hand, despite being 4 years older than his brother, looked stunted in comparison; he simply hadn't grown. And, just like his sister's, his face too was a replica of his father's. An outsized nose protruding from the centre of his face, like a shrine erected to shame, and unfocused eyes surrounded by stubby, scant eyelashes . . .

In short, Veysel had been angry with his brother ever since they were children. He was furious with him for achieving goals that were beyond Veysel's wildest dreams and for forcing him to live in his shadow. And when that whole business of going abroad to study after secondary school had come up, he had gone insane with rage. He had not yet opened his grocery store at that stage. But he had plans in mind. The trouble was, no matter what he had planned for the future, somehow it was never as impressive as his brother's projects. Eyüp didn't only have ambitious dreams, he achieved every single goal he set his sights on. But each new dream he turned into reality drove him a little further away from his family. When the last dream he deigned to share with them came true, he went a long way away from home to university and never returned. In this way Veysel's rage against his brother escalated. "Now that he's gone and become someone in Europe he thinks he's too good for the likes of the people he's left behind," he would mutter behind his back. His jealousy had turned into anger, and his anger into rage. Furthermore, as time passed, it grew stronger instead of weaker. The resentment he built up inside turned into a fight that he was burning to win but could not transform into a punch up in the absence of his opponent. He hadn't, in fact, been fighting with Eyüp all this time, but with himself. Perhaps that was why, even though he missed his brother, he would never say so. He probably feared defeat by him. What was done was done; he had caught the bug for pride and having to win at all costs and now there was no curing him. And strangely enough, he thought it possible to win these battles in which he wounded no one but himself. He didn't know that no one would triumph in this fight, because wars started in a place where everyone had lost long ago, that these futile battles were fought only between losers. Still, on those rare occasions when he managed to park his malevolent feelings to one side, Müesser thought he secretly missed his little brother, whom he hadn't seen for so many years. At least that's what she wanted to believe.

When the car approached the back gate, she saw Perihan waiting impatiently at the window. Please God don't let her show us up like her husband did, she thought. Her sister-in-law loved nothing better than making snide, needling remarks. Then she would act as though she had meant no harm and accuse whoever she had offended of reading too much into the situation. Because she had grown used to these traits, most of the time Müesser let her impertinence pass in silence. She would let off steam by mumbling to herself and try to turn a blind eye and a deaf ear. When all was said and done, Perihan wasn't a bad person either. She was just a bit under-ripe; she needed to mature. But no matter what, she was her brother's wife and, more important still, the mother of her only nephew. Which is why she would never hurt Perihan's feelings. She went out of her way to avoid it, often defending her against Veysel.

"Here we are at our hovel," said Veysel, turning to Pilar. He seemed to be making an effort to look friendly. He had realised the rudeness of his earlier behaviour and, without needing to be prompted, was trying to make amends. Ever since he had been a child he had spoken impetuously without considering the consequences, and, two minutes later, when he had stopped seething, he would writhe with remorse. He would never stoop to apologising, but he did use his initiative to endear himself in other ways that would gain him forgiveness for his blunders. Müesser believed that the biggest handicap in her brother's life was his pangs of remorse. Because his conscience came to its senses only after it was too late. If he had no conscience at all, he would have no qualms about whom he wounded. But he did. He was just in no rush to reason with himself, that was all. And, that being the case, he spent his life weighed down by the burden of the blunt words he had blurted out and the wrongs he had committed. No matter how much he repented his rashness, his regret never stopped him from committing the next wrong. He was 41 years old, but was still like a child who wouldn't learn how to behave.

"What a lovely garden," said Pilar, opening the car door. "I grew up in a house with a garden. I love gardens."

"And I've lived here since I was born," sighed Müesser. "I have no idea what it would be like to live anywhere else."

The moment she said this she regretted it, for fear it may have come across as complaining. But Pilar showed no surprise at anyone's comments, nor, in fact, took any notice of her. Veysel was trying to take Pilar's tiny bag out of the back of the car, but this time Pilar was determined to carry it herself and was preparing to attack the moment he opened the boot.

"Welcome!"

Perihan's impatient voice rang out. Overcome by curiosity, she hadn't even managed to contain herself until the guest came in through the garden gate before she ran out of the door. As she opened the garden gate Müesser replied, "Thank you." Then, turning to Pilar, who was following her, she pointed to the woman waiting on the threshold and introduced her, "Perihan, Veysel's wife."

She didn't know whether to attribute it to anxiety or exhaustion, but the guest looked paler than she had when she first got off the plane. Smiling wearily, she held out her hand to the woman sizing her up with unabashed inquisitiveness. Perihan, for her part, seized her hand and pulled her closer. Smothering her with noisy kisses, as though they had been friends all their lives, she said cheerfully, "There's none of that cold handshaking here, dear sister-in-law. The custom here is to hug and kiss." Right now she seemed as sincere and friendly as she had seemed offensive a moment earlier, when she had been scrutinising her sister-in-law. Veysel asked if the table was set, and they all went in together.

Perihan was an industrious woman. Not even Müesser's own mother's cooking had been as exquisite as hers. Until Veysel had married, the cooking had been allotted to Müesser, in addition to every other household task. And she wasn't a bad cook. But there was no comparing her culinary skills with Perihan's. Which was why, although she undertook any task willingly, particularly cleaning, she had, according to the unwritten house rules, left the cooking entirely in the capable hands of Perihan, with whom she could not compete. Müesser made no attempt to cross that boundary, and Perihan never complained that no one helped her. On the contrary, she was pleased if no one got under her feet in the kitchen, which was her exclusive domain, a competition she had won, and she swelled with pride when, at the dinner table, the family praised all her hard work. Aware that it was expected, Müesser ensured that she complimented her on the exquisiteness of the food every time they sat down to eat and was rewarded with seeing her sister-in-law beam with joy, whereas Veysel, who considered it degrading to bestow the odd kind word on his wife, hardly ever even opened his mouth to say "this is nice."

Perihan had arranged the perfectly rolled dolma she had prepared that morning on a serving dish, which took pride of place in the centre of the table. The spiral-shaped filo pastry cheese and parsley börek, for which she had also made the pastry that morning, presided alongside the dolma. In addition, the table was laden with beans dressed with olive oil, red lentil köfte and, the family's favourite summer dish, sautéed vegetables with tomato sauce.

Müesser was as excited as if this were the first time a visitor had set foot in their home. Furthermore, she was already exhausted by the burden of feeling responsible for everything that might upset their guest.

"Dinner's ready, let's go in," she said, in the self-doubting tone of someone unaccustomed to telling others what to do. She looked hopefully at the guest's face, like a desperate schoolgirl called up to the blackboard, searching for the answer in her friend's eyes. Pilar looked at least as anxious and bewildered as she did and, as no one had invited her to sit down, remained standing, waiting.

"Let's have dinner first, then you can put your feet up and relax. You may want to go and freshen up in there before we sit down to eat," said Müesser timidly.

Pilar, who, like a compliant child, murmured an inaudible "okay," headed towards the corridor Müesser had indicated, in search of the bathroom where she could purge herself of the journey's dirt and grime. At that point Perihan let out a little shriek, "She really does understand everything. But can she speak as much as she understands I wonder?"

Müesser, who heard Perihan's shrill voice from the living room while walking ahead of the guest deduced, when she did not continue, that her brother had silenced his wife by fixing his threatening gaze on her face. She felt sad for the woman. True, Perihan was not exactly what you'd call white as the driven snow, but still it would be cruel to say she deserved what she got from Veysel. She was only 33 years old. She had gone to Veysel at a very young age and become a mother very early too. For all her sneakiness and artfulness and uncouthness, which came from ignorance, when all was said and done, at home she was Müesser's companion. She was so young when she entered this house that you could say she had grown up here.

Although some people said Perihan got what was coming to her for riling her husband even though she knew what he was like, Müesser completely disagreed. Testing your strength on someone weaker, or setting out to knock them into shape yourself with brute force was neither courageous nor just. Presuming to wound another person was the gravest of sins. Furthermore, if she received even the slightest bit of affection from her husband, if she heard just a few fond words, she believed Perihan would back off. But Veysel felt no love for his wife, and was enough of a brute to raise his hand against her. This business of beating his wife infuriated even Müesser, who did not speak her mind easily and didn't protest, even when someone did her a personal injustice. How many times had Veysel unwittingly punched her when drunk, because she had tried to come between him and Perihan. Time and again she had pleaded with her brother, whom, in all these years, she had never once asked for anything for herself, not to raise his hand against his wife. But it was all in vain. Once he'd had a few drinks he got completely off his head, and then all his loyalties to his sister and to anyone else went straight out of the window. Some nights when he got filthy drunk and lost all control, he would fly off the handle at the slightest aggravation and go for his wife. Once he was off on one of his rages there wasn't much hope of holding him back. At first, just as she had done when she was trying to defend Eyüp in the past, she had attempted to shield Perihan with her own body, but had given that up when she saw it sent Veysel into an even blinder fury. Nowadays in such situations she had to make do with taking Bülent away from the scene and sitting with him until things had settled down. Thank God Veysel didn't lay a finger on the child. Mind you, just let him try ... The mere thought of such a scenario made Müesser's hair stand on end.

When they were children her father used to abuse their mother too. Then, his thirst for violence not sated, he would subject the children to a thrashing as well. No sooner had she heard the swishing of their father's belt through the air than Müesser would wrap herself around Eyüp, using her own body as a shield to preserve her brother from the blows. Deep down she knew that what she did wounded Veysel. Because whenever their eyes met at such moments he would avert his gaze, as though denying her the sight of his expression. He felt offended with his sister, who preferred to defend Eyüp instead of him, and jealous of his fortunate brother, whom she always protected and watched over. But what could Müesser do ... Her skinny body wasn't big enough to defend both brothers at once. So her choice unfailingly favoured her younger brother, whom she saw as her own son. Veysel was older after all; he could look after himself. But was the same thing true of Eyüp? Eyüp, whom she had more or less managed to preserve from beltings during those years, probably didn't beat his wife now. This Spanish woman did not look at all like the type who would sit and passively accept a thrashing. But Veysel, whose contact with his father's belt had been all too intimate, had no qualms whatsoever about subjecting his wife to the same thing now. And, like an impudent child, the more he beat her, the more defiant Perihan became; while she was scared stiff of him on the one hand, she became increasingly unconcerned about infuriating him on the other.

First of all, she heard Veysel asking, "Where's Bülent?" followed by Perihan calling her son to dinner at the top of her voice. One of the things that wound up Veysel the most was his wife's wandering around the house deafening everyone with that piercing, ear-splitting voice of hers. And, as though Perihan were intent on enraging her husband even more, she obstinately refused to relinquish the habit. Whenever Müesser ventured to advise her to humour him, and to refrain from provoking that volatile man to vent every bit of his wrath on her head, Perihan would dismiss her with, "Honestly, abla, I wouldn't worry, a dead donkey has nothing to fear from maggots."

Shortly after his mother's voice shook all four corners of the house to its foundations, Bülent came tumbling down the stairs, like a deafening cannonball. His aunt, who had returned from showing the guest the bathroom, cornered him at the top of the stairs and squeezed his cheeks affectionately. Staring after the boy, who wriggled free and ran inside, giggling, she thought, for the umpteenth time, thank goodness for this boy. After all, the only thing that made Müesser's life bearable was his existence. Her nephew was the sole source of happiness in her life. God had begrudged her the gift of a child of her own but had at least had the grace to grant her the chance to raise both Eyüp and Veysel's son. Müesser constantly thanked Him for that. As she watched her doting on Bülent, Perihan would say, "Seeing as you love children so much, why didn't you get married while you were still ripe?" Then she would jeer with, "but there's no age restriction, you never know, if you put your mind to it you may well find yourself some old codger suitable for someone your age." She had been cracking jokes about it for years and still hadn't grown tired of it. Whenever there was a guest or a neighbour in the house, she made a point of raising the subject and making quips until she made Müesser blush.

She took advantage of her sister-in-law's mildness and, certain Müesser would never snap back, never hesitated to ridicule her to her heart's content. But actually, Müesser did feel hurt. Every time the subject came up, and anyone made allusions to the loneliness that was slowly eating away at her like a maggot, she felt completely exposed before others. It upset her to be stripped bare and humiliated. And, suspecting that one of the reasons why Perihan insisted on bringing it up so often was because she didn't want her in the house, she was mortified twice over. True, Müesser didn't exactly adore the desolation of this house that had consumed her childhood, her youth and her whole life either. Like a fruit that withers on its branch, she had gradually rotted and remained trapped here. If only she could turn the clocks back, if only the Almighty had written a different destiny on her forehead ... But this was the life that had been cut out for and imposed on her without consulting her, the punishment she had been obliged to bear, like an item of clothing she had never chosen to wear. An entire lifetime passed, the days that flowed by were at first consigned silently to memory and then, one by one, inevitably, forgotten. How strange it was to go through life like a diary, knowing no-one would remember even its hiding place. ... She was 46 but looked at least 10 years older. Except for her two brothers, one of whom she hadn't set eyes on in years, Bülent and Perihan whom, despite everything, she considered as family, she had no one whatsoever in this mortal world. She carried on living with the patience of one accustomed to resigning herself to her lot in life. Clinging all the more tightly to those still left to her.

She scuttled into the living room after her nephew. They all settled themselves at the table and waited for the guest to return from the bathroom. Müesser believed this woman would bring Eyüp back to the house again.

★ ★ ★

For days I have been following my doctor's advice to the letter, waiting for dreams to come and find me where I lay. Perhaps they do come and visit me, as far as visiting goes, but none of them is willing to wait with me until morning. After coming and bothering me during the night, they leave just as they came, uninvited. All that is left of them is a little sign to prove they have been there. Sometimes it's a lump in my throat, sometimes a pain in my stomach, sometimes it's several kilos weighing down on my shoulders ... Having an early night and a light supper does no good either. These deplorable dreams that have reduced me to resorting to psychoanalysis at this ripe age, when there was an era when it made me roar with laughter, are still stubbornly resisting coming out into the light of day. I say psychoanalysis, but in fact I have no clear idea of the technique my doctor intends to use. I should also confess that I lack the expertise needed to make an educated guess. But still, whenever anyone speaks of dreams, images, the past and anxieties all in the same breath, I can't avoid thinking of Freud. And when that happens, I fear my doctor will stand in front of me one of these days and declare something along the lines of "My dear Mr Bahriyeli, you suffered some kind of elephant-related trauma during an outing to the zoo when you were a child, and as a consequence of certain surmises you made at that age, you came to believe your thingy is too small. That's the reason why you can't sleep at night," or "It all started at the age of 2, when you fell in love with your mother. There's nothing to worry about, it's just a case of bog standard Oedipus complex." Who wants to hear such outrageous things about their dead mother ... Where I come from, anyone who dares to utter such profanities, even if it's a doctor, is badly asking to be beaten in the middle of the street till they're black and blue. I'm no expert on the matter, but the little I do know is that Freud, who was famous for going out of his way to find something fishy in everything, limited himself to a very tiny area when looking for the sources of humankind's troubles. In his obsessive world, the blessed gentleman's hallmark is his searching for the root of the problem — even if someone just has toothache – between their two legs. To some extent, his fixation with that business, his sleeping and waking with phallic symbols on the brain, is normal. Because, if the story isn't an urban myth, the first time he ever had communion with anyone was at the age of 30. After so many years of curiosity and deprivation it's no wonder he thought "down there" was the source of everything. Therefore, because I'm sceptical about his way of handling things, and even about his intentions, I can't say I'm a great fan of Freud's. In other words, I'm terrified that, after having spent so much time and money on this matter, Doctor Carcel is going to subject me to an unwelcome discourse on the subject of my private parts.

What I want to say is this: although I don't know exactly which technique my doctor uses, these assumptions I've made in the light of hearsay irritate me. But then I remind myself that the main reason why I feel the need to see Doctor Carcel is my sleep and dreams, and try to persuade myself that with his recommendation of "My dear sir, we'll just take a little look at your dreams and the rest will be easy," he can't be comparing me with a patient suffering from a lack of concentration. If I had a headache, the doctor wouldn't start off by examining my stomach, I tell myself. If it's my dreams that are disturbing me, then my doctor will naturally begin with them. Inside, my head resembles a rubbish dump; I thrash about, with no idea what to think.

I look at my dream diary from a distance, with the dismay of a child who can't play with his new toy. I want to write something right away. In the end I decided it didn't necessarily have to be a dream I had had recently. Because in fact, I do have a dream. I even described it to the doctor at our first meeting. A patchy, bitty dream I have in fragments some nights, which I know is unsettling just from the way I wake up feeling completely drained. A dream I can never remember completely, no matter how hard I try, a niggling, irritating puzzle. Like the ones in the newspaper that infuriate me when I can't finish them, so I vent my rage on the woman in the middle of the page by drawing a beard and moustache on her. My dear doctor, may I please request that when you're reading my diary you don't get fixated with this beard and moustache business. It is well known that, in certain situations, even your master Freud accepted that a pipe was just a pipe. Drawing a beard and moustache on the women in newspaper puzzles really can sometimes just be drawing a beard and moustache. Just for the hell of it, in other words ... And besides, I'm not keeping this diary so you can judge my words, but so you can read my dreams. In which case you needn't bother reading what I've written so far. In fact, you won't read it! You don't know it yet, but I'm writing these sentences in a tongue you're none too conversant in.

The other day, when I opened the notebook, I started writing in Turkish before I noticed. And, once I realised, I continued. I enjoyed talking to my doctor, or rather to myself, in my mother tongue. I think that knowing I'm not going to give him this notebook leaves me free to gabble on as I like.

Besides, quite frankly, I'm not really accustomed to my sentences reaching others unchecked, that is to say, in the same state as they race through my mind. Even if I occasionally say things that seem tactless or impulsive, anyone who knows me will realise that it isn't by accident but by design, that I am someone who's enough in control not to blurt out everything as soon as it comes into my head. But on the other hand, I naturally haven't forgotten that I haven't started to keep this diary for my own entertainment, but on my doctor's advice. Therefore, yes, of course I'm going to give him the notebook that he requires. The problem is that, as well as seeing clearly that someone in my situation shouldn't hide anything from his doctor, I believe there's nothing strange about my deciding myself how I am going to phrase what I have to say. I am not going to hold back from my doctor the dreams he has charged me to remember and reveal. That's why I'm going to prepare a Catalan edition for my dear doctor, which includes the answers to his questions. In other words, with myself I'm going to share everything, but with him only what he wants to know. I believe it's best that way, that is to say that, despite being doctor and patient, our relationship should be based on respect for our mutual privacy.

Okay, so let's move on to one of the chapters in Doctor Carcel's edition, that fragmented, bitty dream dating back to the distant past.

In my dream we're in the house in Istanbul, in the room I shared with my sister before I started school. My sister is sitting on her bed combing her hair. She's crying while she combs it. I can see her thin shoulders trembling. As she cries she sheds heavy weights from her shoulders. Those weights are Zagor's speech bubbles. One by one, each word flows down. Then it turns into a louse. The words are transformed into giant lice. I know they feed off people's blood and that they're easy to catch. I'm afraid I too might catch them. As they fall out of my sister's hair I feel lighter. The wind blows its breath in through the open window, and, like pregnant women the curtains swell up, then deflate. My sister turns her face towards me, as though she didn't know I was there, or that I was watching her. If she knew I was watching, she would hide her eyes, puffy from crying. So, that means she doesn't know I'm watching her. My sister's face is the oddest colour, it seems almost violet. All that time she spends talking to violets has turned her face violet. I have no idea what time it is. It may be the middle of the night or it may be early morning. There is a chilling desolation hanging over the house. The branches of the tree in the garden are beating against the window. My sister is sitting down combing her hair, her shoulders trembling. I close my eyes to avoid seeing what's falling out of it.

I still have that dream. Or rather, some mornings, even though I can't remember it, I know I have had it because I wake up overwhelmed with weariness. I've done all the things my doctor said would help me to remember my dreams. Just as he told me, I stayed exactly where I was after I woke up, pretending I was still asleep so I could catch it before it slipped away and consigned itself to oblivion, but my mind would not be fooled. The dream about my sister didn't click its fingers for its beginning and end to jump into line before it made its appearance. I can only identify it because of the desolate weariness afflicting me. When Doctor Carcel asked me to explain the feeling, I couldn't. None of the words I knew could describe it. It's not anger, it's not grief, it's not resentment. If I attempted to draw it ... I would draw glass. A glass that has turned into tiny shards scattered in all directions ... Or rather, what remains of the glass. How funny, each of those shards will think it's a glass, but that glass will never exist again. Yes, following that dream of my sister combing her hair whilst crying, I feel just like a glass that has shattered into thousands of pieces. Too many pieces for them to ever be able to join together again, at a great distance from myself, or rather, from the wholeness of the fragments that make me into me, scattered, shattered ... And hand in hand with that sensation is the feeling that nothing can ever be the way it was again. Actually I don't even know what the way it was means. Which is why I couldn't come up with an answer when my doctor asked, "How long ago for example?"

These fragments turn me into a child deprived of his favourite toy, or a badly beaten up adult. That's why I can't tell how far back in the past it is. My doctor asked me what comics and lice signify for me. Yes, I used to read comics as a child, and did catch lice a few times. I didn't remember it too clearly. When he asked about the connection between the colour of my sister's face and violets, I told him she had a thing about violets and that she even spoke silently to the flowers as she watered them. He may have secretly thought my sister was the one who really needed to go and see him. But of course he knows I haven't seen her in a very long time. He asked me questions about my reluctance to go to Istanbul and about my relationship with my family. I told him I had grown up away from home, that after I had gone away to school I had settled abroad and that with time I had drifted away from them. I know he wasn't convinced. No one would be. To this day I've never yet met anyone who's asked me that question and been convinced by my explanation. I don't know why, but no one wants to accept that it's normal for someone to make the choice to renounce the people they are tied to by blood. People divorce their wife or abandon their best friend, but no one is willing to understand someone who is tired of their mother or sister, or who prefers to keep their distance because they can't find anything in common with them. For some reason everyone is bent on searching for profound psychological explanations, periods of your life that require analysis, deep traumas, etcetera at the root of that decision. When someone who has grown up as an only child loses his parents and ends up a lone wolf, that amounts to nothing more than a sad situation; it doesn't call for any major psychological analysis, whereas everyone considers the situation of someone who decides he doesn't belong in his home and feels no need to see his home and family, who believes his family is dysfunctional, as unhealthy. I don't know if it's because he knows how defensive I am about it, but my doctor showed no surprise at my finding it unnecessary to see my family. He only asked what my reasons were. He listened to what I said and jotted down several notes in the notebook in front of him. And I watched him, imagining he had scribbled down a whole lot of nonsense that had nothing to do with the matter at hand. I fancied he was not satisfied by my explanation, that he felt the fact that I stayed away from them had wreaked terrible havoc on my soul; in short, I figured that, exactly like everyone else, he did not believe that someone can renounce his relationship with his family in the same way as he can his other relationships and that that can be a perfectly normal state of affairs. But I also appreciated the fact that at least he was professional enough to spare me any extreme reactions. When, instead of trotting out old women's conclusions like, "You see, you're dreaming about the sister you haven't seen in years, that means you need your family's love," he said, "We're going to try and get you to remember your dreams. Then, that is, when you can recall them well enough, we'll have a chance to discuss why the dream about your sister makes you feel this way," it made me feel, albeit ever so slightly, relieved. Although granted, later on, after I related a childhood memory, he did try and act out the comedy of attributing the reason for my not being able to remember my dreams to my wanting to ingratiate myself with my mother, but still. I mean, didn't they give him that diploma partly for trying his luck with every possibility that entered his head? When all is said and done, I think the poor man's branch of science is partly based on the optimistic principle that nothing's impossible. That's why it's not a good idea to give too much credence to Doctor Carcel.

3

Veysel

I asked you
to come find me take me
put my memory to sleep
wherever you wish.

Birhan Keskin, "Snail"

Today he didn't touch the sautéed vegetables he generally
devoured with such relish; Veysel left those exquisite aubergines,
those crunchy courgettes and those perfect potatoes forsaken
and forlorn on the plate. Although not so much as a single
morsel had passed his lips all day, he didn't feel like eating
anything; his stomach didn't raise even the tiniest objection
to the day that had passed in such unmitigated emptiness.
Waving away his sister, who was reaching for his plate to serve
him some beans, he rescued his plate from the beans, and the
household from the peril of Perihan's tongue, that complained
more about her food being left on the plate than about its
being left untasted. If someone didn't try a dish, it might be
because they weren't hungry, but if they failed to finish a meal
they had already started, his wife assumed they didn't like it,
which meant handing her a conversation piece on a plate and
resigning oneself in advance to an onslaught of protestations
that would invariably persist for hours. He wasn't in the mood
to endure her reproaches right now. As it was, the mosquito
buzzing around the table was doing its utmost to drive him
insane. This house sprayed more insecticide than any other
house in the neighbourhood could envisage; they drew no lines

when it came to measures against mosquitoes. How the insects dared to trespass in his home despite all that was a source of wonder to Veysel.

His mind was all mixed up. If only he could go to bed and drift into a sound sleep. But chance would be a fine thing! Never mind during the day, he couldn't even enjoy decent sleep at night in this madhouse he lived in. What with the boy's relentless racket on the one hand, and Perihan's chin that didn't stop wagging, even for one moment, on the other, and his sister's imposing silence that provoked echoes from all the sounds around them ... And as if all that wasn't already enough, there was this damn guest now as well. And then there was Eyüp's ghost ... Like he really needed it ...

Whenever he imagined his brother, the image of that 14-year-old anxious teenager he met standing at the gates of Galatasaray Secondary School swam into his vision. It was 1976, and Veysel hadn't left to do his military service yet. It was the era when the complaints about his having left full-time education had ended but the recommendations regarding his need to knuckle down and make something of his life had not yet started. Besides, ever since they had buried their father nine years ago, there was no one left whose wrath he feared or who was capable of cowing him. He was well practiced in turning a deaf ear, to recommendations and rebukes alike. At worst, his mother talked incessantly before falling silent, hoping to use the black earth she would be consigned to as a tool for licking her son into shape, constantly reminding him she had one foot in the grave, now that she was a truly old woman. That was the extent of her influence. Veysel was, after all, the eldest son. Even though he hadn't started to earn his living yet he was still, in a way, the master of the house, the backbone of the family.

Most of his friends who hadn't done well at school and had set out to have a stab at the wider world had found some kind of job, thus exchanging leisure for labour. But, using his prospective military service as a pretext, Veysel was in no rush whatsoever to knuckle down and become a responsible citizen.

He lived a life of ease, relishing his layabout existence, aspiring only to prolong it.

That day, he and his friend Salim, who was idle like him, were loafing about Beyoğlu, whiling away the time before the evening's match. It was the end of May, the sky was a deep blue and the sun was shining. A fine, warm breeze tickled the city with mischievous fingers. He could barely contain his excitement as he contemplated the big match Cimbom would play that evening. Two weeks ago they had lost the first cup final against Trabzon 1–0. He had squirmed on the edge of his seat until the referee had blown the whistle. There was little in life that mattered to him as much as Galatasaray.

Coming out of the fish market and walking up the street, he was speculating about the evening's match while eyeing up the girls Salim was pointing out and rating on a scale of one to ten. When they got to Galatasaray Square, Salim indicated a group of some seven or eight boys and girls gathered outside the school and said, "Hey, isn't that your brother over there?" Following his friend's finger with his gaze, Veysel spied his brother convulsed with laughter at something the girl in front of him was saying, looking infinitely happier than he ever did at home with them. He was wearing a navy blue trench coat over his swanky school uniform, and he stood there with one hand shoved in his pocket, looking very sure of himself. Then he checked out the girl his brother was chatting to. She laughed loudly as she tossed her long blonde hair, trying to hold down her skirt that the wind was blowing up. She was wearing the uniform of Saint Benoît secondary school, which they had stood in front of a few hours previously, rating the girls as they were doing the rounds of Karaköy. So she too was the stuck-up, conceited type, just like all the others. Girls that studied in fancy schools like that were all snobs. They turned up their noses at anyone who wasn't one of them, not even deigning to say a simple hello. The Saint Benoît girls had marched past them today, all high and mighty, as if they owned the place. True, he wasn't exactly mad about them either. He had only stood outside the school because Salim had insisted. Otherwise what business did he have hobnobbing with butter-wouldn't-melt-in-their-mouth schoolgirls . . .

The happy group talked loudly, oblivious to passers-by, frequently bursting into fits of laughter. Veysel had taken a step towards his brother, who hadn't noticed him until then, and their eyes met. No sooner had he seen his older brother's face than Eyüp's fell, as though he had just stepped into a house where someone had died. Gone was the child who, just a moment before, had been giggling helplessly, radiating a glow of elation. In his place was an anxious, embarrassed boy trying to crawl away unseen, like a dejected insect. He was thrown off balance, like a boxer who has just received a punch; he turned pale and remained rooted to the spot. He looked at his brother, his gaze desperate. His eyes wide with apprehension, he seemed to be silently imploring him not to approach, to go away. Veysel realised he was embarrassed to introduce his elder brother to his friends. What's more, he perceived this wasn't just a child's tendency to shy away from adults and try to stop them from meeting his friends. Because Veysel couldn't be considered all that old; there were only 4 years between them. There were no two ways about it: Eyüp was ashamed of his brother and that was that. He thought he was beneath him and didn't think him worthy enough to introduce to his friends. Besides, Veysel knew his brother didn't think much of him or, in fact, of anyone else in the family. That he was growing further and further away from them all, that he saw himself as different from the rest of them and remained aloof . . . He went to a swanky school, learned foreign languages, hung out with the sons and daughters of high society and was ashamed of his older brother, whom he felt was inferior. Veysel had plenty of cash. And he could run rings around his brother's snotty, high-society, mummy's and daddy's girls and boys. But deep down he knew that something was missing, that no matter what he did, he could never be one of those adolescents standing a few paces away. The problem was, he couldn't work out just what that missing piece was, or where it came from. Could it be his lack of education, the way he dressed or spoke; he had no idea what it was about him that set him apart from people like Eyüp. What he did know was this, that his brother couldn't bear to have him anywhere near him. Even Salim, who was itching to mingle with that group where there were girls, noticed what was going on, or so it seemed to Veysel. They filled the growing silence between them with the thoughts going through their heads. He neither said "Yes, that's my brother", nor did Salim repeat his question. They just stood side by side, staring silently at the happy crowd. For a brief moment, long enough to despise his brother but too short to love himself, he stared at Eyüp's frightened, embarrassed face with eyes that revealed his resentment. Then, avoiding what his brother feared, in other words, without cramping his style by pestering him, he walked off without giving anyone the slightest indication that they were acquainted. Leaving the laughter of the Saint Benoît girl behind him and muttering a terrible oath under his breath, he headed towards the Tunnel.

Luckily Cimbom won the match that day. Otherwise who knows how Veysel would have purged all that rage; God help them if he'd had to deal with the fury of defeat as well, he would have really exploded. He would never have overlooked his brother's antics then but would have made sure he paid him back without mercy the moment he got the chance. To tell the truth, considering that that memory was the first thing that came to his mind whenever he thought of Eyüp, even years later, you couldn't really say he had overlooked them ... But at least, in honour of Cimbom's triumph, he had turned a blind eye to his brother's insult and decided not to land his fist in the centre of his mouth at the first opportunity. True, it wouldn't have made much difference even if he hadn't decided to spare him; like there was any chance of touching a single hair on the head of that snivelling pampered brat they all fawned over and worshipped. Eventually Veysel had buried his resentment deep inside him, in a place that was much more dangerous. That night he didn't just celebrate the score of the match, but Cimbom's sixth Turkish Cup too, and he had tried not to think of his brother. Boy, that had been some match ...

The supporters were packed like sardines, breathless with excitement, in the then still mixed stands at Galatasaray, which had lost the last match 1–0. Veysel had shouted so much that day he had lost his voice. He couldn't bear to watch the critical shots; he had covered his face with his hands and made do with listening to everyone else's reactions. It was as though, anyhow he watched Trabzon score a goal, as God was his witness, the eyes that beheld it would never recover, but be blighted by eternal darkness until the end of time. Although he relaxed a tiny bit when Bülent's goal at the start of the second half put them 1–0 in the lead, he still didn't heave any sighs of relief. They needed another goal to win the cup. But when 90 minutes were up with still just that one goal, the score had to be settled with extra time. The intervals imposed on them because of power cuts just at that precise moment put a serious strain on his perilously pounding heart. The match, which looked like it would last forever, went on and on, while Veysel, in mortal terror of the rival team scoring a goal, watched with bated breath, dying a thousand deaths, sweating and trembling. At the third power cut he exploded, "For God's sake, if we're going to win let's get on with it, and if we're not, let's get the hell out of here. I swear, my heart will pack up if I hang around here much longer." But neither his protests nor the fans' cries made any difference. It was as if the more they yearned for it to be over quickly, the longer it dragged on. But when no one scored any goals in the extra time either, they had to resort to penalty shots. His heart racing dangerously, the boy couldn't bring himself to watch a single one. They won the match in the end, but when, after those breathtaking 3 hours and 20 minutes– for which he had the power cuts to thank – he felt as though arrows were piercing his heart for days afterwards, he vowed never to go to the stadium again. "I can't bear it brother," he said, and settled for viewing the matches on television after that. It wasn't until many years later that he went back to Ali Sami Yen with his son. The idea was that it would be their first father and son outing and, as such, unforgettable, but, when Bülent's finger got trapped in the car door on the way, their football adventure turned into a God awful nightmare.

His brother didn't go home that weekend. Using his approaching exams as an excuse and claiming he had to study, he had stayed at school. As if he cared whether he came or not! And even if he had come, Veysel wasn't about to demand any explanations from him. And anyway, what would he say? Was he meant to ask, what were you ashamed of me for, or, what have the likes of you got that I haven't? He didn't open his mouth the following weekend either, when Prince Eyüp sent his mother and sister into raptures by deigning to honour them with his presence. He simply watched from afar in silence. His brother had a weary, embarrassed air about him. Veysel couldn't work out if it was because he felt ashamed of his family in front of others, or if he was ashamed in front of his brother for behaving as if he didn't know him ... He certainly wasn't about to bow down before his lordship and plead with him to accept him, to shower him with love and swell with pride when presenting him to his friends. He felt more disappointed than angry, telling himself, it's his loss; if he doesn't want to know me, then I'm damned if I'll have anything to do with him.

During that period Eyüp grew increasingly distant from his family. The two brothers avoided each other and never exchanged words unless they had to. And besides, soon afterwards, Veysel went away to do his military service, and not long after he got back, Eyüp left to go to France, on the pretext of carrying on that education of his that had made him so high and mighty and hell bent on looking down his nose at everyone. And, as they all knew, he never came back. Whenever Veysel thought of him, the image that invariably came into his head was his face that had turned as white as chalk at the sight of him, and his eyes filled with dread and shame, crying out for him not to approach; that and his hoity-toity navy blue trench coat ...

Out of the corner of his eye he glared at his wife making loud chomping noises as she chewed the food in her mouth. No amount of effort had taught the woman to eat quietly. He had nagged her till he was blue in the face and, when she wound him up, ranted and raved at her and, at times, kicked her about, but it hadn't done any good. Whenever he laid into her she would try to calm him down, saying, "All right all right, I'll be more careful," but it never lasted; at the very next meal, as soon as she sat at the table, she would forget herself and start munching and chomping again. Veysel restrained himself. If he insulted her in front of their guest, he would upset his sister. So he held his tongue, not because he gave a damn about offending Perihan, but because he didn't want to embarrass his sister, who worshipped the ground the guest walked on. He had already made his poor sister, who had been fretting and praying there wouldn't be a scene, quake in the car when his tongue had got the better of him. He couldn't make her suffer any more.

As he tried to shut his ears to his wife's infuriating lip smacking, he was startled by the sudden sound of dreadful music. Before he could work out what it was, the guest had leapt out of her seat and rushed to her handbag. After a lot of rummaging, she eventually located her mobile phone and started speaking in a foreign language. Spanish, no doubt. Veysel had heard it from tourists and in films. He listened carefully; although he didn't understand a single word, he loved the sound of it. How beautifully the woman pronounced her h's and sh sounds. She spoke as though she were eating something delicious. She wasn't repulsive, like Perihan; she tucked in with relish, but, at the same time, with elegance …

As he scrutinised the mosquito clinging to the curtain, rubbing its two long forelegs together, he decided that Eyüp's wife didn't look like a bad person. She did get a bit standoffish in the car when she hadn't liked what she heard, but really she'd be doing herself a favour if she got used to that. Actually, what had possessed that idiot Eyüp to make him want to up and leave this gorgeous woman? For the first time it crossed his mind that something terrible might have happened to his brother, and the thought made him uneasy. Of course he didn't want anything bad to happen to him. Okay he may have wiped

Veysel out of his life, he may have wiped him clean out of his existence a long time ago, but they were still brothers. Before Eyüp had turned so unfriendly or, rather, started to be ashamed of them, they had grown up in this house together. No doubt they had had some good times. Even if it had been such a long time ago he couldn't remember, they must have done . . .

The moment he felt that tiny stab in his heart, he immediately pulled himself together. Nothing had happened to anyone. Just like he had walked out on them, he'd decided he'd had enough of his wife and walked out on her as well. And the poor naive woman, who still hadn't realised what kind of man she'd married, had set off after him like a fool. I'm not so stupid, I'm not about to go fretting about whether Prince Eyüp is alive or dead while he's gadding about living it up here, there and everywhere, he thought. And not even his sister feared that something terrible may have happened to Eyüp. All she cared about was that at last, after all these years, her brother was finally in Istanbul. Just like the proverb, while the lamb fears for its life, all the butcher can see is meat, she got herself all worked up wondering if he might come and see them. As if he ever would, thought Veysel. Why would a man who hasn't bothered to come in all these years suddenly up and come now?

"My sister sends you all her regards," said Pilar, as she hung up. "She just wanted to make sure I had got here safely . . ."

"How many brothers and sisters have you got?" interrupted Perihan, sizing up the guest's mobile phone out of the corner of her eye. She wasn't just nosy, she was garrulous too; never satisfied unless she was talking, questioning, prying . . .

"There are two of us. I've just got one sister."

"Me too. But I have a younger brother," said Perihan, steering the subject round to herself, as though anyone had asked her. She spoke with an air of superiority, as though she had scored a victory by having a brother rather than a sister. When she received no answer, this time she ventured to say, "Mashallah, you speak such good Turkish. Did your husband teach you?" Veysel was inclined to land a square punch right in the centre of that jaw of his relentlessly jabbering wife, who so loved talking out of turn. But at the same time he was curious to know what her reply would be.

"I did a course for a year, and I took private lessons. And naturally I practiced with Eyüp too."

Huh, just as he had thought. When had his brother ever been known to move a single hair on his head for anyone else's sake? Whatever this woman had learned was the fruit of her own endeavours. Which meant she loved her husband.

"Oh, what did you go wasting money on courses for?" gushed Perihan, struggling to swallow a huge mouthful that she hadn't had the sense to cut in half. "When you have a perfectly good husband at home . . . he should have taught you, wouldn't that have been better?"

"Of course he taught me as well, but I wanted to take classes too. That way you take it more seriously, and you make the time to study."

"Do you speak to each other in Turkish? Because it's a real pain to learn, unless you talk."

Anyone listening to her would think she spoke seven languages, thought Veysel. His gaze became fixed on the speck of red oil at the corner of Perihan's mouth. She was perfectly capable of poking her nose into everything, whether it was any of her business or not, but it didn't enter the stupid woman's head to pick up a serviette and dab at the corner of her mouth.

"Sometimes in Catalan, sometimes in Turkish. We have a few Turkish friends in Barcelona; we usually speak Turkish when we're with them. And I have a colleague who speaks Turkish, sometimes I practice with her. So you see, I get a lot of practice."

"What's Catalan? Don't they speak Spanish where you are?"

"No, in Barcelona people mostly speak Catalan," replied the woman shortly. She had got Veysel all confused now. Where had this Catalan business sprung from? Did that mean she hadn't been speaking Spanish just now? God, this is confusing, he thought. Why on earth wouldn't a man speak Spanish if he was in Spain . . .

He smiled at his sister, who said, "Mashallah, your Turkish is so good" as she knocked on the wooden table. As if, without that gesture, the woman would suddenly forget everything she knew and be incapable of pronouncing a single word of Turkish ever again. It was his sister's habit, no matter where she was, she made a point of knocking on any piece of wood she could lay her hands on. If there was no wood then metal, and failing that, glass, cardboard, anything within reach . . . If she had heard something good, she did it to ward off the evil eye, and if she had heard something bad, it was to keep it from coming to their door . . .

When, incapable of containing her curiosity, Perihan inquired, "So, what does your sister say then?" Veysel saw red. Although he managed to bite his tongue, he didn't hold back from glaring at his wife in the hope she might get it and let it drop. But Perihan neither noticed, nor so much as glanced in his direction . . . As Veysel hovered on the borders of his patience, Pilar responded politely to Perihan's question:

"She asked how my journey was. And she asked about Eyüp, of course, whether I had any news."

Perihan launched into a lengthy monologue, declaring, "To tell you the truth, you've got a tough job here. What can I say, may God grant you success! Look, I've been married how many years now, and I've yet to see my brother-in-law's face. He shunned all this and took himself off long ago; I really don't think he'll suddenly turn up out of the blue now. But of course, what does it matter what we say, in the end our fate is whatever is written on our foreheads. What's the expression, if it's fated he'll come from India or Timbucktoo, and if it isn't then there's nothing we can do . . ." At the end of his tether, Veysel broke in with, "That's enough Perihan, you don't ever stop, do you!" and he rose from the table and went to sit on the sofa. "Never mind all this now, go and make us some tea. We'd all love some, with your permission."

Reluctant to go to the kitchen empty-handed, Perihan busied herself with clearing away the plates on the table. Then, as if she wasn't the one her husband had just berated, she asked the guest:

"Do you speak English as well?"

Veysel was getting seriously riled by his wife. Anyone would think this is a goddamn job interview. What kind of a question is that, he thought to himself! Judging by the way Pilar limited herself to nodding by way of reply, without so much as opening her mouth, he wasn't the only one who had had enough of Perihan's prattle. But unfortunately his wife didn't have the delicacy to realise she was annoying the guest and give it a rest. And so she went on:

"In that case, aunty Pilar, will you say a few words to your nephew now and then? We send him to a private school, where they teach him English, but we can't practice with my poor baby at home. Because of course, *none* of us knows any English . . ." As she said this, she made sure to turn her head and throw her husband a pointed look. She being a woman, there was nothing odd about *her* not knowing any foreign languages, but it was unforgiveable for the master of the house to be so ignorant. When her husband failed to bite the bait she turned to Bülent, instructing, "Speak to your aunty in English darling. You know your teachers say you must practice, with anyone you can." The child instantly turned the shade of beetroot. He had taken after his aunt; whenever he was embarrassed he immediately went bright red. The sole outcome of his mother's pouncing on the slightest opportunity to broadcast to all and sundry that she had sent her only son to a private school and forcing him to speak English in front of every guest who came to the house was that Bülent had lost all interest in the language. The poor boy was so mortified to be paraded about like a circus animal that, whenever the subject arose, he flushed crimson and wished the ground would open up and swallow him. Veysel was convinced his ridiculous mother would see to it that his son never learned a word of English in his life.

Bülent, cringing and desperate to change the subject, said, "Daaaad," as though crying out for help. "There's going to be an eclipse on Wednesday. Not just any eclipse, but a total eclipse of the sun."

Veysel was eyeing the mosquito that had settled back on the curtain after having done the rounds of the coffee table, the curtain and the dining table. Without taking his eye off the mosquito he nodded, saying, "Really? That'll be nice for the sun."

"It's going to be amazing, Dad. Yekta's family is going to watch it; Aunty Filiz is taking them in her car. Can I go with them?"

Biting his lower lip, as he always did when he was engaged in a delicate task, Veysel grabbed the newspaper beside him tightly and brought it down hard on the mosquito, that looked as if it were stuck to the curtain. But the mosquito had been quicker and flown off long ago. As he put the newspaper down on the coffee table with evident disappointment, he told his son, eagerly awaiting his reply, "Yes son, you go." He stared glumly after the mosquito that had escaped; he wasn't done with it yet.

It was an effort for him not to screw up his face in distaste as he watched his wife walk to the kitchen carrying the empty plates. That's how it was sometimes, when he looked at her, and especially when he touched her, he felt aversion, disgust almost, as though he were touching something dirty. He wondered if other men were as repulsed by the sight of the wives they bedded at night as he was. Although no one walked around broadcasting details of their lawfully wedded wives' smells and secretions, or advertising the positions they did it in, he nevertheless imagined that his friends didn't feel the way he did. He knew as much from his adolescent days.

In those days too he was disgusted by everyone he fucked. On the way out of the brothel, while his friends were describing down to the minutest detail how they had shagged the whores, he was as tense as if he had just been wallowing in putrid mud and felt an urgent need to rush home and purge himself of the filth clinging to him. But, because he didn't want to be the butt of their merciless jibes, he would grit his teeth and join in with their banter. To stop them thinking he hadn't been man enough to do it, to avoid being the object of their ridicule, he would exaggerate everything that had gone on inside, more often than not completely reinventing the entire episode.

The first time, he hadn't been able to get it up. He'd gone with Rafet, who lived in his neighbourhood. Veysel had been 16. It was summer and as hot as hell. He had entered, burning with curiosity and desire; but the moment he came face to face with the woman waiting for him, his desire withered. The woman was a dog, well past it, and sagging everywhere. As though she could tell from the look on his face, she grinned salaciously, baring her unsightly teeth, and asked Veysel, "Is this your first time?" Although he intended to stave off any slurs on his manhood by replying, "Of course not," fear that she would mock his soon to be exposed inexperience made him nod in assent to the whore his mother's age. The events of that day made their mark on his mind as a crimson memory filled with shame and revulsion. Flaming red, sinful scarlet and bloody darkness, all at the same time . . .

Instead of dividing all his experiences into separate cells and trying to remember each one individually, he trusted in colours and what each one evoked. Rather than in all its brutal details, he preferred to recall the past in terms of the colours his mind associated it with. In the mirror that concealed the secrets of his life, every experience had its corresponding colour. For example, his first day at school was yellow, like crestfallen roses. His perfidious relationship with studying and making something of his life was a solitary, lonely colour, purloined from the leaves spread out like a quilt on the route to school. The day his father died was white. They had laid him in the soil that the stark white snow covered like a duvet and returned home, in utter desolation. His mother's death, on the other hand, was a memento of a melancholy day inspired by blue. When he had found Müesser clinging to his beloved mother, for some reason his gaze had drifted outside, where it met the magnificent blue sky. They had laid his father to rest in white-capped soil, but his heart couldn't bear to deliver his mother to the same fate; he had willed the deep blue skies he could see from the window to take the lifeless body before him and make it fly away. The day he noticed Perihan, in other words, the day that bane of his life had wormed her way into it, was pistachio green. Like the blouse with the three top buttons undone that she was wearing on the day she came into his shop and fixed her indifferent gaze on his . . . Whenever he sighted pistachio green, the tedious weariness his wife had imposed on his life intensified. The colour that evoked Eyüp was navy blue. The colour of the fancy trench coat he was wearing that day when they had met at the school gate, that was his colour in the place he occupied in Veysel's heart. Eyüp was so navy blue . . .

Over the years he had accumulated a large number of memories, painted each one a different colour and filed it away. Whenever he chanced upon those colours in his daily existence, his life would unwind before his eyes like a film roll. Only Veysel's dreams were colourless. In his sleep he lived like a dog. In black and white. Free from colours, from joy and sorrow, in the cold embrace of fear. Some nights he would find himself in the midst of a brutal conflict. When he came eye to eye with guns that unknown hands were aiming at his face at close range, he could see nothing but the barrel, growing increasingly larger before his eyes. The barrel would advance, then retreat. No matter how hard he wished to close his eyes and die soundlessly, it wasn't possible. A force he was powerless to resist compelled him to keep his eyes open and trained on the barrel. The morning after those dreams he felt like he had been plunged in filth. He had an irrepressible urge to wash himself.

On that deep crimson day when he had first set foot in a brothel, in that room that stank of sweat and semen, where the walls seemed to bear down on him like gun barrels, he had been so tense and felt so awful, his sole instinct had been to turn on his heels and run.

He had taken a deep breath and tried to calm himself, but in vain. The woman had reclined on the bed like an obese sow, spread her legs and called to him in her rasping voice, hoarse from years of smoking. Veysel had trembled and shivered like a branch swaying in the wind and crawled into bed, almost fearfully. Toil and struggle as he might, he simply couldn't get hard enough to wedge himself between her thighs. Wheezing and rasping, the woman had taken hold of Veysel's member and yanked it up and down a couple of times, but to no avail. "Don't give me a hard time boy, this heat is killing me already. If you're going to do it, then get on with it, otherwise get out," she had said, and closed her legs. Struggling to suppress his rising nausea, his face flushed deep crimson, Veysel had rushed outside and sat down to wait for Rafet. When his friend appeared some ten minutes later, rosy cheeked and grinning from ear to ear, Veysel had not uttered a word about what had happened inside. While Rafet launched into a minute description of all the things he had done to the woman, in the style of an epic adventure, Veysel too, not wanting to seem less of a man than his friend, fabricated some story.

But of course it hadn't always been like that. On his subsequent trips to the brothel they referred to as "school," he hadn't been so timorous. On the contrary, he had turned into a lion; fearless, he had aroused fear; untrembling, he had made them tremble. Once he had tasted domination rather than fear of women, he felt much more powerful. Seeing them grimace with pain as he thrust into them, hearing their cries for mercy, made him feel like a man and put him in excellent spirits. His shoulders became squarer, he grew taller and more majestic. On those occasions he would go outside feeling as though he ruled the world. But at the same time, all the women he thrashed on top of disgusted him. He felt they were all dirty, sullied and stank of spunk. He would part their legs and ram himself in and out, as though determined to dismember them. As though he were driving himself into a cesspit and not their wombs. He would ejaculate inside them as though he were spitting, as though he were vomiting; one part of him floating in pleasure, the other in fetid water. The moment he was satisfied, he felt a compulsion to cleanse himself, convinced that if he didn't have a shower immediately he would never get rid of the stench that he believed clung to him. They were all dirty, every woman that groaned underneath him with pain or with pleasure was dirty.

As she returned from the kitchen carrying a large dish of finely sliced watermelon and melon, Perihan said to Pilar, "Weeell, so when did you and Eyüp meet then? We know you're married, but we don't know anything about how and where it happened." Although his wife's constant meddling in matters that didn't concern her drove Veysel mad, he couldn't suppress his curiosity about the answers to some of her questions. How could he not be curious? ... He knew practically nothing about his brother's life. The ungrateful wretch would phone once in a blue moon, never speak to his sister for longer than a few minutes at the most and then hang up without telling her anything worth hearing. He had informed them of his marriage by phone. When, as usual, his sister had brought up the subject of his coming to visit and asked when they would get to see the bride, he had talked about his impossible workload and said that if he ever managed to set some time aside, he would bring her to meet them. Lies! As if he couldn't have set aside a single day in all these years!

In the beginning Eyüp had invented shamefaced excuses for declining the summons to come. But, with time, it was those who summoned him who started to feel shamefaced. His sister knew that each entreaty to him to come meant he would postpone his next telephone call even longer. Which is why, fearful of stifling him, she was permanently on tenterhooks, even when telling her brother that she wanted to see him. In fact, the lengthening gaps between his telephone calls had nothing whatsoever to do with the poor woman. No matter what his sister did, Eyüp was distancing himself from his origins at breakneck speed. Pretentious little shit, thought Veysel to himself. He had wiped his family clean off his slate, thinking he was too good for them, not even taking the trouble to turn around and look behind him to see what state he had left them in.

When Pilar started to tell them, "Eyüp and I met in France, in Paris. Eleven years ago," he chased away the demons inside his head and listened. No matter how angry he was, he couldn't help feeling curious about this part of the story.

Pilar told them she had done her degree at Milan Polytechnic. After her postgraduate degree, her supervisor, Nicoli Mancini, had proposed sending her to Paris to work on a privately funded project led by a friend of his. She had been excited by the idea of converting an old winery into a contemporary arts museum and in no time at all had hot footed it to Paris, and not long after that had met Eyüp. She had been only 24 years old then, and Eyüp 26 ... He had studied economics at Paris Dauphine University, and, despite graduating with an excellent degree, had been adamant about not wanting to work in that field. He was an interesting, intriguing young man. He worked in a converted garage turned makeshift studio that he shared with a group of artists and crafted objects made of ceramics and glass and tried to scrape a living from his creations.

"What ceramics?" interrupted Veysel.

He knew his brother had studied economics, but wasn't really in a position to hazard any guesses as to which jobs he had done afterwards. When he had telephoned to say he had graduated and his sister had asked, "When are you coming back?" Eyüp's reply had been, "I'm going to find a job and work here for a while." When his sister had told him to come home right away the next time he phoned, saying it would be hard for him to get a job out there and that it would be best for him to return to his own country, he had informed them he was working in the sales department of an automotive company, and thereafter, whenever anyone asked how his work was going he would just say, "Well." His sister must have preferred to imagine her little brother dressed in impeccably pressed suits with razor-sharp creases, sitting behind a desk, because she hadn't asked him anymore, resolved not to delve any deeper. However, that image was not as appealing to Veysel as it was to his sister. The idea of his brother, who had been raised like a prince, living the life of a sultan, while his own unremarkable childhood had been followed by the unenviable existence of a run-of-the-mill shopkeeper needled him. But when, sometime later, in response to his sister's reproachful remark about her brother not even returning to pay them a visit, Eyüp had said he was an illegal immigrant in France and that if he left he wouldn't be able to re-enter, Veysel had smelled a rat. What fancy company would give an illegal immigrant a job behind a desk, in a big shot, VIP position? Eyüp was lying, either about being an illegal immigrant, or about working ... The fact that he had never asked any of them for money was a sign that he had a regular income from somewhere, and that was enough to deter them from delving any deeper into the matter. But he had nevertheless voiced his suspicions to his sister. And she of course had seized on the first opportunity to ask Eyüp. According to Eyüp, he had sorted things with the aid of some acquaintances who had helped him wangle a document or two. Müesser Abla had been satisfied with that information, but Veysel still believed there was more to the matter than met the eye. Nevertheless, for the sake of not upsetting his sister, he probed no further and pretended to accept the mental image of his brother sitting proudly behind a desk. Even after Eyüp had married and moved to Spain, he didn't bring up his brother's immigrant status or job situation, but kept his mouth shut. But now, this talk of ceramics that she was bandying about was turning everything Eyüp had fed them all these years upside down; it was confirming all Veysel's suspicions.

"You know, ceramics," replied Pilar, but, seeing the blank looks on their faces, felt she should elaborate: "You know, clay pots and stuff?"

This time Müesser and Perihan both spoke out in unison:

"What! Eyüp makes pots!"

It was obvious from her whole manner that Pilar couldn't understand what they were so astonished about.

"Yes. As far as I know, he was into ceramics right back from his secondary school days. His teachers even helped him hold an exhibition of his work. Didn't you know?" she couldn't help asking. His sister confessed, in a tone of meek dejection, and with evidence of all the awkwardness occasioned by revealing to a third party that they were not a tightly knit, close, loving family on her face, that no, they did not know. After primary school Eyüp had gone to boarding school. And when he came home for the weekend he didn't like talking about what he did at school. He was a withdrawn child. And so no, he hadn't mentioned the pots and bowls and things. And he hadn't told them about what happened afterwards either. And so, feigning to continue with her account of how she and Eyüp had met, Pilar started talking about her husband's life prior to meeting her. Veysel got the impression that Pilar was pained by Müesser's embarrassment. On the one hand she wanted to fill her in on everything she wanted to know, to throw open the doors to the unknown territory that was her brother, but at the same time she wanted to do it discreetly, without hurting anyone's feelings, without drawing attention to their estrangement ... That was the impression that Veysel got. He could differentiate between good and bad, his nose could discern human nature. "I'm a connoisseur in judging character," he would boast, whenever the subject came up, claiming he could see right inside a man at first glance, and that he never got it wrong. He didn't like people who were pretentious, or full of themselves, or know-it-alls who were out to rub everyone's nose in how much more they knew than everyone else. It was obvious this Pilar wasn't like that. Just look at how considerate she was towards his sister. She seemed to shrink from wounding her. Veysel liked her. Maybe it was the first time he had ever liked something of his brother's without feeling jealous, or flying into a temper and getting into a mood because it wasn't his ...

Their sister-in-law was saying that Eyüp was very serious about this ceramic business. But still, in the beginning, he hadn't regarded it as a livelihood, but rather as a hobby that he could have alongside a serious job which would allow him to earn his living, something he could do for pleasure. When his teachers at school encouraged him to follow that path too, he left Istanbul to study economics. But, once he got to Paris and started studying, he was stifled by the future the university was carving out for him, and at the same time, as he got to know the artists' collectives there, his relationship with ceramics changed. With his artists' group, he started going to workshops on abstract ceramics and working on lithographs; he even attended a few fine art lectures as a visiting student. He developed his natural talent with new techniques. He loved what he was doing so much that he decided, right from his third year, that he would not earn his living from what he was studying, but from ceramics.

"But, as you know, Eyüp is ambitious," said Pilar. That made Veysel laugh to himself. How could he not know? He knew all right.

"He's obsessed with finishing off what he's started. Because he's so used to success, he couldn't bear the idea of giving up his studies halfway through. Despite everything, he got his degree, and a very good degree at that. But, apart from an internship in the sales department of an automobile company that he did while he was still a student, he's never had any job connected to the department he graduated from."

Upon hearing the word internship, Veysel glanced at his sister. Their eyes met fleetingly. Even if their younger brother hadn't been lying to them entirely, he had manipulated the truth considerably when telling it to them. The photograph he had in his head of Eyüp sitting at a large desk in his own office, dressed in pristine suits, vanished, and in its place came an intern boy who ran all the errands, scurried backwards and forwards at everyone's beck and call and made photocopies. So, while he had fearlessly entered the world of business from a young age and become his own boss, his brother hadn't been brave enough to go into a career where even the internship was too much for him, and instead had thrown himself into pots and bowls. To tell the truth, Veysel didn't really understand this pot business, but still, just thinking about it made him want to laugh. It was obvious that no one in the room knew exactly what Eyüp did for a living, but no one had the courage to ask. No one except Perihan that is:

"Now, when you say pots, what exactly does that mean? Who buys those pots over there? How does your husband manage to make any money?"

"He has a small studio where he works by himself. He makes decorative or household objects, like vases, plates and glasses, but also large ceramic panels and three dimensional miniature statues ... Over there people find it fascinating that he uses tiles. We can't say he's famous exactly, but he is quite well known in those circles. For example, last year he made two incredible panels, one for a hotel in Barcelona and the other for the entrance of a large shopping centre in Valencia. Recently he had a meeting with a gallery in Madrid; he may have a new exhibition there in the winter."

As Pilar spoke, the expression on Veysel's face changed. It was obvious that his brother's job was a la-di-da one. The image of Eyüp clad in a suit vanished; this time it was replaced with the image of a full of himself, arty-farty type. Whatever he did, the little shit always landed on his feet. He was lucky all right. He always had been, ever since he was a child. Either he was lucky, or life wasn't fair . . .

Eventually, Pilar deftly brought the subject round to how they had met. She had met Eyüp during her first year in Paris, through a mutual friend. It had been love at first sight. When the project she was working on was complete, she had wanted to return to her own country and had persuaded Eyüp to go with her. Then, when Pilar had found a job in Barcelona, they had moved there together and, some time later, had got married.

"Are you from Barcelona?" enquired Perihan this time. Are your parents there?"

"No, they're in Valencia. But workwise we're much better off in Barcelona. That's why we decided to live there."

"What job do you do?"

"I'm an architect."

"Oh," said Perihan, and then fell silent. She stared at her sister-in-law with acrid envy. Veysel, who was thoroughly enjoying watching his wife's crestfallen expression, said to himself, go on, go ahead, keep asking, you've got your answer, that'll teach you." The disappointment of the woman who had obviously not understood a single word of the stories about converting old wineries into museums a moment ago was written all over her face. Of course she had wanted Pilar to be a housewife, like herself. Someone on her level. Because that way she would feel free to make jibes, or pound her, as and when the fancy took her. But now that she knew she was up against a whopping great architect, she was as out of her league as a third league team playing against the cup winners. Perihan flushed purple and instantly fell silent. She didn't feel like asking any more questions. Pilar, for her part, was totally unaware of what was going on. And she was oblivious of how completely those three words from her had deflated Perihan, nor did she have any inkling of the mixture of malicious ill feeling and intense mortification she had subjected the pitiful woman to.

Seeing that Veysel, who had had enough of this chat, was reaching for the remote control to put the television on, Pilar suddenly cut in with, "What are we going to do now?" It was obvious that the serving of tea, the hands reaching for the remote control, the gestures that indicated life was going on as normal, had upset the woman, who had come all this way and was sitting there going out of her mind because she hadn't been able to get any news of her husband. She wanted to see people running backwards and forwards in a state of panic, hunting high and low for Eyüp. God knows, she had been squirming the whole time, wondering when they would get onto the subject of finding Eyüp, and in the end hadn't been able to stand it anymore and felt she had to ask. Veysel was no fool; of course he knew what was going through the woman's head. And when she said what are we going to do now he knew what she meant as well as he knew his own name. But still, he chose to feign ignorance:

"What do you mean, what are we going to do?"

Pilar's shoulders sagged at this. Clearly she hadn't anticipated such indifference.

"How are we going to find Eyüp?"

"Honestly Pilar Hanım, we explained the situation to you in the car. It's all well and good for you to up and come here, but don't expect us to be able to help you. If you ask why, the man you're looking for isn't mad and he's not crazy. He got on the plane with his own two feet and came to Istanbul. I mean, even if we tried to go and report it to the police, it's not as if he's been kidnapped or anything."

"But—" Veysel continued, without allowing Pilar to voice her objections:

"To tell you the truth, your best bet would have been to sit at home and wait, but seeing as you've come all the way here, then of course you're more than welcome. Only you mustn't expect us to go out and search the streets for Eyüp. Anyway, you can see for yourself that the man has cut off all ties with us. Look, we didn't even know what job he did until you just told us."

"But I thought—"

"You won't get very far just by thinking . . ."

Perihan, her eyes glittering, was following the conversation as though she had scored a victory. Thinking her husband, who wouldn't let the woman get a word in edgeways, was avenging her own humiliation a few moments ago, she was most probably feeling like the cat that's got the cream. Veysel felt irritated when he realised that. Because he was not out to either upset his sister-in-law, or please Perihan. All he wanted to do was make it clear from the start that he didn't want anything to do with any of this, and then he would get on with his own life, that was all . . .

"Now don't go getting all offended and upset with me. If there was anything we could do, we'd have done it. But, I'm sorry to say, we won't be any good to you in this matter. I hope you don't mind," he said shortly.

Just then he saw the look of dismay on his sister's face. Had he gone too far, he wondered, had he behaved like a brute . . . The woman had upped and come because she had felt a closeness to them, because she had regarded them as family. Was it acceptable to say, I hope you don't mind but we won't be any good to you? But what would happen if he hadn't said it; was there actually any action they could take? What was he supposed to do, set out in hot pursuit of Eyüp in this huge great city and track him down like a detective? If his brother were in trouble, if he needed him, then things might be a bit different; but what business was it of his to go after a man who had run away from his wife? No no, even if he had been a bit harsh, he'd said the right thing . . . He consigned the rest of his sentence to silence. Until a submissive voice cut into the acrid soundlessness . . .

"We'll wait."

All their heads turned in unison towards the owner of the voice. His sister spoke with her head lowered. As though she were embarrassed on account of her guest, as though her face were bowed down to the ground . . . It was as though Veysel had shown her up yet again. It makes no difference to me, thought Veysel irritably, after all, you're used to being shown up and I'm used to showing you up . . . It makes no difference to any of us . . . Instead of being ashamed and upset by what I say, why don't you just for once feel ashamed of your brother who runs away from home like a child, for his wife's sake? But he's used to running away from home, just like we're used to watching and waiting for him, don't you think? Everyone is so good at doing what's expected of them in this house . . . Veysel was upset with his sister for being upset. But he didn't make an issue of it; he simply held his tongue.

"We'll wait. The ground hasn't opened up and swallowed this boy, he's bound to turn up somewhere. There's no way he won't get in touch with either you, or us, or someone. If he's come to Istanbul, then sooner or later he'll walk through this door. Don't go upsetting yourself any more. I'm glad you came. We'll all wait together . . ."

His sister spoke with such conviction that even Veysel looked towards the door at one point, as though Eyüp might walk in any minute.

But Pilar protested, "I can't wait." Clearly she was reluctant to trust in any false hopes. And she wasn't like his sister. She wasn't the type who said, if speech is silver, silence is golden; she didn't trust in long silences for comfort. Waiting was not offensive to his sister. She would wait, like a solitary plane tree on the edge of a deserted road, tying her hands, her tongue, if necessary, making her tears flow inwards. She would wait, believing that bowing to her destiny and remaining silent meant she would suffer less. His sister had trained herself to believe the greatest evils would pass only by waiting. That, rather than tearing herself apart to overcome the troubles awaiting her, she needed to wait for the troubles that had already afflicted her to pass, to grit her teeth and endure . . . But this foreign woman wasn't like that, nor could she ever be. She had come here from a completely different world, a completely different family, a completely different history. She was the type that thought waiting was stupid, the type that believed in intervention and struggle. The type that thought herself strong enough to change her destiny, that strove to liberate her life from the slavery of some unknown force and rule over it herself . . . The foolish type . . .

"I can't sit and wait without doing anything. If I was going to do that I wouldn't have left Barcelona. Give me some advice, tell me where I should look for him. Okay, so he hasn't come here, where else might he have gone?" said Pilar, practically sobbing. She had ended up losing the composure she had been trying to maintain ever since she had arrived.

"Listen, yenge Hanım, that's just what I'm trying to say to you. We don't know where Eyüp does and doesn't go. It's been years since we've seen his face. Look, you say he's had exhibitions, that he made pots and bowls at school, we didn't even know about that. It's not just where he might go today that we don't know, we don't even know where he went and what he did years ago, while he was still here," replied Veysel, in his gentlest voice.

At that, Pilar's eyes lit up with anger:

"The missing man isn't just my husband, he's your brother too. Aren't you at all worried about what might have happened to him? How can you be so relaxed?"

Veysel looked pityingly, first at the woman who was refusing to understand what he had just explained to her, then at the mosquito who had committed the folly of circling around his head and then landing on the sofa.

Using the newspaper he picked up stealthily from the coffee table, he flattened the mosquito on the sofa with a single blow. Turning the newspaper over, he briefly examined the remains of the creature stuck to it. His face relaxed with the satisfaction of having saved, if not the lives of the members of his household, then at least their sweet blood. Then, taking pains to avoid sounding harsh, he enunciated each word carefully:

"That is what you don't understand. You have only lost your husband recently, but we lost our brother years ago. When you turned up saying my husband's missing, he'd already been lost to us for a long time. It was nothing new for us. This was always on the cards, but it's only now that you've had to deal with it, that's what it all boils down to. Now calm down and tell us what kind of help you want from us. What are you planning to do?"

The young woman hung her head helplessly. She clearly feared seeing her husband's fate reflected in the mosquito's end and her own future in Veysel's insouciant eyes. She pictured herself accustomed to being without Eyüp, after long years entwined around the habit, and found the image utterly distasteful. She turned resentful eyes on Veysel.

"Okay my dear, do you have anything in mind? Is there anything you'd like us to do?" Müesser had raised her eyes from the ground and was looking straight into Pilar's as she asked. She was offering, within the limits of her capabilities, to walk beside the woman who had refused to follow her path. She was saying, as you're not interested in waiting, then at least don't walk alone, she was offering a shoulder to lean on.

"I would say let's ask someone, but we don't know Eyüp's school friends. If you like we can look up Eyüp's old childhood friends from around here, but I doubt they'll have any news of him. Is there anyone you know of?"

At that point Pilar mentioned an old friend from Eyüp's Galatasaray days. Someone called İlhami Doğru. Eyüp had kept in touch with him despite all the years that had passed. The man who couldn't spare five minutes for his family was clearly the height of generosity when it came to lavishing love and respect on his friends. According to Pilar, after Galatasaray they had also been together in France. But by the time Pilar had met Eyüp, İlhami had long since returned to Turkey. İlhami had gone to Barcelona years later to visit his friend, and that was when Pilar had met him. Trusting in the strength of this friendship that had withstood so many years, the young woman thought Eyüp might be with him. And even if he wasn't, he may have told İlhami where he was. At the very least, perhaps İlhami might be able to suggest something.

"He's the only person I can think of," she said. "I'm going to go and see him first thing tomorrow morning."

"Where are you going to find this İlhami, or whatever he's called?" asked Perihan.

"When İlhami came to Barcelona two years ago, he told us he was about to take over a bookshop. He said the shop is in the passage directly opposite their old school. I remember where it is because Eyüp teased him, saying he was only taking it over because he couldn't bear to tear himself away from their school. I'm going to go there."

"What if he's sold up and left?" asked Perihan, intent on throwing a spanner in the works. Following her recent humiliation, she was no doubt determined to even the score with her unrivalled talent for putting a damper on things.

"Someone will surely know where he's gone . . ."

"What if he never took it over? He may have told you that, and then changed his mind . . ."

Like a preying animal, Pilar glared at the woman before her with glowing eyes. She was clearly trying to work out what Perihan was playing at. I wouldn't bother, I still don't know, even after all these years, thought Veysel, watching them from his seat. The family knew only too well how Perihan was the harbinger of doom and gloom, but the guest, who wasn't familiar with her character, seemed very put out. Perihan always looked on the dark side of things and would cast shadows on everyone's mood by envisaging the most unlikely calamities. When someone bought a new dress, instead of saying, "It's lovely," she would say, "Oh, be careful you don't spill anything on it, that fabric's really hard to clean"; when a couple had a new baby, before she said, "Congratulations" she would come out with, "life is so hard, vallahi, may God come to your aid." They were yet to see her open her mouth to say anything positive.

"I prefer to be optimistic for now," said Pilar curtly, making it clear she wasn't prepared to listen to any more negativity. For her part, Perihan made do with shaking her head knowingly, like a forbearing clairvoyant whose predictions of disaster no one had heeded.

Veysel murmured grudgingly to Pilar that he could go with her tomorrow morning to search for this İlhami person or whoever he was. But, after what she had just heard, the woman must have concluded that her brother-in-law's absence would help her more than his presence, because she declined Veysel's offer of assistance, saying there was no need. If he could just tell her how to get to the secondary school, that would be enough; she would take care of the rest. Veysel was baffled by the woman's confidence and the resilience of her self-esteem, even though her husband had walked out on her. But he didn't insist and merely explained to Pilar where she needed to go. At her request, he even drew the young woman a little map of the place. The little minx might well pooh-pooh all their advice and dig in her heels about going by herself, but she wasn't taking any chances either. There was no question about it, she was a smart woman. Damn you, Eyüp, he thought to himself, you've landed on your feet yet again!

He picked up the newspaper in an attempt to distance himself, however slightly, from this Eyüp business. After quickly skimming the news on the front page he turned straight to the sports page. He wasn't interested in politics. To tell the truth, he wasn't interested in sports either. As far as he was concerned, the only sport that existed was football and the only team Galatasaray, and that was it. Galatasaray was his be-all and end-all. It was his life's greatest passion. Maybe even his only passion ... Two warm colours that shone out of his pallid existence, the sole pleasure that gave him a chance to join the ranks of the winners ...

Of course he had brought up his son, the apple of his eye, to be a Cimbom fan like him. But, for some reason, Bülent had come home one day declaring, I support Fenerbahçe now.

Although Veysel had been horrified, he hadn't shown it, but limited himself to saying, "A young man doesn't change his team. He changes his car, he changes his job, he changes his wife if need be, but he doesn't change his team." He didn't know which friend had goaded his son into that decision, but wanted to believe he would soon be back on the right track. When all was said and done, children's fathers were their role models. Sooner or later Bülent too would come back to his father's team.

No matter how badly he wanted to escape, everything he saw and touched tonight transported him to Eyüp. Even the photograph of Fatih Terim in the newspaper brought back the ennui of bygone days. Once again that maddening day when he had seen his brother in front of the school sprang to his mind. First of all, with a smile flickering at the corners of his mouth, he recalled Fatih Terim's penalty goal. But later, that goal took him right back to that day, to that first moment when the abyss between Eyüp and himself had grown so wide. Eyüp's powers were such that he could make you remember him even when you were looking at Fatih Terim's face. And not only that, but he owned every one of the places where he made you remember him.

It wasn't just Fatih Terim's image, his mother's and sister's love and his father's mercy that he had stolen, he had cast his eye on Veysel's team as well. Enrolling at Galatasaray Secondary School made it seem like he was closer to the boys than his brother. As far as the world was concerned, Eyüp had earned the right to be a genuine supporter from the moment he had first walked through that magnificent door. Whereas Veysel had known and loved Cimbom before he had. Long before ... But his brother had coveted even that. And, like everything he had ever coveted, he had managed to make it his. Even the student card the boy carried in his wallet said Galatasaray in whopping great letters; he couldn't compete with that. But luckily, once his brother went to France, just as with the house and his family, Veysel got Galatasaray back too.

As with everything else, Eyüp had abandoned Galatasaray too. That's what he was like, he couldn't care less about anything except himself. Not about his dead parents' grave, nor his living sister, nor his brother's rage, nor his team's talents ... He had left everything, everyone and gone ...

If this foreign woman hadn't phoned and told them, they would have had no idea of what was going on. Just as they had had no idea all these years. If he hadn't suddenly disappeared, he might have died unexpectedly in an accident two days later. They wouldn't have known about it for months. When, occasionally, his name came up in conversation, they would recall his face in whichever snapshot had taken their fancy. Sitting at his desk in a pristine suit, standing in front of Galatasaray Secondary School, his eyes pleading, please don't approach me ... No one would visualise him rotting in black earth. And anyway, as long as no one visualised him there, he would never die. Even if they themselves died, the Eyüp in their imagination would live forever. As though he had knocked back a whole bottle of elixir of immortality ...

All right, he wasn't mad about his brother, but obviously he didn't want anything bad to happen to him either. As Perihan was always saying, "You're none too pleased when your brother's delighted, but it breaks your heart when his life is blighted ..." Everything could have been so different. If he had shown him just a bit of love and respect, if his stuck-up brother had made a tiny effort to get close to him, he would have been capable of loving him, and even of being glad when things went well for him. But Eyüp was a cold fish. His face was always sullen, his mouth permanently downturned; he was the fiend of his own hell. It wasn't just after he had upped and left, he was aloof even when they were living under the same roof.

For example, he hadn't shed a single tear when their mother had died. And what's more, he was the only one who hadn't cried. Veysel had felt like strangling his brother on the spot. At that time, he had just returned from doing his military service. There was a place he had in mind, in the Reşitpaşa area, for the grocer's shop he was thinking of opening. He was waiting for the tenant to vacate the premises. Eyüp was in his second year of secondary school. Often he didn't even come home at weekends, using homework and exams as excuses, and would stay in the school's dormitory. But as chance would have it, that particular weekend he was at home. He had come after school on Friday. He was wearing his usual sour expression and after dinner had gone straight up to his room. There were four of them at home that night. Eyüp, Veysel, his sister and his mother. Four people had got into bed at bedtime. But the following morning, only three of them had managed to wake up.

The sound of Müesser's scream had startled Veysel out of his wits. He had run to where the noise was coming from, to his mother's room. When he entered, his sister was prostrated over her mother, crying. To tell the truth, he was ashamed of crying, everyone had always told him boys don't cry. In the past his father would get riled when he wept. "Stop crying," he would bark, "stop blubbering like a woman." But still, that day, he had blubbered as though his heart would break. He couldn't believe what he was seeing. He couldn't get his head around his mother's death. For an instant he would forget what death meant and feel calmer, then suddenly it would dawn on him once more that he would never set eyes on his beloved mother again and an inconceivable pain would sear right through him.

He and his sister had knelt at their mother's bedside that morning and wept. There was nothing more they could do now, either for her or for themselves, except cry. Eyüp, who had woken up to the noise, come into the room and stood at the door, his face chalk-white. He stared first at the bed, then at them. And, once he realised what had happened, he had slumped down to the ground and stayed there, motionless. Veysel had hated his brother at that moment, because not even their mother's death was capable of making him throw his arms around them and share their tears. As usual, his arrogant little brother had preferred to stand apart from them, by himself. All the colour drained from his face, he had fixed his wide, staring eyes on the bed. No tears flowed from those eyes, not one word came out of those lips, clamped as tightly as if they had been sealed. Putting even that down to the profound shock her brother had suffered, his sister had disregarded her own grief and endeavoured to console Eyüp. How did his highness always manage to be the centre of attention at all times and in all places . . . To steal even his dead mother's thunder . . .

Never mind sharing life's joys, it wasn't even possible to share the devastation of death with him. When, a year later, Eyüp announced he was going to continue his studies in France, Veysel felt pleased. Although on the one hand he was none too happy to think that his brother would add new triumphs to his already interminable, inexhaustible list, on the other hand he was comforted to know that he was going to put a nice long distance between them. At that time he was busy with the grocer's shop he had opened and he swaggered around, puffed up with his new status of head of the household. If his brother had phoned and occasionally mentioned that he was short of money, that would have inflated Veysel's ego even more, but he never did. Eyüp got some kind of grant or something which allowed him to get by; he never needed his brother. He never gave Veysel the satisfaction of bailing him out.

In the third year after he had opened the grocer's shop, Perihan's family moved to that neighbourhood. She started dropping into the shop more and more frequently. Over time he began to take a fancy to this girl whom he hadn't really noticed the first time he saw her. She wasn't all that pretty, but there was something about the way she looked at him and the way she carried herself. The longer he looked at her, the more Veysel was aroused. From the way she would show up at the shop some four times a day, claiming to have run out of rice one moment, oil the next, he assumed she must be interested in him too. As she did her shopping, entering two items in the credit book for every one she paid for, she would fix her eyes on Veysel's and hold his gaze unflinchingly. As time passed, she got under his skin. He started to dream of her at night. He always thought of her when he sought solitary satisfaction, each time fantasising about different ways of making love to her. One day he squeezed her behind the cheese counter. Wrinkling her nose as she looked at the cheeses, she said, "Don't ask me, ask my mother," and wriggled free, giggling coquettishly. Until that moment, marrying her hadn't crossed his mind, even fleetingly. But suddenly he decided that it wasn't such a bad idea at all. He'd finished his military service, set himself up in work and one by one fulfilled his duties as a man. Wasn't getting married and carrying on his lineage the next step? Goaded by his raging hormones, and guided by the logic "I'll have to marry someone one day," Veysel set his sights on his target and swiftly made up his mind. Before a week had passed, clutching a bunch of flowers and a box of chocolates, with his sister and an older lady from the neighbourhood, Aunty Ümran, in tow, he rang Perihan's doorbell.

The girl's unsightly mother, Fitnat Hanım, whose husband had met his maker many years ago, was honest enough not to conceal from the suitors what a grasping woman she was. Before they had even got to the "by the will of God and according to the prophet's word" stage she had bewailed, with the utmost theatricality, the difficulties of raising a child without a father and made sure they were aware of all the expenses she had had to incur in order to raise her darling daughter to this age, and, although she didn't demand a bride price outright, she saw no harm in intimating that a bit of financial support from her son-in-law wouldn't go amiss.

Although the endless glasses of water brought to her by Perihan partially calmed Fitnat Hanım, who repeatedly dissolved into tears as she related how she had broken her back to raise her daughter in the direst poverty, she did not relax in the full sense of the word until she had extracted a promise from Veysel to the effect that he would support them for as long as they both lived. It was only after Veysel had said, "From now on you are like my mother too, I'll do everything in my power for you" that she was able to take a deep breath, lean back and enjoy the rest of the suitor's visit, as she polished off each and every one of the chocolates they had brought.

The rest all happened so quickly Veysel wasn't even aware of exactly when he got married. If their betrothal and engagement had been a bit longer and the young man had had a chance to get to know the girl he was going to marry, the marriage would most probably never have taken place. But because Fitnat Hanım, under the pretext that people would talk, rushed the young couple to the registry office as though bandits were hot on their heels, Veysel didn't get to find out exactly what kind of person he had married until he was clutching his marriage certificate. During the interval between the day he went to ask for her hand and their wedding day, he saw so little of Perihan that it struck him some nights as he lay in bed that he could barely picture the face of the girl he was going to marry. During her engagement, the street was out of bounds to the girl who used to come to the shop four times a day. It was not until they were married and had entered the marriage chamber that the young couple were finally alone.

But Veysel did not succeed in finding the happiness he sought, either in Perihan or in marriage. To tell the truth, he hadn't given much thought to exactly what he was looking for. Although he didn't know how to go about it and in fact didn't even feel like it most of the time, he wanted to treat his wife differently from the women he had touched until now, to become someone new when he was with her. But because he didn't really know what it was like to have a relationship with a woman outside of a brothel, he would go from getting flustered to feeling tense and keep repeating to himself that making love to your wife must be different from fucking a whore. If Perihan had helped him even a bit, everything could have been different; he genuinely believed that. But that's not the way it turned out.

At first he was as patient as he knew how to be. He tried to get used to his wife, to love her even. He tried to tolerate her faults. He even pretended to have fallen for the trick Perihan tried to pull on their wedding night and never confronted her with it. If he had only felt that she loved him, that he meant something to her, he could have overlooked his wife's defects, her pathetic failings, he might have been happy and, more than that, he may have even tried to make her happy.

But, far from being worthy of so much effort, the woman stoked the fire of every one of Veysel's sinister urges; she seemed to be forcing him to become more depraved.

It didn't take him long to discover that the woman who called herself his wife hadn't married him for love. She believed she had found someone whose pockets were sufficiently lined; she had only cast her eye on him because she saw him as a means of securing her future. Actually Veysel liked people who were weaker than him, and in fact, it was only with them that he felt truly relaxed. He was far from being averse to having people dependent on him and needing him; on the contrary, he liked it. In other words, he could have overlooked that detail, pretended it didn't exist ... if the woman could only have deluded first herself, then Veysel, into believing she loved her husband just a little bit.

He didn't ask for much from this woman with icy blue eyes, who lay underneath him as though it were a duty, who went straight to sleep, without uttering a single word, as soon as it was over, who slept beside him at night like a stranger. Even if she faked it, he would have settled for just a shred of affection, for her to get used to him like she would to any pet she may have owned, to be troubled by his absence, for her to just desire his existence. All he wanted was to feel indispensable to someone. All he needed was to feel that someone loved him, that he mattered to someone, just a tiny bit. But Perihan didn't deign to indulge him in that, not even once.

They had only been married a few months. One day, as he was buttoning up a blue shirt he was particularly fond of, one of the buttons came off in his hand. He called his wife and asked her to sew it back on for him. He made to remove the shirt but when Perihan, who was trying to thread the needle, said there was no need, he put himself in her hands. He watched his wife's hand coming and going, as it dipped the needle in and out of the spot just below the collar. Just then Perihan's hand slipped, and the needle, which was making tiny holes in the fabric as it worked its way in and out, mistook its target and stabbed Veysel's chest. Of course, the pain was not of the agonising, excruciating type that makes your blood run cold but, maybe because it caught him unawares, his eyes instantly teared up. Seeing what had happened, his tactless wife burst into hysterical laughter, as though it were the most hilarious thing she had ever seen. When she said "Oooh, just look at this huge great man, ready to burst into tears at the drop of a hat. How can you cry at such a tiny needle prick? Stop crying like a woman!" that huge great man's teared-up eyes clouded over so darkly with the memory of his father saying, "Stop crying like a woman" that even Perihan fell silent and nervously retreated two steps. Then, without a single word, she hastily completed the sewing and, making some excuse about having to get back to dinner, ran down to the kitchen. As he watched his wife's retreating back, the harsh truth that she didn't, and never would, love him pierced Veysel deep in the heart. He felt an intense rage surge up towards her. A rage as immense as the sum total of all the fury he felt towards everyone who, to that day, had not appreciated him or taken him seriously, or balked at the idea of wounding and offending him. That was the day he changed his mind about overlooking Perihan's faults and ugly traits, about watching over her and protecting her against his dark side. He spat out venomously, through gritted teeth, as though offloading all the rage he had amassed since the day he was born, "It's her loss!"

Once he had satisfied himself that the woman he had wed was no different from the ones he paid to screw, he had no qualms about subjecting her to the same treatment he saw fit for them. He no longer strove to conceal the evil streak inside him, to suppress his depraved desires, to curb his own malevolence. On the one hand he was relieved to be free to release the monster inside him once again, and on the other, because he was resigned to the impossibility of ever being able to love himself, he felt afflicted by a lifelong, devastating illness. He was somewhere between the irremediable grief of someone who has abandoned all hope and the relief felt by someone who has accepted the futility of yearning for the better things he can never have. He wasn't looking, and, like everyone who didn't look, he knew he would never find it, but behaved as if it didn't matter.

His sole aspiration for his own future was to become a father. Somehow, those who haven't enjoyed their own childhood hope to find the solution in fatherhood. To be able to give their child what they haven't received from their own father, to see their child do everything they haven't been able to, to finally get the chance to redeem an unlived childhood ... Veysel had to have a child, even if Perihan were his mother. He wouldn't be like him, he wouldn't be like his mother, his life would be nothing like Veysel's ... He would be the kind of child that would make him say, "This boy can't be mine." As he didn't love himself, he could never love a child who was like him.

Perihan fell pregnant before they had been married a year. But she didn't tell him. Because she imagined that her husband would want the child, she decided to butcher his baby quietly, without telling anyone. If Müesser hadn't found her lying unconscious in a pool of blood, no one would have known about the murder that she denied fervently, even in the hospital room. She might even have died. Veysel wouldn't have been all that upset if she had died, maybe he wouldn't have been upset at all.

Things changed radically after he announced to that woman, who would never be good for anything except bearing him a child, that if they didn't have a baby, he would divorce her. This time Perihan, horrified by the thought of having to return to her poverty-stricken existence in her mother's home and haunted by sleepless nights, sweated and toiled to get pregnant, as though she hadn't been the one who had murdered the first child that entered her womb. It was impossible to know whether it was the wages of her sin, but becoming a mother this time wasn't as easy as the first. She went from doctor to hodja, wore amulets, had melted bullets poured into a bowl of water over her head, commissioned the recital of prayers, paid sorcerers, but for a long while was unsuccessful in resuscitating the withered fertility of her womb so a new life could sprout inside it. If she hadn't managed to fall pregnant with Bülent in 1986, that is, three years after her marriage, she would have been dispatched to the destitute home of the now long dead Fitnat Hanım, to reap the fruits of her crimes. During their marriage there had been two periods in which Veysel had looked at Perihan and attempted to discern a human form there. The first was during those initial few months when they were newlyweds and he had not yet abandoned all hopes of happiness, and the other was during the nine months when Bülent was forming in his mother's womb. Because during those nine months Perihan was not Perihan, but the flesh and bone and nerve shield of Veysel's child. And as such she deserved a bit of – transitory – respect and dignity.

Although Veysel was not exactly born again with Bülent's birth, it did give him the opportunity of a whole new page on which to make a clean copy of himself. Having someone they can love more than themselves is a great blessing for those who can't love themselves. Veysel found a meaning for his life that was the punishment for he knew not which sin, and a reason for curving his lips in the smile he had not seen in the mirror for so long he couldn't remember it. From the moment she produced Bülent from between her legs, Perihan went back to being the old Perihan in Veysel's eyes. He even preferred not to remember where his child had come from; it was better that way. From then on, Bülent was the centre of his universe.

If he hadn't had Bülent, he may not have been all that bothered about the business; he might have settled for what he had. But now he was enjoying working and earning money for his son, planning a future for him based on all the things he hadn't had. That's why he threw himself into his work with much more conviction and zeal than before. Foreseeing in good time that the supermarkets sprouting like mushrooms on every street corner would one by one force all the grocers like himself to shut down, he moved into much bigger premises in the same neighbourhood and started his own supermarket. From now on everything he did was for his son.

"Why haven't you had any children? Or maybe you have, and you didn't tell us that either?" asked Perihan, completely out of the blue. The guest shifted uneasily. She must have truly had her fill of Perihan's relentless bombardment, her overfamiliarity and her complete lack of respect for anyone's personal space.

"We thought it better to wait a bit," she said simply. "We're putting it off for a while."

"How old are you?"

"Thirty-five."

"Ahhh, and you think you can afford to put it off? If you're going to do it, then you should do it now, or you'll regret it for the rest of your life. It's all right for a man, he can become a father at 70, but it's not like that for a woman, is it? A woman who doesn't become a mother will end up dry and withered," replied Perihan. It wasn't just a reply, her words cut like a sword, which stabbed deep.

Veysel looked at his wife, who had been getting on his nerves from the moment he had set foot in the house, and, thinking of the hiding of her life she had earned, told himself, "It's her loss." Pilar refrained from responding to that sharp sword, settling for a barely perceptible, clearly reluctant smile. Bülent wasn't aware of the exact reason why, but he felt an icy wind blowing in the living room and shivered. Müesser stirred nervously and heaved an unhappy sigh, as though it were her womb's secrets that had just been spilled and all eyes were fixed on her expired womanhood. Confounded to be noticed, no matter how hard she tried to be invisible, she shrank back into her seat and sat still. Perihan's poisonous, suppurating, seemingly casual words, which washed over all of them, cast a cloud of tension over the room.

After they had eaten the fruit, which followed the tea, Müesser asked the guest if she was tired. She reminded her that her bed was ready and that she could go up to sleep whenever she wished. Pilar, who was saturated by the endless barrage of questions, didn't wait to be asked twice and, on the pretext that tomorrow would be a very long day, bid everyone goodnight and, accompanied by Müesser, winged her way straight to her bed.

Veysel too was impatient to get to bed. "Pull back the bed covers," he ordered his wife on his way to the bedroom. Never once in all the years of his marriage had he taken the trouble to take off the bed covers in order to get in between the sheets and the quilt. Before they could retire, Perihan had to remove and fold that outlandish satin cover with matching cushions she had put on the bed. Because Veysel thought it was women's work, he refused to do it, standing in a corner like a child, waiting for his wife to take off the covers and fold down the quilt he would use to cover himself. The only job around the house that he enjoyed was slaying mosquitoes. Apart from that, he left everything to the women. As he stood in the corner once again, he thought about the supermarket. He hadn't been able to do anything today. And they had been expecting a delivery in the evening. He had left Bünyamin in charge of everything and gone. As he hadn't been in touch that must mean everything was all right. Still, first thing tomorrow morning I'll check everything and quickly go over the accounts, he thought. He wasn't concerned so much about what Bünyamin might pocket, but about his inability to calculate exactly what he was supposed to put in the till. If it wasn't because Perihan had insisted, not only would he never have dreamed of employing him, he wouldn't have even let the boy in his shop. He was a halfwit, the type who thought he was one step ahead of every cheat. He forgot to do the jobs he was given, and the ones he did manage to keep in his head he did half-heartedly. He had only put him on the till because it wasn't right to hire an outsider when there were relatives at hand; he had put him in charge of accounts when he wasn't there. Veysel pretended not to notice the small sums of cash he filched, thinking no one knew. At the end of the day, that money would have come out of his pocket anyway. That useless Bünyamin would have come pouting and grinning either to him or to his sister and wangled it out of one of them somehow. Veysel wanted Bünyamin to have to pull his weight, even if it was only when stealing, and, if he could find it in his heart, to feel bad about it, which is why he kept quiet.

He let the good-for-nothing waste of space steal and think he was getting away with it.

As his wife was putting the pink cushions from the bed on top of the wardrobe that she used for storage, where they would wait until morning, she said, "Fancy coming all this way empty-handed. Humph, and she calls herself a grand lady from Europe. I'd say a tight arse more like." Veysel glared so hard at her as he got into bed that, realising she should fear for what might be coming, she instantly fell silent and cowered. Those who have been silenced and made to cower love silencing and seeing others cower.

★ ★ ★

I'm in a peculiar place. On one side of me is Adam and Eve's bashful paradise, on my other side is the frightful hell of hideous creatures. As for me, I'm in the world, surrounded by songbirds, luscious fruit and stark naked mortals clad in love and lust. I am at the centre of my journey stretching out on either side of me. Well, it's a dream, isn't it, don't ask me how, but somehow I've found my way into Bosch's *Garden of Earthly Delights*, and I'm lying on my back right in the middle of it. Just then a terrible weight presses down on my whole body and I become anchored to the spot. I am suddenly stifled, as though thousands of tons of weight are pressing down on me, and I can't breathe. I try to see what's going on, but can't locate myself in that huge crowd. I have an unbearable pain in my groin; I have to bite the insides of my cheeks to endure it. My cheeks are rent to shreds and I'm bleeding. The blood trickling from my mouth turns first into a river, then a waterfall. I stand underneath it and bathe in that bloody cascade. When I lower my chin to survey how clean I am, I'm astonished and terrified to see that my tensed stomach has constructed a little mound in the centre of my body. I'm ... pregnant!

I've had a dream! At last I've had a dream! And, more to the point, I can remember it! When I woke up my mind was submerged in fear and my back drenched in sweat. Although one part of me was highly perturbed by the ridiculous things I had dreamed, you could say the other part, the part that acknowledged I had been able to remember my dream, was, to some extent, happy and proud. To tell the truth, walking into a painting and dreaming I was pregnant were the last things I would ever have imagined. But still I was pleased to have remembered it.

Even after I had sat up in bed and picked up my notebook, I still didn't feel entirely at ease. I don't know what made me more anxious: Bosch's disconcerting world, my inability to breathe there, bathing in my own blood, or finding myself pregnant. And, of course, why I would have chosen that of all paintings to enter. It's not exactly a painting that sends me into raptures. In fact, when I first saw the original in the Prado years ago, it didn't make much of an impression on me. The *Garden of Earthly Delights* hung there with its hundreds of figures, its humans with beasts' heads, its innumerable breeds of animal, its heaven, its hell, its innocence, its lust, its sin, its punishment, its yesterday, its today, turning pleasure into sin and suffering into punishment. The left panel depicted the paradise of the innocent, the central panel the world prostrated before pleasure and the right panel the hell where people will go to receive their just desserts after all that sinning. Yes, it was very detailed and was beyond its time and the place where Bosch lived, but still . . . Still, it could never be the kind of painting that would be so close to my heart I would want to lose myself in its details. Only in my dream. Because during my waking hours I'm a hard core Cezanne fan. Somewhere between the impressionists and the cubists, swimming in that ancient Prussian blue winking in the distance . . .

As for that matter of being pregnant . . . How many men in this world dream they're pregnant? When I tell my doctor about this dream I wonder if he'll tell me I have fertility envy, womb envy, I don't know, vagina envy, or something. To my knowledge our elder brother Freud smoothed the way for his fellow creatures in these matters. Usually these kinds of absurd dreams are attributed to women hankering after a penis, to their envy of those who possess one, or to their erotic feelings for their mothers or fathers or whatever. But God knows what kind of analyses a wretched male like me, who has attained the honour of dreaming he is pregnant, and is a pauper when it comes to interpretations, will fall victim to. If they put the literature in front of me now, the place would turn into a blood bath. God forbid, they'd start off with castration anxiety and who knows where they would end up!

Okay then, so why might I have had this bizarre dream? I can think of a few reasons. As someone who doesn't like lifts, buses, planes, in other words, places that imprison me inside them when their doors close on me, I have always had a fear of not being able to breathe easily. What's more, I imagine this fear has found its way into my dreams before. Are you wondering what makes me imagine that? The mornings when I wake up panting and out of breath, with an urgent need to gulp air into my lungs. I have no idea whether pregnant women have difficulty breathing, but I imagine if I were ever pregnant, it's more than likely I'd feel stifled out of my wits. Most probably what was weighing on me in that dream was my pregnancy.

To tell the truth, I'm grateful to myself for not having had a dream that's difficult to analyse. The fact that I dreamt it shortly after Pilar's abortion means there's no need to wrack my brains trying to work out what it might mean. However stifling my imaginary state of maternity was in my dream, the thought of fatherhood in real life was just as unbearable. Although it was Pilar who was pregnant, I was the one who was stifled and unable to breathe by the thought of her swelling belly. My wife was ready to accept full responsibility; she wanted to have the child. For my part I wasn't up for either the child, or the responsibility it would entail, or for Pilar to take on all those responsibilities on my behalf. I did not want any such event to occur in my life. She accused me of being selfish. She talked about how women's childbearing years are limited, and about how she was starting to approach that limit, about how there was no point in putting off having a child, about how, instead of regarding her pregnancy as a calamity that had befallen us, I should see it as an opportunity. She said she feared she was in danger of missing the last train while waiting for me to say I was finally ready. What if she could never get pregnant again? What if she menopaused earlier than expected? If it wasn't selfish to force her to take that risk, then what was it?

Pilar was right. The rules had been made by a force much too solid to oppose, nature had deemed it so. I could become a father whenever I liked, but it was very likely that after a while my beautiful wife would be completely deprived of the right to motherhood.

Not knowing whether that while would be 5 or 15 years was making Pilar anxious. She wanted to have a child as soon as possible so she could be free of that uncertainty. Well, there was no doubt that she was absolutely right where she was concerned. But if there was one thing I knew without a shadow of a doubt, it was that at that stage of my life I could not contemplate having a child, even in my wildest dreams. I could not make such an important decision in one fell swoop just to make my wife happy, just to allow her to experience motherhood before it was too late; I couldn't destroy myself in my attempt to save her. If I did, it wouldn't only be unfair on me, it would be unfair on Pilar and even on the prospective child. There are still so many things I want to do, even though I can't provide a precise answer in response to the question of what those things might be. I refuse to answer that officious question of "And what might they be?" that may come hot on the heels of that sentence. I am not going to feel like a monster and think I have to justify what my heart is telling me, just because I don't want to become a father.

Resolving that I was not ready for fatherhood, I proposed to Pilar that we postpone the business of having a baby until such time as we were both up for it, although I didn't have the foggiest idea of when that time might be. I don't know if she thought me as right as I thought her. She seemed a bit off with me, but still accepted my proposal. Perhaps sensing she might lose me if she insisted on having the child, she felt forced to choose between us. Without any further argument, she aborted the baby in her womb.

I can't say that my mind was entirely at ease after the abortion. I couldn't stop thinking I might have permanently deprived my wife of experiencing motherhood. I hadn't only married Pilar because I loved her, but because I had also realised she was the right person. I want to worship her in the same way as she worships me. I want to make her dreams come true. I'd be capable of doing a great many things for her, maybe even of dying. But anyway, dying for someone is easier than living for them. That's a fact, even if no one wants to admit it. That's why I don't want a baby in my life for whom I will feel obliged to live. Of course I would have liked to have been able to do more for my wife. But alas, I'm not capable of any more than this.

This baby business surpasses what I'm capable of doing for the sake of her happiness.

Besides, toiling away at being happy exhausts me. I don't know what Doctor Carcel would have to say about that, but I think this obsession with happiness is a contagious disease that's exclusive to this era. And it would appear the only ones to benefit from that disease are Doctor Carcel and his colleagues. Oh, and those know-alls who write self-help books that don't help anything except their bank accounts. In fact, this fixation with happiness infuriates me. Probably because I am one of those individuals who believes unhappiness brings people closer than happiness ... It's easy to share happiness, but can the same be said of sorrow? For example, Pilar and I have never had to overcome any major setback together. There has never been any unhappy or sorrowful event to put our love to the test. The biggest crisis in our relationship was this abortion. And now I'm not even sure whether we'll be able to carry on after the damage wreaked by that crisis. I think Pilar has her doubts too. If we're one of those couples that falls apart at the first sign of unhappiness, then we don't deserve to be parents, do we? Doesn't that prove I was right to abstain?

If I were in the company of a close friend who had no qualms about speaking frankly, he would most probably tell me I'm looking for excuses. Because the reason why I renounced that child was not because I don't have faith in my relationship with Pilar. I renounced it because I can't be certain of myself. Can there be anything as ridiculous as blaming Pilar for not having lived a miserable life until now and for hoping for happiness from her remaining days? And is she the only one to have been smitten with the happiness disease? As if I'm not the one who shunned that baby in case it cast a shadow on the happiness it's doubtful I even feel!

When she was agreeing to the abortion, if she chose being happy with me over her maternal instinct, she took that step because she dreamed that one day we would both decide we wanted to have a baby. But alas, I am neither as eager nor as certain as my wife about that day. What's more, I know she is as frightened as I am of the possibility that that day may never come. I don't know if it's because she doesn't feel prepared for what she might hear, or because she thinks I will eventually change my mind, but she doesn't try and talk about it anymore. We mutually remain silent about the thing she most needs to talk about. Perhaps it's only in our dreams that we spill the things that we hide.

4

Perihan

Is it a woman's apparition in a child
Or a child's apparition in a woman
Or just an apparition?

Edip Cansever, "I'm Ruhi Bey How Am I"

Partly because of the absurd dream she had had, Perihan woke up early, while the rest of the household was still nestling in the warm embrace of sleep. She got out of bed and tiptoed from the room so as not to wake her husband. It was only once she had closed the door behind her that she took a deep breath. She had had enough of that man's brutishness. She was how old now and she still had to put up with one kind of abuse during the day and another at night. Last night, when he had been too rough with her, she had threatened to shout and scream, never mind that Bülent and the guest would hear, and to wake the entire household, but the filthy low life couldn't have cared less. Not only had he not left her alone out of respect for the others, but he had flown into a rage and beaten her as well. Her side still ached where he had kicked her. That man hadn't been this out of control in the beginning, but, once he saw he could get away with it, he had got more and more savage. He thought he could do whatever he wanted to his wife; he regarded her as his property. Was that any way to treat the mother of your child? He did it even to the mother of his child . . . just like dogs . . . Remembering what Havva Abla had said years ago, she suspected her husband did it with young boys too. For a while that business had been number one on the gossip agenda of the women who came to the hairdresser's salon at Gülbağ. Seizing the moments when Şenol wasn't in the shop, they talked about how Yıldız's husband Hikmet had got into hanging out with transsexuals in Beyoğlu and how he squandered all their income on them. Whatever, the women said. If he had got bored of his wife, why didn't he go with another woman, they complained; what business did he have with transsexuals. Perihan knew what was really eating them. They were terrified that tomorrow or the day after, they too might find themselves in the same boat as Yıldız. Somehow none of them could be certain their husbands would never do what Hikmet was doing. Once, one of the women in the salon – most probably Seher Abla with the ebony hair – said, as they were talking about Hikmet, "Ok, so the one who gets it is one of them, but, are you saying that the one who gives it isn't? I mean, what it boils down to is that he's more turned on by men than women." All the women in the salon disagreed in unison, saying no, what are you talking about. A real man is someone who goes with whoever takes his fancy. Women, men, he could even pester animals if need be. It would be better if he didn't of course, but that's just how men were; they had too many hormones, their appetites were insatiable and their natures different. But it was important to make the distinction. Opening your legs like a woman was one thing and thrusting in the seed like a man was another. How could you see them in the same light?

Gülizar was the only one to speak out honestly and release the maggot that was eating away at her:

"What if our husbands are going with the likes of them as well? How can you tell?"

Havva Abla supplied the answer with her eyes pinned to the door, as though she were anxious that Şenol, who had popped out to get some supplies, would come back and overhear what they were saying:

"It's easy. That sort harasses their own wives from behind at home as well. Once a bugger always a bugger, ladies."

All the women in the shop had burst out laughing, as though she had said something hilariously funny. When Perihan had presumed to try to join in with their mirth, her boss, who was backcombing Gülizar's hair, had yanked her ponytail so hard she thought each and every strand of her hair had been wrenched out of her head.

"You get on with your work, air head! This isn't for young girls' ears" Havva Abla reprimanded, and dispatched her subordinate to clean the waxing booth. As usual, Perihan had entered the sticky, cloying booth with loathing. Ripping out everyone's hairs from their legs and underarms disgusted her; and especially when someone came to have that part waxed, because she couldn't take a proper deep breath until she had finished, she would emerge from the booth a shade of something between red and purple. She couldn't understand how they weren't ashamed to display all their bodily parts; no matter how many times she did it she could never get used to that job. The things she had seen in that tiny booth. Women splaying their legs wide when they hadn't even managed to wipe the shit off their behind, women with overgrown, matted, pubic hair that looked like spiders' webs, who lay in front of her without feeling the need to trim it even a little bit beforehand, those who weren't embarrassed to have that part of them waxed on the one hand, but protested it hurt and made her blow on them on the other, those who couldn't grit their teeth but screamed the salon down at the tiniest hint of pain ... It was in that booth that Perihan had learned to abhor her own sex. And to despise the smell of wax ... She had suffered a lot on account of smells. When she was born her grandmother had rubbed her body with salt, which was why her sweat never smelled. But when the salt went up her nose and she started screaming, the old woman had said, "My goodness! There was I trying to make an eyelash, but I've gone and gouged out an eye. This nose is going to torment this little child, dear God, protect the little mite!"

Everyone believed she had said it because she thought the salt that had gone up the baby's nose would be ,painful and no one dwelt on it too much. But what the woman had meant was that her granddaughter's nose, which had become sensitive after its accident with the salt, would create an olfactory inferno for her when she grew up. And Perihan really was overly susceptible to smells. Like a hunting dog, her nose picked up every scent. And bad smells in particular, the ones that made her feel sick . . .

Once she had washed her face and was fully awake, the first thing she did was go into the kitchen and switch on the tiny radio on the counter. The singer's beaming voice spilled out into the kitchen as she sang one of Perihan's favourites, "No one is a shah, nor a king" and, in autopilot, she put on the water to boil for tea. As she did so, she considered the weird dream she had had that night. In her dream she was holding a plate full of baklava. She had wanted to eat one of the delicious cakes that were making her mouth water, but the sudden appearance of her enraged uncle, who slapped her hand, sent the plate and all its contents hurtling to the ground. Then Şenol had arrived and, with a hammer, nailed each of the baklavas, which had scattered in all directions, to the floor. She couldn't understand why, after all these years, she could still bring her uncle and Şenol together in the same dream. To hell with the pair of them, she thought irritably. Her uncle would begrudge her even a baklava. But what could Perihan say about Şenol's nailing the baklavas to the floor one by one? Vexed that they still managed to get under her skin after all these years, she hastily wiped those thoughts out of her head. Then she opened the window and filled her lungs with the cool freshness of the early morning. This was her favourite time of day. The morning, the hours she spent alone in the kitchen before anyone else was up. She loved the morning because it was the cleanest part of the day, not yet sullied, not yet tired. She loved being by herself, because throughout her whole life she had never had the chance to be alone. She had always had to live in overcrowded houses, had no choice but to put up with everyone's noise and ill temper and had never had the liberty of conversing just with herself. She loved the kitchen too, because the kitchen was the only place in the house that belonged just to her, where the entire household accepted her absolute and unconditional rule. The kitchen was hers. Because there were so few things in this life that were hers alone, that was the place where she found the most comfort, her kingdom where she triumphed in trivial battles. Perihan was well aware that all charlatans had their secret kingdom. And she was the buffoon of the house and the king of the kitchen.

All her life she had never had anything that was just hers. She had always had to share everything with others, to wait for her turn, which somehow never seemed to come. She was so weary of waiting that, never mind not being able to endure waiting at a bus stop, in a conversation she couldn't even bear to wait until the other person had finished talking before butting in to have her say. It infuriated her husband, who accused her of being bad-mannered, disrespectful and of having grabbed more than her fair share of all kinds of other ugly traits. It was easy for him to talk of course. After all, he had grown up in the lap of abundance, and not only that, he had been a boy. It wasn't possible for him to understand his wife's haste, her fixation with doing whatever she had to do there and then and then quickly making herself scarce.

During Perihan's childhood, on the rare occasions when any fancy dish found its way into their house, they would all swoop down on it to make sure they got their share. They would gather around the table and push and shove to prevent anyone else from getting what was rightfully theirs. Perihan saw nothing odd in that and disliked those who did. People who talked about the beauty of sharing had experienced it as a virtue, not as an obligation. Sharing was all well and good in times of plenty, but being forced to share in times of hardship did not bring people closer together, or strengthen their ties one bit. While the rich regarded sharing as a token of love, people like Perihan despised everyone they had shared with, considering them an obstacle to their happiness. Before, when the household used to gather around that table, no one had any sympathy for anyone who lagged behind, or waited, or dithered. There it was every man for himself; whoever acted fast got the fattest portion. And as her grandmother always said, whoever was last was left out in the cold to freeze. That's why Perihan always ate quickly; it was what she was accustomed to. After she had grown up, and even after she had married and moved into a house of plenty, she still hadn't managed to shake off the habit of gulping her food as though someone were going to snatch it away from her.

When Perihan was a child, the winner in her house was not the one who kept quiet, but the one who spoke out. Because no one was going to go to the trouble of defending anyone else, and because, as her grandmother always said, every man for himself and let the devil take the hindmost, everyone had to wrench their fair share out of everyone else's hands. That's why Perihan didn't like keeping quiet. She believed that every moment she was quiet she was missing something, and tried to get whatever she had to say off her chest all in one go, so she could relax. She asked before the other person did, and supplied the answer before they could. What Perihan knew for sure was this: whoever provided the food and spoke out wouldn't easily lose their place in life's queue.

She didn't expect her husband to understand all this. No matter what, a full belly could never understand what it was like to go hungry; someone who had never suffered hardship didn't understand the language of the poor. And Veysel couldn't get his head around why his wife was so possessive of the kitchen. Whenever she wasn't around, he loved bellowing, "Is that woman in the kitchen again? What's keeping her in there so long? Is it covered in shit or what?" How could someone who had had his own room right from when he was a baby understand that a place where she was the only person who entered through the door could feel like a castle, a temple even . . .

Perihan had grown up in a cramped, overcrowded house. When her father had died shortly after her mother had fallen pregnant with her brother Bünyamin, they had moved into her eldest uncle's house, and they and her uncle, her aunt, her cousins and grandmother had all lived on top of each other for years. At night she slept in the living room with her grandmother, her mother and her brother Bünyamin. That didn't change even after she had grown into a fully developed adolescent. She never had her own room where she could close the door and take refuge. When, at age 17, she left her uncle's house and they moved to a neighbourhood several streets away, she, her mother and her brother settled into a squalid, two-room house. This time she began to sleep with her mother. Even being able to turn off the light when she wanted to in the room where she slept was a rare luxury for her. When, in the same year, she married Veysel and moved into this spacious house, she rejoiced about never again having to live nose to nose with anyone. But no matter how much wider the area of the house where she lived became, her soul continued to narrow; that was her destiny. Whereas before she used to sleep in the same bed as her dear mother, now she lay with her husband at night. She may have still not had a room of her own, even amongst so many square metres, but, with time, she took over the kitchen. She threw herself into the cooking, purely for the sake of having somewhere she could call her own. She buried herself under mounds of recipes and, by preparing a host of spectacular meals, each more sumptuous than the last, she earned herself the control of the kitchen. It was unheard of for Veysel to set foot in the kitchen, even to get a glass of water. And her sister-in-law didn't trouble herself to say no, you take a break, I'll cook today. That way, in her seventeenth year, Perihan finally got her own little room. Because they had never suffered enough overcrowding to appreciate the value of being alone, neither her husband nor her sister-in-law could comprehend Perihan's love affair with the kitchen.

And for years they ridiculed her determination to defend what was hers. Veysel mostly accused her of being a deprived, covetous upstart. She had been deprived, yes, which was why she knew how to appreciate everything she attained in later life, and to enjoy it. Whenever she bought a new outfit she would deck herself out like a child on the morning of bayram and not be able to sit still until she had run out to parade herself before the neighbours. A child accustomed to going to kiss the neighbours' hands dressed in new clothes every bayram probably wouldn't understand her behaviour either. For years she had had to make do with the hand-me-downs of her uncle's two daughters. If they hadn't received their own hand-me-downs, then any new clothes that were bought were always for her uncle's eldest daughter, Sultan. The clothes that Sultan outgrew went to her sister Sabiha, and whatever was cast off by Sabiha eventually went to Perihan. Her dresses, her school smock, even her school books for which she had no use after primary school were hand-me-downs from her uncle's children. By the time she inherited them, the trousers had holes in the knees, the jumpers' sleeves were worn out and the dresses were faded. Because she had always had to partake in what others had owned and been forced to be grateful for what they had tossed to her out of charity, ownership meant a very very great deal to Perihan. Her husband ridiculed her openly, while her sister-in-law Müesser belittled her with the look on her face, privately judging her. How blind they were to what they thought they could see. How could they appreciate the value of ownership ... How could they understand the magnitude of her fear of losing what she had attained later on in life ...

Flaunting what she owned before others was Perihan's way of confirming it really existed, which she still couldn't believe. But it was impossible. How could someone own anything in this life, when they were entirely, body and soul, at someone else's mercy? Perihan knew and she knew only too well; never mind the kitchen in the house, or the gold bangles jangling on her wrists, not even the feeble breath she took was hers. Her fate was permanently in the hands of others. The true proprietors of what she took on loan and utilised were her masters too. Those masters were totally ignorant about giving rewards, but generous to a fault when it came to doling out punishment. Their favourite threat was to take back what they had given. They were forever making sure she knew that the future lay trembling between their two lips, like a frail bird, and that they were the ones who controlled it.

Once upon a time she was an unwelcome burden in her uncle's, and now in her husband's, house. Her uncle had thrown her out the very first time she had strayed from the path. Right at the beginning her husband had threatened to send her back to her mother's if she didn't give him a child. Masters snatched back with a ladle what they had dished out with a spoon, and Perihan wasn't just pitiable in poverty but when swimming in abundance too. Accordingly, what she endured in this house was the ransom for what she took on loan and utilised. As she got into bed with her husband, with whom she would never have lived under the same roof so meekly if she had had anywhere else to go, she felt the only thing that differentiated her from a prostitute was her scrawled signature in the marriage book. But she never repeated that truth, even to herself. Whenever it was necessary, she talked of the sanctity of the family and fabricated falsehoods designed to heal her wounded pride. Like everyone who couldn't bear the bleakness of truth, she too required lies.

The only thing in the whole world that belonged to Perihan was her child. In the beginning, in the hope that there might one day be another way out for her, she hadn't wanted children. But then, once she had realised she was liable to lose what she had ... she had had a child. And on the day she gave birth to Bülent she had also accepted that she would never be able to change her life. But even her child, for whom she had condemned herself to eternal unhappiness, was not hers alone. It was one thing to share her son with her husband, but when another woman in the house had the presumption to usurp the role of mother, it made her livid. Not satisfied with loving the boy as a nephew, her sister-in-law did her best to worm her way between him and his mother, like a sly drape.

There was one thing about Müesser that got on her nerves. Yes, all right, she was kind, as kindness goes, but still Perihan never felt at ease around her. She made people feel beholden to her with her kindness, and she intimidated people with her silence. And most irritating of all was the way she doted on

Bülent. She didn't know her place; she tried to behave more like the boy's mother than his aunt. And when that happened, Perihan would think how dare she try and mother a child who already has a mother, and see red. If she was so keen on being a mother, then why hadn't she got married and left? Why did she insist on being a millstone around their necks? Instead of trying to mother other people's children, why hadn't she had a child of her own to take into her arms? And naturally she didn't keep any of this to herself either; she offloaded each and every one of her grievances whenever she sat down to gossip with the neighbours.

She opened the cupboard and started taking out all the breakfast things. She wondered what the guest might like. Last night when she was going to bed Perihan hadn't asked her what she wanted for breakfast. Mind you, anyone brave enough to dare to ask that grim woman any questions was better than she was. It was like a tiny hill giving itself the airs of a mountain; that stuck-up madam was so puffed up with her own importance she thought no one was good enough for her. Because Perihan had to bend down whether she liked it or not, she couldn't stand the sort who were so arrogant they wouldn't bend down to pick up their own nose if it fell off.

When her sister-in-law had put the telephone down she had opened her eyes wide and said, in a near stammer, "It seems Eyüp's in Istanbul." Perihan too had been excited about her brother-in-law being in Istanbul. The first thought that had crossed her mind was what the reason for his lordship's visit might be. She didn't think there could be anything auspicious about his suddenly upping and coming now, after all these years, and was convinced there would be a catch at the bottom of it. But what did anyone in this house care about what she thought? If they had cared, would her sister-in-law have grabbed the phone and called Veysel before she had even had a chance to open her mouth and say two words?

But Perihan didn't take it personally; after all, that was just how the woman was. Anyone looking at her from outside would take her for a complete pushover, but in fact she was a real wolf in sheep's clothing. It was always the same, whenever there was anything concerning the family, she made a point of excluding Perihan. She loved making it understood, in her underhand way, that the real owners of this house were her brother and herself. Perihan would never forget the day when they had come to ask for her hand. Her sister-in-law had entered the house practically on tiptoe. She hadn't disguised her aversion, either as she trod on the carpet, or as she was putting on the slippers they handed her, but instead looked down her nose at everything around her. And especially when her mother was explaining all the hardship she had endured whilst raising her child, instead of having some empathy and commiserating with the poor woman's troubles, she had sat and listened with her lips set in a superior straight line. Perihan knew her sister-in-law had never erased the thick line she had drawn between them. Whenever she witnessed or heard anything from Perihan that wasn't to her liking, she would fish out that line straightaway and plant it on her lips, reminding her sister-in-law of her place. Far from being the serene, reconciliatory creature she seemed on the outside, she was actually devious and ill-meaning.

On the first day Perihan had set foot in the house she had said, with what she tried to pass off as a gentle smile, "Welcome my daughter, this is as good as your house too now." Since when have I been your daughter, Perihan had thought, there were only 13 years between them. And what did she mean as good as? Weren't they going to live in this house together from now on? Wasn't she now undeniably wed to the master of the house? In which case didn't that make her status even higher than that of her sister-in-law's?

But she got her comeuppance all right; whatever Veysel said to her that day had made her hang up in a fluster, her face flushed deep red. Then when Pilar Hanım had gathered momentum and phoned a second time, saying, "I'm coming" things had really hotted up and the mood in the house changed radically. Perihan liked guests. She was very proud of her house and loved showing it off, and piling the guests' plates high with her sumptuous dishes. Regardless of her husband's menacing face- pulling and hard glares during all of last night, he couldn't fault her hospitality to her sister-in-law. She had welcomed her at the door, thrown her arms around her in response to the frosty hand Pilar had held out to her, prepared a table laden with lavish dishes and served her with more than generous portions. But of course, it wasn't very nice when a person didn't reciprocate with even half the friendliness they received. The woman didn't deign to open her mouth to say a single word about all that food she had put in front of her. Okay, so her husband was missing, okay, so she was miserable, but, just like she hadn't been too upset to wolf down all that food with such gusto, she should have been able to find the energy to say a couple of words about it too. Perihan was accustomed to people ignoring her, but she wouldn't stand for anyone ignoring her food.

She was proud of her talents in the kitchen. Besides, that was her only accomplishment that nobody could fault. While she was forced to share even her role as a mother with her sister-in-law, she was the sole ruler of her creations in the kitchen. She had enjoyed cooking as a young girl too, but, just as with everything else one did in poverty, there wasn't much pleasure in it. When she no longer had to cook according to the ingredients she had available, but could finally look at whichever ingredients she needed for what she was going to cook, then cooking had turned into the most enjoyable occupation in the world. Once she had sent Bülent to school and Veysel to work, she would enter the kitchen compulsively, not to carry out her daily tasks, but to fulfil the duties that would appease her soul. If she didn't clean, her sister-in-law would immerse herself in embroidery or crocheting – though for whose trousseau was a mystery – and allow her to do whatever she wanted in the kitchen at her leisure, without bothering her, or getting under her feet.

Perihan would go into the kitchen with the same feverish excitement as an artist who is undecided about what she is going to paint when she picks up her brush. When the door reopened, sending magnificent aromas wafting into the house, nobody had any idea what might come out. One day she might emerge bearing acemkebab, another day with Circassian chicken with walnuts, and on another a simple pasta dish. She did not categorise the meals as difficult or easy, but classified them according to how they touched her heart.

On the days when she was angry she preferred to cook meat dishes. She took out the pain of the rage she couldn't vent on the person it was really directed at on the meat she slapped down on the sturdy chopping board. By slicing and dismembering the whole pieces of flesh lying before her with the aid of a Bursa knife, she endeavoured to free her heart of its burden. If the wrath boiling inside her didn't look like it would be pacified easily, she started kneading köfte. She would plunge her hands into the large bowl in which she had placed minced meat, stale bread and all the other ingredients and, sometimes kneading, sometimes pinching, purge herself of the pain that had been inflicted on her. She added generous quantities of cumin to the köfte mixture. She would knead the minced meat until she was drenched in sweat and her arms ached, and at the same time inhale the strong scent of the cumin. Perhaps that was why, whenever she smelled cumin, she would remember all the wrongs that had been done to her and feel as though a fist had punched her in the stomach. Since she had started to spend long periods of time in the kitchen, she had understood better that certain smells hide amongst certain memories. The smell of oranges reminded her of the orange peel placed on top of the heater in the middle of her uncle's living room; that heater, for example, reminded her of the pain she had felt when she had accidentally put her hand on it as she was dodging her mother's slipper. And the appetising smell of chargrilled peppers took Perihan back 25 years. It reminded her of the picnic on Meriç beach shortly before her father's death, when they were still living in their house in Edirne. After her father had cooked the meat on the barbecue, he had chargrilled the peppers. Apart from the memories of a happy day, the smell of peppers made her nostrils ache with grief for those who were never coming back.

On the days when she was in a good mood she preferred vegetables to meat. She loved washing the colourful, shiny vegetables, lining them up on the wooden board and chopping them into perfect, even sizes as she listened to their fresh, snapping sounds. On those occasions she would not wreak revenge on what she chopped, but derive an almost childlike pleasure from it. She found a miraculous significance in the purple of aubergines, the red of beetroot, the white of cauliflower, the orange of carrots, and gave thanks to be alive with each stroke of the knife. When she wanted to remind herself that just being alive was reason enough to be happy, she would arrange the multicoloured fruits she had carefully cut up on a large dish and serve them to her family. The water melon was always the fruit most willing to impart its high spirits. Whenever Perihan opened its bright green casing and encountered its blood red contents, it was as though she had obtained a crucial piece of information, as though she had cracked a vital code and discovered the meaning of life. Even if she compared herself to the black seeds that everyone tried to get rid of, the joy of being in a blood red world made struggling against all the suffering in it worthwhile. That's how Perihan felt on the days when she was content.

Far from being a chore she had got lumbered with, cooking was her sole means of expressing herself. A universe in which she owed no one any explanations for what she slit and dismembered, what she took into her hand and pinched until it had breathed its last, what she burned to a cinder or what she closed the lid of tightly and stored, a universe where she was free, that was hers alone ... The kitchen was like a miniature world. And Perihan and the things in her head were its sole occupants.

Once she had transferred the Seville orange marmalade, strawberry jam, pumpkin marmalade and acıka she had made with her own hands into porcelain dishes, she added the water, which was rising in rebellion because it had not yet been united with the tea, despite having boiled for some time, to the metal teapot. She pondered what she might make for some time, before eventually deciding on cheese lavaş, the griddled flat, cheesy bread Leman had given her the recipe for. At this point the silence in the house gradually began to lift. From the creaking of the floorboards on the first floor, she imagined Müesser to be the first to have woken up. Her sister-in-law walked slowly, pausing after every few steps. Perihan knew that during these pauses she was listening, trying to sniff out whether there was anyone else awake or whether she was disturbing anyone with her noise. The footsteps continued all the way to the upstairs toilet. When the toilet door closed carefully and gently, she had no more doubts about the identity of the person who had woken up.

As she was arranging the breakfast things on the dinner table in the living room, she wondered whether the guest would get up late, thinking please God, don't let her be one of these people who loaf about in bed till lunchtime. It made her angry when people were late coming to the table. It put her in a bad mood when the food got cold and the tea turned bitter. She hated standing beside the food she had prepared and summoning the household to do her the honour of gracing the table. Her sister-in-law, who came downstairs a few minutes later, stuck her head round the kitchen door and whispered "Good morning." Then she went into the living room to wait for the others to wake up. Perihan laughed to herself as she imagined her settling down on the two-seater sofa, after she had checked on her violets lined up on the windowsill, picking up the lace table cover she had started last week and beginning to crochet the pattern Mad Adalet had given her, after making her promise to keep it to herself. How could she not laugh? Like there was any chance of finding a husband this late in the day, or like they had daughters of marriageable age, she and Adalet did nothing but sit and crochet all day till they were blue in the face. What's more, Adalet palmed off the patterns she wangled from other people on Müesser, making out she had designed them herself. Her dim sister-in-law didn't realise it, but it was obvious that's what she did. Otherwise, how else could that old crone come up with so many different patterns all by herself . . . And then, the way she would only give Müesser her patterns on condition that she swore she would never show them to anyone else, and then insisted on unveiling them in the strictest secrecy drove Perihan mad. It's not as if Perihan had a daughter whose trousseau Müesser could prepare. And even if she did, who would ever stoop to their ugly patterns. To spite them, whenever Adalet came over to drink tea, Perihan would mock the two friends, who claimed to be like sisters, by exclaiming, "Oh, it's the weekly gathering of the old maids' brigade! Haven't you managed to save up enough coupons for a husband yet girls?" Adalet wasn't as hopeless as her sister-in-law of course. She at least had been married once. But she had been widowed while still newly-wed and hadn't ventured to remarry. As for her sister-in-law, never mind getting married, she had never once in her life even hankered after anyone from afar. Unless you counted her love for Tarık Akan, of course. Perihan found it hilarious the way she became glued to the screen, spellbound, whenever she was watching a Tarık Akan film on television, and by the way she flushed red and turned pale whenever anyone mentioned her infatuation, like a young girl caught red-handed writing a love letter. For God's sake, was it normal for these two women, one of them widowed for donkey's years, and the other whose amorous adventures amounted to idolising a movie star, to sit side by side all day making lace?

By the time Bülent's door slammed shut, the breakfast was ready. As always, the child made a tremendous noise as he hurtled down the stairs. He switched on the television that Müesser had kept off for fear of disturbing the others, and started zapping channels. Shortly afterwards she heard Veysel's voice, asking his son to bring him water. So, he too had got up and gone into the living room in the meantime. Just as she had feared then, their starting breakfast was going to depend on their guest's whims. She approached the living room door and asked everyone, "When do you think Pilar will get up? Should we sit down to breakfast without her?"

Her husband stared indifferently. No doubt his head was filled with supermarket accounts and he hadn't reserved any space for the question of whom he might encounter at the breakfast table. But Müesser, her eyes popping out of her head as though she had just heard the most unspeakable outrage, said, "It will be rude, let's wait for her."

"Huh, what are we supposed to do then, sit here and starve, with a child in the house?" objected Perihan. In fact she wasn't even hungry. Her nose had simply been put out of joint by her sister-in-law's instant Pilar idolatry, when Pilar had only been there five minutes, and, by the way the woman had arrived yesterday, seized the reins the moment she had set foot in the house and changed the household's entire routine. A proper guest should know her place and fit in with everyone else. Before she could touch upon that subject, Pilar appeared at the top of the stairs. Sly fox, sneaking up on us like that, thought Perihan. Had she heard her saying she didn't want to wait for her for breakfast? Well so what if she had, it wasn't as if it was rude to be hungry!

The woman had put on a light, airy, ankle length, khaki green dress. The outfit made her seem even taller than she had looked yesterday. It was obvious she had been in a hurry when she gathered up her wavy hair in a bun on the top of her head, because several unruly curls had escaped from the hair grips and were poking out in all directions. She looked attractive, even though she wasn't wearing any make up. In contradiction of Perihan's often repeated comment that all attractive women had been born again thanks to make up. She herself was not beautiful and never had been, and she knew it well. As someone accustomed to despising not what she couldn't have, but the people who did have those things, she also had a particular aversion to beautiful women.

Involuntarily, Perihan's eyes went to her own outfit. She hadn't felt any need to examine her appearance since she had got up. The faded t shirt she was wearing was full of bleach stains. The too short sweat pants with the holes in the knees were so tattered even a circus clown would ridicule them. It wasn't that she didn't have the money to buy new clothes; what she wore in the house was the height of inelegance because she believed that particular look was more fitting. Thinking it reflected how hardworking she was, she walked around looking as unkempt as possible. When she was at home there was no need to wear matching colours or worry about looking good. But now, as her sister-in-law glided down the stairs in her khaki green dress, she felt self-conscious about her own appearance.

In the past, that is, in the days when she was condemned to wear Sultan's and Sabiha's hand-me-downs, she used to love films about poverty-stricken young girls who got their own back on the boys who looked down on them by turning into beautiful fairy princesses in a matter of days. She always identified with the servant girls who learned how to play the piano in two days, the gypsy girls who took classes in etiquette from refined Greek ladies, the factory workers who put on evening gowns created by renowned dressmakers that transformed them into ravishing beauties; like them, she fantasised about undergoing a sudden metamorphosis and becoming someone completely different from herself. Someone extraordinary in every respect, in the way she dressed, the way she sat, the way she stood, the way she spoke, the way she carried and expressed herself ... Even more than for the power it would give her to make an impression on others, she wanted to change so she could finally cast off that downtrodden feeling she carried inside her. During those years, Perihan had not managed to transform herself into someone else. She had walked around in a state of permanent irritation, narrowing her dull blue eyes, planted like two tiny dots on the face that not even her tightly pulled back blonde hair could make beautiful. But, after she had moved to Reşitpaşa, married Veysel and come to this huge house as a bride, for the first time in her life she had had the chance to become someone else. She was able to buy new dresses and behave as though she were someone new. And she did, in her own way. On the days when she was going out, or going visiting, she got dressed and made up to the nines, but somehow still couldn't attain the beauty she dreamed of.

Every time she looked in the mirror, she tried to find what was lacking in her face. She was lacking in eyes and over-endowed where her nose was concerned, but it was something else that prevented her from looking beautiful no matter what she did, something that went deeper. After spending years searching in mirrors for the feature she lacked, she eventually realised that what had penetrated so deep inside her she could never wipe herself clean of it was her past, her past that she believed, in her heart of hearts, was what she deserved. She knew now that you didn't become a rich person simply by marrying a rich husband. She knew only too well who she really was, and even more, whom she had been born to be. Even though she had changed her surname with a signature, guaranteed her new life in her own way by having a child, at moments when she was certain that no one was looking at her, she was still Fitnat the charwoman's orphan. That was the reason why, when she was at home and could be herself, she derived comfort from these tattered old outfits that no one would blame her for throwing away. This destitution had worked itself so deeply inside her that neither the jewellery she put on when she was going out, nor the make-up she wore could wipe it away, nor add any beauty to her remaining existence. She could not compensate for what her soul lacked with money and possessions, jewellery, clothes and finery. Whatever it was that Perihan lacked, her sister-in-law, walking down the stairs swaying her hips, had it. Her sister-in-law was nothing like her. Perihan despised people like herself because she knew what nasty pieces of work they were, just as she despised those who weren't like her, because she disliked everything that was unfamiliar.

As her sister-in-law descended the stairs, tossing her skirts, she called out "Good morning" to them. Veysel, who was channel hopping, remote control in hand, made do with turning his head briefly in her direction and nodding, but Müesser, who was bending over backwards to please the guest, seemed to be practically begging for forgiveness as she asked, in her gentlest, warmest voice, "Good morning. We weren't too noisy I hope?" Perihan was sick and tired of this fawning and cringing.

Because she herself had sat in a corner without a murmur, by asking we weren't too noisy I hope, she meant the rest of the household, but by behaving as though she was taking all the blame herself she was drawing attention to her own saintliness. Perihan knew her so-called good intentions and serenity only too well; she could pull the wool over everyone else's eyes, but not hers. An artificial smile, similar to Müesser's, appeared on her sister-in-law's lips. That infuriating smile seemed to be saying, don't worry.

"No, of course not. I always wake up early anyway."

Hmph, some early! thought Perihan. She herself had got up before everyone else, sorted out the breakfast, laid the table, got everything ready, but was yet to open her mouth. And as for that woman, never mind that the table had been laid for hours, and never mind that she was the last one up, she still thought she could stand there barefaced, boasting about how early she got up. The whole world hankers after a madman, and I after someone sane, she thought. Then she remembered her grandmother's favourite expression: "If I planted a flag in front of every madman there'd be no cloth left in the bazaar."

The household started tucking into the breakfast eagerly. Bülent and Veysel, who loved cheese lavaş, polished them off one and two at a time. Extolling the virtues of the orange marmalade she had picked up, Müesser mentioned that İkbal had tasted it last week and loved it, and said let's give her a small jar too. But, far from being pleased by the compliment, Perihan pulled a sour face and thought, haven't you got better things to do than think of İkbal. She didn't like the woman; she only associated with her because she was the only one out of all the neighbours who envied her. The only reason why she had anything to do with her was to know how it felt to be envied . . . But İkbal attracted the evil eye. Anything she admired in the house inevitably suffered a terrible fate. Less than a week later, the vase she had sighed over, breathing "Ohhh, how loooooooooovely," was smashed; the brand new stereo, which she looked at and said "I wish we had one too," broke; the spinach böreks that she had pre-ordered before her arrival by saying "Yours are always so delicious", burnt. And no doubt it was just to spite her that Müesser insisted on pandering to that doom merchant.

Everyone else was eating with relish, but her cold fish of a sister-in-law had hardly touched a thing. She had smeared a bit of chocolate and hazelnut spread on a thin slice of bread and was picking at it half-heartedly. The high and mighty madam couldn't give a damn about all that lavaş and all those jams and those different cheeses she had spread out before her. When Perihan tried to put some lavaş on her plate, she shook her head in refusal, without even deigning to open her mouth.

Eventually, unable to bear it any longer, Perihan asked, "Don't you like it?" and immediately felt Müesser's eyes on her. The woman was quaking in her boots, in case her faithless little brother's cold fish of a wife heard a home truth or two . . .

"No, everything looks delicious, it's just a bit early for me."

"What do you mean, early?"

"To eat."

"Why? Don't you eat breakfast?"

"I do, but usually just something small. I can't eat much in the morning."

Hark at her highness, thought Perihan. Her ladyship can't eat much in the morning! You'd think she could just taste it out of politeness, so she didn't look so rude. To hell with her, she thought, popping a piece of lavaş into her mouth. But nevertheless she still said, "Tell me what you eat and I'll make it for you tomorrow morning." She couldn't bear anyone to leave her table dissatisfied.

"No no, there's no need for you to make anything for me. I just have coffee in the morning. Sometimes with a bit of cake or a croissant, that's all."

At this, despite all her objections to Pilar, Perihan got up, went to the kitchen and returned with a cup of coffee.

"Here we all drink tea in the morning, that's why it didn't occur to me. Tomorrow morning I'll make you a cake too. We'll have to make do with this for today," she said. While Pilar was protesting, embarrassed to have interrupted her hostess's breakfast and made her leave the table, that there was no need for her to make cake, Perihan observed her sister-in-law's face, squirming with awkwardness as she sipped the coffee that had been prepared and placed in front of her at a single word from her, and heaved a deep sigh. No one could leave her table dissatisfied ...

After breakfast Bülent removed himself to the street to play football with his friends, Veysel to his supermarket because he couldn't relax unless he was there to oversee it himself and Pilar to Beyoğlu to find her husband's friend's bookshop. The woman's boldness was really something! She thought nothing of going out scouring the streets for her husband all by herself in a completely strange country. No matter how much Müesser and Veysel had pressed her, she had refused all their help and declared she could go by herself. She had even stubbornly rejected Veysel's offer to drive her to Beyoğlu and insisted on taking a taxi. Her refusal had been so self-assured that neither Veysel nor Müesser had dared object. Helpless and resigned to their defeat, they had given up. As someone who complained that no one took her seriously, Perihan envied her sister-in-law and wondered what it would feel like to be heeded so absolutely. For that to happen would she have to wear a green dress, or be born in a different country? Or would she have to be an architect, drink only coffee in the morning and walk around intimidating everyone with her withering look? Was there still a chance she might ever become such a person?

★ ★ ★

I seem to be in some kind of coffin that I barely fit into. But I'm neither in a coffin nor in my own body. I'm a colourless, scentless plant in a pot. Somehow I can observe myself from the outside. What's more, I see nothing strange, either about being in a pot, or about my transformation into an inane plant. I am completely nonchalant about the whole thing, as if it were the most normal situation in the world. I feel neither surprise nor fear, just loneliness.

Just then there's a sudden flurry of activity nearby. People I haven't seen for a long time come and stand in front of me, each of them holding a glass of water. My sister is the first to appear before my eyes, then Madeleina. When they vanish, İlhami arrives with a glass of water in his hand. Just like the others, he stands and stares without uttering a word. Before I can work out what's going on, he too disappears, just like the others, and Vehbi takes his place. One familiar face after the other appears, then disappears. I'm happy they have come to share my loneliness, but I'm also wary of the water they want to pour on me. I wish it would occur to them to forget about all that water business and just stand next to me. If I could speak, I'd tell them I don't expect water from them, that just having them near is enough, but, just like every other potted plant, I too am mute. I can't speak. The silence I am imprisoned in fills my chest with putrid pus; it becomes a rusty vice that clamps my soul, I'm suffocating. I want to rip my chest open and fling out everything that's built up inside it. I can't do it. Somehow I'm simply not capable of explaining that I don't want them to water my body that's been transformed into a pretty plant, or to strengthen and fatten up my roots that barely fit into that tiny pot anyway. I think I'm afraid of growing, of the pot I'm in being too small for me, of fading away in that narrow space. I squirm under the pressure of the grave choice that lies before me. Must I consent to the water, or resign myself to loneliness? I don't know what I dread most, perishing or ending up alone.

I woke up with a familiar sensation of helplessness. Or rather, let's put it this way, I woke up from one helplessness and opened my eyes in another. At that moment I felt that the endless, boundless anxiety to which I had surrendered was my way of paying the ransom for the space I occupied on the face of the earth. This wasn't the kind of anxiety that would vanish once I had realised it was all just a dream. Because I did not by any means feel as though I had had a dream that didn't bear even the slightest semblance to the truth. Worse still, once I had passed from one state to the other, for a moment I wasn't even certain which of the two was a dream. Was I a potted plant who had dreamt it was a human, or was I a sorry excuse for a human who had dreamt he had become a plant? I couldn't tell.

It was the same when I was a child. I would sometimes believe I was in a dream. I would think, what if the dream isn't what I had at night, but what I think happened to me during the day; if that were the case I was furious with everyone who had fooled me into believing there was any such thing as a land of make-believe. Those were the lucky days when I wasn't deprived of sleep, of dreaming, nor of being able to remember my dreams. But they passed.

Why did I have that dream? My doctor wanted me to write it down. Before, when he was still my doctor, that is. But he isn't anymore, at least not for a while. No, it's not as if, like every know-all patient who thinks it's clever to mistrust their doctor, I've read a handful of books on the subject, decided behaviourists are better than psychoanalysts, thought, for goodness sake, it's not as if dreaming is an illness and severed all ties with him. On the contrary, because I was so pleased about the interest he was taking in my night life, delighted at the prospect of sharing with him the dream I had had the other night, I went to see him on Friday, at the time agreed at our last appointment. He should have been in his consulting room, waiting for me with an understanding look on his face that did justice to the money I pay him. It pains me to be constantly complaining about the fees I pay my doctor, but that sum alone gives me some clues as to the nature of my condition. The amount for which I am invoiced makes me think that only the middle and upper classes can allow themselves the luxury of dream-related anxieties. I can't be certain whether it's a privilege or just plain stupid to throw buckets of money at the doctor because I can't remember what I dream at night, but even if it's a privilege, I get the impression that those who don't have that privilege generally don't need it anyway. Probably because poor people do jobs that tire them out more during the day, at night they tend to sleep like babies or, shall we say, like bricks. Of course it's not as if I live in the lap of luxury. But, when all is said and done, I'm one of those middle-class types who thinks squandering money on pointless enterprises will improve his quality of life. Where were we, ah yes, Friday, which is a holy day where I was born ... Yes, Doctor Carcel should have been there waiting for me. But he wasn't. Reach not the conclusion that I went all the way in but still didn't get to see him. When I got there, because there was no answer when I rang the bell, I couldn't even enter.

When no one answered the door, my first thought was that perhaps the doctor hadn't reacted to my humour, which doesn't generally inspire great enthusiasm, with quite as much understanding as I had at first imagined. But still, because it was perhaps taking myself a bit too seriously to presume that instead of making a quick telephone call to cancel our appointment he had preferred to lock up the office and abandon the country rather than see me, as soon as I got home I telephoned the office, in the hope that someone would answer and explain why I had been left standing at the door. An irritating answering machine message in the doctor's secretary's voice greeted me. She announced daintily that Doctor Carcel had suddenly been taken ill, undergone emergency surgery and would be convalescing at home until such time as he felt well enough to return to work, and that he would therefore be unable to attend any appointments for the next month, although he would be very pleased to recommend another doctor colleague of his to any client who requested it. When my anger provoked by the secretary's failure to deign to make a few telephone calls to either cancel or postpone the doctor's existing appointments prevailed over my concern for my doctor's health, I hung up, muttering. To be honest, I still can't decide whether it was a stroke of good or bad luck. I don't know whether not being able to present my dreams to my doctor for interpretation just when I had started to remember them was a blessing or a curse. Because my aversion to someone setting out to analyse the kind of person I am on the basis of my dreams is as strong as my desire to remember them. Given that my remembrance mechanism, which I hope will continue to function at its present rate, has somehow started to work, I suppose there's no rush for me to draw my final conclusion on this matter. Because I am not obliged to make Doctor Carcel read my dreams each day, I can continue to keep notes until he recovers. I mean, I have plenty of time to decide whether or not I'm going to share these notes with him. Because I don't have the foggiest idea of what else I could do during this period, I'm going to continue to use the methods he recommended.

To be honest, even this explains why people who have information are so unwilling when it comes to sharing what they know. If you look at how I seized upon the two or three sentences I had picked up by hearsay and then presumed to be my own doctor, it really would appear that knowing little is a dangerous thing. I mean, maybe the people who know should be extremely careful when disclosing information to those who don't. Before I take matters further and get embroiled in stuff like hypnotism, which, fruit of my self-administered sessions, will lead me to embark on journeys from which there is no return, I pray to God that either my doctor gets better, or my anxieties end of their own accord. Anyway, let's not detract from the subject just because the doctor's not here and the coast is clear; let's proceed to conjecture as to why I might have had this flower pot dream . . .

Yes, why could I have had that dream? Why do I dream of myself as a plant stuck in a pot? In fact, perhaps I don't dream it, perhaps I just remember it. Maybe my dreams aren't sentencing me to a flower pot, maybe they're just reminding me of where I am. That's right, tonight's not the first time I've thought that being a potted plant befits me. During the first few years after I had left my country, while I was acclimatising myself to being away from the places and people I knew, I would look at the clay pots I had made and impose myself on them. After a while people imagine themselves inside everything they look at.

During those years I used to think I had no more roots than a plant in a pot. And I probably wasn't the only one to think that. Because on my birthday, an ex-girlfriend of mine, Madeleina, who graced my dream with her presence tonight, accompanied her warmest wishes with a small potted plant. Her intentions were good, and the plant was exquisite. Just like Madeleina ... But alas, when that beautiful, exquisite young woman heard some time later that I wanted to leave her, she flew into a rage and yelled in my face that I was no better than the plant she had given me that time. You see me here, right? Well, apparently I'm no different from a decorative plant, condemned to dry up and wither all alone on the windowsill, that's what she said.

I have witnessed many a time how, in defiance of their shrill voices that sound like air escaping from a balloon, enraged women make extremely grandiloquent statements. If I were them, I would capitalise on that talent by devoting myself to politics or something. But they generally prefer to squander their most flamboyant metaphors and their most colourful words on the man they accuse of having wasted the best years of their life. Just like Madeleina. Because such women prefer to view their relationships as power struggles and their lovers as conquered territory, I didn't let those words, which epitomised the customary wrath of complex-ridden females who consider being dumped as an affront to their pride, get to me, but instead let them run off me, like water off a duck's back. I laughed them off, not just the uttered words, but the person who uttered them too. She was neither an important character in my life, nor a lover who had made a permanent mark on it.

For years she didn't enter my thoughts once, or at least that's what I presumed. But if I can link the dream I have just had to the events of that day so many years ago, it must mean I haven't really forgotten her. If I absolutely have to find an explanation for my dream, I suppose I could blame it on my sister's potted plants. But somehow this dream doesn't remind me of her violets, but of my own small plant that I received as a birthday gift. My sister spoke to her violets as if they understood her, and watered them conscientiously, whereas I heartlessly neglected my plant, which was presented to me in honour of my birth, condemning it to wither and fade. Never mind talking to it, it didn't even occur to me to give it enough water. I was frivolous, both about its entry into my life, and its death and departure from it. I forgot all about it. Or so I thought.

When I graduated from secondary school I was still practically a child. And when I arrived in France, my head full of dreams, a foreign child. İlhami was the only person close at hand whom I trusted. Although I never formally made the decision, I think I knew from the outset that I would never go back. Maybe that's why, at the times when I felt most alienated and lonely, instead of consoling myself with the thought that I'd eventually go back home, I forced myself to get used to being a permanent stranger in this foreign land, where I would never truly belong. And to the fact that being rootless, being a long way away from one's roots, was not such a terrible thing. I had seen people who clung to their land, who strapped themselves to it tightly and did not move. As well as those who guaranteed their unhappiness as much as their happiness by anchoring it to one place. I didn't want to be like them. To be honest, people got stuck in something different, most probably in themselves, in each different place they went, but still, it was good to be able to go.

Once it was confirmed that I was going to France, I was carried away by elation. I walked around inflated with my own smugness, secretly feeling superior to everyone I was leaving behind. According to my way of thinking in those days, there was I, about to embark on a sea of colourful adventures that would be so thrilling they might as well take place in a land of make believe, and there were they, wallowing in the desperation of not having been able to shake themselves free of the miserable lives that oppressed them. I did not have the slightest doubt that those who appeared to be satisfied with their lot had not yet grasped the gravity of their situation. By the time I realised that many of my friends whom I had secretly pitied, thinking they were stuck in the rut of Istanbul, actually didn't lead a life they felt they needed to get away from, and that the only one who led a miserable life and was therefore to be pitied was me, the ones who were left behind had probably long since stopped pitying me and most likely even had trouble remembering my name. In comparison with the period in which I woke up to the truth, I can safely say that I slept much more easily by far during the period in which I believed in my lie. Believing in those sorts of lies does everyone good, and what's more, it's extremely wise. Isn't aggrandising our own situation and believing our tedious lives are bearable just an intelligent solution invented by our brains, which are forever devising ingenious games to stop us from committing categorical suicide? While we wear life as though it were a bespoke kaftan, and live it in a state of permanent commiseration and pity for the poor wretches around us, we prefer to shut our eyes to the fact that those poor wretches entertain very similar feelings towards us. That's why an old man and a young boy sitting opposite one another on the bus each harbour an insincere compassion and a heartfelt loathing towards the other. While the young boy looks at the old man and, thinking he is living his last days, gives thanks for the years that lie ahead of him, the old man prefers to recall that when he was the young boy's age he was a simpleton with no idea of what the world was about and is grateful for the maturity conferred on him by age. But, apart from the truths that each has brought to the other's mind, they both secretly despise one another. While one sees his own demise in the other, the latter looks back on everything that is now lost to him. Both are sullied with the stain of death's sly shadow, but both the young boy and the old man prefer to turn a blind eye to their observations and continue to feel smug about being the one who is better-off. That's the way it is. And a good job too. Because otherwise suicide figures would most probably reach a peak on the statistics tables.

Well, it must be because I too possessed my share of the mechanisms that subscribed to and advocated that kind of life, because I thought hotfooting it out of Istanbul immediately after secondary school, without knowing exactly why I was leaving, was something to gloat about, and firmly notified my friends who wittered on about homesickness, that I knew as well as I knew my name that I would never ever experience it, even in its mildest form. When one of them said he couldn't understand what all the fuss about returning to one's homeland was about and mentioned that he wanted to know why a peasant who had left his dung stinking village and settled in Berlin was so determined to go back home, without hesitation our Vehbi chipped in with the answer I dreaded hearing:

"My brother, it's because in the place where he's gone he's a second class citizen, but in his own village he's a king. And especially when he goes back, he's a high and mighty king who's been and seen the world but still chosen his own homeland in the end. What else can he do but return, and love the place he's returning to?"

Even before I went, I knew perfectly well I would never completely fit in where I was going, and tried to hide from myself the price of the inferiority complexes from which I assumed I would suffer in the future. Not even the fact that I was going for the sake of my education made me feel any better. In terms of not fitting in, that didn't give me a single advantage over the peasant who had been cited as an example. But, unlike many of the people who remain strangers in the place where they go, given that I had not been able to form any attachment to the place I was leaving either, I wanted to believe I didn't have much to lose. When all was said and done, I was no king in my own home either. I felt more like a clown unaware of anything that was going on in the world. And not only that, but, because he made no effort to make anyone laugh, a good-for-nothing clown, whose existence wasn't even capable of filling any gap ...

Where was I, ah yes, while all this talk of homeland and nation was flying around, a bright boy from our class called Murat said, "At least you're going with İlhami. If you find a few more Turks there you won't need your country and stuff anymore. When it all gets too much for you, you can make yourselves feel better by meeting and talking a bit of Turkish together. Because the worst thing is not being able to express yourself. How well can you ever express yourself in a language that you've learned later on? I think people miss sounds more than their land. The sound of their mother tongue. Your homeland is your language my brother, it's as plain as your nose!"

When I heard the last sentence I was perplexed at first, then I argued that I had no intention of meeting any Turks other than the friends I already knew, and that the only possible way of adapting to life in Paris was by mixing with French people. Language could never be an obstacle for me. I didn't learn until later that experience is the fool's wall of shame. Throughout all those years when I felt like an unopened box, when, no matter how much I spoke, I couldn't convince myself of having unburdened myself of everything that was burning me up inside, I remembered again and again how foolish I was to think that way, as though looking back on my own personal era of ignorance from a distance. When not even my own language sufficed to make me open up, how could I hope another language would heal my wounds? A long time has passed since those days, a lot of water has flowed. I think I speak very well now, but am incapable of explaining anything. I think that, by keeping it all bottled up for so long, I must have forgotten how to express what I feel.

I didn't put any pressure on Pilar to learn Turkish, but when she decided to learn, it made me even more happy that I felt brave enough to teach her. There is no doubt that I got a buzz from being able to speak the language of my childhood at home. But alas, that made no difference to the stark truth that the parts of me that spoke sincerely about myself had long been mutilated. Even if there were anyone who would listen to me, I was no longer qualified to explain what was inside me. It was as though I hadn't only forgotten how to explain, but also what it was that I was supposed to explain. It's hard to describe, but that was how I felt. It's as though the words have all squeezed into the coffin of my past and are now doing their best to destroy my present.

Why have I written all this? Yet again, I wanted to say something, but I don't think I've succeeded. As I said, I don't just not know how to explain, I don't even know what to explain anymore. Like my dreams, my innermost thoughts have remained in the dark too. Maybe shedding light on one will bring the other out into the open too.

5

Pilar

The soil swelled furtively.
Ahmet Hamdi Tampınar, "From the Winter Garden"

When the taxi Müesser had called arrived, Pilar departed from the house in Emirgân, with warnings of, "Oh, take care, whatever you do" ringing in her ears. She couldn't put her finger on exactly what it was about that house that was so oppressive, but she felt she would have suffocated if she had stayed there any longer. If Eyüp's sister had not worn down her resolve by insisting she stayed, she would have grabbed her bag and checked into the nearest hotel. But because she didn't want to upset that poor woman she braced herself to put up with Eyüp's infuriating brother and his odd wife for a bit longer. Besides, she hoped her husband would come knocking at the door any day now and that this bizarre adventure would very soon be over. She felt as though she were in a cheap horror movie where everything would turn out to be a dream in the end. What's more, last night it had pained her considerably that Eyüp's notebook which, by the look of things, wasn't doing much good as far as his therapy was concerned, mentioned his ex-girlfriend, the fact that he didn't know when he would feel ready for fatherhood and that he supposed the reason why his wife had stopped pressing him was because she was afraid of losing him. And as for his complaint that they weren't a couple who had been put to the test by severe hardship . . . Those were just the rantings of a sick mind that regarded pain as a form of discipline and derived pleasure from being hurt.

While she was waiting for sleep to bear her away, she asked herself whether she regretted coming to Istanbul. Before elusive sleep came and knocked on her door, every imaginable scenario had stormed the corridors of her mind. Separations, deaths, betrayals, desertions, all manner of stories, all of them connected to Eyüp's disappearance. And especially after Paz's phone call . . . That had just been the icing on the cake.

Her phone had rung about an hour after she had retired to her room. She had only remembered that morning's conversation when she saw Paz's name on the screen. Of course, her friend was planning to go to the hotel that day to find out what Ramon was up to. Paz had launched into the conversation by protesting she had phoned earlier but hadn't got through. She explained that she had weighed up a million times whether or not she should go to the Majestic. She was happy with her husband, and, as Ramon kept saying, they would be even happier if she could just get all those madcap, unfounded stories out of her head. She didn't want to complicate her life by obsessing over groundless suspicions anymore.

"That's why I didn't go to the hotel. Even despite that 'I miss you text.' I thought I'd trust my husband just this once."

Then she had suddenly broken down into tears. Somehow she just couldn't get her words out through her sobs; she was trying not to remember the story that was the reason why she had phoned in the first place. Pilar knew that feeling. People thought if they kept a terrible experience bottled up inside them, they would be able to convince themselves it had never happened. Wasn't that one of the reasons why she was trying to stop anyone from finding out about Eyüp's disappearance? According to what Paz had eventually managed to tell her, instead of going to the hotel that day, she had stayed at home and busied herself preparing cod. Suddenly there had been a knock at the door and she had found herself standing face to face with an unexpected guest. "Her name is Elsa, not Marc. She came to tell me my husband was waiting for her in room 312 at the Majestic Hotel. That I could go and see for myself if I wanted . . . That they have been together for a year, that

Ramon can't pluck up the courage to tell me because he's afraid I might harm myself ...Which is why she decided to do it herself ... She said I should let him go, that I should show them some consideration, that I should stop coming between two lovers. That I have no right to use my personal weakness as an excuse to make my husband stay with me." Paz had asked the woman to leave. And she must have gone to the hotel and told Ramon what she had done because he had phoned her in a panic. He sounded terrified when he asked how I was, as though expecting me to say I had slit my wrists and was bleeding to death, or that I was just about to jump out of the window; when he heard his wife was still alive and kicking he announced he would be right home. But, with a self-possession she never knew she had in her, Paz told her husband, who was taking deep, anxious, furious breaths through his nose, to calm down. From what she gathered, his fury was directed at the thoughtless Elsa, who had dared to go to his house behind his back, and his anxiety at his poor wife, whose state of mind was weighing on him. When Ramon said he had been a fool, that he was really sorry and wanted to come home and explain everything, Paz had asked him to give her some time and requested he didn't come home until she had managed to pull herself together sufficiently to call him. Now that everything was finally out in the open, Pilar imagined a multitude of messy reactions from her friend, ranging from packing up her things and leaving home, to trying to end her life. But Paz had simply decided to telephone Ramon, summon him back home and, after she had listened to him, to forgive him, despite everything he had done. It was only then that Pilar understood why Paz hadn't gone to the hotel. The woman who had spent all that time trailing her husband like a detective in an attempt to catch him out had always wanted to believe that nothing would come of all her efforts. And when, for the first time, she had felt she was a hair's breadth away from the truth she had always feared, she had preferred to ignore it rather than face up to it. Paz had known from the beginning that Ramon would be there with a woman, but had refused to go and see it with her own eyes.

Pilar could sense it wasn't advice Paz wanted from her, but approval. She would probably stop her ears to all the interpretations she didn't want to hear and do what she thought best, no matter what Pilar said. Even if her husband really did end his affair, she would never be able to trust him completely, but, because she couldn't contemplate such a major life change, she wasn't going to file for divorce. She would rather live with that constant, eternal, poisonous pain gnawing at her than endure the hardship of trying to grow accustomed to a life without Ramon, and her suffering would thus consume her, drop by drop, day by day. But, at least for now, Pilar didn't tell her friend what she didn't want to hear. She just limited herself to advising her to be calm, to listen to what Ramon had to say and not to make any rash decisions. Paz was happy to hear that, and Pilar thought she was comforted. But actually she could only feel as comforted as a child who has found a partner in crime. Because the crime still existed. When she eventually hung up, Pilar thought her friend, who believed her to be in Seville, would have no trouble at all working out that she had made an international call once she received her telephone bill. But that would doubtless be the least important of the realisations Paz would come to with time . . .

After that upsetting telephone call, her own troubles and Paz's became confused. The possible reason for Eyüp's disappearance that everyone in the house had been hinting at since her arrival now took on a whole new meaning. Right now she couldn't say if she would be more upset if Eyüp had abandoned her or if something terrible had happened to him. She didn't know what to think, or what to believe.

In that house filled with malevolence, no one except Müesser thought there was any likelihood of Eyüp turning up, and not just that, it was as though they didn't want her to find him. They had observed her dejected face with expressions that said, fool, when will you get it into your head that he's left you. They had intimated that she was a senseless woman who preferred to think her husband was dead rather than entertain the possibility that he had walked out on her. That was the gist of their message, from everything they had and hadn't said. Veysel and his wife, the pair of them, with their refusal to understand the situation, and their ruthless interpretations, had left her with a heavy heart. Worse still, they had confused her and infected her too with their malicious theories, like a contagious disease.

How could those two know what Eyüp's true intentions were when it had been years since they had even seen his face? When she used to ask Eyüp in the past why he didn't see his family, he would say it was because they didn't get on. That because he had gone away to boarding school he had grown distant from them from a young age, that they had never really been all that close anyway ... Nevertheless Pilar still argued that even a loose tie meant they should meet occasionally and criticised her husband for neglecting his brother and sister. Besides, she was curious about the house he grew up in, his siblings, his world. But Eyüp hadn't offered to bring his wife here even once, and every time Pilar had suggested it, he had refused. At first, partly under the influence of Paz's theories, she had wondered whether there might be something in his country that he didn't want her to see. An ex-fiancée or, even worse, a current fiancée. A lover and maybe even a child ... But the more she got to know Eyüp and the more she shared his life, the more she realised how out of the question such a possibility was; in fact, with time, she forgot she had ever even entertained such suspicions. They spent all their days together. She always knew exactly what her husband was doing, and where and when he was doing it. And that being so, there was no way he could keep any long-term secrets from her. With time, people eventually got used to things they found strange at first. As time passed, she too considered Eyüp's not seeing his family as less odd than she had in the beginning. She even learned how to regard him as friendless and alone.

Although the business with his family had ceased to be an issue, Pilar's desire to visit Istanbul, which raised its head from time to time like a recurrent illness, had driven a wedge between them for years. As someone who loved travel and had been to countless cities, it was natural she should want to visit Istanbul, that everyone loved so much and couldn't praise enough, and which was moreover the birthplace of the person she loved most in the world. But Eyüp who, in the beginning, used the excuse that if he entered the country he would be marched straight off to do his military service, and then, once that was sorted out, declared he didn't like Istanbul, always refused whenever she pressed him. Once, Pilar had been so frustrated by the ridiculousness of the situation she had said, "Fine, you don't have to come. I'll go and explore it by myself." Eyüp had laughed it off at first, but, once he realised his wife was serious, he had hastily planned a trip to Turkey, although he had excluded Istanbul from the itinerary, claiming that "The heat is unbearable in the summer." They had had a wonderful holiday together in the south. Pilar, who had loved Antalya and been swept along by that languid holiday feeling, had not felt the need to insist that she had to go to Istanbul. That was where she had met İlhami for the first time too. When Eyüp had told him they were in Turkey the man had gone straight to Antalya without giving it a second thought. After that he had been to see them in Barcelona, once by himself and once with his wife. The two friends had spent many years together, first at the secondary school, close to which she was now heading, and then at university in France. Perhaps they didn't meet very often anymore, but they were still close friends. Pilar had sensed it, despite only having met İlhami three times. She had noticed that her husband regressed to his childhood when he was with him, and that he was more cheerful, relaxed and talkative than he was with any other friend. That alone had been enough to make her like İlhami. As far as she could recall, his wife, Eda, too was a quiet, serene, kind woman.

Pilar was beginning to understand why Eyüp didn't feel the urge to see his family. If they had been the same since time immemorial, she could hardly blame the man for trying to steer clear of them. But then, remembering Müesser's anxious eyes, she felt ashamed of having thought such things. The poor woman had gazed straight at her and overflowed with affection for her. Anyone would have to be blind to all sentiment not to see the love she felt for her brother. But why had Eyüp turned his back on such love? Could not being loved at all sometimes be preferable to being loved so much as to feel indebted? No, maybe she was misjudging these people. Couldn't even the tedious questions fired by Perihan, whom Eyüp had never met, simply be her way of trying to bond? Right now she was oversensitive and inclined to blow everything out of proportion. All right then, had she misinterpreted Veysel's thunderous looks too? Hadn't his eyes flashed with lightning fury every time he had mentioned Eyüp? And wasn't it those looks that had irritated Pilar even more than his thick-skinned oafishness? Those scorching eyes had most probably remained rooted in an untold part of a story completely unknown to her. That's why she thought she shouldn't be too angry, even with him. But everything was so new and had all happened so suddenly ... Right now she didn't want to be someone who thought logically and made decisions based on common sense. She wanted to like some, loathe others, be angry with some, offended with others, but no matter what, she wanted to have faith in Eyüp. "Damn!" she said, "damn!" Her head felt as though it was about to explode.

"Did you say something, abla?" asked the amiable taxi driver, looking at her out of the rear-view mirror. She replied sharply, as though intent on venting all her spleen on the poor man, whose only crime had been to pose a question:

"No I didn't! You just concentrate on your driving."

After a long drive along a coastal road, the taxi turned up a hill. It went down narrow streets and ascended steep slopes.

"Did you say in front of Galatasaray Secondary School, abla?" asked the driver, opening his mouth for the first time since her rebuke.

"Yes, I understand there's a passage there with second-hand bookshops."

"Oh yeah, the used book dealer, you mean Aslıhan. Look, the building on the right is the secondary school. And the passage is straight ahead. Wait, let's go right up to the entrance," he said, moving the car a few metres forward. He pointed to the passage they had stopped in front of.

"There it is."

After checking the taximeter, she put her hand in her bag and took out the Turkish lira she had changed yesterday as soon as she had got off the plane. She counted it and held it out to the man. With a wave of her hand she dismissed the driver's attempts to return her change and got out of the taxi. She knew very well it wouldn't redeem her earlier uncalled-for rudeness, but she couldn't think of any other way of showing she was sorry.

No sooner had she set foot in the passage than the person she was looking for appeared, as though they had arranged to meet. She would never have thought finding him would be so easy. She was delighted and, for the first time in days, felt her luck was changing. Dressed in multicoloured shorts, and looking more like a tourist than a shopkeeper, İlhami was standing in front of a table outside one of the bookshops near the entrance, arranging books. He turned around when he heard his name and couldn't believe his eyes when he saw Pilar before him. Once he had got over his astonishment, he approached her with a broad smile revealing his sparkling teeth and hugged her happily, saying to his unexpected visitor, "Where on earth did you come from?" As soon as he opened his mouth, Pilar realised he didn't know anything. And right there her last hope was dashed, like a crystal vase. Totally oblivious of any broken glass, İlhami was impatient to see his friend.

Pilar scrutinised from top to bottom the man eagerly looking around him, saying, "Weeeelll, where is he?" Both his astonishment and his impatience were completely genuine. Instead of replying, she asked for a seat, sat down on the tiny chair he offered her and started telling him what had happened.

When she had finished she looked at her husband's friend with pleading eyes:

"Will you help me?"

Together, they had wracked their brains as to where Eyüp might be and tried to think of ways of making enquiries without raising everyone's suspicions. İlhami had no idea what was going on, but believed the situation was a tricky one and that, at least for now, it would be best if they didn't go broadcasting it to all and sundry. If, when he eventually turned up, Eyüp saw that everyone was talking about his disappearance, he would no doubt be furious. Because they were both aware of how exceedingly protective he was of his privacy. They were well accustomed to him keeping his mouth tightly sealed in all matters concerning himself, and to his insistence on resolving his own problems by himself. But this latest stunt was complete folly. When İlhami learned that his friend hadn't been feeling too well recently, and that he had even been to see a doctor, he suggested that the source of the situation may well be some kind of psychological breakdown. Perhaps he just wanted to be alone for a while and had chosen to go somewhere familiar, somewhere he knew. No matter how inexplicable his mysterious disappearance might be, at least that possibility explained his coming to Istanbul and not contacting him.

But İlhami said they should still inform the police, just to make sure that nothing worse than what they imagined had befallen him. Remembering Veysel's couldn't-care-less attitude towards Eyüp's safety, Pilar shot the man a grateful look. "Yes, let's," she said. "I think we should."

İlhami told her to wait for him in the shop and, should any customers arrive, to sell the books at the price pencilled on the inside page. So saying, he sprinted to the nearby police station to file a missing person's report. While he was gone she ignored the telephone, but did what she could to serve the customers as well as she was able. Although there weren't really any customers, apart from an old man looking for Sevgi Sosyal's novel *One Afternoon in Yenişehir* and a young woman who wanted to know the price of a Marilyn Monroe biography she had found whilst rummaging through the books on the stand. She limited herself to telling the man, who stared at her from behind filthy lenses that made her want to whip them off his nose and wipe them clean, that the shop's owner had popped out and that she didn't know where the books were kept; and had sold the book to the woman, whose miserable face increased her own dejection, at the price written on the inside page, exactly as İlhami had instructed. The woman, who started walking off in a semi-daze after she had put the book in her bag, was just about to exit the passage when she turned back, as if she had remembered at the last minute, and enquired about a Sylvia Plath book, whereupon Pilar repeated the sentence about the shop's owner having popped out. When no one else called in during the time she was alone in the shop, it struck her that dealing in old books was not particularly lucrative, and tried to remember why İlhami had gone into this line of business. Of course, he too had studied economics, just like Eyüp. As far as she knew, he had spent a term lecturing at the university. But Pilar didn't know what had happened to make him give that up. Either İlhami hadn't mentioned it, or it hadn't interested her enough to make her pay attention. The only thing she remembered was İlhami's excitement at the prospect of taking over the shop and his talking about the book-dealing business at great length.

İlhami, who returned 20 minutes later, panting and out of breath, said the police hadn't shown much interest, that they had said they needed to confirm matters before they began the search and that they had requested the contact details of the missing man's family so they could ask them a few questions. So, they obviously weren't going to accept that he was missing without speaking to his relatives. Pilar got to her feet immediately, intent on going straight to the police station, but İlhami dissuaded her, saying it wasn't necessary for the time being. He had called the shop to ask for the numbers, but when Pilar hadn't answered he had had to come in person. Pilar regretted not having answered the telephone when it had rung a few moments ago. But she hadn't had the foggiest idea that the call could have been for her. Much as her instincts told her to get up and go to the police station, concluding that İlhami knew how things worked in this country much better than she did, she made do with merely writing the family's home address and telephone number on a piece of paper. At the last minute she said, "Take this too, just in case" and added her own mobile phone number. When the man, who had taken the piece of paper and run back to the police station returned, puffing and panting, he said he had given them all the information they needed and the police would now handle the rest.

Although they hadn't made even the tiniest shred of progress, Pilar still felt better than she had in the morning. At least she was with someone familiar who shared her concern and was going out of his way to do something. İlhami had so much delicacy and consideration that he had steered clear of all questions that may have intimated that Eyüp's disappearance might be linked to any marital problems. That being so, there wasn't much else they could say on the subject. They wracked their brains over and over again, analysing the same possibilities and trying to come up with new answers to the same questions, but alas, to no avail.

After a while, İlhami stood up, having decided that Pilar needed some distraction.

"Come on, we've been sitting here for hours. Aren't you hungry yet?"

"No I'm not. Besides, it's too hot, I really don't feel like eating."

"In that case we can go for a drink. We can get some air and clear our heads."

"What about the shop?"

"Forget the shop," he said, shrugging his shoulders. "I don't guard over it every single day from morning till night anyway."

Pilar reluctantly followed this kind, easy-going man, who was doing his utmost to try and cheer her up, however slightly. They went out into a crowded street.

"This is İstiklal Caddesi; it's a bit like your Las Ramblas. It's always buzzing, day and night. All of Istanbul's nightlife is in the side streets here. Look, there's our Raval down there, Tarlabaşı."

Pilar looked around without enthusiasm, wobbling despondently in this bustling crowd, like a decayed tooth. She tried to protect herself, as though afraid of being swallowed up by the tumultuous swarm of people surrounding her. But before that could happen they cut through a side street, walked down towards the boulevard and got into a taxi.

"I'll start off by taking you away from all this chaos," said İlhami. "Let's go somewhere quiet and picturesque. We can drink tea as we look out over the Golden Horn. Take a look at Istanbul and see what you make of it."

Then he leaned over to the driver and said:

"Take us to Eyüp."

When he noticed Pilar's questioning look, and her eyes grown wide in their sockets, İlhami first finished instructing the taxi driver: "Take the back streets to Pierre Loti." Then he turned to Pilar and explained, "Eyüp is the name of a neighbourhood." From what he said, they had to go through a cemetery to get to their destination. The best way to go was on foot, weaving through old gravestones as they climbed up the road, but this time they would have to drive up the hill, because of the heat. There would be a spectacular view of the Golden Horn waiting for them when they arrived. Once she realised the place where they were going had no connection with her husband, Pilar lost all interest in it. What's more, deriving pleasure from walking amongst gravestones was a pastime fit only for necrophiliacs. She had no eyes, either for the hill or for the view, but because she didn't want the well-meaning İlhami, who was bending over backwards to help her, to think she was ungracious, she kept quiet. And besides, once they got out of the taxi, she couldn't see anything all that fantastic anyway. They walked up a few steps and came out onto the terrace of an ordinary-looking café. Once they had passed the road that stretched out before them like a corridor, they reached a courtyard that was much bigger than it looked from the outside. It was furnished with dozens of tables and chairs. And immediately in front of them was the most breathtaking, spectacular view. Pilar, who had been taken completely by surprise, stared, awestruck. She wished Eyüp were there now; if only they could sit and admire it together.

They did not talk much as they sipped their tea. They sat side by side and contemplated the Golden Horn in silence, both of them most probably thinking about the same person.

When their glasses were empty, İlhami sat up in his chair and remarked: "A friend of mine, Vehbi, has a tea garden in Beyazıt. We were at school together. All his friends call him Boss. He's the type that always keeps his ears open; he knows everything about everybody. If you like, we can drop in on him and see if he knows anything. You never know, he may have heard something about Eyüp . . ."

Pilar remembered the name from the letters that arrived from time to time. She had never met the man, but Eyüp said he was unique. Whenever he mentioned his name his face would light up with a smile. As far as she knew, they had not seen each other since school, but had kept in touch by letter. This man they called Vehbi had made it his duty to write and keep his friend, who was estranged from his homeland, updated on events in his country, as well as on the news and gossip about their common acquaintances, and sometimes he even sent little gifts, like music and books. For a moment Pilar's face shone. Of course, as one of the very few people with whom her husband had not cut off ties, Vehbi might be able to help them. Amazed that it hadn't occurred to her before, she willingly agreed to go and see her husband's penfriend. She felt much happier.

After they got out of the taxi, they entered a courtyard filled with book stalls. They walked until they reached a rundown coffee house with a few tables and chairs dotted about its tiny garden. The inside was as colourful and cheerful as the outside was unkempt and dingy. On the walls were a lot of mostly black-and-white photographs, haphazardly hung newspaper cuttings, a Pink Floyd poster with torn edges, a huge Fenerbahçe flag, a poster for the film *La Haine* and a Palestinian flag. There were newspapers and magazines on the tables, where groups of three and five people were engaged in heated discussions. Pilar couldn't help wondering how exactly this place had come to look the way it did. İlhami summoned a young boy and asked him, "Isn't Vehbi around?" When the young boy replied that he was at the mosque and would soon be back, he ordered two teas and headed for one of the free tables. Pilar was about to say "I'd better not drink any more", when a lanky youth a few tables away stood up and ran to them, exclaiming, "Professor, how are you?" By the time İlhami had managed to get rid of him after a brief conversation, the tea had long since arrived. Pilar reached out for hers without protest.

Shortly afterwards a sweat-drenched man entered the coffee house. He puffed and panted, as he mopped his face and neck with a tissue. His vertical curls that elongated his head, the scraps of newspaper poking out of his shoes, his huge rucksack that had long had its day and out of which he removed a large stack of newspapers and magazines, all looked incredibly odd.

"I got these books really cheap, a man up the road was selling a whole cartload. Look at all this, André Gide, Maupassant, I've even got Brecht's ThreePenny Novel here," he explained. As he spoke he heaped the war spoils he had taken out of his bag on an empty table. As he was speaking into the void, Pilar couldn't work out exactly whom he was addressing. Looking at him, he seemed to know everyone there and might have been talking to everyone at the same time. He put one of the books in front of a young boy sitting at one of the tables at the entrance.

"Simone de Beauvoir's *She Came to Stay*. Didn't you have a feminist friend? You can give it to her."

Then, taking an ordinary pencil out of his bag, he gave it to the other young boy. "Here, this is for you, you can write with it."

And, with a completely straight face, he also put a used eraser on the table:

"And then you can rub it out if you want."

Completely oblivious to Pilar's astonished looks, this strange man, who, like some kind of Father Christmas, distributed gifts to everyone who crossed his path, exclaimed, "Uff, it's as hot as hell in here!" and proceeded to put new scraps of paper inside his shoes to replace the ones that had disintegrated with sweat. "I swear, if I had a bit of money I'd buy a summer house and spend my summers in Ardahan. Anyone who stays in Istanbul in the summer is mad," he continued, to himself, or perhaps to everyone. Everyone in the coffee house exchanged looks and laughed.

Someone quipped, "Abi, didn't you do your military service in Ardahan? Enlist in the Turkish army, then you can take up where you left off." Father Christmas pretended not to hear. He was too preoccupied with trying to cool down by mopping his brow and neck with the wet wipes he had taken out of his pocket. But when his eye caught the table where Pilar was sitting, he tossed the wet wipe aside and rushed over to them.

"İlhami! I didn't see you, when did you get here?"

"We've been waiting for you for the last two hours Boss, what is this never-ending worship! I was beginning to think you'd go straight to heaven, without ever coming back here."

And that was how Pilar realised that this peculiar man was the one they were waiting for. Of course, she thought to herself, it's totally to be expected that someone who still writes letters after all these years, and not only that, but also goes to the trouble of sending little gifts now and again, should turn out to be Father Christmas. This saint, who was a martyr to the heat, continued speaking to İlhami as if he hadn't noticed her at all.

"Ah no abi. After the mosque I went to see a friend to wish him luck. He's an old friend, he opened a little motel in my area not long ago. Somehow I just never got round to going and seeing him. So I called round, he gave me tea and it's done and dusted now."

Then he lowered his voice and added confidentially:

"Abi, he's invested all that money, he's set up his business, you'd think he'd at least give it a decent name, wouldn't you? But no, he went along with his wife and called it Razzle Dazzle Palace, what do you make of that! Because razzle dazzle means sparkling and glitzy, it's meant to make people think of a shimmering palace. . . . But it sounds like Ramshackle Palace or even, at a push, Rat Ridden Palace. It's a crazy name, it turns people right off wanting to go and stay there, I swear."

The man, who had changed his mind about standing up and settled himself at their table instead, kept up his monologue. As though Pilar too were an old friend, despite not having ventured to introduce himself to her, he kept his endless torrent of words flowing, jumping from one subject to another, moving from Fenerbahçe one moment, to newspaper columnists the next. Eventually, unable to bear it any longer, İlhami exclaimed, "What are you like! Any normal person would at least show a bit of interest in the lady sitting with us! From the way you're rabbiting on and on, anyone would think you've known her all your life. At least meet her first."

"Sorry, abi," replied Vehbi sheepishly. "I thought it was all right to rattle on because I figured that no one who comes with İlhami can be considered a stranger," he continued, eyeing Pilar apologetically. Then, casting his embarrassment aside, he scolded his friend:

"And besides, why do I have to ask you, it's your job to introduce her, seeing as she's with you."

"Ok, I will then, Pilar. Our Eyüp's wife."

"Eyüp's?" The man stared at Pilar with questioning eyes. "Which Eyüp?"

"My son, how many Eyüps are there?"

"Loads, abi. Which one do you mean?"

"I mean the only one we both know."

After scrutinising his friend with vacant eyes for a few moments, his face a picture of bewilderment, he blinked and asked, "You mean our Eyüp from Barcelona?"

"Yeeeees, our Eyüp from Barcelona."

"Ohhhhhh," said Vehbi, as though he had just woken up. "Our Eyüp's wife! Welcome." He reached over and shook hands with Pilar. Casting off the confusion that gave him a childlike air, he smiled warmly. The first thing he asked was whether she had already been to Istanbul and which parts she had liked the most. Pilar responded concisely. From the way he said, "Weeeelll, where's Eyüp then?" after he had showered praise on the young woman's command of Turkish, it was obvious he too had no idea of what was going on.

"He had some business to see to. As soon as he arrived he dropped Pilar off here and went to Ankara," improvised İlhami rapidly. Pilar couldn't help wondering if he had prepared the lie about Ankara beforehand, or if he had made it up on the spur of the moment. These past few days she too had been resorting to the same measure with alarming frequency, but still, ever since her childhood she had feared people who could fabricate lies at the drop of a hat. İlhami, who had no idea what was going through her head, said, "As you can see, I haven't seen him yet either. Pilar and I met up first, and, when Eyüp comes back, we'll all get together." Then he added, as though it had just occurred to him:

"Tell me, does he know about your coffee house?"

"My coffee house ..." After he had stared at the ceiling, frowning, for a while, as though the answer were written there, Vehbi said, "Of course he does. We write to each other from time to time, I told him about it. Why? Are you going to invite him here?"

"For God's sake, I can't invite him anywhere. I told you, the man isn't in Istanbul. I just thought if, when he gets back, he happens to come to see you before he comes to see me, I want to know, so I can nip over."

"Oh sure, if he phones I'll make sure I let you know," said Vehbi allusively.

Having low expectations of people reduced the risk of disappointment. This man, who expected nothing except letters from his friend, with whom he had been corresponding for years, didn't even resent him now for not telling him he was coming. He expected nothing, which meant that, when he received it, he never got upset or offended. If only I could be that way too, thought Pilar.

Once Vehbi had discovered the identity of the guest sitting at the table, he asked where Eyüp was and what he was up to, and, the moment she had delivered her brief replies, he returned to his potpourri of chit-chat, ranging from the heat, footballers' transfers and politicians' blunders, to how there weren't any good films on at the cinema during the summer season. Pilar, whom the knowledge that this table wouldn't be providing what she sought either had long since sent into mourning, her eyes on the two men and her mind floating in the distance, had long ago migrated to her own dream world. She came back down to earth when İlhami nudged his friend, saying, "Look who's here." It was a tall man with a slightly receding hairline, so thin he looked as though he would fly away if you blew on him.

"Are you looking for someone, brother?" Vehbi called out to him. When he noticed them the man exclaimed, "Oh, two birds with one stone! How are you İlhami Doğru?" and came to their table, grinning. "I thought I'd just look in on the Boss but it turns out you're here too, what a treat."

Pilar was instantly introduced to the man who had just arrived. It was their friend Müjdat, from secondary school. When İlhami was headed for France with Eyüp, he and Vehbi had gone to Ankara to study political science. İlhami made fun of the pair of them for doing jobs that had nothing to do with their studies.

"Their poor parents wasted their money sending these two to school. One sells coffee and the other sells newspapers."

"Did you want me to be a district governor?" laughed Müjdat.

"You could have tried your hand at being a mukhtar at the very least."

"What are you like! Anyone listening to him would think he's a Wall Street broker and that he's got the New York stock market twisted round his little finger."

Ignoring Vehbi, who chipped in with "The Gordon Gekko of Arnavutköy!" İlhami repeated the same story he had fabricated for Vehbi to Müjdat, explaining that Eyüp couldn't join them because he had some urgent business to attend to. He even elaborated the story a bit by inventing a huge pile of paperwork that couldn't be dealt with in any place except Ankara. Müjdat, who was more interested in Pilar's presence than in the absence of his old friend whom he hadn't seen in years and whose existence he may well have forgotten, deftly managed to steer the conversation towards politics, and asked Pilar if anyone in her family was of Basque origin.

For some reason he was delighted to hear that her father's side of the family was Basque.

"Really? That's great!"

Pilar, who couldn't understand the reason for such irrational satisfaction, limited herself to giving him a wan smile, as she had done so many times over the course of the day. It wasn't just Eyüp's family that were strange, but his friends too. After a while İlhami rose to his feet and said, "Boy, we're hungry, come on, let's go and get something to eat." The man couldn't sit still but was constantly hatching new plans. Despite Vehbi's protests on the grounds that they couldn't go out in that infernal heat, they all got up. Once the men had decided on the destination amongst themselves, they set off through narrow streets and came out opposite a large building.

"This is the Süleymaniye Mosque," said İlhami. "In the past an architect's greatness was measured by his domes. You must see Süleymaniye's dome." Pilar, who was thinking to herself, oh yes, my sentiments exactly, all we need now is to go on a tour of the city, cut him short with a point-blank refusal. She hadn't vetoed the idea of lunch so as not to be a killjoy, but she certainly wasn't going to stretch to touring mosques and studying architects. When they saw how reluctant the guest was to tour the city, they walked through the mosque's courtyard at a leisurely pace and sat down in one of the many kuru fasulye restaurants lined up in a row opposite the mosque's garden wall. While Vehbi was ordering, İlhami launched into an explanation of how he and Eyüp used to go there a lot when they were students. Ali Baba served the best kuru fasulye in the city. And it was cheap. For that reason, Eyüp would always demolish the contents of his plate as though he had come from a land plagued by famine. Once, unable to slow down, he had wolfed down three portions one after the other, and then hadn't been able to move for the rest of the day.

While the friends at the table laughed out loud as they reminisced over the old days, Pilar too savoured the pleasure of reliving the same memory shared with the man she loved. Years ago, when he was a child, Eyüp had sat at one of these tables, perhaps even at this same table, and dipped his spoon into the dish she was about to eat. Even if it were at different times, when all was said and done, they were still in the same place. In the same memory ... in the fragile shadow of a lost moment. That alone should have brought the two of them closer together. She fantasised that she was approaching the place where Eyüp was, that she would find him soon ...

When the aromatic, steaming kuru fasulye, with plenty of tomato sauce and just a hint of chilli, arrived, Müjdat proclaimed, "It's here! You should really eat this bugger in winter, but if it's kuru fasulye you're after, then the rest is academic" and dived eagerly into his dish. Pilar followed suit and was astounded to see that her appetite made short shrift of the bean stew in front of her in ten minutes flat. This really was the most delicious kuru fasulye she had ever had in her life ...

After lunch İlhami suggested meeting up with Eda and going to Beyoğlu for a few glasses of rakı. The moment he heard the word rakı Müjdat said, "Count me in." For her part, Pilar, who was quite finished with behaving as though everything was completely normal, refused, saying, "No, I've had enough fun for one day." She wasn't capable of acting like a social butterfly when her head was so mixed up and her heart so troubled. She couldn't bear to sit at a table or join in with their banter. What's more, to her eyes, everyone who didn't understand what she was going through, everyone who set out to enjoy life, was offensive. Besides, she hadn't come to this city to go out and have fun ... Using the excuse that the family were waiting for her at home, she tried to wriggle out of going. But İlhami leaned across and whispered in her ear, "I know you don't feel like doing anything. But you'll be better off spending time with us than sitting at home and fretting, it will be a distraction for you. Besides, we can't do anything else right now except wait."

He was right. It wasn't much fun witnessing the happy laughter and chit-chat of these men who were unaware of the fears gnawing at her, but it might be better to kill time outside than go back to that bleak house so early. Instead of being bombarded with Perihan's relentless interrogation all evening and night, or Veysel's impertinent quips, she would be lulled by this false story in the company of Eyüp's old friends for a bit longer. And who knows, a few drinks might even do her tattered nerves some good.

"All right then. But I can't stay long."

And so they all rose and accompanied Vehbi to his coffee house. Pilar telephoned the house in Emirgân from the public telephone in the coffee house to tell them she'd be late, but, as no one answered, she couldn't let anyone know. While İlhami was telephoning his wife, Vehbi, who wasn't going to join them because he didn't drink, invited Pilar back to the coffee house another day. If she had a chance she must go back and let him treat her to some more tea. And, like a dejected child, he added, "I hope Eyüp will be with us too next time." From the shadows that gathered on his face as he said those words, Pilar realised he was hurt that the man with whom he had been corresponding for so many years, and whom he regarded as a friend, hadn't told him he was coming. So, the extent of people's expectations didn't bear much relation to how offended they got with those they cared about after all. Perhaps grief was just a side effect of love. If only the poor man knew the truth, he would most probably forget about himself and pity Pilar. Just as they were about to say goodbye, he said to Pilar, "Wait, hold on, hold on" as though he had had an afterthought, and headed towards that huge bag of his standing beside the counter. He returned some time later, clutching a tiny red notebook.

"Here's a small keepsake from me. In case I don't get to see you again . . ."

Of course, Pilar had forgotten about the Father Christmas traits she had witnessed earlier. When she remembered, she smiled sincerely and thanked him. As she was putting the notebook in her handbag, she wondered whether she would ever see this curious man again. Would seeing him again be an indication that everything had gone back to normal, she wondered, or that nothing would ever be the same again?

They met Eda in Taksim Square. According to İlhami, she had been delighted when he had telephoned and told her Pilar was in Istanbul. And when they met she hugged her tightly, as though they had been friends all their lives. Pilar found it both odd and gratifying that Eda should greet her so warmly even though they hadn't seen each other since her visit to Barcelona. Ploughing through the crowds in İstiklal Caddesi, they advanced to Çiçek Pasajı, close to her first stop that morning. They sat down in a tavern where Pilar imagined, from the waiters' hearty welcome, that İlhami was a regular, and ordered rakı. Had Pilar ever tried rakı before? Yes, of course. Eyüp always kept a bottle handy at home, and occasionally he produced it and had a few drinks with feta cheese. Although it wasn't Pilar's favourite, she had been known to join her husband for a glass.

"You Spaniards have a drink that's similar to rakı don't you?" asked İlhami.

"Yes, *Cazalla*. It's transparent, like rakı, but turns white when you mix it with water. It's mostly drunk in Valencia. My mother, for one, loves it." The moment she uttered that last sentence she remembered she had to call her mother. Otherwise, sooner or later, Vicky would telephone to find out how things were going. Unlike Paz, she probably wouldn't even have to wait for her bill to arrive to realise that she was making an international call. Her ears would prick up at the tiniest sound coming from outside, for instance. As Pilar, made uneasy by these thoughts, grabbed her telephone and was heading for the toilet, the friends sitting at the table had long ago changed the subject from *cazalla* to *ouzo*.

The toilet was empty. Once she was satisfied that it was sufficiently quiet, she dialled her mother's number. Vicky, who only managed to answer the phone at the sixth ring, had just come back from shopping and was putting the food away. The first thing she asked, as though deliberately rubbing her nose in her lie, was what the weather was like in Seville.

"Hot."

"Very hot?"

"Very."

She was afraid of detecting a pointed reproach in Vicky's voice. Her instincts, or her whatever it was that they were called, were acute beyond imagination. Since her childhood, Pilar had never been able to lie to her. Following the principle "few words few lies," she kept it brief, saying everything was fine but that she had to work very hard. Then, saying "I won't keep you, seeing as you're busy," she hastily rang off. She quickly phoned Isabel too. Apart from reeling under the kicks of the little rascal playing a one-sided football match inside her, her sister was well, but concerned for Pilar. Pilar gave her too a summarised report of the day's events and told her not to worry. And while she was stuck in the telephone traffic, she tried Eyüp's family again, thinking it wouldn't be right to stay out without letting them know. When she received no answer a second time, she felt annoyed. What was going on? Where was everyone? No one had said anything to her. If she got up and went home now, would she have to wait outside? Then she thought no no, even if the others went out, Müesser would definitely wait for me. There must be a problem with the landline. If that were the case, the police wouldn't be able to reach anyone either when they phoned to corroborate the missing person's report. The thought left her feeling very glum. Finally, for the millionth time since he had disappeared, and with the absolute certainty that she wouldn't get through, she called Eyüp's mobile. The voice she had heard the most these past few days explained yet again: "The person you are calling can't come to the phone right now." She returned to the table feeling slightly more dejected than when she had left. And, unlike when she had left, the table was now laden with a large selection of meze. İlhami was topping up the rakı, while Eda was absorbed in an animated story she was telling Müjdat.

"Look, I don't want to cast aspersions on her character but . . . You just can't help wondering."

"Wondering about what?" asked Pilar, feigning interest. As she'd agreed to come, she wasn't going to spoil everyone's mood by being a wet blanket. Even if it was just out of politeness, she needed to join in with the conversation occasionally, or at least pretend to.

Pleased to see Pilar's interest, İlhami stepped in before his wife:

"There's a girl whose novels are published by the publishing house where Eda works. Eda isn't mad about her. She thinks her novels might be written by someone else and keeps coming up with heartless conspiracy theories."

"Honestly!" laughed Eda. "They're making fun of me. I didn't say that, but if you see the girl, she's so young ... And when she's talking she can't string two words together. I can't get my head round how she writes those books. It's true I know a lot of writers who gush with eloquence when they're writing but are struck dumb when it comes to talking, but, I don't know, this is different. And of course, when you consider that her daddy's loaded ... you start imagining all kinds of things. And anyway, how many ghost writers are there? I mean, it's not impossible ..."

Even as she asked, "What are her books like?" Pilar thought to herself, what's it to me, it's not as if I'm going to be reading any of them. But that was the nature of socialising, it constantly forced people to ask questions when they knew they wouldn't listen to the answers.

"Well, I don't know, they're not bad. I wasn't crazy about the first one, but she delivered another one two months ago and I liked that, for example. It's about a circus acrobat; we're going to publish it this month. In fact, that's what I'm working on right now," explained Eda obligingly. For her part, as she stared blankly at the woman's face and smiled, Pilar wondered where she would have to go to look for her husband tomorrow. These bleak thoughts were interrupted by Müjdat's rich baritone while he tucked into the mezes with relish, as though he hadn't been the one who had polished off all that fasulye earlier.

"Will you shut up and eat. Pilar, you can't get these mezes in Barcelona; eat them while you have the chance. He who lags behind gets left out in the cold, I'm warning you."

İlhami, who obviously liked sparring with his friend, and was looking for an excuse to liven things up, seized his chance:

"You're giving our guest the wrong idea about our rakı banquets. My dear Pilar, don't take any notice of this man; he's famous for the inconsistency between the amount he eats and the sum total of the surface area he occupies. At school they used to call him the Insatiable Samovar. Not only did he eat everything in sight, but he also drank tea by the litre. In other words, he's not exactly a good example when it comes to food. For instance, at a rakı banquet it's not the done thing to attack the mezes and devour them as though you haven't had a square meal in weeks. On the contrary, you're supposed to eat them slowly, while you savour the conversation."

Although Pilar muttered to herself, I wish you would talk slowly too, so I could understand what you're saying, she didn't show it. When she was alone with someone they always pronounced each word slowly and carefully, but when they were in a group they accelerated, completely forgetting she was a foreigner, and spewed one word she had never heard before after another. But still, she wasn't bothered. She wasn't particularly interested in listening anyway.

"What's this? Have you suddenly become an expert in etiquette? Why don't you teach us all how to hold a knife and fork, and how to play the piano too while you're at it?" huffed Müjdat, as he reached out for the dish of salted tuna.

When İlhami said "Besides, Spaniards are no strangers to the meze culture. They have their tapas, don't they, Pilar?" Müjdat cut in as though it were his turn to launch an attack:

"Man, will you stop going on about Spaniards. Her father's Basque. She might not even think of herself as Spanish!"

At this, all three heads turned towards Pilar. She, for her part, was far from pleased that the conversation had done the rounds and eventually stopped at her.

"My mother's Catalan, and my father's Basque but—"

"Aha! You see, our friend is anything but Spanish!" interjected Müjdat.

"Hah, just the subject you were craving! Not satisfied with dissecting the Turks and the Kurds, now you're going to sink your teeth into the Spaniards and Basques as well! Go ahead, talk on all our behalf; tell us what you decide."

"Oh, and of course you're talking on your own behalf, aren't you? In that case don't ask me, ask Pilar."

Because she didn't want to prolong the discussion, Pilar, who had only half followed the drift of the conversation, tried to respond diplomatically:

"I don't really have any strong political views on the subject. And most of my family aren't really politically inclined either."

While İlhami was giving his friend an "I told you so" look, Müjdat had long ago pounced on the clue that had caught his attention and wasn't letting it go:

"Ahaa, *most* of your family isn't bothered, but I'll bet there's one person at home who's a bit of a black sheep."

Although she could have pretended not to hear, or lied, Pilar smiled at Müjdat's perspicacity. "Yes, my uncle."

"Well, what are you waiting for, tell us about this uncle of yours," pressed Müjdat. "Was he a member of ETA?"

"Yes."

"You don't say!" Müjdat cried out so loudly the people sitting at the other tables turned and looked at them. İlhami felt obliged to warn his friend with, "All right man, turn that foghorn down a notch."

"Okay okay," he said, in a calmer voice. Then, turning back to Pilar:

"Tell us Pilar, my friend. Tell us about what goes on in your part of the world."

"What can I tell you about him?" asked Pilar, at a loss. "My uncle was a Basque nationalist. He wanted an independent Basque state—"

Müjdat must have realised that his persistence might not have gone down too well because he felt the need to interrupt Pilar with an explanation, "Don't mind my curiosity. ETA is really well known here. Well, it is and it isn't. We're always comparing it with the PKK. We compare the PKK with ETA and Batasuna with the People's Democracy Party, HADEP . . . We're always looking for someone to tell us about it."

At that point Pilar looked into his eager eyes. If he wanted to hear about Uncle Ander, then let him be her guest.

She started speaking in a fragile voice that she had just taken out of its red velvet box, as though the person she was talking about was not her father's brother, but a storybook hero left over from her childhood. As she spoke she reminisced, and as she reminisced she yearned for Uncle Ander and the days they had shared together . . .

In 1968, Txabi Etxebarrieta, a leading member of ETA, was killed following a skirmish that broke out when the police tried to stop him whilst driving. Of course, because Pilar was only 4 years old at the time, there was no way she could remember the incident. But, partly because she had heard the adults discussing it so many times, and partly because the consequences had repercussions not just on her family, but on the history of a whole nation, she knew all the details as though she had been there in person.

The organisation did not take Etxebarrieta's death lightly. They retaliated by murdering the high-ranking police officer Meliton Manzanas. Thus, 16 militants, including Uncle Ander, were charged with the death of Manzanas and put on trial.

Even if it were from behind a cloud of smoke, Pilar felt as though she had witnessed those days. She seemed to recall them all going to see Aunty Izaskun together. Isabel was still a baby. Her cousin Raul, who was much older than her, was trying to entertain Pilar in the garden to keep her away from the living room where the adults were engaged in a heated discussion. She could hear raised voices coming from inside. Aunty Izaskun was crying, Uncle Ramirez spat out his wife's younger brother's name with fury, shouting at the top of his voice, "That lawless lout will bring trouble on all of our heads." Her father was trying to calm things down, while her mother was closing the windows so they wouldn't be overheard. Pilar watched her mother from the garden. Whenever their eyes met, Vicky would give her an insincere smile, as though there was nothing at all to worry about. The false curves of that smile Vicky resorted to in an attempt to hide the truth stuck in Pilar's mind as the trademark of the years during which her family tried to deal with her uncle. And in her own adulthood, whenever she was in a tight situation, she took refuge behind the same curves.

While the family members were helpless to do anything more than wring their hands, grieve and rant, the organisation had long since rolled up its sleeves to devise a way of saving Uncle Ander and the others. In their struggle to prevent their comrades from being tried for murder, the militants kidnapped the West German consul in San Sebastian. Eventually the situation grew so tense that Franco had no option but to retreat and convert the death sentence that was originally going to be served to the authors of Manzanas's death, into a prison sentence. Although Pilar squeezed the day her uncle entered prison in with all her other hazy memories, she could remember the day he came out, two years after Franco's death, like it was yesterday. Like a birthday gift, Uncle Ander had come to Valencia on the day she turned 13.

When she was younger Pilar had always imagined him as a rebellious, vagrant, bushy-bearded type, with wild, overgrown hair. Maybe that had a lot to do with the adults wearing the expression of people talking about a mischievous child whenever his name came up. Which is why she was genuinely taken aback when she saw Uncle Ander in the flesh. He was far from being a greasy-haired, slovenly man with an unkempt beard. He was impeccably groomed, elegant even. He was very smartly dressed, with his wavy hair combed to the side. Anyone would think he hadn't come from prison, but from a soirée where he was the guest of honour. What's more he bore no resemblance to the loud, argumentative, intransigent, unreasonable man of her imagination. On the contrary, he spoke in velvety tones, always looking straight into the eyes of the person he was addressing, his look inspiring trust. No matter what the age or size of the person before him, he always took them seriously, listening to them with care and attention, as though he would learn important, valuable lessons from them. At first Pilar thought the adults had done her uncle a great injustice. Were they trying to tell her that this was that hot-headed, headstrong, obstinate younger brother! But with time she realised that although Uncle Ander listened to everyone very attentively, and appeared to take their words on board, he always did exactly as he wished. He let everyone have their say, but in the end still did what he wanted. But he did it with such gallantry it was impossible to be angry or offended with him. He wasn't like anyone else she knew; he was altogether quite extraordinary.

"Weeell, so what happened to your uncle?" asked Müjdat. "You tell us he was this and he was that, did he die?"

"I don't know."

She didn't. Uncle Ander had stayed with them in Valencia for a while, and then disappeared, as stealthily as he had arrived. That night Pilar had found a beautifully wrapped book under her pillow. *Alice in Wonderland*. Inside was inscribed, in midnight blue fountain pen ink, "A belated birthday present." Pilar had loved Alice, but she knew only too well that her real birthday present had been Uncle Ander himself. She engraved his image, that had the magical aura of a storybook hero, on her memories. Adults wanted to prune everyone until they looked like themselves, but children had the courage to love heroes just as they were. That's why she wasn't offended with her uncle for going away and leaving her; in her own way she understood him. The only thing she didn't understand was why he had never contacted them from wherever he had gone.

Pilar wondered where her uncle was, would he ever come back? Occasionally she used to ask her father, but she never got a straight answer. Although no one ever told her as much, over time she realised that he had died, or rather been killed somewhere. Rather than going in pursuit of a graveless corpse, the adults in the family chose to forget him and behave as though no such person had ever existed. Uncle Ander and the dazzling memories he conjured remained in her mind as her favourite thirteenth birthday present . . .

When Pilar finished speaking, a brief silence descended on the table. Müjdat became thoughtful, Eda drifted off into the distance, rapt in the memory of who knows which loss. İlhami raised his glass slowly:

"Let's drink to all the beautiful people we have lost, and to their undying memories."

The others followed suit: "To eternal memories!"

Just before 9:00 p.m. Pilar said she had to get going, as everyone at home must be frantic with worry by now. As it wasn't her fault the landline didn't work, they couldn't hold her responsible for the concern her staying out so late would cause Müesser in particular. But still, out of courtesy, she believed she should return at a decent hour to the house where she was, after all, a guest. She had no doubt that if it had occurred to her to give them her mobile number before she left, Müesser would have telephoned her countless times by now. Maybe it's a good job I forgot to give it to them, she thought, and laughed. She point-blank refused İlhami's offer to accompany her home and, just as she had done that morning, said she would hop into a taxi. Müjdat, who thought Eyüp was in Ankara, asked Pilar to give his friend his regards and tell him he definitely wanted to see him before he left.

"Of course I will," said Pilar, with a smile that, under the rakı's influence, made her stop feeling sorry for herself and start seeing the funny side of her predicament. Her eyes met İlhami's. He gave her a reassuring look, as if to say, "Don't worry, we'll sort it out," or at least that's how she chose to interpret it. Eda said, "You must come to our house one evening before you go, we're expecting you," and hugged her warmly again. İlhami left with her to make sure she got into a taxi safely. They walked side by side in silence until they found one waiting for a customer. After he had opened the door and told the driver where to go, İhami said, "I've got your mobile number, here's mine", and handed her a business card. Yelkovan Bookshop/ İlhami Doğru. Before the taxi pulled away, he leaned in through the open window and said, "We'll be in touch again tomorrow. Don't fret. Our mad Eyüp will show up soon." Pilar wanted to believe him with all her heart.

All the way home her head throbbed as she replayed the events of that day in her mind. Her leaving the house that morning, her finding İlhami without even having to look for him, the mini tour they had taken together, Vehbi's coffee house that was as curious as its owner, then Müjdat's sudden appearance, the splendour of the Süleymaniye Mosque, the exquisiteness of the kuru fasulye, and then Eda's warmth, Uncle Ander's voice, the trip down memory lane, the rakı-induced relaxation ... She had done so many things today ... The only thing she hadn't managed to do was find Eyüp. Gazing at the lights rising from the opposite shore of the sea, she sighed, "Ah Eyüp. Come out of wherever it is you're hiding!"

Unlike his counterpart that morning, it didn't occur to the taxi driver that she might be addressing him. Either he was turning a deaf ear, or he really didn't hear her.

When her father had said, "He's my brother, how can I throw him out of my house?" her mother too had turned a deaf ear. But Pilar had been too ashamed to tell them that at the table today. Not even Eyüp knew that Vicky was the reason why Uncle Ander had left. He might be less fond of her if he did. Pilar too must have been afraid of loving her less, because she didn't repeat what she knew, even to herself, and, because she kept it bottled inside herself, she never forgot it. "I've got two children, I have to protect them," Vicky had said. "Ander's friends and his enemies are all beyond me. I don't want him in my house." And Uncle Ander had departed post-haste. Not only did he himself never come back, but no news of him ever came either. Pilar knew that loss was one of the first injuries her heart had sustained. But the world was a place where injuries were considered ugly; to become beautiful, she had kept it secret.

When the taxi dropped her off she was uneasy about returning so late. As she entered the front garden and started walking towards the house, where every single light was switched on, she noticed the shadow outside the door. As she approached nearer she realised the shadow consisted of a huge pile of shoes heaped in rows . . . Wondering what might be the reason for this sudden onslaught of guests, she pressed on the infuriating doorbell which grated on the ears with its frightful bird sound. A strange woman opened the door. Just as she was beginning to wonder if she had come to the wrong house, Müesser appeared behind the woman. She had aged 10 years since the morning. Her silent eyes were swollen and bloodshot. She stared at Pilar with those eyes and spoke to her with that silence. But Pilar didn't understand. Once the woman who had opened the door had gone inside and was out of sight, she said, "What's up Müesser? Has something bad happened?" She wasn't sure she wanted to hear the answer.

Müesser clearly tried to open her mouth, but failed. She looked as though she could barely stand; it was as if she were liable to collapse if she didn't hold on to the door.

"Müesser, stop frightening me. What's happened?"

Pilar listened to the sounds coming from inside. Someone was murmuring a song. Except it wasn't like a song, it was more like something you would hear in a religious ceremony, with its sombre melody . . . When the song ended and she heard a chorus of female voices all saying "Amin" at the same time, Pilar held Müesser's arm and squeezed it.

"Will you tell me what's happened?"

Müesser opened her mouth with great difficulty, as though mustering up all her remaining strength. Her dried, chapped, bleeding lips, that had stuck together, parted, opened. And finally a voice, though very faint, came out of the space:

"He's dead . . ."

Pilar felt as though boiling water was pouring off her back. She couldn't make sense of what she had heard. What had happened to Eyüp? Was this a bad joke she was hearing? She wanted someone to tell her what was going on this minute, in her mother tongue. She couldn't get her head round this Turkish anymore; her head was in a whirl. Her brain began to throb, and she started to feel dizzy. She leaned against the door for support and remained staring at the face of the woman opposite her, which had been reduced to two eyes.

"He's gone," repeated Müesser, as though exhaling her last breath. "My brother's dead."

★ ★ ★

I am inside a foggy winter's night. The stench of sulphur hangs thick in the air . . . Beside me is a friend whom I haven't seen in years, Vehbi. His mouth keeps moving, but I can't hear a word of what he's saying. I look like I do now, whereas he hasn't aged a bit; he's exactly the same as he was when I last saw him. When I look at his face carefully I can read his lips. "From now on you'll walk alone. Don't forget what I told you, all right?" he says. "Whenever you call me . . ." And then he vanishes abruptly. I'm left by myself. I slink into a side street, when I come to a three-storey stone building, I freeze. It's as though I'm waiting for someone who will never arrive.

Just then I suddenly smell the most wonderful fragrance. I fill my lungs with the scent, as though I don't want to miss the tiniest fraction of it. I say I wish every soap in the land could smell that way.

When I turn towards the source of the fragrance, I see her. She is standing before me with her pale face, her black eyes and her dark auburn hair. When I am face to face with her I realise I have found the person I've been seeking for so long. Strange! She's standing before me like a diary, with her black eyes that have the whole of my past accumulated inside them, yet I still can't work out either her name or how I know her. All I know is that I love her madly. It's as though she's either always been with me, or always will be. I want her to have either given birth to me or to give birth to my child. Then I remember with great pain: But she doesn't love me! I begin to weep. When my tears become a flood and soak her feet, she leans over and whispers in my ear that she loves me. Then she vanishes, taking her wonderful fragrance with her. I hear the sound of her heels growing faint. Didn't she say she loved me, so why is she leaving then? Tears stream down my face. Suddenly I recall her name, and let out a blood-curdling scream:

"Maria Puder!"

The sound of her heels falls silent. She carves a passage through the fog by tossing the hem of her fur coat. Then I see myself in her black eyes. She leans over and whispers slowly in my ear:

"I'm leaving now. But whenever you call, I'll be there."

When I wake up it's as though a snowman has melted on my pillow. It would appear that I, who am incapable of crying during the day, fulfil that particular need at night. I have woken up to a wet pillow before, but this is the first time I clearly recall crying my eyes out in a dream.

When I complained of not being able to remember my dreams, I had no idea that what I was lacking was Sabahattin Ali's imagination. For a long time I couldn't get *Madonna in a Fur Coat*, which I read just before heading off to Paris, out of my head; for years it was the answer I gave anyone who asked what my favourite book was. But it was in fact a cruel story, guaranteed to dampen the enthusiasm of a youth unversed in the art of love. Maria Puder was an angel, while I, who had had the audacity to think ill of her, was a devil. I was somebody who did not try to win because I believed I would lose, somebody who could not love because I was afraid of not being loved. Just like Raif, I had lost my faith in anyone being able to love me, and I knew it was those who had made me feel worthless who were responsible.

During those years it was as though all women spun round me like propellers, and I couldn't decide which one to choose: I believed I could only fall in love with someone like Maria Puder. Whereas usually boys of that age will settle for any woman misguided enough to throw them a sideways glance. I couldn't really be classed as choosy when it came to fleeting fancies. But I did believe that it was only a woman like Maria Puder that I could love and spend the rest of my life waiting for. Even if she never arrived . . .

For some reason the first time I set eyes on Pilar in Paris, Maria Puder sprang to my mind. There was no physical resemblance between them. But the moment I saw her I thought she could be my Madonna in a Fur Coat. She was someone who would never surrender her innocence and dignity to any of my paranoias or ulterior motives. For that reason alone she was the right person.

Yes, that's the kind of person I am. I have eyes that look at my inside one way and my outside another, and I have many different faces, all with an aptitude for rubbing everyone up the right way. I'm a fretful, lying wretch. But can the same be said of Pilar? Well, she is at ease with herself. She and I are like the bleary-eyed readers of newspapers that print two pictures side by side and ask them to spot I don't know how many differences between them. She is always looking for our similarities, while I'm always looking for our differences. I am as addicted to melancholy as she's full of joie de vivre . . .

For example, Pilar talks about the time when we went on holiday to Lisbon together. Whenever the subject of holiday arises, she always cites that one. For her, it's special and romantic because it was our first holiday together. As occurs with the holidays of every couple newly in love, that holiday passed smoothly, in radiant happiness that imbued even the most mundane moments with miraculous significance. Whereas I always think of my favourite as being the holiday we spent in Rome a year later. The holiday when all our money was stolen on our second day in the city, in front of the Fountain of Love no less . . .

When I put on a pair of shorts without pockets and expressed my reluctance to carry a manbag, poor Pilar was forced to put not just her own wallet in her bag, but mine too. Thus our prospective pickpocket was able to kill two birds with one stone and no doubt praised our generosity to the heavens during the banquet to which he most likely treated himself. We only realised our wallets were missing when we tried to pay for the sumptuous pizzas we ate in the fancy restaurant in the Piazza de'Mercanti in Trastevere. I still smile when I recall our romantic trip that turned into a nightmare; boy did we sweat!

Pilar always pulls a face whenever I mention that holiday. She doesn't like remembering it. Whereas I much prefer overcoming obstacles together to exasperating bliss and sickly sweet romanticism. That is one of the most striking differences between my beautiful wife and me. Of course my insistence on siding with darkness and the fact that Pilar can only be happy in the presence of light doesn't mean she's going to move out at the first sign of a power cut. Otherwise I probably wouldn't have married her, believing she could be my Maria Puder.

That immortal woman whom the protagonist of the novel, Raif, talked about years later with regret, the real Maria Puder, retained her place in my memory as my first love. I can see this morning that it was a love true enough for her to enter my dreams and find me, in other words, to come back, like she said she would.

Vehbi gave me that book when my friends and I got together for a farewell party two days before I went to France. And, if I'm not mistaken, he also gave İlhami, who is a Galatasaray supporter, a tattered old Fenerbahçe kit that was falling apart. As one of the school's few Fenerbahçe supporters, he had carried out a failed campaign to try and win over supporters right up until the last minute, making us laugh for years. He wasn't a fake, but everyone knew a lot of his eccentricities were designed to make his friends laugh. He was one of those rare people whose reward is knowing how to grow bigger by giving. He would walk around with a huge battered bag and give everyone little gifts, whether he knew them or not. People were both bewildered and delighted by his bizarre range of gifts, which varied from house slippers to old newspapers or embroidered handkerchiefs. With time, every present he gave, even the strangest seeming, occupied an important place in the recipient's life, or at least that's the impression I got. From what I gather from his letters, the years haven't changed him one bit. Despite his education, he refused to think becoming someone important meant the same thing as we do. Which is why, unlike the rest of us, he really did succeed in becoming someone important. He opened a coffee house in Beyazıt and apparently has customers from all walks of life, from students to pensioners. It makes me happy to imagine him there.

I haven't seen his face even once since secondary school. But we still write to each other after all these years, exchanging all kinds of inane chit-chat. I send him postcards and posters from here, and he sends me cassette tapes, interesting newspaper clippings and such like . . .

Okay, but why did I have that dream after so many years? Was I missing Maria Puder, or just things from the past in general? If we also take into account the fact that I recently dreamt of my rootlessness, it wouldn't take a great deal of talent to imagine that my dear doctor will conclude from his analyses that I'm feeling homesick. If I tell him all this, he'll ask what Maria Puder signifies for me. Love, suffering, longing, fear, hope . . . A lover who will come running whenever I'm having a hard time. Someone from whom I'm far away, but who will never abandon me . . .

When he was giving me *Madonna in a Fur Coat*, Vehbi had said, with a huge grin on his face, "I'm leaving now. But whenever you call I'll be there." As I hadn't read the book I didn't understand, but just stared at him blankly. I only understood once I'd read it. In fact, when it was apt, I didn't hesitate to appropriate it, I purloined it. Mostly I said it to girls I was trying to abandon tactfully during the years when my inexperience in love sent me out looking for a good time. I lied. To tell the truth, I was more interested in hearing it than saying it.

But no one ever said it to me, even insincerely. Apart from my secondary school friend's big smiling face, no one told me they would be there whenever I needed them as they were leaving. Worse still, I don't think anyone ever loved me enough to come back and find me still there. Or am I the one who's got it all wrong? Ah Maria Puder, look at what you've done to me!

6

Müesser

Night, still night, still night,
Right now I wish I were a reed in a stream!
Ahmet Haşim, "Wish at a Day's End"

Müesser was thinking about tombstones. How silent they were, and how heavy ... It was as though the whole world had renounced its spite and melted into them, as docile as a sick cat. Was that why they were as burdened as if they carried the secrets of the entire universe, as sorrowful as women who have never given birth and as weary as women who have given birth too often? Was that why those with a great deal to say cloaked themselves in their reproachful silence? They stood haughty and rigid, as though they were not finished, but only just starting ... Müesser thought of the terrible darkness of those stones, that would be erected over the heads of everyone who had ground themselves in the rubbish dump of existence, everyone who had ever set foot on the face of the earth. Since her childhood, she had quaked and trembled more at the thought of others' tombstones than of her own. Her mother didn't have a tombstone on the day she was consigned to the earth. Had her father – who had bought that vast family plot as though he cared more about the deaths of his nearest and dearest than he did about their lives – known when she was going to die, he wouldn't, no doubt, have restricted himself to merely sharing and reserving his wife's resting place, but would have placed a stone over her head too. But, he had no idea, just as he didn't know when his own time would come ...

After they had had a tombstone made for Hafize Hanım, Müesser took to talking to it every time she went to the cemetery. She fancied that even if the body the maggots had lustfully eaten away was now mixed into the earth, from there it would have flowed away to the water, to plants and other destinations. The earth was now completely empty, and as dark as the terror-filled nights of her childhood. But could the same be said of the tombstone? It had sucked up whatever was left of her mother's soul and was heavy with its weight. Whenever she looked at the tombstone she felt as though she could see her mother's weary form there. Whenever she ran her hand over it, it was as though she was touching the sorrowful lines on her face . . .

She remembered when, years ago, as a small child, she saw two cats on the road on her way home from school one winter's day. Two tiny kittens lying on the side of the road. One was dead and lay there completely still. The other was clinging to it from behind and looked as though it were crying. It was shaking the dead body, that would never move again, to make it wake up. It had pressed its own tiny body against the dead kitten's, striving to turn the two of them into just one cat, to make them come to life together. The day Müesser had found her mother dead in her bed, she too had thrown herself on top of her. Just like that cat. And again today, yet another time . . . How many more times would she throw herself in vain on top of a loved one lying before her with no breath in his body?

Müesser thought of the tombstones lined up side by side. Of the solid, silent walls erected around the large family plots . . . Of the thousands of tons of weight of lived days attacking the tombstones lined up within those walls . . . She thought of the reason why she disliked family plots. She couldn't say whether the occupants' cages were their graves, or their families. Then she thought of the rough surface of her parents' gravestones, standing side by side. And the new one that would soon be joining them, Veysel's . . .

Ahhh, she sighed to herself, ahh, if only I hadn't answered that telephone! If only I had taken my last breath before

I could answer it. If only I could have died without hearing what I heard, or seeing what I saw ...

That morning after breakfast she had felt strangely oppressed. She had put it down partly to the ominous dream she had had last night, and partly to her regretting having allowed her sister-in-law to go to Beyoğlu by herself. In her dream she had been in a garden full of bushes on a dark night. She could hear the cries of animals and trembled with fear as she imagined the savage creatures that she couldn't see in the dark; she had cowered under a tree, terrified, awaiting her fate. Just then a fairy-tale king appeared before her. He was wearing a majestic crown encrusted with precious jewels, and a long cloak glittering with gold hung from his shoulders. At the sight of the king, Müesser felt comforted. The fact that she didn't know him at all wasn't all that important. He was, after all, from the fairy-tale world of her childhood; he could protect her. The king had a gentle face, embellished with a benign twinkle in his eye. He approached her, unperturbed by the blood-curdling noises all around them. He reached over to the branches of the tree Müesser was leaning against. It was then that Müesser noticed the peaches on the branches. Sensing that her saviour wanted to eat them, she picked one and held it out to him. The king accepted the peach and devoured it, the juices running down his chin. Somehow looking at him now made Müesser feel nauseous. She wanted to retch, but stopped herself. Then the king found a hosepipe from somewhere. First he washed his face with the water that gushed from it, then, fully dressed, he wet his entire body. But somehow he couldn't get clean. The sticky peach juice had turned him into the dirtiest, ugliest person in the world. When he noticed the look of disgust on Müesser's face, his eyes darkened with fury. He raised the hosepipe high in the air, aimed it at Müesser's face and started to squirt water on her. Müesser emitted a piercing scream as the pressurised water stung her face. Then she woke up with a start.

She was sick and tired of these nightmares. Some nights she grappled with giant snakes, others she was lost in vast forests.

The dreams stifled her so much, she didn't even attempt to interpret them in the morning.

But this morning's sense of foreboding was not just on account of the bad taste the dream had left in her mouth. She was more anxious about Pilar's having gone all the way to Beyoğlu by herself. When she had refused to allow Veysel to accompany her, Müesser had asked her to at least allow her to go along, but Pilar wouldn't hear of it. Not that Beyoğlu was an area she knew, mind you. But still it would have been better than sending the woman by herself. However, Pilar was as obstinate as her husband; she had dug in her heels and gone alone.

She's a grown woman, and not just any woman but a European, she must know a thing or two, thought Müesser, doing her best to reassure herself. Then, picking up the lace cover she was crocheting for the coffee table, she settled herself on the two-seater sofa in the sitting room. Just then Atiye had turned up, bursting to talk. Perihan loved having this gossip-mongering woman over. Müesser had told her several times that, "Anyone who gossips to you about other people will gossip to others about you," but Perihan hadn't listened; maybe she thought Atiye liked her too much to gossip about her. But Müesser knew that leopards don't change their spots. In God's eyes the sin of calumny was equal to eating your own brother's flesh – and no one who had tasted it once would recover in a hurry. Müesser felt irritated whenever Atiye launched into tales of Hüsniye's husband from the next neighbourhood hobnobbing with prostitutes, or Cevahir the baker gambling his car away. She had no interest in other people's secrets and didn't want anyone to discuss hers. That's why she felt uncomfortable whenever Atiye came to sully their home with her malice; she would sit in a corner with a long face, in silence.

Atiye's demand of "Weeeell, where's the guest then?" the moment she set foot in the sitting room, wearing her leering smile gave away the reason for her visit.

"She's gone," said Perihan. "She's off to find her husband's friends in Beyoğlu, apparently. She hasn't even got their address, the clever clogs just thought she'd try her luck. I hope no one films her wandering up and down Beyoğlu searching high and low."

Atiye burst into hysterical laughter. Müesser didn't know whether to be angry at Perihan's tasteless joke, or offended with her for being so quick to blurt out their private family business to all and sundry. When had she had the chance to tell Atiye about Pilar's visit? Why had this outsider been notified of her brother's leaving home?

The more she thought about it the more inclined she was to believe Eyüp had left his wife. But because there was no kind way of saying as much to the woman, she had preferred to keep quiet. Müesser had liked Pilar; she thought she and her brother made a good couple. And maybe Eyüp would come back and they would make up. But her real concern was whether or not she would get to see her brother during all of this. She was upset with Eyüp for depriving her of the sight of his face for so long, but if she were to see it just once, all her upset and anger would vanish in an instant. If Pilar could only find her husband, take his arm and bring him here. That would be the end of all the hurt and resentment; the rest would be pure rejoicing and celebration. But what had got into Perihan's head to make her repeat all this to that garrulous Atiye . . .

"Weeeelll," said Atiye, settling herself on the armchair immediately opposite Müesser. "How would you rate her? Is she blonde?"

"Not really, auburnish."

"And how did you communicate? Can she talk at least?"

"Oh don't ask. She's mastered Turkish all right, but it's too much effort for her ladyship to talk. You have to wrench the words out of her with pliers. I practically got a hernia just trying to get her to say two syllables," replied Perihan. She had obviously rushed post haste to tell her friend about Pilar's phone call the moment she had hung up. Didn't they have anything better to do than talk about who was coming? What difference does it make if she's blonde or brunette, thought Müesser. What was it with all this sudden nose poking and envy . . .

"How are you, Müesser Abla? How do you like your sister-in-law?" said Atiye, turning to Müesser. Her mission being first and foremost to gossip, it had only just occurred to Atiye to greet her.

"I'm fine," said Müesser curtly. She was not about to share what she thought of her brother's wife with this offensive woman staring at her with eyes glittering with spite.

But the woman insisted with, "Yes but what did you make of your sister-in-law?" It was obvious she wasn't going to relax until she had a fresh news item to spread about the neighbourhood.

"We loved her," said Müesser, looking straight into Atiye's eyes. Then, having gained momentum, she fired the fatal arrow into Perihan, who was sitting in the corner grinning as widely as a boiled sheep's head.

"We even said, enough of all this living in foreign countries away from your family. We said move back here and we can all live happily together here."

When they saw Müesser's flaming eyes, the two women fell into a bewildered silence. They didn't even ask if she was joking or serious. After all, they were completely unaccustomed to seeing her angry. Never mind her erupting like a volcano that has been seething inwardly over the years, it was unheard of for her to allow even the tiniest hint of wrath to slip out of her. Muttering an excuse of some job in the kitchen Perihan needed to finish, they made their escape. Müesser knew as well as she knew her own name that, once there, they would whet their appetites with all the ins and outs of Pilar's husband leaving her, next on their agenda would be Müesser and what a ridiculous old maid she was and then they would sink their teeth into every juicy titbit about everyone and anyone they could think of. But she said nothing. At least not to them . . .

To avoid swelling up until she exploded with everything bottled up inside her, Müesser often talked silently to herself, trembling and unwinding, like a weary ball of wool made from an unravelled old sweater. She reasoned that everyone with many motives for not speaking did the same. She thought if no one but herself heard her voice, the poison she was unable to spew out would become purified inside her. When she came face to face with those she had fought with inside her head she was ashamed, as though the people before her knew of the altercation that had taken place in her mind, and shy, as though they had heard the sentences she had never actually uttered. Years ago her dear mother had once said, "You fight with all of us inside your head. And then you get offended with us because we haven't heard what you've said to yourself." And she had thought, if I were to repeat the things I say to myself to your faces, none of us would ever be able to look each other in the eye again. But because she said it to herself, her beloved mother was never any the wiser.

When the whispering in the kitchen turned into a buzzing that pounded inside her brain, she wondered if she should go out and see Adalet. Everyone around her was all too ready to swoop down onto a sorrowful day, like a hawk, and pull it to shreds. But Adalet wasn't like that. She didn't just notice when Müesser was troubled, she suffered with her, but still never probed until Müesser opened her mouth and mentioned it. What Müesser liked best when she was with her was for the two of them to sit together in long, uninterrupted silence.

But thinking that, should Pilar came home early, she didn't want her to be at home alone with those two busybodies, she changed her mind about going out. She placed her hand on her constricted heart and listened. Something bad was definitely going to happen today!

Every time she felt a mild pain in her heart, something terrible inevitably befell her. As though every evil in the world were spawning inside her ... News of goodness, kindness, gratitude never winged its way to the doorstep, but cruelty, evil, ugliness, always manifested themselves in advance. Perhaps that was the reason why she remained wide eyed on some nights when she was a child, the reason why she resisted sleep. And the reason why, in later years, as a young woman, she was reluctant to open her eyes to the mornings that lay ahead of her... Nowadays she mostly had that pain in the afternoons. After all, the inevitable occurred at inevitable times. At each stage of her life the darkness appeared at a different time of day. When she was a child it was the nights that were black, when she was a young woman it was the mornings, and now the afternoons . . . Being anchored neither at midday, nor evening, but somewhere halfway through the day, was like being a blind man without a stick, a child without a mother, or a lover without time. Like being suspended in limbo.

Only this time that familiar oppression hadn't waited for the afternoon, but lodged itself inside her from the morning. Müesser was more bothered by this unwelcome guest confusing the time than by its imposition. She searched for an activity to distract her, to keep her hands occupied. Actually, the house needed cleaning. If she could polish the windows, the doors, the floorboards, she would feel better, but they had a guest, it would be rude to turn the house upside down. Otherwise, Müesser loved throwing herself into cleaning when she was annoyed, or when something was weighing on her heart. Some days she launched into her chores as though obeying some mysterious command, in a near frenzy. At those moments there seemed to be a grim determination in her eyes, a tense expectancy between her eyebrows, and a black fate stamped on her forehead, a fate that, despite years of scrubbing, she hadn't managed to remove. Once she had embarked on a job, she wanted to feel the dirt, the rust, the water, the soap, everything. Because anyone who didn't feel the dirt didn't appreciate the value of water, and anyone who didn't feel water didn't understand the power of dirt. She would wring the cloth she had soaked in a pink plastic tub full of foaming water until her hands hurt, squeezing the water out, then slap it down onto the wooden floorboards, which had long ago lost their varnished sheen. Slap! Anyone who saw her would think she was challenging those floorboards to a fight. Then she would tightly clasp the cloth that was awaiting the order to slowly creep up on the target and take action, press it down onto the wood with all her might and start scrubbing. She would rub the same spot for several minutes, as though struggling to clean a phantom stain visible to no one but herself. Until her white hands turned red and chapped, until the green veins in her arms swelled, one by one, until her tightly clenched jawbone succumbed to a red ache . . .

Given that cleaning the house was out, she went into the bathroom, thinking, well, in that case I'll clean myself. Besides, abandoning herself to the serenity of the water would do her good. She soaped her head three times, as she always did. She had learned as a child that Allah gives you three chances. She drank water in three stages, she soaped her head three times, after picking up bread that had fallen on the floor she kissed it three times and pressed it to her forehead. Müesser felt kindly towards soap, but, as with the house, she used a rough hand when cleaning herself. She clawed at her scalp with her nails every time. Boiling hot water scalded the wounds on her head, making them sting and smart. And, once she got hold of the bath glove, there was no stopping her; she would scrub her body raw, tearing at her skin until it peeled. Her entire body would turn bright red, burning like an open wound. She would take the foaming sponge and scrub between her legs with grim determination. As though that were the dirtiest part of her body. It seemed she wasn't out to clean it as much as to rip out and tear apart that cursed body part where her Maker had not seen fit to place a baby's head . . .

When she emerged from the bathroom with her skin so chafed and raw it would be covered in scabs in two days, Atiye was still there. Perihan must have finished what she was doing in the kitchen because they had both settled themselves in the living room and were watching a romantic drama. Müesser entered silently and sat down on the two-seater sofa. Neither they nor Müesser said a word. Not only did they behave as though there hadn't been any tension whatsoever between them just now, but as though Müesser wasn't even there. She, for her part, picked up her interminable lace coffee table cover and forced her fingers to work faster.

When she was startled by the sound of the telephone, her first thought was that Pilar was lost and was telephoning the house to ask for directions. As though that were the most terrible thing that could happen to them at that moment ... She put her crocheting down and sprang from her seat. She raised the receiver in an absurd fluster, as though it were a question of now or never. She didn't know that some telephone calls should never be answered, some news never be received.

"Hello?"

"Müesser Abla?"

It was Perihan's brother's voice. He sounded both meek and out of breath ...

"Yes, it's me Bünyamin. How are you, my child?"

"Abla ..."

"Yes?"

"Abla ..."

Bünyamin wasn't exactly what you would call razor sharp. But normally when he telephoned he could at least convey his message in one go. This strange behaviour did not bode well.

"Tell me child, what's the matter? Are you all right?"

"No Abla, I'm not. Abla, I'm all right but ..."

His voice sounded hoarse, as though he were sobbing. And he seemed afraid to tell her what he had to say; somehow he couldn't get the words out.

"Bünyamin, will you tell me, my son? Has something bad happened?"

Realising it was her brother on the other end of the line, Perihan had rushed to Müesser's side and was tugging at her arm, demanding "What's up, what's he saying?" How could Müesser tell her when she didn't know herself. All she could do was repeat her question.

"You're frightening us my son, what's happened?"

All Bünyamin could manage was to rasp "My brother-in-law ... Abla, my brother in law ..." Whatever it was that he couldn't say was making the boy groan like an agonising patient and cry like a tortured cat. Whatever this ominous news was, it was too shy to come out of those lips. Müesser trembled with trepidation, shuddering from head to toe.

"Tell me! What's happened to Veysel?"

There followed several seconds of silence, which seemed like years to Müesser. First she heard Bünyamin's irregular breathing, then his desolate voice, like lava that had cooled instantly after erupting from a volcano:

"We've lost him Abla ..."

Ever since she had been a child she had always felt secretly guilty about Veysel. Her belief that she had abandoned him was a dark stain on her conscience. But in actual fact they had spent their whole lives together. They were partners in adversity. When it came to secrets, trials, burdens, they had shared them all. But they had been mute when it came to discussion, reticent when it came to love, defective when it came to confession. And that being so, they had neither been able to look each other straight in the eye, nor find the strength to make a clean break and leave.

Veysel had been a good reason for living, he had always been her guarantee against loneliness. While one by one, all the others had left this house, and her, he had held on tightly to his sister. Now that he too was gone ... Like everyone who loses someone near, the one they presume will always be there, whilst yearning for those who are far away, Müesser was incredulous. She had thought Veysel would never do that, never leave.

They had an unspoken agreement never to leave each other, to endure life together. If Veysel had wanted to, he could have broken that agreement in his early youth, in protest against the desolation he suffered compared with the attention showered on Eyüp. He could have left this mothball-ridden house and saved himself. But he didn't. What's more, Müesser knew her brother stayed so she wouldn't be alone. But even still, at every opportunity she made Veysel aware that she loved her youngest brother more than him. Love was apportioned so indiscreetly, even if one wanted to, it was hard to hide it. And for some reason, people always reserved their greatest love for those who spurned it.

One year before her father died, Müesser had gone to stay with her mother's elder sister, Aunt Habibe, who lived in Adapazarı. Or rather, she hadn't gone, she had been sent. When Aunt Habibe had fallen ill and become bedbound, Müesser had been entrusted with the duty of waiting on her, her uncle and her two cousins. She spent her days serving a sick woman and three males, one an adult, cooking their meals and doing their chores. She resented being despatched to be the servant of these relatives whom she never saw, but nothing could equal her grief at being separated from her tiny Eyüp. At that time Eyüp was just 4 years old. During those four years they had never once been separated, even for a moment. But still, he had not once cried for his sister during the two and a half months she spent in Adapazarı. That's what her mother had said; "Eyüp's fine, he's not fretting for you. He hasn't made any fuss." This explanation, which was intended to reassure her daughter, however slightly, had put a lump in Müesser's throat. She had felt dejected, like a sweater whose stitches have come undone, like a knitting needle inserted into the wrong hole, like a piece of yarn that has snapped because it has worn too thin. While she was grieving over her absence not making the slightest difference to her little brother's life, it was thanks to Veysel, then aged eight, that she eventually returned to Istanbul at the end of two and a half months. He had fallen and broken his leg whilst playing football outside and, made irascible by his injury, had screamed "I want my sister." When no amount of reasoning, scolding or beating made him see sense, her father had ended Müesser's visit to Adapazarı. Thus it fell on the youngest sister, Aunt Maide, who lived in Bandırma, to take over her duties at Adapazarı. And a good job too. When, in the second week after Müesser's return home, Aunt Habibe had gone to meet her maker, the young girl had felt secretly pleased not to have been with her when it happened. She rejoiced to be reunited with Eyüp, but quickly forgot that it was Veysel she had to thank for being allowed to return. She had never worked out if it was because he thought his burden would be heavier without her, or because he believed they would be stronger together, but ever since he was a child Veysel had wanted to sleep under the same roof as his sister. He neither let her very far out of his sight, not went himself . . .

But as it turned out, even those one thought would never leave could up and go. And what's more, when it was least expected. At a moment when, far from fearing their family would shrink, she was nursing a hope that it would grow . . . And now, with Veysel gone just as Eyüp was about to come . . . Müesser felt even guiltier about not being able to share out her love for her brothers fairly. Sometimes she thought just because one was big and the other small, one was near and the other far, one was dependent and the other brutish that did not justify treating Eyüp as her real brother and having a permanently guilty conscience where Veysel was concerned. Could it be that she felt close to one because she regarded him as an empty page and distant from the other because she regarded him as a diary that reminded her of the things she wanted to forget? Okay, but even if that were the case, how was Veysel to blame? He wasn't . . .

Even when he did the most unforgivable things, Müesser did not judge him in the same way as others did. She always understood him and looked for different meanings in what he said and did. And most of the time she found them . . . No one chose their life. No one chose either their body or the temperament that would inhabit that body, nor where and with whom one would come into the world . . . As if Veysel would be Veysel given the choice. Had she herself chosen to be Müesser? Take that poor Perihan, for example; was she happy in her own skin? And that being so, Müesser would say to herself, who had the right to resent Veysel for being Veysel?

Apparently, when Veysel had arrived at the supermarket that morning the first thing he had done was check the accounts. Then he had sat down on the stool he had placed outside Tevfik's furniture shop opposite his supermarket, and they had drunk tea and played backgammon. They had played for a kilo of ice cream, and when Veysel had lost the game, he had walked down to the beach road to buy it from the renowned Roma ice cream parlour. The tragedy had occurred on his way back, when he was trying to cross over to the other side of the road. His journey and his life had been cut short by a 22-year-old youth by the name of Cüneyt and the navy blue Citroen he was driving. According to eyewitnesses, the car had not been going too fast. Veysel had leapt into the road in a great hurry without looking. Was he rushing so the ice cream wouldn't melt?

From what Müesser discovered only once she had got to the hospital, the youth, who managed to stop his car, albeit too late, all the local people sitting in the coffee house on the street corner, the tiny eyes of the birds perched on the branches, all ran to Veysel in fear and panic. Before he had died, Veysel had gazed into the youth's face, not with anger or fear, but almost with affection, and said, as though speaking to someone he knew very well, "It's you! I'm so glad you came." Those had been his last words. "I'm so glad you came . . ."

As Veysel was swaying between fantasy and reality, death and life, in that split second before he departed from his present and floated towards infinity, there, in limbo, he had seen someone else, perhaps someone he knew, in the face of the man who had killed him . . . It had been a strange death, but he had died happy.

Müesser had heard before that the angel Azrail appeared to each person in different forms. Once, Perihan had even told her a story she had heard from Fitnat Hanım: "Before he died my grandfather kept talking about a black cat that walked around his room. Sometimes it slept in the drawer and sometimes it wandered around his death bed on its tiny paws. But no one except him could see that cat. According to my mother, Azrail appeared in a different form before each person whose life he was going to take. But only before that person, no one else . . . In other words, my grandfather died at the hands of a black cat."

As Müesser listened to how Veysel had looked into his murderer's terrified face and, seeing who knows who there, had said "I'm so glad you came," she was not at all interested in what Cüneyt, who had long since been taken into custody, looked like. What really interested her was what her life without Veysel would be like now.

Entrusting Perihan, who was having fainting fits in the corridor, to Atiye, who had rushed to the hospital with them, she followed the man in the blue gown down to the basement. She accompanied him down a long corridor. Perhaps it wasn't as long as it seemed, but it seemed to stretch out endlessly before her. To be honest, she had no wish to reach her destination anyway. She could walk like this for hours, for days.

How had it happened, she wondered? Had he died in the way it was written in the sacred books, for example? Had that white light that those who had returned from the brink of death talk about appeared to Veysel as well? But Veysel didn't like white; he didn't even wear white shirts. "White shows the dirt too much," he would always say, but what would it matter if he wore it, he wasn't dirty. If a beam of white light had come to get him, he would have definitely resisted, he wouldn't have wanted to go. He thought of himself as dirty; he avoided white because it exposed his dirt. And had he gone to heaven? Müesser knew, she could imagine, the sins he was sullied with. But still she didn't hold her brother responsible for any of them. Whatever Veysel had done, he had had his reasons. Were God's angels too simple to see that?

After the walk that had seemed to last for years, they reached the end of the stark white corridor. Yes, white did show the dirt. This hospital was dirty, with its walls with peeling plaster, finger-marked doors, pungent medicine smells and diseased, cracked columns, because it was white … The man in the blue gown stood at the end of the corridor, outside the white door on the left. It was a door that was even whiter than the rest, or so it seemed to Müesser. Then the man looked at her face, as if to ascertain whether or not she would be able to deal with what she was about to see. He was obviously afraid she might fall down in a faint and make extra work for him. His expression enquired whether they should go in, did Müesser still wish to enter? Müesser didn't want to enter; she wanted to wake up with a start and realise it had all been a dream. But nevertheless she bowed her head slightly forward to show she was ready. When in fact she was not at all ready for what she was about to see. How could someone prepare herself for her brother's dead body?

Just then a hairless head poked out of the slightly opened door, followed by a male body so thin it would topple over if you blew on it. He was wearing a green gown made from some strange material that looked like a plastic raincoat. The man was a hairless, beardless, moustacheless, colourless, lifeless, sickly-looking thing. From his exchanges with the man in the blue gown, Müesser understood he was in charge of the dead bodies. So, he had become a living corpse from spending so much time in the company of cadavers. Those who kept vigil over the dead, washed them, carried them, made the coffins they were to be carried in and manufactured their tombstones, might well fatten up their book of good deeds and secure their place on the other side, but it was obviously at the price of progressively weakening their connections with this world. What proportion of a person so completely steeped in death could be alive?

The man with the plastic raincoat opened the door wider for the new guests. After a brief hesitation, as though it wanted to say something but, fearing it wouldn't be able to, had changed its mind, the white of the stammering door opened all the way. Behind it Müesser thought she would find the kind of darkness where lightning strikes, but the dominion of that unnerving whiteness that had seeped into every corner of the hospital leered over her here too. She felt as though an imperceptible wind were licking her face, and, immediately afterwards, was startled by the smell of death that is unlike anything living.

Like their bathroom at home, the floor and walls were covered with gleaming white tiles. The uniformity of the whiteness was broken only by the rows of cold steel deposit boxes. Müesser shuddered when she saw them, as though noticing them for the first time. Her brother, now stone cold, would also be inside one. That was all well and good, but what was the thing they called a morgue? Was it a kind of limbo between the street and the grave, for example? Was it a resting place for stopping and catching one's breath before the body went into the earth and the soul could relax completely? Or had the soul long ago completely abandoned that faithful body that had been its home for so many years? If that were the case, then did that make these morgue deposit boxes no different from a dumping ground? What if it were to explode one day, like the large dumping grounds outside the city, and long, lifeless arms, legs, kidneys and guts were to rain down from the skies onto the living ... Ugh, what am I thinking, she said to herself, unhappily banishing the thoughts from her mind. It was then that the man in the blue gown eyed her once again with suspicion. He wanted to be certain she would not swoon onto the floor. When he noticed the resolve in the woman's feet, separated and planted firmly on the ground, he motioned to the man in the plastic raincoat gown. The latter held on to one of the deposit boxes and, using all his might, pulled it towards him ...

When the glinting steel opened, a two-layer berth appeared inside it. Instead of beds, there was only a long stretcher in each section, in the style of a drawer. The top segment was vacant. The man in the blue gown pulled out the bottom segment. If his eyes hadn't been closed, she would have come face to face with Veysel, lying stretched out, his face the shade of the chalk white he so disliked ...

The first thing Müesser noticed on her brother's now completely wan face was the smile frozen on his lips. As far as she knew, a person went over to the other side under the effect of the last thing he saw. What could her brother have found to smile about in a car that was heading straight towards him?

In a programme she had watched on daytime television recently, Müesser had learned that a person's death throes can last a few minutes, or a few days. A doctor in a white gown sitting beside a glamorous singer had said that phase was slow and drawn out in the case of chronic illnesses and ended very quickly in the case of sudden deaths. When Müesser remembered Aunt Habibe, for whom she had cared when she was on her death bed years ago, she had prayed her own death wouldn't be of an illness, but of old age, or a sudden accident. She hadn't wished it for her brother, she had wished it for herself . . . But this is what God had willed . . .

The doctor had explained that when a person is in the throes of death, their bodily systems shut down one by one. First their eyes, then their ears abandoned them. Their eyes, their light now extinguished, rolled upwards as though they were looking at the ceiling – though who knows what they could see there. Then, there were sometimes beads of sweat on their forehead and tears in their eyes . . . as though they were crying . . . Finally the body cleaned itself by freeing itself of all secretions. Sweat, mucus, urine, faeces, saliva, even semen . . .

The doctor, whom she had watched knowing full well she wouldn't like what she learned, had said the colour would drain from the deceased's face in the first 120 minutes. Veysel's face, which didn't look much like him anymore, had also turned pale; it was the colour of lime. The doctor had added that after someone died, their body temperature dropped too. Her brother's hands, which she held between her two palms, were stone cold, just like their mother's had been. She lifted those icy sculptures to her lips and kissed them, then, unable to bear it any longer, she clung to her brother . . . It was then that the two men beside her decided the visit should end. The one in the blue gown raised her up by the shoulders. The one in the green gown reached straight for the drawer. When she saw he was getting ready to close it, Müesser gazed affectionately at her brother's motionless face one last time, at his pale smile . . . For some reason she remembered a summer's evening long ago . . .

It was the summer of the year which marked the end of the school chapter for Müesser and its beginning for Veysel; it would have been July or August. The heat that summer was unbearable . . . And the mosquitoes . . . Oh those mosquitoes

. . . They buzzed around their heads all night. Müesser reached the point where she could hear nothing but that buzzing sound and would start scratching furiously before the mosquitoes had even touched her body. Despite the great pains she took to never harm animals, when it came to mosquitoes, killing them was almost enjoyable. It wasn't mere revenge; Müesser actually derived pleasure from slaughtering them. It gave her great satisfaction to flatten the ones who weren't content with just her blood, but had the audacity to bother her beloved little Eyüp. The walls were dotted with tiny blood stains, but somehow there was just no rooting those mosquitoes out.

The mosquito nets her father had fitted in the wide open windows, the plastic mosquito rackets swinging through the air like death machines . . . As she was trying to think of a speedy way of exterminating the mosquitoes, a malevolent plan took shape in her head when she noticed Veysel running past her. Her face deadly serious, she called her brother and informed him that a war had been declared in their home between mosquitoes and humans. If they didn't succeed in wiping out the mosquito race on behalf of the human population, then those outrageous mosquitoes would carry out their evil plan, starting off by taking tiny bites out of the inhabitants of their home, and eventually taking over the house, the neighbourhood, the country, the entire world even. Feigning terror, Müesser had explained the nature of Veysel's mission in this great war. His role in the battle was vital. Just like he could save the whole world at one fell swoop and be promoted to the ranks of hero, the tiniest mistake on his part might be playing right into the hands of the enemy and could get him branded a traitor . . . Veysel had listened solemnly with wide-eyed excitement as he tried to assimilate the importance of the mission he had undertaken. Although he knew it was a game, he was still convinced there was a little bit of truth in it. His sister realised it when she saw the despairing look in his eyes. He feared he might not be up to it. It was then that Müesser wondered fleetingly whether the game they were playing was unfair. Even if they were just pretending, was she putting more responsibility than was reasonable on the shoulders of such a small child? But eventually, concluding that her brother had understood it was all just a game and that she was only doing it to make it more fun for him, she continued to outline the battle plan. Perhaps at that moment she had cared more about ridding the house of the constant buzzing than about exploiting Veysel. And thus, after carefully explaining the action plan, she despatched that toy soldier into the ruthless battlefield. Clutching a long-handled mosquito racket, Veysel ran up and down the house in pursuit of mosquitoes for several minutes. By killing the mosquitoes that didn't upset him as much as they did his sister, he wanted to achieve something, to be a hero, to earn his family's admiration. But somehow, later on, who knows whether it was because he ran out of steam or because the novelty of slaughtering wore off, he lay down on the floor beside the dinner table in the living room, motionless. He shut his eyes tight and waited for his sister to come and find him there. Although it took a while for her to notice him lying immobile on the ground because she was busy putting Eyüp down for his afternoon nap, his elder sister did eventually approach her weary warrior.

"What happened?" she asked. "Have you stamped out the mosquitoes?"

". . ."

"Are you tired?"

". . ."

Müesser understood the game her brother wanted her to play with him.

"Oh my poor darling, just look at him, he's worn himself out so he could save us! Now he deserves a hero's medal."

The young Veysel was so pleased to hear this that his lips, which he was struggling to keep closed, parted slightly and extended all the way to his cheeks.

★ ★ ★

I can hear water . . . The sound of sploshing, flowing water fills my ears. I want to abandon myself to its music and relax, to float in its tranquillity, but it's impossible. Far from making me lie back peacefully, this sound, which arouses feelings of serenity in everyone else, moves me to protect myself, to be constantly on the alert. Whatever you do, don't be taken unawares, says a voice squirming anxiously inside me. I am so tense that every muscle in my body is strained, my nerves are in tatters, my arms and legs start to ache with an indescribable pain. I remind myself that it's crucial I open my eyes before something terrible happens to me. The sound of the water is telling me I have to wake up. I must wake up before I am swept along by its melody and let myself go, before I am deluded by the fantasy that I'm not in bed but in the toilet, and wet myself. I absolutely must wake up.

When I woke up, my entire body stiff and tense, the first thing I did was grope the front of my pyjamas in a panic. I could not take a deep breath until I had convinced myself there was no wet patch there.

Once I had got over the initial shock, I couldn't stop myself from laughing. I must have made some noise because Pilar turned over in bed, opened one eye and threw me a questioning look. But that one eye closed before I had a chance to say "It's all right darling, go back to sleep." I have always been in awe of the magnanimity of my wife's sleep. Unlike mine, it does not make its proprietor suffer. She is someone who, when not feeling very ill or in low spirits, goes straight to sleep the moment her head hits the pillow. It's impossible to watch her sleeping as peacefully as a baby without envying her.

Once Pilar had taken up her sleep from where she had left off, I concentrated on my dream again and started thinking about that feeling I know only too well. I became acquainted with that familiar apprehension, which had not visited me for many years, during my time at boarding school. There were a number of stupid jokes that were rife in the dormitory. The bed-wetting joke being one of the main ones. Several lads would get together and gather around the bed of a victim who had been singled out that morning. They would make trickling, sploshing sounds by pouring water from one glass into another, until the little cherub, sleeping soundly, oblivious to what would soon befall him, fell under the delusion that he was in the toilet and, responding to the needs triggered by the sound he was hearing, peed in his pants. Everyone who has been to boarding school has been either a victim of that prank, or a spectator, or a cunning friend, at least once. The victims generally get their turn over with and can relax after that, but the fear of not knowing when they will be next turns the nights of those in the spectator and cunning friend categories into living hell. I too belonged to that group that seemed fortunate from the outside, but was actually cursed. Every night I would get into bed thinking today might be that day, crippled with the fear that the cunning lads who would make me wet my bed might visit me at any moment, causing me to listen to sploshing, trickling sounds inside my head day and night!

I never told my family about my fear of wetting the bed. Because right from the start they hadn't been all that keen on my being a boarder. They almost didn't allow me to go to boarding school because of some tale of my sleepwalking a few times as a small boy. My sister tried to brainwash my mother by reminding her that they had found me asleep in a different part of the house several times after putting me to bed, and got all anxious saying, oh, imagine if he leaves the dormitory and wanders off. If on top of that she knew of my anxiety about the children making me wet the bed at night, who knows what tragic torture scenes she would imagine, and would no doubt argue it was madness for me to stay there when I had a perfectly good home. Whereas I, even if I peed myself, or even if I shat myself, was very happy to be away from home with the other children.

The truth of the matter was that despite the allure of the freedom gained by leaving home at an early age, life at boarding school was actually not all that easy. Living in the same building, with the same people, day and night, being removed from the cushy comforts of home ... No matter how much a child of that age may behave as though he doesn't, I think he still needs his family's love. Otherwise there most probably wouldn't be any children running away from the school they were delighted with at first, crying for their mothers. The two categories into which boarders were divided were not those who needed their parents' affection and those who did not, but those who could adapt to the new situation and enjoy it and those who could not and suffered. If I hadn't had the good fortune to fall in with a fun-loving group of friends, I could have easily been miserable, put my name down in that second category and maybe even been promoted to honorary member. But luck was on my side, and I not only got on very well with my friends, but with my teachers as well. We weren't a family, but we were like a family. For me, for many reasons, it was better than being with a real family. I still believe that being like a family is more fun than being a real family. My doctor will most probably disagree, but I also believe it's healthier ... Because while a child who has grown up with his family thinks he will never be able to get away from them, boarders have the peace of mind of knowing they can always go back to their families when things get really tough. To my way of thinking, what makes a place good or bad isn't so much the life one leads there as the question of whether or not one is going to be stuck there. Wherever one feels imprisoned, wherever it's hard to get out, is bad. Even if it is a warm home composed of the loving people I have mentioned here. Because saying all homes are warm would amount to taking hell, and saying they are all loving, would amount to taking the devil lightly.

I was happy to be a boarder. Our family at home was small, at school it was large. At home we were silent, at school we were boisterous ... Our home was bleak, while school was bursting with joie de vivre.

If I hadn't been at boarding school, I wouldn't have been able to escape to school when I had had enough of home, but as a boarder I could spend the holidays at home whenever it took my fancy. But alas, no matter where I slept, I lived in mortal fear of waking up to the trickling of water.

If I try to attribute the source of the problems that turn my nights into a nightmare to my childhood sleep, I may reach the conclusion that getting into bed during that period of my life with the fear of wetting myself caused me to acquire a whole series of habits that distorted my sleep patterns. Of course, if I'm still having these problems at my age because of a fear of wetting myself, then that really is a bugger.

I managed to get my school years over without committing a wet mistake that would have made me cringe with shame. But now I think that instead of spending all those years in mortal fear of drifting into a sound sleep and in constant tension, I wish I had let myself get caught out by one of those jokes just once and wet myself. Maybe then I would have got my share of humiliation over and done with and finally discovered what it was to sleep soundly and peacefully.

7

Perihan

Your jailers have changed but so what
Come on undress and beat yourself with your own
branches once more.

Cahit Zarifoğlu, "The Era of Battle with Ourselves"

Perihan, whom the neighbours had taken to her room so she
could rest and get a bit of sleep, not only couldn't sleep, she
couldn't even close her eyes. What she feared was not so much
closing her eyes, as opening them again. She imagined that
every time she opened her eyes she would see her husband's
head on her lavender-scented pillow, with his face that looked as
if it were attached to that head by mistake, his eyes fixed on her
like an obscene curse. When she had bent down and whispered
as much in her ear, Atiye had said, "How can anyone be afraid
of her dead husband girl?" So, not even Atiye understood her
then. Given how much he had intimidated her even while he
was alive, what could be more normal than quaking at the
thought of him dead?

The way all the women in the neighbourhood had crowded
into the house as gleefully as if they had suddenly come into a
fortune had really set her nerves on edge. She remembered how
her grandmother used to say people delight in the troubles of
others; how right she was. She knew full well what these people,
who had supposedly come to offer their support and share their
grief, were really after. For many of them a house where there
had been a death gave them more food for merrymaking than
a wedding hall. That was the source of the juiciest gossip. Did

the dead man's relatives cry, and if they did, did they mean it, who was the first and last to cry, was the house where death had suddenly visited as tidy as it always was whenever they called in or was everything all in a mess and all over the place ... There was plenty to discuss. Oh, and wasn't there anyone who held her tongue? Yes of course there was; when all was said and done, not everyone was completely evil. But it was naïve to think that even they came running to offer their condolences. Most people came to the dead man's house to give thanks for still being alive themselves. Visitors who remembered that death wasn't just a misfortune that struck others, and that there was no getting round that truth waiting just round the corner for them as well, weighed up their sins in a mad rush, repented and spent the whole of their visit fretting about their afterlife. Except for the dead man's closest relatives, no one was in any fit state to offer prayers to ensure the departed would rest in eternal peace. Perihan knew from the number of times she had gone to houses where other people had died and rubbed the hands that she had opened wide to pray for the deceased over her face, after supplicating God to grant her own child and herself a long life. The guests grieved for their own deaths, or those of loved ones they had lost in the past, while the family grieved for the newly deceased. The dead man had long ago taken himself off to a completely different world; the problem was the life the ones left behind would live without him. In the dead man's house so many people cried until their eyes were bloodshot and all their energy was spent, but not many of those tears were shed for the dead man himself.

Perihan was crying after the departed, but everything had happened so quickly she still didn't know what exactly she was crying for. Maybe it was fear of how she would adjust to this sudden change in her life; of all the things she was feeling, that was the one that crushed her the hardest. And then of course you had to think that, no matter who it was, you still got used to someone you had lived with in the same house for all those years and slept with in the same bed. A selfish pang of anguish after the departed stabbed at her. It seemed she was more put out by the dead man's not being in her life anymore than by his no longer being alive.

It was obvious Veysel wasn't the kindest person in the world, and it was a fact that he wasn't the best husband in the world. But still, thinking of him flattened on the ground like those mosquitoes he was always slaughtering made Perihan feel all peculiar inside. As for him being gone forever, like a child, she still couldn't believe it. Inhaling the scent of lavender on the pillow, Perihan thought from now on she would sleep in this bed by herself. And suddenly it dawned on her that, for the first time in her life, she was going to have her own room. At any other time that thought would have made her happy, but now . . . Grief, fear, even yearning, every feeling she knew assailed her in quick succession. Before, she used to love fantasising about a life without Veysel. But not one of those fantasies ever involved her husband being mangled under a car.

Now the thought that she was going to have her own room for the first time in her life made her feel more anxious than happy or sad. She wasn't as upset about Veysel's death now as she had been when she first heard about it. And anyway, what she had felt at that moment was closer to disbelief than grief. When her brother had called the house and his tongue hadn't found the words to spit out the news, she had known something was wrong and, convinced she was about to hear something terrible, was already prepared to fling herself to the ground. And, she had in fact received the worst news anyone could receive under the circumstances, as it happened, someone had died. The only thing worse than that would have been if it had been someone she actually loved . . .

But still, when she heard her husband was dead she had screamed and howled and writhed on the floor. And what's more she hadn't even faked it; she had actually done what came naturally. And when they had gone running to the hospital it had been even worse; she had had fainting fits. She hated hospitals anyway. She had never liked them, but she hated them even more after that incident, when they had rushed her to hospital . . . Whenever she caught a whiff of a hospital she was overcome by total desperation; ever since that day she had been terrified of being all alone in the world. That's what Veysel had said once; "I'll divorce you. If you're not capable of giving me a child, I'll divorce you. You'd better pray you haven't ruined your womanhood by going and being so stupid. Else I swear to God I'll divorce you." Perihan had quaked with fear then. She was gripped by the terror of being a poor wretch cast off by her husband, of being all alone, and going back to those miserable, destitute days of her past. She had regretted what she had done a thousand times, but what good was that now . . . Not only had her secret come out into the open but she had got herself into a complete mess as well. The last thing she remembered was the blood trickling down her thighs, then the strong hospital smell and Veysel's furious face. "I wish you'd died as well, you child murderer," he had said. He had practically spat the words in his wife's face. Perihan couldn't stop herself from thinking, well, look at us now, I'm still alive, whereas you, you've gone for good. . .

As she pondered the idea that Veysel would never walk through the door again, for some reason she remembered a famous saying of her grandmother's; mortals don't die unless the Almighty decrees it, the Almighty won't decree death unless the mortal's depraved . . . And no one could deny that there weren't many mortals more depraved than her late husband, who had aroused the Almighty's wrath over and over again . . . As the news of his death began to sink in, Perihan started to see what had happened in a different light. She had suffered at Veysel's hands for years. There had been times when she had felt like rebelling against her fate, thinking why does all this have to happen to me. Then she would conclude that she was paying the price for the sins of her past. But she doubted her sins were terrible enough to warrant the cruelty he had inflicted on her all these years. If all the hardship she had endured was her punishment for her sins, then maybe the sudden demise of the person responsible for that hardship was the ransom for what *he* had done. The thought lightened the weight on her chest. May God keep it from their door, it wasn't right to rejoice over anyone's death, but still, her husband leaving home in the morning to go to work and not returning home in the evening wasn't by any means the worst thing that could happen to her.

Had Veysel ever shown her even a tiny bit of appreciation, ever once treated her like a human being? Hadn't they even done *that* like dogs? Hadn't he got blind drunk and forced his stinking body on her all these years? Had he ever tried to make her happy, or win her over, even once? While she was with him Perihan hadn't been able to enjoy either her youth or her femininity. Even Hikmet, whom they all talked about for carrying on with boys, even he had the decency to tuck Yıldız under his arm and treat her to a day out at the shops. But that Veysel, who was so charming in the street and such a monster at home, had never once taken her on his arm and shown her off as his wife, never mind in the street; he had never even respected her at home. Oh, but he was quite capable of jumping into the middle of the road because he had to buy ice cream for the shopkeeper. Of course he had brought ice cream into this house too, many times. But the trouble was, he had created such an atmosphere they had all choked on it. No, thought Perihan to herself, if it's a sin, then so be it; but after everything he's done to me I'm not about to go crying after him just because he's dead.

And besides, she had learned early on in life that shedding tears is a waste of time. No matter how heartsick you were with grief, when all was said and done, your life would be whatever fate had cut out for you. If that weren't the case, then wouldn't Perihan have liked to change absolutely everything? What worried her most right now was being left marooned, without a man to protect her. Because all their misfortunes had been the result of having no man to protect them. Everything had started with her father's death. They had been poor while he was alive too, but still, their lives had been different. However, after he died everything was overturned, shattered, they became objects of pity. The unfortunate man had been a building labourer who worked for a daily wage. He hadn't been able to leave them either savings or a pension. And, that being the case, they had packed up all their possessions and moved to Istanbul to live with her uncle. She had never managed to shake off that feeling of being an unwelcome presence that had clung to her in that house. And because she had neither sufficient brains nor money, she hadn't gone to school for long either, but had left after her seventh year. At the age of 14 she had started as a manicurist at Havva Stylists, not far from their house. Right on the very first day, Havva Abla had said, "I'm going to teach you a profession that will serve you for life, so you'd better be grateful to me." What she called a profession was clipping the hulking great hooves and ripping out the hairs of the stinking, sweaty women who came to the salon. Women with claws for fingernails and peasant's hands thought they would come out of their manicure session looking like a top model, and when they didn't they blamed it on the manicurist's incompetence. Flat-faced, ugly women with drooping eyebrows insisted they wanted arched eyebrows, and no one could persuade them their eyebrows would never comply. They would march in with photographs of celebrities cut out of newspapers, or fantasising about something they had seen on the neighbour and thought that just by ripping out two hairs and removing some cuticles they could look like them. And when they didn't, all hell broke loose. On those occasions, even though she knew the truth only too well, Havva Abla, who was forever reminding her that the customer is always right, invariably sided with the customer. She would make a big show of explaining to her subordinate what she had to do and then, admiring the new result, which was identical to the previous one, would declare, "A-haaah, *now* it's perfect, madam's beauty has come shining through" and pack off the happy customer with her confidence in her good looks restored. Perihan liked neither her job nor Havva Abla, who never got off her back. And besides, she handed over her entire puny wage packet, untouched, to her uncle. She was furious about not even being able to buy herself a blouse after all that hard work. Every time she tried to treat herself to something to wear, her aunt would say, "Look, you already have this", and toss her some hand-me-down from her cousins.

There was no point in being wasteful and buying from outside something they already had at home.

Besides, Havva Abla was a rare beast. She took back with a ladle what she had dished out with a spoon. Non-stop rebukes, and even slaps at times, were part of Perihan's everyday existence. Her body had developed early, and Havva Abla was angry even about that.

"Stop walking like a horse girl, you're wobbling everywhere. Bind those breasts of yours good and tight, I'm not having you going around looking like a slut," she nagged. She thought bras didn't do the job well enough and handed her uncut waxing fabric to bind her breasts with tightly. According to her, it was for Perihan's own good. Because, being an orphan, she fell into that category of prey that rapists were always hankering after. When there was no man to keep tabs on her and make any scoundrel pay, it was easy to harass innocent young girls and have designs on their honour. Especially the flirtatious, coquettish girls, who walked around with everything hanging out ... That's why Perihan had to be cautious. She mustn't give anyone cause to speak badly of her boss or of herself. She wasn't all that much to look at, but still, she mustn't rely on that. If they were desperate enough, the male of the species would climb on top of a donkey's head; they weren't particular about beauty when it came to *that*.

That's what she said to Perihan, but it was all right for her to wear clingy dresses or short skirts. Never mind squashing her breasts flat with waxing fabric, she went out of her way to flaunt and make everyone notice them; she wore tight blouses with plunging necklines that didn't just show off her breast bone, but most of her cleavage too. At that time Havva Abla was in her forties, practically the same age as Perihan's mother. But, unlike her mother, she wasn't haggard, her hair wasn't grey and she hadn't let herself go. She was an attractive, well-groomed, flirt of a woman. Was it because she had a shop and money that rapists didn't have any designs on her honour? Perihan didn't know why, unlike herself, Havva Abla didn't need to be afraid; she didn't dare ask. So she bound her breasts firmly with the waxing fabric. Just as she had been so strictly instructed, she squashed her breasts down from the top, until they were flat.

Then Şenol arrived. Havva Abla, who went on and on about his legendary cutting skills, started off by employing him as her premier stylist. He was good at his job; he had worked at a fashionable salon in Şişli, but hadn't got on with his boss and had walked out after an argument. He had an entourage of devoted clients, whom he claimed would follow him wherever he went. Şenol was a 33-year-old loner who had never married. From what Perihan had heard, he was also a first-class rake. He flirted with all the mature clients in the salon in Şişli, and the moment he spied a woman with a bit of cash, he would make a beeline for her. He had been sacked when one of the women's husbands had erupted into the salon. He wasn't handsome as such, but he did have the gift of the gab. And even though he didn't manage to bring all his old clients flocking after him, he did quickly make himself popular with the salon's own clients. What's more, contrary to all the gossip Perihan had heard, he didn't try it on with a single customer, but steered clear of womanising. And he was talented. He made such a good impression on Havva Abla that, within a few months, they were married. Perihan's mother said, "That Havva woman didn't bring Şenol to her shop for nothing; she obviously had her eye on him right from the start. Well, and don't say he hasn't got himself a cushy number as well; he's been hunting high and low for a woman with cash. But what is Havva thinking of, what's she going to do, treat that boy who could be her son like he was her baby!" But Perihan knew very well that her boss certainly didn't treat Şenol like her baby. When there weren't any customers in the shop they always played around, and Perihan pretended not to notice. Besides, whenever they wanted to get up to anything Havva Abla would always pack her off somewhere. But Şenol was different. He seemed to enjoy flirting even more when Perihan was around. When there weren't any customers in the salon, when Havva Abla was sitting at the till, for example, he would go up to her and stroke her thighs. His hand would move higher and higher. Havva Abla's eyes would glaze over with pleasure, and a huge grin would spread across her face. She thought Perihan couldn't see, but Perihan always saw her boss's legs opening like the mouth of a hungry beast. And she understood that Şenol's fingers were parting the woman's sagging lips. Because she was the one who waxed her, Perihan knew what Havva Abla's looked like. She always walked around perfectly waxed and smooth, but hers was the type that Perihan found most repulsive. It was ugly, a hideous colour between black and purple, like rotten meat. And, just before her period, it stank like off cheese. Couldn't she smell it too, or did she think that just because she counted out her wages week after week she didn't need to feel embarrassed in front of her employee, and maybe that was why she was so eager to open her legs, Perihan had no idea. But because they reminded her of those and other days, she couldn't bring herself to eat any of the cheese recipes she prepared, even years later.

Everything in life left its mark on a person. For a long time Perihan had been unable to see herself through all the marks and stains that clung to her. She remembered the razor scars on Şenol's arms. Who knows which pain they were the stains of? It would seem that sometimes, while someone was trying to wipe their own marks clean, they could leave deep cuts and large stains on the lives of others. That's what Şenol had done.

From the first day he had set foot in the salon she had noticed the way he looked at her. But it hadn't taken her long to see Havva Abla's special interest in her new employee. And because she had no intention of inciting her boss's rage, she ignored Şenol's hungry looks, his loaded laughter. Besides, he was cautious when Havva Abla was around; he saved his impudence for when she wasn't there. When she had called him abi on the first day they had met he had pretended to scold her; "Call me Şenol," he had ordered. And half an hour hadn't passed before Perihan had needed to ask for something and had called the young man by his name. No sooner was the sentence out of her mouth than her boss's face had contorted with contempt, and she had let rip, shouting, "What do you think you are, the same age? Have some respect!" Şenol had had a mischievous look on his face. He hadn't bothered to confess his share of the responsibility in the matter, but he had looked at the young girl as though the two of them had a secret they needed to keep. And so Perihan had started to call him by his name when they were alone and abi in front of Havva Abla. She thought of it as a harmless game and enjoyed the unspoken rule between her and Şenol. What she liked most was the feeling that the two of them were united against Havva Abla in that rebellion started by that tiny conspiracy. The feeling became even stronger after the two of them were married. Şenol hadn't distanced himself by lording his status as the boss's husband over her and behaving as though the salon were as good as his; he hadn't renounced their little games. And for Perihan, that was a victory over her boss.

Havva Abla was equally oblivious of their complicity and the thoughts going through their heads. She didn't even seem to entertain any likelihood of her husband regarding Perihan as a woman and showing interest in her. But nevertheless, she berated the girl more than she ever had before and relished bringing up her incompetence and her ugliness at every available opportunity. Perihan, who was inwardly becoming more and more resentful of her boss's increasingly hostile treatment, occasionally caught Şenol eyeing her with desire, and, far from making her uncomfortable about how furious Havva Abla would be, his furtive glances gave her pleasure. As far as she was concerned, as long as she was careful, there was no reason why she should deprive herself of this tiny thrill. She was young, and the only place she ever went was this salon, where she worked like a slave six days a week. Şenol was the only man she ever got to speak to in this madhouse they called a workplace, and she wasn't about to feel guilty because she secretly enjoyed the interest he took in her.

She had had enough of always having to hump the blame for other people's faults, like some kind of porter, and of being the butt of everyone's contempt, like a scapegoat. In this life people should only have to pay the price of their own sins.

But it was as though everyone was out to wreak revenge on Perihan for crimes she hadn't committed. Why was she always the one who got hurt? Because the strong inflicted pain and the weak bled. How she would love to have the power to make someone bleed. Was it any small thing to be strong enough to harm someone? But that was out of Perihan's league. She had always been tricked by the people she thought she had tricked, she had been cheated every time she thought she had got the better deal. Just so she could feel ever so slightly intelligent and get her own back, even a tiny bit, for all the bullying and berating she endured, she had hoped for solace just from calling Havva Abla's husband by his name when she wasn't around, but the punishment for even that harmless game had gone way beyond anything she could have expected.

If Havva Abla hadn't gone to Amasra for a few days to sort out some inheritance business to do with her rights over a plot of land her late grandfather had left her, none of what happened would have come to pass. But she did. And she went, entrusting the salon to her husband. No sooner had she left than that lecher Şenol's lust raised its head. His silver tongue spouted every trick of persuasion in the book. He told Perihan how he despised his overripe wife, who didn't excite him one bit, how Perihan's nymph-like fresh beauty, gliding through the salon, dazzled him, how he was planning to stake all his bets as soon as he could and divorce Havva so they could be together openly, with nothing to fear from anyone, and talked about a whole lot of other things that Perihan knew full well from the start were lies. Perihan lied to herself, deceiving herself into believing the lie that she had fallen for those lies. As she lay beneath Şenol in that tiny waxing booth on the third day of Havva Abla's absence, she pretended to believe she would soon be his lawfully wedded wife. Because if she had declared she didn't believe him, but opened herself like a gift-wrapped parcel and offered up her body to Şenol anyway, then that would have made her a whore. What was it her grandmother always said; steal one loaf and you're a thief, steal one kiss and you're a whore ... How could a woman make love to a man just because she felt like it? She could only be deceived, only be duped by promises of marriage, only open her trembling legs whilst dreaming of the wedding ring on her finger. Because Perihan knew that tedious rule only too well, she pretended to believe what he had said. But in fact she was intelligent enough to realise that the marriage dream in question would never come true and, no matter how much she feigned otherwise, she never once fantasised about herself at Şenol's side dressed in a flowing white dress. What she felt when she looked at him was limited to a strange tingling in her groin and the satisfaction of getting her own back on Havva Abla. The things that happened in that waxing booth that day had gone some way towards healing both the tingling in her groin and her pride, torn to shreds by Havva Abla. And as for worrying about the future, well, she would worry about that in the future. But for a young girl there was no yesterday or today. The first thing she had to think about was her future.

What would happen now? Now that her virginity, which she had been instructed to preserve like a priceless treasure, had been spent like loose change by this man who would clearly never marry her in a million years ... So, to be intelligent it wasn't enough to merely divide dreams into either unrealistic or realistic. That meant all those young girls out there should be called intelligent for managing to resist the tingling in their groins and the fire of vengeance smouldering inside them. Because they, unlike Perihan, didn't deceive just themselves, but, with astounding virtuosity, succeeded in pulling the wool over the eyes of an entire universe, made up of fathers, elder brothers, uncles, shopkeepers and all the young boys in the neighbourhood. They pretended they had no curiosity, no groin and no desire for revenge, that their only aspiration in life was a white wedding dress, and they believed their pretence. To avoid sustaining any more injuries in this game, for which their fathers, elder brothers and uncles had made the rules, they hid inside a white wedding dress. That was the way life went. And, this flawed beginning notwithstanding, Perihan's life too had been more or less shaped in the same way.

Two weeks after Havva Abla's return, all hell broke loose in the salon. While they were out drinking, Şenol had bragged to Halil about what he had done, as though it was something to be proud of, and he in turn had informed his loud-mouthed wife Remziye, who hadn't been able to eat or drink or rest until she had spread that juicy titbit all over the neighbourhood, and eventually, news of the forbidden affair reached Havva Abla's ears via one of her regulars, Sabahat. When she first heard she said nothing for several seconds, then suddenly started flying round and round the salon, like a released balloon. Finally, her wrath began pouring down in a torrent of fury. To her husband she limited herself to shouting, "Is this idiot the best you could do?" but she yanked Perihan down onto the street in front of the salon, like a lamb to the slaughter, and laid into her until she had vented all her rage. The local shopkeepers must have thought it a well-earned thrashing because not one of them intervened to separate them. Havva Abla beat her, and they watched. Perihan protected her head with her two hands and, as she observed the number of shoes that had gathered to gawk, concluded that what made Havva Abla so furious wasn't so much that her husband had slept with another woman, but that that other woman was her. What's more, the problem wasn't that she had given her work and kept her fed for years. The real issue was that she had attributes that made her preferable to Havva Abla. Perihan's most prominent memories of that beating were of İsmet the butcher's muddy shoe with its back trodden down, and Dürdane the grocer's wife's tights, that were laddered from the ankle all the way up to the knee. Those two must have had the best view of that improvised street theatre.

When she arrived home, she discovered that her news had preceded her. Her mother, her aunt and her cousins had sat at home and waited for her to return, fully aware that she was receiving a public beating in the middle of the street. So, now things had gone this far, as far as they were concerned, it made no difference whether she came back alive or dead. They were all staring at her with hatred, as though they would tear her to pieces at any moment. Only her grandmother seemed more grieved than angry. She fixed her elderly eyes on her granddaughter and, instead of coming out with one of her terse sayings, recited prayers that Perihan didn't understand, with slowly moving lips. She was afflicted with the pain of knowing in advance what awaited her granddaughter. When her uncle came home in the evening, Perihan yearned for the blows that had flown from Havva's strong arms and landed on her face. Her uncle flung her against one wall and then another, pounding the young girl until blood was pouring out of her mouth and nose and she passed out. He asked her again and again if what they were saying was true, but Perihan refused to say a single word. The next morning, they forced her to go and be examined by a doctor. On the way back they changed their route to avoid passing in front of the salon. But they couldn't avoid the shopkeepers' accusing stares. It wasn't just the people in the street, the members of her own household too fixed hostile eyes on her. Even the 9-year-old Bünyamin glared at the bloodshot eyes of his sister, who had dragged their sacred family honour through the mud, with fury and hatred. On their way back from the doctor her uncle had said to her mother, "Don't turn me into a murderer for the sake of this whore. Take your children and get out." And so, to avoid turning the man of the house into a murderer and leaving his family destitute and bereft, they had packed up everything they owned in a few days. Perihan, her mother and her brother hastily moved into a two-room house in Reşitpaşa. The move was only made possible by the money her grandmother had somehow managed to put aside, though no one could work out how, for her burial shroud. But the meagre sum the poor woman had squirrelled away over all those years was only enough to pay for the removal and the first month's rent. After that, mother and daughter would have to fend for themselves. They would send Perihan to work in a salon and Fitnat Hanım would clean houses, that way they would be able to pay their rent. But they weren't able to find either a salon for Perihan or any houses for her mother to clean. They were staggering under the weight of unpaid rent and crippling debts when, on their way back from buying food one day, Fitnat Hanım looked straight into her daughter's eyes and said, "I get the feeling that grocer has his eye on you." And she started sending her to the shop several times a day. Perihan didn't have much choice. Perhaps because she had heard it from her family so many times, she had accepted that she was no different from a piece of faulty merchandise, a rotten apple or a pair of tights cast aside as export surplus because they had a little tear in the corner. The best thing she could do at that point would be to palm herself off on someone. And if that someone happened to have a bit of money, then what more could she ask of life?

But she had never loved Veysel and never wanted him. She hadn't loved Şenol either, but she had had reasons for wanting him. Under her mother's influence, with time, she came to believe she had reasons for wanting Veysel too. But she had never once looked on him as someone she might be able to love one day. There had been times when she had looked on him as a saviour, a tyrant from whom she needed to escape, a fool she could easily dupe, or a means of guaranteeing her possessions, but as someone she could love . . . never.

Things went according to her mother's plan, and Perihan married this man whom she had no plans to love. She put on her wedding dress with the widest of red ribbons tied around the waist, stepped into a car decked out with flowers and was driven to the reception hall. That wedding dress had the power to salvage both her honour and their family bonds. If that were not so, then would her uncle, who had refused to even look at them during all that time, have ever come to the wedding? That night he had danced and made merry, pinned a gold coin threaded with a ribbon on her dress and kissed her on her forehead. Perihan had observed all of this in wonder. So, she had had the misfortune of catching the disease of unchastity, for which the only remedy was marriage. But look, she had been cured in the end!

She had been instructed on what would come next over and over again, as though it were a lesson she had to memorise, and her mother had even made her repeat it to make sure she understood. On her wedding night, once she had removed her wedding dress, she told Veysel, who was hovering over her impatiently, that she wanted to go and get ready first and had fled to the bathroom, clutching her bag. She had dipped the piece of sponge that she took out of her bag into a small medicine bottle filled with chicken blood and, once it was completely soaked, pushed it firmly inside her. The blood had trickled down her legs and she had badly wanted to be sick. After she had cleaned herself up she had tiptoed back into the bedroom and lain down beside her waiting husband. She knew that any sudden movement would make the sponge inside her contract, and expel all the blood it had absorbed. For that reason, she had been afraid to even sit down on the bed, but had lain down slowly, taking care to keep her pelvic bone slightly raised. When Veysel, wearing his hideous wedding pyjamas, had reached for her, his eyes burning with lust, and leapt on top of her, Perihan had instinctively pulled her knees up. When she felt the sponge, which she hadn't inserted properly, slipping out of place, she had panicked. As her husband's hands wandered over her body she prayed to get this over and done with as quickly as possible. And she had made it as obvious as she could. As she was pulling up her nightdress she thought she had seen a red stain there and immediately clicked off the lamp that was still on, even though her mother had instructed her to turn it off the moment she went into the room. Once Veysel was done, Perihan had run back to the bathroom in the dark. She had stuck her fingers inside her and pulled out the sponge that had gone up even further than where she had inserted it; then she had leaned over the toilet and been violently sick.

When she had returned to the bedroom she had found her husband sitting up in bed naked, with the light switched on. He was smoking a cigarette as he contemplated the red blood stain on the crisp white sheet . . .

Veysel had collapsed to the ground in a pool of blood, lying spread-eagled in the middle of the street – that's what they had said. He wouldn't be coming home tonight, or ever again. And most likely, Perihan wouldn't miss him one bit.

"Are you looking for a worse punishment from God? What do you mean by saying you're not happy?" her mother had said. If a woman had enough to eat and her husband didn't bring home a second wife and his violence didn't go beyond a few slaps every now and then, saying she was unhappy was just being downright spoilt. And her mother never passed up the opportunity to remind her that Veysel had taken on faulty goods. Perihan should go to bed every night and get up every morning rejoicing in her good fortune; she should offer up prayers thanking God for being respectably married, after all the trouble she had brought on her head. And that's what Perihan did. Even when she was at her lowest, she never once contemplated giving up what she had and dreaming of something better. But still, it was as though she harboured some unnamed hope for the future inside her because, when she fell pregnant a year after her marriage, she flew into a panic. Despite her mother's constant reminders that a child would seal the guarantee of her future, she had decided she didn't want to have it. She didn't know why, but a voice inside her, and a strong voice at that, was telling her not to have the child she was carrying.

She didn't discuss her pregnancy with her mother or her husband. She knew full well that if she told anyone she would completely lose all powers of decision. Mentioning it would mean the child, her belly and the decision would all be Veysel's. Wasn't marriage a handing over ceremony anyway? Perihan had been placed in her husband's charge, along with her belly, her arms, her legs and her womb. If she told him now that she didn't want the baby she was carrying, her husband would treat her like a thief he had caught stealing money from his wallet. It would be as though she was deciding on the fate of something that belonged to Veysel. That's why she decided to deal with the problem quietly and discreetly. Using the methods that she had overheard from the women while she was still working at the salon . . .

Once, there had been a disagreement amongst the customers over the issue. One faction had argued that home abortions were dangerous and primitive, while the other had reminded them that in the past, before people were able to go to the doctor every five minutes, their mothers and grandmothers had handled their own business by themselves, and accused those who thought otherwise of having airs and graces. It was only later that it became fashionable to go running to the doctor at the drop of a hat. But actually a lot of the time our ancestors' methods were much more effective, and better for one's health. Doctors dished out medicines that cured one thing and damaged another, and patients who had gone to them perfectly healthy, were sent home sick. Fahrünissa Abla, who was a staunch supporter of old-school methods, had explained how when, after her second child, her husband had gone to prison over some business to do with a debt, she had aborted her baby herself, without having to go running to any doctors. "My husband wasn't around, and no one knew when he would come out. So I trusted in God and, begging Him not to mark it as a sin, I dealt with my own business with my own hands," she had said. First of all she had skipped in the house with a rope at great length; when that didn't work she had lain on the ground and rolled a camping cylinder over her stomach. Then, just to be on the safe side, on top of everything else, she had boiled an onion thoroughly and drunk the water. Eventually, the thing inside her had popped out. And there hadn't been any long-term damage; once her husband got out she had had no trouble at all getting pregnant again. Another woman who heard the story about boiling an onion – most probably Sly Türkân – said, "That's what my sister-in-law's neighbour did," and told them a story that made Perihan want to be sick just thinking about it. Apparently, this sister-in-law's neighbour who, despite trying every trick in the book, hadn't managed to get rid of the thing in her womb, had finally resorted to inserting a whole onion inside her. She had lived with that onion in her body for some time. But then, the onion grew and grew and wrapped its shaggy long roots around the foetus inside the woman's belly. When the roots had truly bound the baby, which had lodged itself firmly in her womb and was putting up a strong resistance, the woman grabbed hold of the onion and yanked it out. The arms and legs of the foetus, which had fought so hard against coming out for all that time, slowly began to appear and were ripped out of the woman along with the onion. Perihan had almost thrown up when she heard that story. But, partly because she didn't think much of the woman who had told it, partly because she knew very well that you should never trust stories that had happened to the such and such of so and so and partly because she didn't want it to be true, she hadn't believed it.

That day one of the women at the salon, Solmaz, who argued that using old-women's methods to abort brought nothing but trouble and who, because she couldn't have a child herself, couldn't even understand those who aborted in hospital, let alone at home, and accused them of not being satisfied with the fortune God had granted them but of kicking it back in His face, had told tales of women who had dismembered their wombs trying to abort and had not just permanently lost their ability to bear children, but their lives too. But because her tales, just like Türkân's, were stories of things that had happened to the such and such of so and so, Perihan had doubted their authenticity. In one of Solmaz's stories, when a certain woman discovered she was pregnant, she had stuck a knitting needle in her womb to abort the baby, but had lacerated herself in the process - and had never been able to bear children again. Solmaz had concluded her tale with, "Weeell, God has His own way of punishing sinners." Hamiyet, who was having her hair permed, had added, "For God's sake, everyone knows about the knitting needle, and it doesn't do any harm at all. It's no more dangerous than what the doctors do! One of my relatives aborted her baby with a knitting needle, not just once, but twice! She even said, the second time, I aborted the baby, lay down to rest for a couple of hours, then got up and went to the market and did my shopping. It's that easy in other words. The woman you're talking about obviously didn't calculate properly. You mustn't stick the needle all the way in, you just have to jiggle it a bit. If it hurts you, you should stop straight away." Of all the methods they had mentioned that day, Perihan had liked that knitting needle technique the most. And, when the time came, that was the one that had stuck in her mind.

All she had to do was look out for a moment when she could be alone in the house, so no one would discover her secret. When her sister-in-law said she was going to Adalet's for tea, she feigned a headache and stayed at home. And the moment Müesser stepped out of the door, she started looking for her knitting needles. Although Müesser, who rarely went out, occasionally went to visit Adalet, she usually kept her visits short, rushing back quickly as though someone were waiting for her. Because she knew this, Perihan wanted to set to work without delay. She took out the wicker basket where her sister-in-law kept her multicoloured balls of wool and her knitting needles of all different sizes, and examined each needle in turn. She had no idea how thick the knitting needle was supposed to be. Size two seemed much too thin and so did size three. As she wavered between sizes four and five, she decided on size five, to be on the safe side. Anyone who saw her cool-headedness would think she shifted a different baby with a different knitting needle every day.

Just as she had done on her wedding night, she ended up in the bathroom. Perhaps because it had witnessed so many incidents, she didn't like it in there one bit. She particularly disliked the huge mirror hanging above the washbasin ... It was an enemy that recorded everything that went on in here, slyly absorbing and retaining all the images that Perihan wanted to forget the moment she turned her back. She was terrified that it would spill all its secrets, including hers. Perhaps the best thing to do would be to break the mirror and hang up a new one, after this new crime it was about to witness. Perihan thought that wasn't a bad idea at all and smiled as she opened her legs wide and bent her knees. Then she seized the size five knitting needle that she had just selected, like a deadly hunting weapon.

When she was done, she didn't even have the strength to open the door and leave the bathroom, let alone break the mirror. An excruciating pain kept her rooted to the spot. She wanted to be sick; the bathroom's white ceiling spun above her head like a propeller. She was afraid of passing out; all she wanted was to pull herself together and get to bed as soon as possible. Just then she noticed the blood trickling down her legs. And then the blood forming a puddle on the white tiles ... It was as though her own body was shrivelling up as the blood flowed out of her. So much blood coming out of me, she thought in wonder, as she lost consciousness and drifted into a long, long sleep.

When she opened her eyes she was in hospital. "I wish you had died too, you child murderer!" Veysel had spat. That was the sentence that had jolted her back to the land of the living. Veysel had threatened to divorce her if she couldn't get pregnant again soon and give him a child. Fitnat Hanım, who had rushed to the hospital when she learned what had happened, had said, "You're a fool, you haven't come to your senses, you haven't come to your senses one bit." She told her that if Veysel got it into his head to divorce her, they would be left out in the street without a penny. Okay, so the man had refused when they had proposed that his wife's mother and brother move in with them, but, from the first day since his marriage he had promptly paid Fitnat Hanım's rent and even given her a monthly allowance. If Perihan were left without Veysel, it would plunge the whole family back into destitution. And there was no point in her relying on maintenance either. "If you slaughter the chicken that lays the golden eggs, it won't be your share of the gold you'll get, if you get anything at all it'll be its shit. Don't push your luck Perihan, pull yourself together," her mother had said. In that hospital room, Perihan had believed that getting divorced was the worst possible thing that could happen to her. She had cringed with remorse. She remembered the woman Solmaz had talked about. Her minor operation hadn't gone too well. She had managed to abort the child, but damaged her womb in the process. What if she would never be able to get pregnant again, just like that woman? Veysel's voice spitting "I'll divorce you. If you're not capable of giving me a child, I'll divorce you. You'd better pray you haven't ruined your womanhood by going and being so stupid. Else I swear to God I'll divorce you" kept ringing in her ears. When she opened her eyes she heard her husband's enraged voice; when she closed them she saw the pool of blood on the white tiles . . .

Blood . . . There was so much blood in her life. The blood she had left on the couch in the waxing booth, the blood she had soaked into a sponge and inserted into herself on her wedding night, the blood she had shed on the white tiles so she wouldn't have her first baby . . . It all had a strange smell, like a rusty nail. That smell brought with it nothing but regret and panic. And fear . . . Perihan thought of Veysel. Of his dark red blood that she imagined forming a puddle in the middle of the road . . . Despite the lavender-scented pillow, she smelled the rusty nail. She suddenly realised with horror that what the smell of blood evoked was Veysel himself, and perhaps even the form of all men. Regret, panic and fear . . .

Her mother had died two and a half years ago. Her mother, with whom she had traipsed from doctors' doors to hodjas and all manner of healers in order to be able to bring a child into the world after that incident . . . If she hadn't died, she might be upset even now, saying you've been left all alone with no husband. Although she hadn't been cast out into the streets without a penny to her name, and had come into possession of everything her husband owned and more, Perihan too was afraid of what this new, completely unfamiliar life had in store for her. She could hear the neighbours' voices from the next room.

"Widowed so young, the poor lamb," said one.

"I know, I know, she's only 33."

As she was surrendering to the warm arms of sleep whilst inhaling the scent of lavender mingled with the smell of rusty nails, Perihan paused and pondered on a bridge somewhere between dreams and reality, which stretched from apprehension to curiosity. How would things be now, she wondered. Russssssty nails! – Is it really all that hard? – The deep scent of lavender – Or maybe it isn't? With no man to protect her, fending for herself . . . Without regret, panic or fear . . .

★ ★ ★

I'm standing at the gate of our secondary school. I'm surrounded by my friends, there's a lot of banter, noise, laughter. But I feel troubled; I know something bad is going to happen. Just then, I have no idea how, but I suddenly turn into a sheet of paper. There is a light breeze blowing, and I am absolutely terrified that it will tear me into two. But no one has written anything on me yet; before getting torn I want someone to scribble something on me, however small. After I have been blown about by the breeze for a while, I go back to my own body. My friends haven't noticed my absence and are still engrossed in their hilarious conversation. Their mirth disgusts me, I want to get away from them. Just as I'm about to stalk off, high walls suddenly spring up in front of me. I remain dumbstruck. I look at my friends, no one but me cares about being trapped behind the walls. They're still cheerful enough to make me loathe them. I despise each of them in turn, for not being able to see my unhappiness. I am so angry that this time I turn into a knife. But I can't make anyone but myself bleed.

Just then someone calls out my name. Excited, I turn around and look. I come face to face with my brother standing behind the wall watching me. I can see him, despite the wall separating us. Just as I can see the reproach, the anger, the hatred even, in his eyes. He is angry with me, with the walls all around me, with the fact that I am not smashing a hole in the wall and going to stand beside him. The flowers of his wrath are beginning to sprout on the wall between us. The wall becomes covered with an obstinate vine. Everything turns green in an instant, and I lose sight of my brother. But there was something I wanted to tell him. It was vital that we discussed it. I call out his name to the other side of the wall. He doesn't reply.

Like everyone forced to bottle up the things they want to say, I awoke with a terrible feeling of oppression. When I was a child too, I used to wake up some mornings with a similar sense of unease. Forget about being able to translate that feeling, I don't think I can even express it in Turkish. Which is why, even if I were about to explode, it doesn't look like there's much chance of my being able to explain it to my dear doctor. To tell the truth, I doubt we'll ever come face to face again. As someone who has believed for years that it's not patients that need doctors but doctors that need patients, Doctor Carcel's sudden illness may have opened my eyes to certain truths once again. Either that, or starting to remember my dreams has gone to my head and made me conceited enough to think I don't need him ... If I have to be honest, I believe that what is really coming between me and my doctor, who is at least as sick as I am right now, and who is at home resting on the advice of his colleagues, is my reluctance to share the things I remember with him. But I am not going to allow him to note that opinion on the confessions page of his little notebook.

Let's come to that strange dream that my dear doctor will probably never hear about. I awoke from this brother and wall-ridden dream with tons of kilos weighing down on me. If I tried to describe that feeling, I could, for example, compare myself to a fat cloud that will never rain. I was like a flood that didn't fit into a dam, but couldn't overflow either. Like a fire that burns itself first and foremost. I was oppressed, I was troubled, I was guilty and very sorry. My trouble was a strange creature, with no beginning and no end. It was an ill-omened disease, born from childhood guilt and adult regret. A little frightening, and very ugly ...

This dream reminded me of that day when my brother collared me at the school gates. To tell the truth, I can remember that day without the need for any nonsensical dreams. Because of course you can't remember things you've never forgotten.

Like every healthy student, I too used to occasionally skive off school. And, like every sensible truant, I didn't tell my family about those little adventures.

But, as bad luck would have it, on one such day when I had used the excuse of a free lesson to skive off school, as my friends and I were chatting and trying to decide where to go, I happened to run into my brother right outside the school gates. When I noticed him he was standing a little further ahead, his face a picture of rage, reproaching me for my wrongdoing.

As someone who had repeated time and again that he had had to abandon his own schooling so that I could study, fire darted out of his eyes, as they say.

We were okay financially but, according to my brother, one of the men in the house had to act as the head of the household. And, in order for me to be able to continue at school, he had taken on that sacred duty. He had sacrificed himself, like the older brothers in Turkish films. And he had thrown that magnanimity in my face so many times I started to nurture an uneasy feeling towards him that may have been gratitude or guilt, I wasn't sure which. That's why I was mortified with shame for having skived off that day. I wanted to hide, for the ground to open up and swallow me. If the look on his face had given me the slightest hint of encouragement, I would have approached him and begged his pardon with my tail between my legs. But his expression was anything but inviting. The tornado howling between us was so hostile that, never mind approaching him, I didn't even have the courage to raise my head and look at him. It wouldn't have been like that if I had bumped into my mother or my sister. But I had always felt slightly guilty and embarrassed around my brother. Because I knew very well that he blamed me for not having been able to lead a different life, I always felt humbled and uncomfortable around him.

As far as I can recall, my brother had never been a good student. But I never knew if he had left school because he genuinely wanted to or because he had uncomplainingly taken on the responsibilities that had been hoisted onto his shoulders. That's why, for years, I felt as responsible for the life he hadn't led as I did for the one he had. I spent a part of my childhood desperately trying to repay what I had stolen from him with my achievements at school. It was like I wanted him to see that his good deeds hadn't been in vain. But, far from making my brother happy, my achievements seemed to make him even more angry. I was most probably reminding him of everything he had given up. Even if I was naïve enough to search for the reasons for his unhappiness in myself, I wasn't stupid enough not to see that my achievements didn't make him happy. He was angry with me. Always angry . . .

But in fact I wanted him to love me so badly. However, when I couldn't work out how to make that happen, with time I eventually gave up, both on him and on trying to prove myself to him. I chose the path of trying to calm his anger, not by trying to make him notice me, but by trying to make myself invisible to him. In that way, the more time passed, the bigger and longer the dark tunnel between us became. That well, out of which we managed to escape, swallowed up our ties of brotherhood; of the two of us added together, there remained only two separate beings. In my brother's remoteness I learned not only to think that every wrong was my fault, to constantly run away from things, not just to not be loved, but not to love either. But we could have loved each other a lot. And then we would have been stronger, more united. But it didn't happen; for some reason, we couldn't even manage something that simple. When I was departing from Istanbul, we took our leave of each other with unspoken words. We added new unspoken words to our old ones. I've not seen my brother since. And I didn't want to see what he thought of me. Maybe he's finally forgiven me for the life he thinks I stole from him. Or maybe at least for skiving off school that day, who knows . . .

8

Pilar

But fear grows by suckling on its own breast.

Bilge Karasu, "Variations of Fear"

Pilar sat in the living room, stunned and dejected, with no idea of what to do. That morning she had thought this was a gloomy place. In fact it was only now she was discovering what gloom really was. As mumbled prayers mingled with whispers, and sighs with loud intakes of breath, she felt the gloom and the catastrophe right down to her bone marrow. In the past few days she had considered herself to be one of the most woebegone and desperate people in the world. Now, as she sat in the centre of the living room, like a tortoise hiding in its shell, she realised she had been wrong about that too, that she had attached far too much importance to herself and her own troubles. The world was a place where, no matter how miserable you were, there was always worse suffering and, no matter how happy you were, there was always someone happier. While history defeated people with fate and other people's harrowing stories, that truth manifested itself over and over again. And in the most unexpected ways . . .

At first she had thought it was Eyüp who had died. Her eyes had clouded over, and the ground had slipped from under her feet. Those few terrible seconds, during which she had believed he was no longer alive and had shaken like a victim of malaria, had taken perhaps 10 years off her life. Then, once she realised Müesser was talking about Veysel and not Eyüp, her relief had been indescribable. Her heart had unclenched, her face had lit up, she had stopped shaking and her eyes had shone again. Just then she had seen her own selfishness reflected in the bloodshot eyes of the wretched woman before her and felt ashamed of her own happiness. That's why she hadn't even been able to properly enjoy the elation of discovering it wasn't Eyüp who had died. The tragedy of Veysel's ill fate quickly put an end to anything resembling happiness. Once again her heart constricted and filled with poison. If life were a card game, then most likely grief would always come out on top of happiness in every hand until the end of time. But the fact that happiness always triumphed despite that was an unsolvable, bizarre equation.

The knowledge that someone she had seen only that morning was no longer alive wasn't just upsetting, it was disturbing. Under those conditions, perhaps what really disturbed the living was not so much the absence of the deceased as the impassive, unconditioned presence of death. Because every time death paid a visit, it injected fear in the hearts of those who were still alive and raised uncomfortable questions about their own mortality. The existence of someone who was there one day and gone the next was like the bloom of a delicate orchid that was at the height of its beauty now but would fade and wither in the next moment. It all happened in the blink of an eye.

Pilar thought about Veysel, as though trying to confirm he had once existed. From what she had seen of him, he was an odd creature. Eyüp may well have been the only connection between them, but Veysel seemed to have rejected that and seized every available opportunity to show he couldn't care less about his brother. It was as though he wasn't bothered so much by Eyüp's disappearance as by the idea of someone going out to look for him. This behaviour of his reminded Pilar of the warped minds of killers in detective movies. The types that, after killing their victims and hiding their bodies, did everything in their power to dissuade everyone who set out in search of the missing person ... But in those films the murderer always revealed where he had hidden the victim before he died. Veysel hadn't said anything.

To tell the truth, there was a childlike side to him, despite his mean streak. Pilar had noticed that about him last night on the way back from the airport. No matter how much his face said the opposite, he was like a little boy who was excited by the prospect of having a guest in his house. He had even taken it upon himself to act as her tour guide, in an attempt to get her to notice him. But of course that wasn't reason enough to make her remember him fondly.

If she had accepted his offer to drive her that morning, then perhaps Veysel would still be alive now. That was the first thought that had gone through Pilar's head as Müesser was telling her how he had died. If they had gone to Taksim together, his plan for today would have changed completely. He would have got to the supermarket later and perhaps, because he was running late, he wouldn't have played that game of backgammon with the shopkeeper. And if he had insisted on playing, it wouldn't have been until at least an hour later, the sun would have been at its hottest, his opponent would have made a couple of bad moves whilst wiping the sweat off his face and maybe it would have been Veysel who beat him. No, but even if he had still lost, he would have gone to buy the ice cream an hour later. That car wouldn't have been there anymore, that tragic encounter would never have taken place. If they had left the house together that morning, then Veysel would be alive now.

His death had been so bizarre. How many people paid the price of losing a simple game with their life? Only someone who was both childlike and extremely unlucky . . .

Pilar had trouble keeping track of the human traffic in the living room. New people kept arriving to offer their condolences, while others left, imploring God to grant the family patience in their mourning. But somehow they all looked alike. It was as though a dead man's house was a mirror submerged in secrets and the only thing it reflected onto the forms standing before it was death. Voices mingled with voices and breath mingled with breath; in the end death was the only discernible presence in the crowd. Its colour was somewhere between yellow and green, it had an acrid smell, and tasted of mould. It swaggered and strode arrogantly around the room, smug in the knowledge that all those who were wrinkling their noses at it today would one day inevitably taste it. Those who heard its footsteps creaking on the wooden floorboards hoped the whispered prayers they clung to would bring them salvation.

The family was in a state of complete desolation. Poor Perihan had taken to her bed, while little Bülent was evading all the adults who were trying to show him compassion and attempting to grieve by himself. Müesser was the only one sitting in the living room with the guests. But she was in such a daze and stared so blankly into space that the well-wishers were worried about her. Some of them rubbed rose water on her wrists, while others ran back and forth fetching her glasses of water in the hope it would help her relax. Pilar wanted to say something to her, but couldn't find the right words. Eventually, aware of how absurd it would sound, she voiced her feelings:

"I know how hard it is for you, but please, don't be upset."

Müesser smiled sadly and dried her eyes on the corner of her headscarf. When Pilar looked into her face she got the impression that, more than tears, what was gushing from her eyes were all the things that had remained trapped in a weighty vat of secrets. And, unable to retain them any longer, she had shed some.

"How can I not be upset? Veysel was all I had left. Now he's gone too. I'm left all alone, with nobody."

Pilar couldn't think of anything to say. She wanted to spout a platitude like, "You're not alone" but couldn't bring herself to. Müesser's loneliness was so starkly obvious that, more than someone left all alone, she likened her to an abandoned building. A building that was deserted, forgotten, where no one had set foot for years, where even rats did not deign to tread . . .

"Whatever you do, don't end up alone Pilar, don't end up alone whatever you do," Müesser whispered in her ear, as though she feared someone would overhear them. "Make sure you have a baby, don't grow old childless."

Last night she had kept quiet during the discussion about having babies. It was clear she wasn't someone who was in the habit of bringing up sensitive topics and giving advice gratuitously. But now, more than offering counsel, she seemed to be expressing regrets, confessing sins.

"Don't be like me. Do you know what 'Müesser' means? The author of a work. But look at me. What work do I have to leave behind? I don't even have a child who looks like me. Don't do what I've done, don't end up alone, whatever you do."

When at last Pilar went up to her room, it was gone midnight. She had waited until all the guests had left before going upstairs. She didn't know why she had felt responsible for staying, but she had waited as though she were a part of this household; she had not abandoned the living room that felt like the deck of a ship on the point of sinking on the open sea. But in fact, the mere idea of being a part of this household made her shudder.

When the guests eventually departed, ceding the house to those who would grieve in it, a weight was lifted from her chest. But when she looked at Müesser's face she realised that, rather than being left by herself, she would have preferred to be swallowed up in that mayhem. When Pilar announced she was going to bed, she too, under the pretext of not wanting to leave her nephew by himself, but probably because in actual fact she herself didn't want to be alone, headed for Bülent's room. She would sleep there tonight.

Pilar couldn't understand why the neighbours had stayed so late. They must have thought the restless crowd could fill the void left by the departed. It couldn't. All they could do was try to drown out the sound of suffering with their noise. But alas, like their solution, they too were transitory. And besides, where was the sense in running away from something they would have to face up to sooner or later? No matter what it was, and regardless of the circumstances, Pilar always wanted to face up to whatever trouble she was in as soon as possible. She was a staunch believer in letting all hell break loose without delay. If we're going to be upset, then so be it; if we're going to cry, then so be it, but let's get it over with as soon as possible. It was this impatience that had driven her to up and come to Istanbul. All this haste wasn't because she had no fear of what might happen, on the contrary, it was because she feared it a great deal.

But, right from when she was a tiny girl, Vicky had told her not to fear anything, that bad things migrated to addresses that they chanted to themselves over and over again. That's why people should protect themselves accordingly, take precautions against any possible dangers but, once they had done everything necessary to safeguard themselves, they should push any negative thought out of their minds. She always used her sister as an example. Because Aunty Concha was the perfect example of a self-fulfilling prophecy. She listened to her body so closely she managed to hear a voice from wherever she happened to train her ear. And then she would convince herself that that part of her was riddled with a terrible disease. She would run backwards and forwards to the doctors for days, weeks, having tests and X-rays, doing her utmost to prove she really did have the illness no one believed in and everyone laughed off. It wasn't that her family and friends didn't love her or care about her health; it was just that they had had a lot of practice when it came to her phantom health scares. But poor Aunty Concha was both angered and offended by their attitude. So much so, that when the test results came back she would have rather gone home clutching a report certifying her illness than one saying she was perfectly fit. And as though they were witnessing a miracle, the entire family had seen how Aunty Concha had the power to will herself ill. The illness she couldn't prove to anyone because of the all clear reports she brought home, invariably ended up afflicting her some time later. She would go to the doctor with the same complaints at varying intervals and when, after one of those visits, she discovered she did indeed have what she had feared, it almost came as a relief. Despite being two years younger than Vicky, she suffered from a whole range of illnesses that didn't affect anyone in the family except her. For example, when Pilar was still a child her aunty was convinced she had goitre and went running to the doctor to have all the necessary tests. She would get herself all worked up about some illness or other practically every year.

"Look at the way my hands sweat. People who've got goitre sweat a lot, just like this," she would say, for example. Uncle Hernando's reply would always be the same:

"It's your nerves."

As far as he was concerned, if nerves were at the source of the problem, then that made everything fine. The important thing was that there shouldn't be anything physical the matter. To tell the truth, Aunty Concha must have thought the same, because hearing that her illness was caused by nerves would make her fly into a rage for not being taken seriously by anyone and send her in hot pursuit of evidence to prove that the cause of her illness was physical.

"Would you say my neck looks strange, Hernando?"

"No it doesn't."

"Don't you think it looks swollen?"

"No."

"But my eyes definitely aren't normal, look. It's as though they're popping out of my head. When I look at old photographs of myself I can see I didn't look anything like this before."

"What do you mean?"

"My eyes didn't use to bulge like this. I'm telling you, it's a sign of goitre."

"That's how they were when we got married. You're exactly the same Concha, nothing has changed."

"You mean I had bulging eyes when we got married? Is that what you're trying to say?" she would say, and have a mini temper tantrum. For some reason, any family members who happened to witness these incidents would find them extremely entertaining. Her hypochondria and the indifference her husband adopted to help him cope with it seemed very funny from the outside. As she got older, Pilar realised that neither her aunt's symptoms nor her uncle's reactions were in the least bit funny. That, in fact, because she felt undermined for being misunderstood, and he was at the end of his tether for thinking he could never understand, their marriage was a nightmare. One scare after another had led to Aunty Concha suffering from a whole host of illnesses, ranging from goitre to diabetes, from heart trouble to breathlessness, from an ulcer to haemorrhoids. And that definitely wasn't at all funny. Whenever Vicky was talking about self-fulfilling prophecies, she always used her own sister as an example. "Whatever you do, don't beckon to your fears," she would say. "And besides, fear is much more terrible than many other things that could happen to you."

Her mother was right. Paz, for example, had lived in mortal, deadly fear that her husband would be unfaithful. She had nurtured her fear day and night, and in the end he had been. Perhaps Pilar was in the state she was in because she too lived in terror of being without Eyüp one day. Of course, during the time of that business with the baby, hadn't she cowered in silence for fear she might lose her husband if she insisted? Hadn't she buried the one thing she wanted most badly inside her just so she wouldn't lose Eyüp? From what he said in his dream diary, he too knew that only too well. Pilar paused for a moment. Had Paz been gripped by the fear that her husband would be unfaithful because she had sensed he was deceiving her, or did he deceive her because she had feared he would? She couldn't answer that. And she absolutely, definitely didn't want to apply the same question to her own case.

She was contemplating picking up Eyüp's dream diary and taking up from where she had left off, when there was a knock on the door. She knew immediately who it was, not just from her calculations of probability, but because she could tell from the restraint of the knocking fingers. When the door opened and she saw Müesser's head poke through it, and her sorrowful, anguished face, she straightened up. Grief always inspired more respect than happiness; deep down, the suffering of others was good for those who wanted to console themselves with their own good fortune.

"Don't get up, don't get up, sit down."

"Is Bülent asleep?"

"No, he wanted to be with his mother."

Just as she had imagined, the poor woman couldn't bear to be by herself. Once Bülent had gone, she had come here. And she had her excuse already prepared.

"I didn't get a chance to ask you, what did you do today?"

"I saw several of Eyüp's friends, but none of them knew anything."

"Several of his friends? How did you find them?"

"Well, actually I only found one of them. He found all the rest."

"And what did you say to them?"

Judging by her interest in how much she had told them, Müesser too cared about who knew what and to what extent.

"Nothing."

"What do you mean nothing?"

It suddenly dawned on Pilar that her answer to that question would seem absurd. When you were searching for a missing person how could you not tell the people you were asking that he was missing!

"I . . . we, I mean Eyüp's friend İlhami and I, we didn't tell his other two friends the whole truth. They don't know Eyüp's missing."

"Okay, but why not?"

"I don't know. We just didn't tell them. We didn't want everyone to know."

Müesser's lips curved into a despondent smile.

"You're like me. You're ashamed of things that aren't your fault. You want to hide them. Don't. It's the things they hide inside them that wear people out the most and make them dirty."

It was unbelievable that the most discreet person in the house could undergo such a metamorphosis in a single night, and, as if her blurting out everything on her mind wasn't already incredible enough, she had suddenly been transformed into a poet too. But the woman had, after all, lost one of the people she loved most in the world. Or rather, yet another one . . . You could hardly blame her for turning into a completely different person in a single night. What would I do if anything ever happened to Isabel, thought Pilar. She couldn't bear to even imagine such a horrendous possibility. It would be unendurable.

"And if they know he's missing, they might be able to think of places where they could start looking for him," continued Müesser. She wasn't talking about herself or Pilar anymore, but about her missing brother.

"They might."

They remained looking at each other for a while.

"And we also went to the police today. Or rather, İlhami went. He gave them your home number. They said they would call you."

"Were they going to call today?"

"Probably."

As though the answer to controlling her tears lay there, she clamped her lips between her teeth as she said, "Even if they did, as we weren't at home after twelve . . ." A teardrop trickled out of her eye. She was asking about Eyüp, but crying for Veysel. She seemed uncertain of which one to think about and which one to cry for first.

"They'll probably phone again tomorrow," said Pilar, in an attempt to console Müesser. Then, unable to slow down now she had got started, she said, "We'll find him Müesser, you'll see."

"You'll find him and bring him to me won't you?" The woman was like a wounded soldier stripped of his heavy armour, or a wretched cat that has had its tail amputated and been flung out into the street. Pilar told her what she wanted to hear, in the hope that she too would believe it:

"Of course I will."

At that moment, anyone looking at Müesser's face might have mistaken the profound grief etched between her two eyebrows for a prayer.

After her sister-in-law had left the room, Pilar didn't know what to do with the tiny seed of suspicion that Müesser had unwittingly sown in the darkness of her mind. Should she water it, or try ignoring it? For a while she was undecided. Eventually the darkness of the suspicion availed itself of the vacuum and grew and blossomed of its own accord.

The suspicion that had suddenly germinated in her mind was called İlhami. İlhami and his odd behaviour. Odd behaviour that had aroused her attention several times throughout the day, but that she had seen no need to dwell on, or that she had deliberately shied away from, to avoid muddying the waters of her mind . . .

Couldn't this man, who so deftly spouted lie after lie to his closest friends, and even to his wife, without batting an eyelid, have deceived her too? Pilar had no idea. And now, in this room in her head that had only just been illuminated, it suddenly hit her hard that she didn't know him well enough to answer that.

Then she considered the question Müesser had quite rightly asked, but couldn't find a sensible answer to that either. Why indeed had they kept Eyüp's disappearance from the others? Okay, she had kept it secret in Barcelona, but she had had good reasons for that. But here in Istanbul, where she had come to find Eyüp . . . How could they find a man when they didn't even know they were looking for him? İlhami's determination to handle the matter in such a cloak-and-dagger fashion couldn't just be explained by his respect for Pilar's decision. Common sense would dictate that he should at least have expressed his opinion, given some advice, but he hadn't . . . What's more, Pilar didn't even remember how they had reached that decision now. Had it really been her idea to keep Eyüp's disappearance a secret between just the two of them?

When she started to think in that way, the whole issue with the police began to seem strange too. Why hadn't İlhami wanted her to go with him? Was it again out of courtesy? If they needed a member of the family for the missing person's report, then why had İlhami gone to the police station the second time, instead of her? For the first time Pilar wondered if he had even gone. Had he really gone?

Her mind was all in a blur. She tried to think of a reason why İlhami would do such a thing. Why would he trick her with such a heartless game? Maybe Eyüp was with him or, at the very least, İlhami might know where his friend was hiding. Besides, hadn't she clung to that possibility when she was leaving the house that morning? Hadn't she told herself that if Eyüp wasn't with his family, then he must be with his closest friend? Yes, it must be exactly as she imagined, but the only thing that hadn't occurred to her in the beginning was that, if that were the case, İlhami would naturally help his old friend, not her. If Eyüp didn't want his wife to know where he was, then thinking İlhami would give his friend away was the kind of optimism only a fool would entertain.

Obviously, instead of helping her and revealing Eyüp's hiding place, İlhami would look for ways to keep his friend's secret. And of course he hadn't gone to the police or done anything of the sort. He had just stopped Pilar from going – that was all. While Pilar was imagining him filing a missing person's report at the police station, he may well have been drinking tea somewhere, or phoning his friend from the telephone box around the corner to update him on events. And she didn't know whether the reason for his supposedly going to the police station twice was to make his game seem more convincing, or to kill time. If they had to go to the police, he had been the one to go; if they had to look for Eyüp, he had been the one to look. The result had been a day out touring the city without Eyüp. Pilar was angry with herself for falling for such a game, for spending a day doing nothing but admiring views and eating kuru fasulye, drinking tea and rakı and broadcasting her childhood memories, for behaving in front of the people who may have been able to help them as though there was no one missing, instead of telling them there was, instead of looking for Eyüp, tracking him down. She was furious with herself for being so stupid.

She suddenly recalled the moment of her encounter with İlhami that morning. How easily she had found him, as though she had put him there with her own hand. It was more as though she hadn't found him, but that they had arranged to meet. It was as though İlhami had been waiting for her in front of his shop because he knew she would go. He had been surprised to see her but, for whatever reason, had got over it very quickly. He had talked about finding Eyüp all day, but not thought it necessary to delve into the reasons why he might have gone missing. And Pilar had stupidly put that too down to courtesy. She was obviously fixated with courtesy. All right, she thought to herself, even if that were the case, how did İlhami know I would go and look for him this morning? Who could have told him? Müesser? Perihan? Or Veysel, who wasn't even alive anymore? Which person or persons could have spilled the beans? And more importantly still, was Eyüp closer to all of these people than he was to his wife? Why had he done this, why was he doing it? Pilar felt like she was about to explode; she couldn't get her head round so much intrigue.

In that case, what everyone kept hinting at was true. Maybe all the people who kept saying it knew something. Nothing terrible or anything of the sort had happened to Eyüp. Maybe he really had just run away from Pilar. But why? If she knew that, she wouldn't be here. But still, she wracked her brain, trying to find an explanation for the whole absurd situation.

The only problem between them was the baby issue, which they had decided to shelve for a while. They had gone through a very bad patch because of that unplanned pregnancy. She had wanted to have the baby, while Eyüp had said he wasn't ready for fatherhood and not only that, but that he didn't know when he would be. Eyüp was so unshakeable on that issue that, once she had realised she wouldn't be able to make him change his mind, she had decided to give him some time and had had a termination. But the gynaecologist had stressed that she was at risk of menopausing early and informed her that if she wanted to have a child she needed to act quickly. And Pilar had been fretting ever since. And naturally Eyüp didn't like this constant, silent pressure he was under; he didn't like it one bit. Pilar remembered what she had read in his dream diary. He found the thought of fatherhood so terrifying it took his breath away. And he knew full well what an injustice he was doing his wife with his cowardice. But it was beyond his control. Or so he had convinced himself. Now, at this time of night, Pilar realised that, just as everyone had tried to hint, Eyüp may well have run away from her. Perhaps, because he knew that sooner or later the baby issue would crop up again and he didn't want to take on the responsibility, he had upped and disappeared, while there was still time. Feeling unable to face the music, he had run away, and not only that, but he had done it in the most callous way imaginable. As if vanishing without a word wasn't already enough, he had colluded with his old friend to play games with his wife. These thoughts made her eyes sting with tears. She drowned out her sobs on the pillow. It was strange, but being abandoned, especially like this, really was more hurtful than something terrible happening to the man she loved. Could someone prefer a dead hero to a living coward? Was this love or selfishness? Or were they both the same thing? On the one hand she thought, if things really were as she thought, then all this worry and effort were completely wasted on Eyüp, but on the other hand, she was yearning to find him and hear the truth from his mouth. She needed to understand him now more than ever. She picked up her husband's dream diary once again, as though the answers to her questions might be there.

★ ★ ★

It's a cold winter's night . . . My mother is carrying plates to the table. One, two, three . . .

One for my brother, one for my sister, one for my mother. But what about me, what about my plate? For some reason there's no place at the table for my plate.

I feel forlorn, dejected. I can't bear to look at the table where no one sees the need to lay a place for me. I bow my head, embarrassed at being overlooked. My eyes, battling to suppress the tears that have suddenly welled up inside them, wander over the tassels on the rug; one, two, three, four . . . I start counting them. But I keep getting stuck at four.

When I raise my head my eyes lock with my mother's. She is staring straight at me, her gaze fixed. At first I think she has realised I am upset and is doing her best to be kind. I feel loved, even if it's just a tiny bit. But then I realise immediately, the expression in her eyes is not affection!

What's more I realise, even if it's rather late in the day, that the path of those eyes does not cross with the path of mine at all. My mother can't see me, she is looking straight through my face and staring at something behind me. I turn around to see what her gaze is focused on. I find myself face to face with the black-and-white photograph of my father on the wall. The photograph version of my father is sitting in the middle of the three-seater sofa in the living room and staring at me.

Doctor Carcel wanted me to write how I felt when I woke up. Fine, I'll write it in that case. Sadness . . . When I woke up I felt like the last leaf on a tree, that somehow can't fall down.

If I could share this dream with my doctor he would doubtless ask me questions about my mother. And most probably he would take out the little black notebook where he jotted down notes during our conversation on our first meeting and refer to them. The first time we met he asked me whom I tend to share my dreams with. Provoking me to repeat for the umpteenth time that if I could remember my dreams well enough to be able to share them with anyone, I wouldn't need to see him. So he encouraged me to remember the days when I did recall them. For example, to whom did I describe my dreams when I was a child . . .

It didn't take too much effort to come up with the answer to that one. The answer was easy: No one . . .

"Why not?"

"My mother told me not to."

"I don't understand. What did she say?"

"She said you mustn't tell anyone about your dreams."

My doctor found my reply terribly interesting and asked me to elaborate, as he busied himself jotting down notes in his black notebook.

"I hope you're not going to tell me that by forgetting my dreams I'm trying to endear myself to my late mother," I said, well aware of the risk of making myself unpopular with the doctor. Instead of marvelling at the ingenuity of this inference, he retained the impassive expression on his face. And I, for my part, fulfilled my duty as a patient and elaborated.

At that time, I would have been 4 or 5 at the most. One morning when I awoke from a particularly unsettling dream, I ran as fast as I could to the bed of my still sleeping mother. She must have been disgruntled about my waking up at the crack of dawn and demanded an explanation, because I launched into a description of my dream, determined to prove my fear was justified. As I related it, my mother grew distressed and her face became drawn, as though I were transferring the weight of that dream to her shoulders. Then, interrupting me mid-sentence, she grabbed my arm and pulled me towards her. She held onto my arm so tightly it hurt. It was one of those unnecessary occasions when mothers feel the need to address their children very seriously, as though imparting an invaluable life lesson, even when they are saying the most banal things. She looked straight into my eyes, as though about to confide a vital secret, or give me an essential piece of advice I must never forget on any account, and declared it was wrong to tell others what you have dreamed. When, rubbing my painful arm, I presumed to ask the reason why, she replied, "It's not good to describe your dreams."

"What else did she say?"

She said, "When you tell others about your nightmares they come true, and sweet dreams turn bitter too. Don't forget, no matter what you dream, keep it to yourself; you mustn't tell anyone about your dreams."

Doctor Carcel listened to me with great interest, not neglecting to take notes in his beloved notebook. A few seconds after raising his head, he warmed my heart with an intelligent question:

"Do you remember the dream you had that day?"

I couldn't stop myself from laughing. "You surely can't be asking about a dream I had some 30 years ago?"

"The very same. The one you told your mother about."

"Are you pulling my leg doctor? I come to you complaining about not being able to remember the dream I had this morning, and there you are asking me about a dream I had 30 years ago."

Instead of being offended, he chose to smile gently, before enquiring about my relationship with my mother. Well, I can hardly blame him, I mean, I had asked for it by talking about my mother. I spoke briefly, because I didn't want to prolong the conversation. We didn't have any major issues; my relationship with my mother was fine.

"Is that all?"

"Yes."

"Okay, to whom did you feel closer during your childhood? Or, let's put it another way, who spent the most time with you?"

"My elder sister."

"And what about your mother?"

"She spent time with me too of course. But she had three children and a house to run; she couldn't devote all her time to me. It was mostly my sister who was in charge of looking after me."

"When you were a child did that bother you at all? Would you have liked your mother to pay more attention to you and spend more time with you?"

"Oh no, I doubt it. I mean, I might have done, but don't all children always want more attention?"

That small confession, which I made as though it meant nothing, actually signified much more for me than I let on. I had spent my childhood thinking my mother loved me less than she did her two other children. That is the truth of the matter. I grew up under the permanent impression that the rest of the family were part of a community that excluded me. When they were together they were members of an alliance, to which I did not belong. My mother wasn't the only one I felt distant from. What I really felt distant from was the family they formed when they were together. During the times when my sister was away from that alliance, she was more of a mother to me than my mother was. She loved me, she doted on me. But, when all was said and done, she too was part of that family. And, although I didn't understand the reason why, I could see clearly I had no place in it. It was as though there were something that drew the three of them together. I had not had my share of whatever that was, and that was why I wasn't one of them. Once my mother joked, saying they had found me in the mosque courtyard. And I of course didn't forget it for years. If I didn't look so much like my mother, I would have blamed that mosque for their excluding me. Not even our blood ties were enough to make them accept me in their midst. And, as soon as I was in a position to do so, I went far away from the house, and their exclusive, inaccessible alliance.

My mother ... Yes, I wanted her to love me more when I was a child. Just as I wanted to crack the password that would allow me to join the fraternity she had formed with her other children ... But I never did.

9

Bülent

They washed him and took him away
I never expected that from my father I was blinded.
Cemal Süreya, "Has Your Father Ever Died?"

Bülent stared at the börek his mother had thrust into his hand. He was fussy about what he ate. It wasn't just the food itself that mattered, but who had prepared it too. He searched for the sumptuous taste of his mother's cooking in every mouthful; every time someone invited them to their house, he left the table hungry. Now it was impossible to look at this rock-hard börek the neighbours had brought without protesting. Usually his mother would cook him whatever he wanted, he never had to ask twice. But today she refused to even fry chips, insisting her son eat what the neighbours had brought.

"No," she said. "I can't go into the kitchen, or cook, for three days."

"Why not?"

"Because I can't. You can't cook food for three days in a house where someone has died. Otherwise it's as though you're cooking the dead man's flesh, apparently."

Bülent grimaced and dropped the börek he was holding on the table. The thought of his father's cooked flesh had made him feel sick.

"My son, will you eat, are you going to starve yourself? Please, don't upset me Bülent. Look, I can barely stand up as it is," said his mother to his departing back. No, there was no way he could eat anything now, what he had just heard had filled him up.

He had no idea where his mother got those awful expressions that no one else ever used. He didn't remember ever hearing his friends' mothers saying things like that. For example, he couldn't even begin to imagine his classmate Yekta's mother, Aunty Filiz, talking about cooking a dead man's flesh. She always spoke about nice things and chose gentle, polite words. And it wasn't just her words, everything about her was elegant and sweet. Her silky, golden curls tumbled to her shoulders and, probably because she was always smiling, there was a permanent dimple on her right cheek. She wore cheerful, vibrant clothes, like a young girl, and looked impeccable at any hour of the day. She was more charming and more beautiful than any other woman he knew. And her breasts were like the breasts of the women in the magazine Osman had brought into school. But she could be a bit careless too, which is why once, she accidentally brushed those breasts against Bülent's hand whilst putting something on the table. Against his right hand. Bülent had been devastated that the palm of his hand hadn't been facing upwards. Yes, Aunty Filiz was a fine woman, but she wasn't very perceptive. For example, she hadn't noticed her son's friend was in love with her. And it was a good thing too; otherwise how could Bülent ever go to their house again? Whenever he got the chance he rushed over to the house of that whining Yekta, whom he only put up with for the sake of seeing Aunty Filiz, on the pretext of studying together. Aunty Filiz contributed to those study sessions with light-hearted chatter, dishes of fruit and tasteless, home-baked biscuits that she carried to the children's room. Occasionally, she would run her fingers through Bülent's hair as they chatted, or stroke his cheeks, as though petting a lapdog. At such moments Bülent would hold his breath, convinced his wildly beating heart would leap right out of his chest. Whenever she came into their room, he tried to keep his head within easy reach of her hand, in case she felt like running her fingers through his hair again. And especially after that fateful day, he always kept the palms of his hands facing upwards, as though offering up a never-ending prayer. He always went home from Yekta's in a dreamy daze. His uncle, who sometimes noticed the state he was in, would tease him by saying, "Matters of the heart again, is it?" Bülent never answered; who would ever take him seriously if he confessed to being head over heels in love with a woman his mother's age?

Although they were more or less the same age, his mother was nothing like Aunty Filiz. Bülent had a feeling that had something to do with his father not being anything like Uncle Reha. He didn't like Uncle Reha, who was a deputy director general at a bank that was advertised on television; Bülent never wanted to go to Yekta's house when he was going to be there. Besides, whenever he was at home they usually had a family day out. Because such a thing was virtually impossible in their house, Bülent regarded all the outings, the holidays and the cinema trips they had with wonder. He marvelled to think that mother, father and son could all do so many things together.

He didn't hold it against either his mother for not being like Aunty Filiz, or his father for not being like Uncle Reha ... He wasn't upset with his father for not being someone like Uncle Reha, but he did resent him for being the person he was. He knew his father loved him. But it was hard for him to love someone who hurt his mother.

Some nights when he got into bed it occurred to him that one day his parents would die. The thought took his breath away, just like when he puzzled over where everything was before the world existed. Bülent believed the power that made the world exist out of nothing was the same power that made someone who existed into nothing. Whenever he thought about that, his heart started beating wildly. When he first learned at school that the world and everything in it were formed at some later point, he had been stunned with confusion and fear and had gone running to his aunt as soon as he got home.

"Aunty, when was the world created?"

"A loooooong long time ago, my precious."

"How?"

"The creator deemed it fit and created it."

"But how?"

"In seven days, He created the entire great universe in exactly seven days."

"Yes, but how?"

"He created it in order, everything in turn. In the beginning there was nothing. Neither this world nor the next, neither heaven nor hell, neither beasts nor man, neither light nor darkness . . ."

Bülent couldn't imagine a place where there was nothing, or something that was nowhere; that strange abyss he couldn't even start to visualise took his breath away.

"On the first day the Lord created light, to light up the darkness that engulfed everything. He created day in light and night in darkness. The next day He created the heavens. Then He covered them with the sky and created the place He would illuminate with the light He created on the first day. He created earth, water . . . He created huge chunks of land and the boundless seas. In the beginning the soil on the face of the earth was barren, but then He adorned it with lush green plants, wonderfully scented flowers and sumptuous fruits. In one day beech, cedar, cypress, hornbeam, plane, linden, poplar, pine and fir trees sprouted from the ground and turned into huge great trees. Plum, morello cherry, cherry laurel, cherry, peach, hazelnut, apricot, apple, mulberry, palm, fig and olive trees grew in one day and bore fruit. On the following day He placed stars in the sky so the earth would always have light. Then on the fifth day He looked long and hard at all that He had created and, to make His magnificent painting even more beautiful, He filled the seas with fish and the skies with birds. Dolphins, whales, spotted ray, dogfish, john dories, tenches, roaches, sea bass, blue fish, whiting, carp began to dive and frisk on the surface of the water."

"And sharks too?" he interrupted his aunt, fascinated.

"Of course, sharks too."

"But they eat all the other fish, they even eat people. Why did God create them?"

"He gave everyone and everything He created a purpose, a meaning. There is a reason why every single person in the world is here. No one is here in vain."

"Not even sharks?"

"Not even sharks. They're not here for nothing either. Everything has a duty to fulfil."

"What about mosquitoes?"

"Mosquitoes too ..."

"But we keep killing them."

Unable to think of a suitable reply, his aunt had gone on with her account of the creation of the universe:

"He created the birds on the fifth day too. Crows, ducks, quails, partridges, goldfinches, pheasants, seagulls, swifts, thrushes, sparrows, vultures, turtle doves, cranes, storks, kingfishers, hoopoes, swallows, pigeons, all of them ..."

"So when did He create people then?"

"On the sixth day. But He created the animals before that. All different kinds of animals. Cats, dogs, lions, tigers, wolves, hyenas, elephants, ants, snails, hedgehogs, lizards, bears, insects, cockerels, cows, weasels, chimpanzees, all of them ... Then, when all that work was done and dusted, He looked at the world that He had filled with all those living things and created Adam."

"What did He do on the seventh day?"

"Nothing."

"Didn't you say He created everything in seven days? What did He create on the seventh day?"

"He didn't do any work at all on the seventh day."

"In that case I think we should say He created the universe in six days."

"Maybe He created the seventh day so that all the things He created could rest too. All he built that day was the little garden where He was going to put Adam, He invited Adam to enter."

"I know, he eats an apple there. And then God sends him to the world."

To tell the truth, Bülent didn't care about Adam or Eve. His real concern was making the darkness from before the universe existed, that unimaginable vacuum, less incomprehensible, and overcoming the fears that thought provoked. What his aunt had just told him was no different from the stories she had been telling him for years. But what he had learned at school once he got a bit older wasn't like anything he had heard to that day. He had listened to his teacher saying it had all started with gas clouds. That in the beginning, the world was a mass of hot air, then, over time, as it revolved, it had cooled down from the outside inwards ... Okay, but where had those gas clouds come from? What was the start, the very beginning of everything? The more he thought about it, the deeper he was plunged in infinite darkness; his brain felt like it was about to explode. His teacher, who hadn't said anything worth hearing about what existed before the gas clouds, had told them the sun was even older than the earth. The sun and the solar system, including the earth, were the first to form. Bülent, who wracked his brains endlessly to find the answers to a great many questions to do with where people, animals, plants, mountains, streams and everything he could see around him had been waiting before the creation of the universe, thought the only witness of that whole adventure was the sun. If the sun could speak, then maybe the things it could tell him would illuminate the darkness in his mind.

What he learned at school wasn't enough to answer all the questions that puzzled him, and as for the things his aunt told him, all they did was frighten him even more. Feeling helpless before these great unknowns, he made every effort not to think about them, as he did, for exactly the same reasons, with the knowledge that his mother and father would die one day. Last year, when Caner's father had died of a brain haemorrhage, they had all felt sorry for Caner. His mother had said, "Don't pity him, or you too will need to be pitied." But in the eyes of the neighbourhood children, a child without a father was no different from a green alien waving to them from his space ship. And now he too had boarded that space ship. His mother had been right: he too needed to be pitied.

While he was alive, Bülent had been very angry with that man, who, with his death, had put his son in the pitiful category. Occasionally he would even inflict little punishments on him, as far as his powers permitted. For example, once, his father had wanted to take him to a Galatasaray match. He had whimpered and whinged because he had caught his finger in the car door on the way and, using the pain in his finger as an excuse, had sat there with a long face throughout the match. He had put a damper on the excitement of the poor man, who was only trying to have a fun day out with his son, man to man, like the smiling, handsome fathers in films.

Actually what was eating him that day wasn't really any pain in his finger. When he had got up to drink water the previous night he had gone past his parents' bedroom, and, hearing strange sounds coming from inside, had stopped to eavesdrop.

"Don't give me a hard time, Perihan. I'm not going to sit here and wait till you're in the mood, I know how to force you," his father had shouted. Then he had heard his mother groaning in pain. Although his hand had instinctively gone to the door handle, he hadn't managed to pluck up the courage to go in. There had been times when his father had knocked his mother to the ground with a single punch, and when he had dragged her across the floor ... But that night it occurred to him for the first time that he did more than beat her, that he forced her to do things she didn't want to ... His mind filled with images he couldn't stomach. For some reason, the thought of *that* traumatised him more than the thought of his father beating his mother and dragging her across the floor. That's why he hadn't been able to sleep for a long time after he had gone back to his room, as he struggled to cast out the all too vivid images in his mind. He couldn't bear to think of anyone harming his mother, but the fact that that someone happened to be his father complicated everything. For example, if someone he didn't know hurt his mother while they were walking in the street, he would fly at him and make him pay for it by kicking and punching him. He might not be strong enough because he was still a child, and he might even get a beating on top of it, but he didn't care; at least he wouldn't have just stood there, he would have defended his mother. But it was another thing altogether when the enemy was his father ... He hadn't avenged his mother with kicks and punches, but by ruining his father's day when they went to the stadium together the next afternoon. He had completely spoiled the match for him. And, not content with that, a few days later he had announced at the dinner table, just to hurt him, that from then on he was going to support Fenerbahçe. His father had turned all shades of purple and delivered a long sermon about how young boys don't change their team. Thinking about all that now, Bülent felt guilty. He may have been angry with his father, but he hadn't wanted him to die.

Last year in the week before father's day, his teacher had set the class an essay for homework. Everyone had to describe their father's good points and say why they loved him.

When he got home he couldn't think of anything to write about his father. What was there to say about him ... He had a supermarket he never left, even at weekends, a football team whose matches he never missed, that was it ... You can write about the good times you have enjoyed with your father, your happy memories of him, his teacher had said. But Bülent had never experienced any such good time. He couldn't think of a single happy memory worth writing about. What were his father's good points?

My father is very strong. He's so strong, that once he grabbed my mother with one hand and knocked her against the wall, with his other hand he restrained my aunt, who was trying to stop him. My father is very strong. My father is so strong that he split my mother's lip and made bright red blood pour from it.

No, he couldn't write that. Bülent didn't want to describe his father; he wanted to write a good essay and get a high mark. He opened his exercise book. He turned himself into Yekta and his father into Uncle Reha and started moving his well-sharpened pencil over the white pages.

When his teacher had finished reading out his essay she had said, "Give your classmate a round of applause." Then she had kissed Bülent on both cheeks.

"Congratulations dear, you've written an excellent essay. You're very lucky to have him for a father, and he should be very proud to have you for a son."

Bülent's essay got the highest mark in the class. His mother had made sure all the neighbours got to hear about it; his aunt had thrust 10 million lira in his pocket as a reward. As for his father, he had been very happy at first and asked to read it. But then, as he was reading, the happiness had slowly drained from his face. When he had finished, he had said, without looking at Bülent, "Well done son, this is worth drinking to" and had brought a large bottle of rakı to the table. And, when he had drained the last drop in the bottle, he had turned on his wife on the pretext that she was making too much noise with her chewing gum and struck her twice across the face.

Since yesterday, the heavy air of mourning had reigned over the household. They barely spoke, and, as if noise were a sin, whenever they had to say anything, for some reason they whispered. His mother's and aunt's friends, their neighbours and relatives wandered around the house with long faces, weeping and talking about what a good man his father had been.

"Ah the poor lamb, he's been left an orphan when he's still such a tiny boy," said one of the neighbours, patting his back. Another woman whom he had never met seized him and hugged him tightly, the stench of her sweat making him feel sick. His friend Furkan's mother, Aunty Sündüs, murmured some verses from the Qu'ran and then, looking straight at him, said, "When he came into the world our Prophet was an orphan too." Bülent had no idea whether she was telling him that to try and make him feel better, or to make the other women in the room notice her. But he resolved there and then never to go to Furkan's house again. He hated all these people who were discussing him as though they had nothing else to talk about and, rather than hear what they thought of him, he wanted to run away, to hide, to be by himself.

Last night, stifled by all the crowds of people and the guests who had taken over the house, he had tried several times to slink away into a corner, but had been collared each time by someone different who had pursued him, thinking it her duty to soothe and comfort him. Even after he had gone up to his room, people had entered, patted his back, hugged him to their chests and wept. When he had gone downstairs to drink water, the women in the living room had practically assaulted him. Everyone had tried to play their part in consoling him. Just when he thought he had finally escaped from their slobbering compassion, Aunty Pilar had crossed his path. She looked beaten, but what was casting a shadow over her face was more confusion than pain. Bülent didn't think much of this guest, for some reason. Once he realised that she too was going to try and hug him like all the others, he ran to his room before she got the chance. No, he didn't want anyone's attention, or their pity. In his short life he had understood that adults were at their cruellest when they were pitying you.

It was only after all the guests had left that he had been able to relax a bit. Just as he was preparing to go into his mother's room, the door had opened and his aunt Müesser had entered, her eyes puffed with crying. She had drawn the boy's head towards her chest, as she had done dozens of times throughout the day, and then, overcome by grief, had broken down and wept. Bülent loved his aunt. But because he felt as though he was betraying his mother by loving her, he tried to save his affection for when they were alone. He could sense his mother didn't like it when he got too close to his aunt.

"Do you want me to sleep with you tonight, my darling?" His aunt couldn't bear to see him suffer. Often she was even kinder to him than his mother. His mother was full of rage, while his aunt was like cotton wool. His mother liked punishing him, while his aunt would never dream of it. When he disobeyed her, his mother had no qualms about reporting him to his father, while his aunt had never snitched on him even once. But despite all that, Bülent knew his mother didn't love him any less than his aunt.

"No, that's all right."

"Let me stay darling."

"I'm going anyway."

"Where are you going?"

"To sleep with my mum."

"Your mum's asleep."

"It doesn't matter, I'll sleep with her."

"All right then."

If it had been his mother she would have been offended and angry with her son for preferring someone else to her. But his aunt just gave him an understanding look. She was never resentful or offended; she just went on loving him. Safe in that knowledge, Bülent headed for his mother's room. He remembered the nights when the sounds he had heard as he walked past that room had made him quake with fear. He realised he preferred the sound of his mother's silence as she slept alone to the sound of his father inflicting pain. With that realisation, a wave of guilt larger than himself swept over him.

His mother had surrendered the room to her shallow breathing and was sleeping as though unconscious. Was she afraid of the dark, he wondered. The faint light from the bedside lamp lit up the room. The trick of the light made several shadows flicker on her face. Bülent thought his mother looked like the corpses in films. She was lying motionless on her back, her arms stretched out on either side of her. She seemed either exhausted, or totally relaxed.

"You'll get some peace at last," Aunty Atiye had said to her mother. Bülent had heard her when he had come back from school, just as he was about to go in through the half-open door. Then he had peeped in. "You'll be free of him, you can make a new life for yourself."

"No Atiye, I can't do it. I can't get divorced with nothing to fall back on."

"You'll get your maintenance, and a house, and then you can go your own way. Are you any better off the way you are? And especially if you tell the judge about *that*, he'll grant you whatever alimony you want and you won't even need to ask twice; you'll be divorced in a single hearing."

Bülent's ears had pricked up when he heard the word "divorce." There were some children in his class whose parents were divorced, but to that day it had never crossed his mind that anything like that could ever happen to him. For example, Şeyda's parents were divorced, and ever since they had split up she had lived with her mother and her brother had lived with her father. She hardly got to see her brother or her father anymore. What if my parents get divorced too? Which one will I live with, thought Bülent, horrified. He listened hard to their conversation:

"But how can I tell the judge that?" his mother was saying. "I'm too ashamed. I can't talk about that in front of all those people."

Aunty Atiye removed her slipper, turned it over and placed it upside down on the coffee table. "That's all you need to do" she said, pointing at the slipper. "You don't need to explain anything. Turn your shoe upside down and put it in front of the judge; he'll know what you mean. And once you've done that, he won't even ask you any questions or make things difficult for you."

"Uff, where did you get this idea about getting divorced, Atiye? Honestly, you've made me wish I'd never told you," his mother had said. And the moment she said it, she noticed her son standing at the living room door and got into a fluster. "My precious, when did you arrive? Are you hungry? Shall I get you something to eat?" she had stammered.

"No I don't want anything," Bülent had said and gone up to his room. He had been tearful at first, but had calmed down when he thought about what his mother had said. If Aunty Atiye was so interested in these things, then she could go to the court herself. She could be the one to get divorced and live away from her children. What Bülent had feared most that day was not being left fatherless, or never all being together as a family again, but being separated from his mother. Being away from his mother was even more terrible than being in the category of children whose fathers had died. Perhaps that was why he felt ashamed when he thought of his father now. But that was all he could do, and that was all he felt like doing. He couldn't help it . . . Everyone should have someone in their life whom they loved more than anyone else, and he had chosen his mother.

When he entered the mosque courtyard, he shivered right down to his bone marrow, despite the stifling heat. It was so hard to believe his father was lying in the coffin waiting at the end of the courtyard. When he looked at the coffin he thought his father wasn't as tall as he had imagined. Even though, when he had sat on his shoulders as a small boy and risen into the air, he had felt like a giant, and looked down on everything from above. At that time he had thought his father was the tallest, biggest, strongest, most intelligent man in the world. He had upheld that belief until he had started to believe his mother was the most unhappy woman in the world.

He knew now that, before they had brought him here, the man lying there so still had been laid out on the white tiles and, like a child who hasn't yet learned to be ashamed of his nakedness, allowed others to wash him. In fact, it wasn't until one of their distant relatives, who loved poking his nose into everything, had arrived that morning and said, "Your son should be at his father's side too" and his mother had replied , "What business does such a small child have in a ghusal room?" that he had learned about this washing business. Feeling curious about this place where his mother was so adamant he should not be by his father's side, he asked his aunt what a ghusal room was and frowned when he heard the disturbing reply.

"It's the place where they wash the dead."

"What sort of a place is it? Where do they wash the dead?"

"On a marble slab."

"Have you ever been inside a ghusal room?"

"Yes I have."

"When?"

"A long time ago, before you were even born. When your grandmother passed away."

"What did you do there?"

His aunt shuffled uneasily, unsure of whether or not to answer. It was obvious it wasn't something she liked discussing, at least not with him.

"What did you do, aunty?"

"I washed my mother."

At first Bülent couldn't believe what he was hearing. He tried to picture it in his mind, but couldn't. And, like everything else he couldn't picture, he pushed that too out of his mind. What an awful thing, to have to wash your mother's dead body!

"I'm never going in there."

"Don't say that," said his aunt calmly. "We're all going to end up in there one day."

Bülent froze with horror when he realised what his aunt was saying. His mother, who had heard that last sentence, ran up indignantly to whisk him away him from his aunt.

"I don't believe this! What kind of a thing is that to say to a child!"

"What have I said now?"

"For God's sake, don't you start now. I can barely stand up as it is. There are things you can say to a child and things you can't," she said, striding off, tugging Bülent after her. As she swept past, she muttered through clenched teeth, "You'd know if you were a mother."

Now, as he looked at the coffin at the end of the courtyard draped with a green prayer rug and which, for some reason, looked shorter than his father, Bülent remembered Veysel's green sweater that had shrunk to a tiny size in the wash. His father had shrunk like a green sweater and been tossed to the end of the courtyard. He had been washed by strangers. His mother, who used to force him into the bath when he was little, hurt him so much as she washed him. Who had washed his father today, he wondered? Who had hurt him? Bülent's eyes filled with tears. He wished he could have loved him more and been able to tell him so. When he thought of his father now, instead of the anger he used to feel, he was filled with guilt. Perhaps that was the only thing anyone could do for someone who had departed. As he was gazing at the coffin in the distance, that distant relative, who had said that morning, "He should be at his father's side" pushed Bülent all the way to the end of the courtyard. When he was finally allowed to stop, he was level with the coffin.

He took another look at the coffin placed on the coffin rest directly in front of him. The only thing separating him from his father was a flimsy piece of wood. He was amazed that although he was standing so close to him, his father had gone to a place that was so far away he would never be able to return. This man who, just yesterday morning, could stand on his own two feet, was now laid out in front of him. He would never walk or talk, or laugh or cry again, but had embarked on a journey to another universe. Bülent's lips parted and, involuntarily, let out a weak cry: "Daddy!"

This was the first time Bülent had witnessed death at such close quarters. As he contemplated everyone who was left behind, he remembered what his aunt had said that morning and shuddered with the terrifying thought that he too would one day be carried to the mosque courtyard in a coffin like this one. The thought that he too would one day die was too hard for him to bear. Much harder than the thought that he would never see his father again . . .

When he turned around, he saw the courtyard had suddenly filled up. Relatives, neighbours, the shopkeepers from near the supermarket, they had all crowded in at once. The throngs of people at home had driven him mad, but this was different. He felt proud to think so many people had gathered here just for his father. He wondered if there would be more people if Uncle Reha were to die . . .

The women had retreated to the back of the courtyard, while the men stood in line directly in front of the coffin. His Uncle Bünyamin stood on one side of him, while Aunty Maide's husband, Uncle Sezai, who had come from Bandırma that morning, stood on his other side. Uncle Sezai put one hand on his shoulder and asked if he had ever performed the funeral namaz. No, never. He had never even been to a funeral.

He couldn't take his eyes off the thick hairs sprouting out of Uncle Sezai's nostrils. Even they were white. He was so old he must be certain he didn't have long to live. Bülent was amazed that, despite that, he could still stand in front of a coffin without being afraid. As if he had read his mind, the man bent down and whispered in his ear, "Don't be afraid. You mustn't be afraid of death. Only sinners should fear death. They're the ones who will burn in hellfire. There's no need for a good Muslim to fear death." He doubted his father had been a good Muslim. As for his sins, he had witnessed some of the many he had amassed with his own eyes. Was he bound for hell then, where he would be consumed by red-hot angry flames?

This time Uncle Sezai asked, "Do you know the prayer they're going to recite?" He was looking at him as though he would think it a terrible thing if he didn't. Perhaps if he didn't know it, he wouldn't be regarded as a good Muslim and, when his time came, he wouldn't go to heaven, but be sent to join his father. If that were the case, then Bülent would be very angry with all of them for not having taken the trouble to teach it to him in all these 12 long years. How could his mother and aunt have overlooked something so serious?

"No," he said in a frightened whisper. And immediately he was overwhelmed by the shame of his ignorance. He directed his gaze at the ground and at the tips of his shoes, instead of Uncle Sezai's face.

"I'm going to recite it, listen carefully," said Uncle Sezai. Then he repeated in his croaky voice, without pausing:

"Allahummaghfir lihayyina and meyyitina and shahidina and gaibina and . . ."

When he had finished, the elderly man looked at him as if to ask, well, do you know it now? Not only had Bülent not memorised it, he hadn't understood a single word.

"Well, just hearing it once isn't enough anyway. Make sure you learn it, don't forget. You're not a child anymore."

Bülent didn't like suddenly being saddled with all this responsibility. As it was, his father was dead. As it was, he had been left fatherless. As it was, they had taken him away and washed him. As it was, they had laid him out on marble slabs. Wasn't all that enough, without all these hell punishments, prayer duties and torments in the grave? He inched away from Uncle Sezai, to avoid spending another moment in his company, and went towards his Uncle Bünyamin on his other side. He leaned lightly on his uncle; it made him feel a bit safer. He would be fine, even if he didn't know the right prayers; his uncle would sort it out, his uncle would protect him.

★ ★ ★

My heart is pounding with fear as I walk submerged in a night shrouded by fog. I cling to my father's hand to avoid tripping and falling. I squeeze his huge hands with all my might.

It's impossible to see anything through the dense fog. I don't notice the dogs circling us until they are right under my nose. There's nothing as dangerous as not seeing danger, I know. But still I'm safe, I'm in my father's hands.

I trip on a stone I didn't spot in time and lose my footing. First I ascend into the air, and then I approach the ground again. Every second is multiplied by 10, by 100. My taking off from the ground, my flapping my wings like a bird and then my bracing myself for nosediving back down to the ground go on forever, like a slowed down film frame. I close my eyes tightly; I want to scream, but the only sound that comes out of my throat is a helpless wheezing. Just as I am about to hit the ground, a magical bird catches me and pulls me up. It takes me soaring up towards the sky. I open my eyes, I am in my father's arms. He is carrying me, his decisive footsteps tapping on the ground as he strides. He splits the night and the fog into two. I didn't fall. I am in my father's arms, at the centre of the earth. I'm safe.

My father would often enter my dreams when I was a child. I always used to dream of him watching at my bedroom door, like a guard from bygone days. He was responsible for the soundness of my sleep and the brightness of my mornings. Whenever I was in a fix he would rush to my aid and leap to defend me against whichever obstacle crossed my path. And, like a superhero, he could fly when necessary. His breath, which enclosed my dreams, gave me added protection. I felt more relaxed, both during my nights and during my days. But later, for some reason, he retreated from my dreams. Because a large proportion of my childhood was spent fatherless, after a while I had difficulty finding memories to nourish my dreams. I remained without him, during my nights as well as during my days.

The older I got, the more difficult it became for me to remember my father, but whenever I thought of him as a child, for some reason I always remembered the black leather slippers he used to wear in the house. Did my father drag his feet as he walked, I wonder; why did I constantly hear the rustling of his slippers in my ears?

It must have been because no one but him wore them, because they were too precious to be offered to any guest – when in our house we usually reserved everything we considered too good for ourselves for strangers – that I loved putting on those slippers and dragging my feet along the floor.

My father had a single-sided, fine-toothed brown comb that he always carried in his pocket, which I also remember, as though that were the one vital memory that it was crucial to transfer from childhood to adulthood. Not some long-winded piece of advice that one should never forget, or a life lesson, but a piffling little comb . . . One bayram morning, he had parted my hair from left to right with that comb. And what's more, he hadn't dug it into my scalp as he combed me, like my mother used to, but had done it without hurting me at all. For some reason, the women in our house believed getting clean had to be a painful process. That's why my poor scalp was scalded from being scrubbed with boiling water every bathtime, and my skin turned bright red and chafed, and stung and smarted from such vigorous scouring with the bath glove. Both my mother and my sister washed me as though they had declared war on an army of invisible germs. My father wasn't like that; he was calmer. He never bathed me, but if he had, he would never have hurt me. He was bound to have sponged my arms as gently as he had combed my hair. He wouldn't have gone into a frenzy like my mother and sister. Perhaps because he was the family member I saw the least, my father was the person I trusted most when I was a child.

I was just 5 years old when he died. That's why I always believed my life would have been different had he lived. Being deprived of a role model I could look up to and try to emulate, I was left with no option but to choose my own path. As far as Freud was concerned, under those circumstances I should have turned aggressive, or become overly attached to my mother.

Because he believed the existence of the father created a balance in the clinging relationship between mother and child. But Freud was fortunate enough not to live in our house, and for that reason he didn't go out of his way to try and work out what the consequences of the absence of a father would be in circumstances where there was no clinging relationship between mother and child. Lucky him!

10
Bünyamin

Our job is to fill and empty a full emptiness,
With the dead, with nights, with hyacinths.

Melih Cevdet Anday, "Hadn't These Swallows Left?"

When Bünyamin noticed his nephew leaning gently against him, he moved closer to him. As someone whom no one had ever needed but who, on the contrary, had always needed others, he liked the idea of being Bülent's rock. As long as he was with his nephew he wasn't unnecessary.

When the imam took his place in front of the coffin, the rows of mourners in the congregation also squeezed closer together. Looking first at the coffin, then at the congregation, the imam asked, "What kind of a man was the deceased?" Bünyamin joined in with the crowd, who all chorused in unison, "A good man." He blinked quickly, like he used to do as a child when he told lies he was convinced the adults would never swallow. In those days he was not such a master in the art as he was now. Before, it wasn't just when he told whopping great lies like this one; even if he deviated from the truth a tiny bit, his lashes would blink and his face change colour. His mother didn't give him too much trouble, but any time Rahmi Boss caught him out in a lie he would grab him by the ear and go on and on about what a terrible sin he had committed. Because he wouldn't let go of his ear until he had concluded his sermon, Bünyamin would heap hearty curses, both on the duration of the warning, and on the inefficiency of his boss's jaw, that wasn't capable of uttering more than 10 words per minute. But he knew that even just thinking evil was at least as sinful as speaking evil. If the truth was bad and lying a sin, there was no doubt a place in a prime location awaiting him in that hell his boss described so vividly.

He believed the real sinners in the mosque courtyard weren't those who testified to the saintliness of the deceased and lied outright in the house of God, but the people who forced them to do it. That meant the sin he had just committed should go straight on the tab of the imam who had asked the question. Seeing as it couldn't go on the tab of he who had made him ask it in the first place . . .

No, Bünyamin would not say his brother-in-law was a good man. What's more, he couldn't understand what God, who saw everything so clearly, was doing asking another mortal about the character of one of His creations. His brother-in-law was a downright monster. If even he, Bünyamin, knew that, wasn't it crystal clear to He whose wisdom cannot be questioned?

This time the imam asked, "Do you give him your blessing?" "Yes!" rang out one voice from the congregation. Bünyamin wondered how many years this man had been leading funeral namaz, how many times he had contemplated the corpse of someone he had never met in his life, followed by that corpse's nearest and dearest, and repeated that question. Had anyone ever said, even once, "No, I don't give him my blessing" or "The deceased was a real shit. He eyed up my wife, he saddled me with huge debts, he barefacedly cheated an orphan" or anything like that? Bünyamin doubted it and he knew the reason why. Lying beneath their zeal to keep their true feelings about the deceased to themselves and to try and convince God of the lie that the dead man wasn't a bad person, was the worry of knowing that one of these days it would be their turn. It was all right to swindle a living person out of the last penny of their inheritance, to steal what was theirs and say to hell with justice, but no one could be ungenerous to the dead. People attacked everyone who crossed their path and stamped on their throat as long as they were alive, but their generosity towards the dead knew no bounds. The imam asked again, "Do you give him your blessing?"

"Yes!"

"Do you give him your blessing?"

"Yes!"That's right, go ahead and give it, so that any day now when it's your turn you won't be quaking in your boots on the as-sirāt bridge on the day of judgement, thought Bünyamin.

The imam, who had made sure everyone heard that the deceased had been a good man so they could all pray for him, said, "Allahuekber" in such a deep voice it made his nephew jump: "For the love of God we go to namaz, for the love of the deceased we offer prayers, I yield to the imam, ready to carry out the good man's will," said Bünyamin to himself. He recited the prayers he had learned in the past parrot fashion, without forgetting a single word, but they didn't move him in the slightest. He said the first Allahuekber and recited the Sübhâneke, adding, "Ve celle senâüke." With the second Allahuekber he moved on to "Allâhümme salli and Allâhümme bârik." And at the imam's third "Allahuekber" he began to recite the funeral namaz. One after the other he automatically regurgitated the words that had worked their way into his brain from hearing them repeated so often by Rahmi Boss, in whose coffee house he had worked as a dogsbody during the summers while he was living at his uncle's house. He had no idea what any of them meant, but he did a perfect job of reciting them without once slipping up. He had received no end of slaps across the face and been nagged and harassed ad infinitum whilst trying to learn them; that's why they were etched on his memory. And, like a wound-up clock, once he had started, he always carried on to the end. The greatest effect on his day-to-day life of his boss's taking it upon himself to teach a fatherless boy his religious duties by making him accompany him to every funeral namaz in the neighbourhood, was to make him start wetting the bed again, after years of being dry. His mother would give him a good hiding when she saw the wet sheets in the morning, but she never once demanded to know why Rahmi Boss frightened the life out of the poor child by forcing him to rub shoulders with the dead. In fact, even if no one cared, it wasn't just the coffins he was made to stand in front of at such a tender age that frightened the young Bünyamin, but the imam's booming voice too. At night he dreamed he was playing hide-and-seek with the dead. And the dead found him every time. He knew now that children shouldn't be allowed, either in mosque courtyards or at funeral namazes. If it were up to him, he wouldn't care if it was his father's funeral, he would take Bülent right out of that courtyard. And he would ban all games of hide-and-seek. He came back to his senses at the imam's fourth Allahuekber. He took a deep breath and, placing his hands on either side of him, turned his head first to the right, then to the left, and said "Selam." At last it was over.

Once the coffin was placed in the hearse, he got behind the wheel of the car which, until yesterday, had belonged to his brother-in-law and which he would most probably drive from now on. Bülent sat next to him, and his sister, his brother-in-law's sister and the newly arrived foreign woman sat in the back. His sister's face looked tired, Müesser Abla's sad and the foreign woman's disappointed. As for Bülent, he didn't seem to know which of the dozens of feelings churning inside him was the right one for the occasion; he appeared to be looking to his uncle to set the example. He loved his nephew; in fact, there wasn't anyone around him whom he loved more than that little boy. After all, Bülent was the only person who looked up to him with admiration. He knew from his own childhood how much boys that age hero-worshipped older boys.

As a child, he always imitated the greengrocer Saffet's son, Yaman Abi, and yearned to be like him. The young boy, who would have been about 17 or 18 at that time, was the flashiest dude for miles around. He was a regular at the local karate club and had got as far as a blue belt. In those days, to stop them from getting under their parents' feet after school, the local children were sent to karate classes, or to Quran classes, or both. Although Bünyamin had badly wanted to go, his family had never sent him to karate classes and, after everything he had suffered at the hands of Rahmi Boss in his old neighbourhood, he had put his foot down about Quran classes. That was why, every time he went past the Arslan's Karate Club next door to the greengrocer's, he would sigh with longing and gaze enviously at the people waiting outside. Any time Yaman Abi wasn't chasing girls or swaggering about playing the tough guy, he spent either at his father's shop, or at the karate club. Those who went to the karate club learned the most essential moves from the owner, Tatar Hikmet Arslan. But the classes had one basic rule that everyone knew. All those moves the pupils learned on the tatami mats were taught to them solely on condition they would never use them outside in the street, or to harm anyone. Overcoming someone at a lower level than you was considered particularly disgraceful. That's why, although Bünyamin often watched young boys showing their friends the techniques they had learned, he never got to see any sign of karate in a real punch-up. For example, whenever Yaman Abi was going to beat someone up, he would ignore Bruce Lee and go for Muhammed Ali's methods instead. He wasn't a tyrant, he was brave; he wasn't aggressive, he had powerful fists. He didn't pick a fight with anyone for no reason, but he beat the shit out of anyone who stepped out of line or was cheeky. But still, no one in Reşitpaşa regarded him as a hooligan. And one of the main reasons for that was the way he related to the people in the neighbourhood. He was so charismatic he knew how to get on the right side of people of all ages, all walks of life, and quickly made friends with everyone he met. He was someone whom children admired and looked up to, adults loved, even when they disapproved of him and his peers adopted as their leader. Bünyamin's most grandiose childhood fantasy was to grow up and be like him.

The growing up part occurred of its own accord, but the rest didn't quite conform to his dreams. Besides, with time, he too had packed up his dreams of being a hero and put them away on a high shelf. He neither had anyone who required his heroism, nor the gumption in his veins to fulfil his expectations. As an adult he remained as weak as he had been as a child. He carved "unnecessary" deep into his forehead with an invisible knife. If he avoided looking in the mirror, he might have forgotten about it, but the people around him didn't allow him to forget it. For example, he toiled like a slave in his brother-in-law's shop. But anyone who saw the man's arrogance would think he was giving him charity instead of paying him for his work. His late brother-in-law had always regarded him as an unwanted raffle prize his wife had brought in her trousseau, and had never bothered to hide the fact. If that hadn't been the case, would he have begrudged him one little room in that huge, great house? He was so precious about his possessions anyway. Whenever Bünyamin took over the till he counted the money a thousand times. He thought that way nothing would escape his notice. But Bünyamin wangled it so he could pilfer what he considered he was entitled to. After all, that supermarket belonged partly to his sister too. His sister's husband hadn't been much of a sharer during his lifetime. But ... now that he was dead ... the house, the supermarket ... It's poetic justice, thought Bünyamin.

Now her husband was dead, the whole house was as good as his sister's. It wasn't just so he could live in a better place, his moving in there was only fitting, so his sister wouldn't be by herself. No doubt his Yaman Abi, who had given up the ghost at an early age when, by a filthy coincidence, the elder brother of a girl he had taken to the cinema to fool around with happened to have chosen the same film, the same screen and, tragically, the same session, stabbed him to death, would have done the same thing. But still, there was no need to rush things. He wasn't having people saying he had swooped on the man's possessions the moment he was dead. He would bring it up with his sister when the time was right.

When things had settled down and everyone took up their lives from where they had left off, would his sister commit another outrage, he wondered. He remembered only too well how she had put her foot in it as a young girl and the disgrace she had brought on the heads of the whole family. After she had got married no one had ever mentioned the matter again; everyone had tried to convince themselves it was all long forgotten. But Bünyamin still remembered. He remembered, and was weighing up the possibility of his sister going back to her old ways and bringing disgrace on him, as the new head of the family. Maybe, before tongues started wagging, before any low life had a chance to come sniffing at their door, in short, maybe the best thing was for him to move in to his sister's without beating about the bush. When all was said and done, it wasn't right to leave a widowed woman by herself.

His head filled with these thoughts, he drove the car to the cemetery in silence. Although it was a large, convoluted place, finding his brother-in-law's family plot was easy. Because it was very close to an important personage to whom unmarried girls came to pray for a husband and childless women for a baby. That's why there were always people on the next road making wishes, weeping or sighing deeply as they offered up long prayers. Everywhere you looked, there were arrows indicating where the holy cemetery was, so that anyone looking for it would have no trouble finding it. The person who had haphazardly painted arrows on trees and walls in green oil paint and written "DDDD," the initials of Doctor Devran for Dames in Distress, must have been some kindly person who had benefitted from the personage's benevolence and wanted others to get their share of it too. Müesser Abla pointed at the people outside the window and said to the foreign woman, "Look, all these people come here to pray to an important saint so they will find the solution to their problems. My Veysel is going to rest near a very important personage." Who knows where the woman's mind had drifted to; she just gave Müesser Abla a distracted look and smiled weakly.

Once he had parked the car in a suitable spot, Bünyamin went to join the hearse that had accompanied them. Muttering Bismillahirrahmanirrahim, he went to help carry the coffin.

With the men walking ahead and the women, who, for some reason, were prohibited from touching the coffin, behind, they arrived at the burial spot reserved for the Bahriyeli family. Bünyamin couldn't help wondering how much money Rifat Bahriyeli must have had to cough up to keep his family together even after they had died. Money wasn't just important while you were alive, but when you were dead too. Poor people, for example, stuck their bodies, that were counting the days to rot, into the first hole they could find. But could the same be said for rich people? As if they were going to contemplate the moonlight from their resting places, they would snatch up the best hilltops with sea views while they were still in the prime of health and have magnificent graveyards built for themselves. To avoid having to hobnob with the riffraff, they would erect marble walls to segregate themselves from strangers. As if marble would keep their flesh, which had no other aim in life now but to hang off its bones in shreds, intact; as if the earth wouldn't make sure it mingled, not just with all the other corpses, but with maggots and worms as well ... The well-off loved having the whole family resting in the same place. So, they couldn't bear to be apart, in life nor in death. Either that or, anticipating their idle relatives might use the excuse of the distance between the graves to deprive their souls of Fatihas, they put all their dead in the same place, to ensure they got as many prayers as possible. As Bünyamin eyed the Bahriyelis' marble-interwoven family plot, he wondered how much affection they had felt for one another while still alive. Because the worst hell fantasy he could imagine was being condemned to endure eternity with people he had hated while he was still alive. In such a hell there would be no need even for fire.

After the corpse had been lowered into the ground, Bünyamin picked up the shovel and threw soil on the coffin. Then he passed the wooden handle of the shovel to his nephew. Thus poor little Bülent had no option but to join the brigade of children who had covered their fathers with soil from which they would never be able to rise. As the shovel was being passed around from one person to another, the sound of strange music from somewhere at the back of the crowd suddenly pierced the air. Every head turned angrily to search for the source of the sound. They quickly ascertained the cause of the untimely interruption, and all eyes stared at the foreign woman, who was at the funeral by virtue of being the deceased's sister-in-law. Both because it had rung at a completely inappropriate time and place, and because, despite having become so common, people had still not managed to adapt to the mobile phone, the mourners at the funeral reacted to the strange ring tone coming from the foreign woman's handbag with confusion and disapproval.

The moment the music ceased, every one of the heads that had just turned around in such disgruntlement turned back towards the grave. But then, faint tutting sounds rose up from the crowd. On the pretext of wanting to see his nephew, who, together with his mother, had retreated several paces once he had thrown soil on the coffin, Bünyamin walked towards the source of the sound. When he joined them, he saw the foreign guest was covering her mouth with one hand and heading further into the cemetery whilst talking on her mobile phone. His sister bent down and whispered in his ear, "She probably came out of her mother attached to that phone. Anyone decent would shut the thing up. She's shown us up in front of everyone. You tell me, is this the time or the place?" Not content with what she had said, and as though on a mission to make sure everyone knew she had played no part in the crime, she added audibly:

"Of course, she's not Muslim. What would she know about our customs? Tut–tut."

Müesser Abla, who heard the final tut-tuts, twitched uneasily. Bünyamin couldn't work out whether she was put out by the recent display of bad manners, or by the judgement that had been passed on it. He knew his sister disliked her sister-in-law. But actually the poor woman was completely harmless and always minded her own business. She had never said a single bad word to Bünyamin, or been rude to him. And she was an angel compared to her brother.

Bünyamin had gone to his sister's wedding dressed in a miniature suit. He remembered as though it were today how proudly he had strutted around in it and how the serious air he believed that outfit gave him made him regard himself as a man. It was his brother-in-law's elder sister who had brought that suit round before the wedding. Because she had guessed Bünyamin's measurements when buying it, she said she was worried the trouser legs might be too short, and asked Bünyamin to try on his new outfit immediately. That same day Bünyamin decided he would like Müesser Abla, without needing to look for any other reason. When people were children, their hearts were big and their love generous. But as they got older, they couldn't be bothered to like anyone. That must be why his fondness for this woman, who had never once done anything to hurt him, diminished as he got older, until it was finally replaced with indifference. Now, when he looked at Müesser Abla's face, he didn't see someone he liked, or to whom he felt indebted, but a poor woman who had never once harmed him to this day and who minded her own business.

His sister always said she was a wolf in sheep's clothing. Most probably because she didn't approve of her brother's liking Müesser, she always jumped on any opportunity she got to bad mouth her. Years ago, when she was telling him what a nasty piece of work Müesser was, she had said, "You can tell how degenerate she is just by her name. Do you know where she got her name from?"

Bünyamin didn't. How was he supposed to know?

"Apparently, before their mother, their father was in love with another woman. He asked for her hand, but her family wouldn't give it. So he married Hafize Hanım. When his first child was a girl, he named her after the lover he couldn't forget. But he didn't bother to keep it secret, never mind his wife, he didn't even hide it from his daughter. Apparently, every so often, he would tell her he had named her after the love of his life. What good can ever come to anyone from a girl whose father flagrantly humiliated her mother by sullying her with the name of his old lover? Someone like that can neither be a good daughter, nor a good person . . ."

When Bünyamin heard that story he had felt sad for Müesser. He imagined that every time her mother called her, Müesser felt embarrassed for her. But no one could ever feel genuinely sad for anyone else, and Bünyamin soon forgot all about it.

When the foreign visitor had finished her conversation and returned to her side, Müesser Abla threw her an enquiring look. At least the guest realised how rude she had been.

"I'm so sorry. But I had to answer."

The reply was enough to drain the colour from Müesser Abla's face.

"Was it bad news?"

"No, actually it's good news," answered the guest in a whisper. This reply had the effect of making Müesser Abla practically forget she was in a cemetery.

"Was it news of Eyüp?"

"No, no. It was my sister's husband. He and my sister are the only ones who know I'm here. I've been in touch with my sister, but when I saw Paco's number I got worried, thinking he would never call unless it was urgent."

"What was it?" asked Müesser Abla with concern. Bünyamin and Perihan listened too, without bothering to hide their curiosity.

"My sister Isabel has had a baby! I have a niece!" While Perihan pursed her lips, as if to say, is that all, and turned back to the crowd, Müesser said, "May she grow up with both her parents. May God grant her a long life." Then, unable to resist, she added sadly:

"One goes, and another comes. That's the way of the world."

The guest didn't know how to reply. She launched into an explanation that wasn't really appropriate, given the occasion:

"It was completely unexpected. She still had two months to go. Apparently, she went into labour suddenly. But he says everything is fine, the baby's healthy. And then my phone ran out of battery so I couldn't finish talking."

"A seven-month baby then," said Müesser. Inwardly she seemed to be equating untimely births with untimely deaths.

Oblivious to what was going through Müesser's head, the guest went on, "I was a seven-month baby too. My niece is like me . . ."

She paused for a moment, trying to remember the word she was looking for, then it came to her:

". . . she's going to be impatient."

After everyone had left one by one, two by two, and no one except a few relatives remained in the cemetery, Müesser Abla knelt before the fresh grave. Bünyamin saw her hand caressing the soil affectionately, as though it were a child, and her lips moving, but couldn't discern what she was saying. Her lips did not stay still, yet not a single sound made its way out of them. She seemed to be directing her words inside herself, bidding her brother farewell inwardly. As Müesser Abla stood up again, wiping her eyes with a tissue, she called out to Bülent, saying, "Come and say goodbye to your father, darling."

While the boy advanced nervously towards the grave, his mother complained, "The boy is beside himself as it is. I'm asking you, is there any need for this . . ." For several seconds Bülent stood silently in front of his father's grave, beside his grandfather and grandmother, but with no gravestone as yet, uncertain of what he should do. Bünyamin got the impression that he didn't say a single word, either inwardly or outwardly.

The time had come for them to depart and leave Veysel alone in the company of his own eternity. Bünyamin was just about to round up his troop and lead them back to the car, when he jumped at the sound of a voice saying, "Excuse me young man." He looked, the person speaking to him was a graveyard watchman doing the rounds of the rows of graves where the funeral had been held. Naturally he had realised Bünyamin was the man of the house. Whatever it was the man had to say, he had chosen him to say it to.

"Go and sit in the car, I'll be there in a minute," he said to the women and scuttled off to join the watchman.

As he walked back to the car a few minutes later, he wondered what to make of the watchman's words. When he opened the door, a heat still more unbearable than that outside licked his face. Inside it was like a sauna. As he sat behind the wheel, privately heaping curses on the heat and all its ancestors, and to hell with showing respect in a cemetery, his sister asked, "What did the watchman want?" Imagining his answer would make the women, who were anxious to find something to fret about, wring their hands in agitation, he replied frankly, without beating about the bush:

"He didn't want anything. He just said, 'I think you should know, some man has been hanging around your plot for the past few days.'"

★ ★ ★

In my dream I'm standing on the threshold of our house in Istanbul, looking in. I'm late for dinner and afraid I'm going to be told off. But no, no one is telling me off. I wait for a voice to call me inside. No one does. I leave my muddy shoes outside the door and go in. Everything looks so alien . . . The Hereke rug in the living room with the tulip design has gone, and in its place are black-and-white tiles that look like a chess board. All the photos on the wall have been taken down and replaced by faces I don't know. I look around helplessly at the house where I spent my childhood. I think sadly that it's not just a missed evening meal I'm too late for.

Then I go out into the street again, in the hope of seeing something familiar. I see a small child before me. He's weak, sick, exhausted. He has thrust his little hands, purple with cold, into his pockets and is gazing into a shop window as though contemplating the most beautiful view in the world. Then, he takes his frozen hands out of his pockets and starts cutting out coupons from the newspaper. Coupons of all sizes, printed with pictures of the most wonderful dreams, float in the air. I reach out and try to catch one, but the moment I touch it, it turns to ash in my hand. I hear a familiar tune playing in the distance; it's the sound of a guitar, which breaks my heart. That sound takes me back to an Istanbul I knew long, long ago. Suddenly I become that child. I stare inside that shop window, fascinated. But I can't see inside; all I can see is what is reflected onto the shop window from outside. Suddenly the shop window turns into a cinema screen. The first person I see there is Metin Akpınar, holding plastic bags filled with blood. Then Adile Naşit walks anxiously across the screen. Just then Halit Akçatepe comes out of a pavilion, hanging his head. Tarık Akan, wearing a tatty old cap and a faded coat, follows behind him. Then the cinema screen turns into a shop window once again, and the guitar music in my ears gets closer and closer. I go right up to the shop window and place my hands on the dirty glass. My breath mists up the window, but I can see inside. There is a small television on a raised platform, with dancing ants on the screen. Then a warm feeling spreads through my entire body. I set out on a long journey. If only there weren't any journeys with no return, I tell myself. I wish everyone could return from wherever they go, whenever they want. Just then I hear a voice coming from the depths of the earth:

"Wait. Let's get it set up and working, and *then* we'll wake him up."

I woke up feeling utterly dejected. Neither the movie stars from the Yeşilçam studio nor my wife were beside me. But I didn't want to bear my grief alone. I felt the weariness of awaking from childhood into the body of a fully grown man, and the shame of awaking from being a dead child to being a living man. I felt both guilty and as though I had been the victim of some terrible injustice. I remained in my bed without stirring, as though grieving for everyone whose death I had put off mourning, all at the same time. Then, incapable of finding any better way of purging the sorrow that had coiled itself around my insides, I started to cry, as though unwrapping a gift that had arrived late.

I was about 11 or 12. My sister and I went to see that film together. She had chosen it because she loved Tarık Akan. The poor thing was hoping to see a love story. If she had had any idea it would be like that, I'm sure she would never have taken me to see it, for all the Tarık Akans it starred. When I settled back into my seat clutching my Walls ice cream, I had no idea of what was in store for me either. Just then the lights went out and I watched that film, every scene of which I still remember after all these years, or rather, which was powerful enough to etch every one of its scenes on my memory.

Kahraman Kıral, the child called Kahraman in the film, badly wanted a television. He cut out as many coupons from newspapers that gave away televisions as he had dreams. But they were so poor that Tarık Akan, who played his older brother, had to sell his blood, just so he could take him out for dinner in a restaurant. Metin Akpınar, who trafficked with blood, starred in the film too. He fed on blood, like a vampire. Adile Naşit was also in it, playing Kahraman's teacher. She borrowed the lump in my throat as she gazed after her pupil, with tears in her eyes. Then there was Halit Akçatepe. He was the one with the best flair for sharing what the poor shared the most, poverty. The most frequent image in the background was Istanbul. In the film Istanbul brought herself to life.

Then Kahraman got leukaemia. The poor died much more easily than everyone else. But his child's mind didn't fear death as much as the adults did. Which is why, when his friend asked him what would happen to his marbles after he died, Kahraman was able to answer him with complete composure, saying, "When I'm dead, come and get them from my brother." To which his delighted friend replied, "Bless you, you're the best!" I too was a child when I watched all that. A lump, almost as big as the one I have now, inched its way into my throat. I wanted Kahraman to have all my marbles. But he was slowly going away, like a brightly coloured little sphere. The entire cinema was flooded with tears, and the sound of sobbing drowned out the music.

The sound I heard in my dream, the last sound I heard at the end of the film, and then the film's soundtrack that became the background music of my dream ... It was as though they somehow represented everything I kept bottled up inside me. Which is why I woke up feeling like a glass that has been smashed to pieces. It was the same that day in the cinema too. My sister and I both sat there and cried our eyes out. Everyone in the cinema cried, but we two were the ones most embarrassed by our tears. We hid them even from each other. Oh, how deep we hid them!

I think, if people dream about their childhood, it means they did something wrong while they were growing up. As Ursula K. Le Guin says, "An adult is not a dead child, but a child who survived." If we're not going to die, then we should grow up as gentlemen. But where? By burying our heads in the sand ... We've grown up, but all the heroes are dead! Clean notebooks are filled with scribble and all the clocks have been put forward. That's why, when people look at the secret-filled screen of the past, maybe it isn't so much their childhood they miss, but their lost innocence.

Now, as I write down this dream, this film, or, how should I know, maybe the memory, I can't help thinking. A person can stop themselves from missing someone or, at the very least, turn a blind eye to their longing. Especially if there aren't any audacious triggers to set the memory in motion. Streets that you walked with the person you're missing, films that remind you of them, or of those days, songs and perhaps, most dreadful of all, dreams.

Now, as I write these lines, I can no longer pretend I don't miss my sister, who was trembling beside me that day like a wet cat. I can't try and make myself swallow the lie that I have completely forgotten Istanbul, where I haven't set foot in so many years. I can't help wondering if it has changed very much. Why am I so worried about things changing? It's not as if I've forgotten something I need to fear I won't find in exactly the same state as I left it . . . But still, I can't help wondering.

Do you know, he is in one place, and you
Where are you and what on earth am I.

Şeyh Galip, "The Coming Out of Hidden Secrets"

"Could it be Eyüp?" squealed Pilar inside the car.

"It might well be. He may have wanted to come to the family plot and see his mother and father after all this time. He hasn't been able to visit their graves for all these years, it must have been playing on his mind," said Müesser, joining in with her excitement.

Pilar thought of his dream diary. His parents had figured a lot in Eyüp's recent entries. Perhaps it was as his sister said . . .

"No, you two have really lost the plot with this Eyüp business. Tell me, is it more normal to start off by visiting the living or the dead? It's obviously some creep who hangs around the cemetery day and night. Don't go getting yourselves all worked up about some vagabond waster," said Perihan, dampening their hopes and causing Müesser to fix her wounded gaze on her, before replying:

"You may be right. But what if you're not?" Then, saying, "What exactly did the watchman say? Tell us what he said again, nice and slowly," she made Bünyamin repeat the story. And he, seeing he had no choice, reluctantly reiterated what he had just told them:

"Well, he only said there's a man who's been hanging around your graves for the past few days. He said, at first we thought he had come to pay his respects, but then, when we saw he kept coming back, we got suspicious. Two different watchmen both saw him. The other watchman was about to approach him to find out what he was up to, but the man took to his heels and legged it. That's the whole story."

"What was he like? Did he look like Eyüp?"

"My sweet abla, I've never set eyes on Eyüp Abi in my life, and neither has the watchman. How are we supposed to tell whether he looks like him or not? As they didn't get suspicious straightaway it must mean he's not some down and out. And anyway, the watchman said it's nothing to worry about, but I may as well let you know now I've seen you; I'm only telling you so you're aware. He was most probably hoping to earn himself a little tip by making sure we knew how seriously he takes his duties."

"Should we maybe go back and ask what the man looked like?" asked Müesser, but Perihan stepped in:

"That's enough! I can't believe the things you're going on about, on a day like this . . ."

"I wonder who it was . . .," repeated Müesser. It was obvious from everything about her that she was desperate for some good news.

"Don't obsess about it Müesser Abla, it could have been anyone; forget it. Don't make me wish I hadn't told you. That kind of thing goes on a lot in graveyards anyway. They're a magnet for mad people, drunks, tramps, thieves. The watchman said so too. Whenever he sees them he chases them away."

"Honestly . . .," said Perihan, so no-one doubted she agreed with her brother. "We've only just this minute come back from a funeral. Haven't we got anything else to talk about? Anyone would think we need some troubles to spice up our lives because we haven't got a care in the world . . ."

And, much as Müesser attempted to say, "But what if it was Eyüp?" Perihan had gained momentum and wasn't about to stop now:

"Oh for God's sake, I'm about to explode, will you please stop? I've just lost my strapping young husband, and all you can do is talk about the graveyard idiot. I can barely stand up as it is,

I swear, this nonsense is all I need now." The conversation ended there. Under any other circumstances, Pilar would have wanted to get to the bottom of even the remotest possibility. But what could she say to a woman who had just buried her husband?

As it was, she had wanted the ground to open up and swallow her when her phone had rung in the middle of the ceremony. She had whipped it out of her bag in a panic to switch it off, but when she had seen Paco's name on the screen her curiosity had got the better of her and she had pressed the answer key. At first her heart had pounded in fear of receiving bad news. Then, when she heard about the baby, a lovely warm feeling had spread over her. She had a niece! Isabel's daughter . . . She made a mental plan to go and see her as soon as she got back; she was wild with excitement. Left to her own devices, she would have prolonged that moment of rejoicing over the baby's arrival. But one look at Perihan's hostile face after she hung up and returned to the funeral . . . The woman was obviously annoyed about her taking the phone call just at the moment when they were burying her husband; Pilar didn't blame her. This was her sorrow, and of course she had to respect it.

But she hadn't been able to restrain herself when Perihan's brother had mentioned what the watchman said. She didn't know if the man in question was Eyüp, but she was beginning to feel convinced he wasn't far away. What's more, it was her he was running away from. Perhaps Pilar should have given up long ago; perhaps she should leave this city. That's how she had felt last night. Then, as she was drifting off, clutching Eyüp's notebook that she somehow couldn't finish, she thought, all she wanted was to find him as soon as possible, look him in the eye and ask: Why? But she wasn't doing too well in accomplishing any of her missions. She couldn't make herself see reason, she couldn't find Eyüp and speak to him, all she could do was allow herself to be dragged along this uncertain path. And, as with everything else she couldn't control, Pilar was angry with her own life too.

Her inability to get to the end of that notebook was also beginning to irritate her. Okay, so she wasn't used to reading in

Turkish. Okay, so deciphering Eyüp's handwriting was no easy matter. But deep down she knew, the real reason for this tardiness was none other than herself. Despite all her curiosity, she was, somewhat consciously, taking her time over reading it. Because the notebook was breaking her heart, just like her husband who had abandoned her ... She was afraid of what she might find there; already everything was overly strange and disturbing.

If anyone had told her just a week ago that, in a few days' time she would hear the news of her niece's birth in a cemetery in Istanbul, she would have doubted the speaker's sanity. But now it was her own sanity she doubted the most. What business did she have in cemeteries with people she didn't know? What ignorant courage had plunged her into this adventure? She thought of İlhami. Had she been being paranoid last night, or had she really been wrong to trust him? A voice inside her told her she had been very badly duped and that Eyüp was with him. Yet Pilar still couldn't bring herself to go back to Barcelona. Didn't she at least deserve an explanation? Didn't Eyüp need to look her in the eye and tell her why he had done this to her? Why he had run away from her? She couldn't come up with a logical answer to that question that had been going round and round in her head relentlessly for so many days now. Couldn't she really? Or was she simply pretending not to understand what she didn't want to understand? Why did the facts in her head keep changing shape? Again, she remembered Eyüp's notebook. That dream diary that he may have left behind deliberately ... The things he couldn't bring himself to say to his wife's face ... The more she thought about it, the more confused she became.

When they got home, an elderly woman opened the door. Before she had even opened it fully, overpowering odours and infuriating whispers wafted out from inside. Pilar had thought the funeral ceremony was over, but when she saw the throng of people in the house, she realised that was far from the case. She had just walked into the living room when one of the women sitting there said, "It's most probably for your foreign sister-in-law" and showed Müesser the phone in her hand.

"Someone phoned while you were out too, but of course, not speaking the language, we couldn't understand what they were saying."

When she noticed Pilar, she raised her voice to its maximum volume and, practically spelling out the words, "It mussssst beeeeee for y-ouuuu. Quuuuuu-ick quuuuu-ick taaaaaaa-ke it, sp-eeeeak!" handed her the receiver. Bewildered, Pilar reached out for the phone. She hadn't given the landline number to anyone except Isabel. But why would a woman who has just had a baby phone her, and on this number at that? She placed the receiver to her ear with a sense of foreboding.

"Hello," she said nervously. Because she knew, this was how bad news always arrived.

"Pilar, is that you?"

"Mum?"

When she hung up, her face was flushed a deep red, all the way to her ears. She was about to go up to her room to be alone for a while and collect her thoughts, when Müesser appeared before her.

"Is there any news?"

"No, none at all."

"Who was that on the phone?"

"My mother."

"Ohh."

Pilar added, as though it had only occurred to her as an afterthought:

"She asked me to give you her condolences."

"Thank you."

"I'll just take my things to my room," said Pilar, and went upstairs with her handbag. She went into her room and sat down on the bed with an odd sensation of relief.

Vicky had at first been worried, then angry, then baffled. She had telephoned her daughter to talk about her granddaughter's arrival and share her excitement, but had been forced to play a game of hide-and-seek inside a huge lie. Pilar's mobile phone was switched off. So was Eyüp's. When she hadn't been able to get through to either the house or the studio, she had called her daughter's office to at least get the number of the hotel where she was staying, or of the building site. She had imagined all kinds of things when she discovered that Pilar wasn't where she had said she would be. And that word "funeral" especially had frightened her out of her wits. A funeral they had kept from her! The first person she had thought of was Eyüp! If Pilar had been in her mother's place and had found out from the people in her office that Eyüp had lost one of his relatives, she would have found it hard to understand why her daughter hadn't told her the truth. But she still would have believed what she heard. Or at least, she wouldn't have automatically jumped to the conclusion that Eyüp was dead. But that was just the kind of woman Vicky was. Even if she couldn't work out exactly what the trouble was, it never took her long to find someone to assign it to. She listened in silence as Pilar explained that Eyüp had disappeared without trace and that she had hidden it from them to save them from tearing their hair out. Neither did she utter a word as she listened to how her daughter had come to Istanbul and met her husband's friends. But when she heard that Eyüp's brother had died, she said, "Deceive anyone you want to Pilar, do whatever you like. But don't ever tell a lie about anyone dying again. Sometimes death comes just because someone calls it."

And that was how Pilar realised with horror that the lie she had told the people at the office had come true. Of course, she had told them Eyüp had lost his older brother; of all the lies she could have chosen, she had had to go and pick that one. There was no need for her to feel guilty anymore about not having let Veysel go with her yesterday morning; after all, she had done something much worse than that. She felt as though she had played a part in these terrible events. She had summoned death, without thinking for a minute it would hear her ...

But Vicky didn't give her a chance to wallow in her guilt; she rapidly drew her a road map.

"What do you think you're doing over there? Instead of being here for your niece's birth, you're at the death of a man you don't know. Stop being so stupid and come back."

Pilar loved her mother; she loved her very much. But she didn't like her habit of deciding who should stay where and for how long. Yes, she wanted to protect her children, but why didn't she care about anyone else?

"What about Eyüp?"

"Okay, we'll find Eyüp, but not like this. What business do you have there? As if you're to blame, all by yourself, without telling anyone . . ."

"I told you, Eyúp came to Istanbul."

"That's right, you did eventually deign to tell me, how kind of you."

"Mum!"

"Listen to me, Pilar! I'm saying this for your own good, to protect you. Your going over there all hush-hush is stupid enough as it is. Please stop all this nonsense right away and come back."

" . . ."

"Do you hear me?"

"Did you try many times?"

"Try what many times?"

"Calling here. We were at the cemetery; we've only just come back. Did you try calling many times?"

"No, this is the first time I've called this number. And stop all this working out how many times I've phoned and listen to me. There's nothing you can do there. Please come straight back."

When the elderly woman was passing her the phone she had said someone had called her several times before too, but Pilar hadn't dwelt on it. There were more important matters at hand. She took a deep breath and released it, together with the two sentences she had been wanting to say since she was 13 years old:

"Please stop being the one who decides everything mum! Stop protecting me from the people I love!"

Vicky put the phone down feeling completely baffled. Pilar was rather baffled too, but also relieved.

As she lay on the bed, she thought her mother had always been so protective of her that she had learned to always protect herself first, whatever the situation. She was only just beginning to realise that not having something more precious than oneself made one utterly destitute. But people should be able to feel concern for others, even when they themselves weren't directly affected; they should be able to regard the act of loving as something independent of being loved. For example, had she really come here because she was concerned about Eyüp, or was she more worried about the future of her relationship? What was she most afraid of? Pilar didn't want to think about it, she wouldn't like the answers. When she noticed she was still holding her handbag, she remembered her mobile phone. It had run out of battery while she was at the cemetery. No sooner had she plugged in the telephone to charge than the tune that had made everyone at the funeral tut rang out. Paco's name flashed on the screen.

"Paco?"

"Pilar, Vicky knows you're in Istanbul!"

She didn't even get a chance to tell him not to worry. He reeled off his explanations in a great fluster.

"I phoned you over and over again, but your phone was switched off. And a woman who didn't speak English kept answering the number you gave Isabel. I said your name, but she didn't call you. I had no idea how to let you know."

Pilar felt guilty about forcing him to guard her secrets on one of the most important days of his life.

"Okay okay, don't worry. My mother called, we talked; it's fine."

"I gave her the landline number," said Paco guiltily. "She was overjoyed when she heard the news about the baby. I think she wanted to speak to you straight away," he explained. "When she couldn't get through on your mobile she phoned Eyüp's number. When she saw his phone was switched off too, she tried the house and the studio. When no one answered she phoned your office to get the number of the hotel where you were staying, or the building site ... When she asked for your number in Seville the woman who answered the phone said you weren't in Seville but in Istanbul, and that you had gone to a funeral. And of course, Vicky couldn't believe it. And when she heard the word 'funeral' she was worried sick because she didn't know what had happened, or to whom. She phoned me to ask if I knew anything. I wasn't going to tell her at first, but she was so worried . . . You gave Isabel this number. And she said well, my mother's found out now, she may as well hear Pilar's voice and relax and asked me to give her the number. Please don't be angry."

"Never mind, Paco; it's happened now. How's Isabel?"

"She's well, very well. She's sleeping. She's just fed the baby. She fell asleep when the nurse took the baby away."

Imagining her sister breastfeeding a tiny baby that had come out of her body made her emotions turn cartwheels. The feelings rushing through her were an incredibly intense combination of happiness, longing and excitement. A little baby had come into their lives. Isabel had become a mother and she an aunty.

"Who does she look like Paco?"

"Right now she doesn't look like anything much," replied the voice on the other end, laughing.

Pilar wanted to be with them, to be part of that miraculous tableau.

"Give them both a big kiss from me. I'll be right there the moment I get back."

"When are you coming?"

"Very soon." Naturally she wasn't going to stay here forever. She would return, with Eyüp, or by herself . . . She would be the one who decided when.

"Okay, lovely. Keep us updated. Let us know if there are any developments . . ."

"I will do. See you."

There was no knowing when she would have a child, or even if she ever would. Before, it never used to enter her head to even imagine herself with a baby. A child was a huge responsibility, a lot of trouble. It meant devoting the rest of your life to looking after it. And a lot of the time they turned into bad-mannered, rowdy, spoilt brats. Although she flashed false smiles and feigned interest in her friends' children, they inevitably wound her up after a few minutes. Particularly the ones who felt loved and constantly wanted to play games, and the ones who perceived they weren't loved and wreaked revenge by making rude faces and kicking out, she couldn't stand any of them for very long. She went out of her way to invent excuses not to visit her friends with either dogs or children. Dogs jumped all over you and licked you, while children were a complete turn off because they demanded endless attention. Pilar had no tolerance for such things. But later on, her ideas, or rather, her expectations from life, changed. Just like her fears . . . With time, the woman who used to fear being ordinary gradually began to dread being lonely and different from everyone else. It wasn't only her feelings about motherhood that changed, but the person she wanted to be as well. She reached the point where she yearned to be someone else, to lead a different life. A child would complete everything that was missing in her life, only a child could provide the missing pieces. Before, she used to think of motherhood as a renunciation of herself, but nowadays she equated it with finding herself. She envied her friends who woke up in the middle of the night to the howling of babies; she craved the far-off days when she would change her baby's nappy.

When she fell pregnant, albeit by accident, Pilar realised she had never wanted anything as badly as she wanted that baby. But she must have wanted Eyüp even more badly, seeing as she didn't just renounce the baby she was carrying so she wouldn't lose him, but also half of the person she wanted to be. Although at first she consoled herself with the thought that she would fall pregnant again, with time, intense anxiety started gnawing at her. That child she aborted had been a miracle, and most miracles occurred only once. And perhaps the miracle of motherhood was moving further and further away from her womb, just like a departing train . . .

But now this baby had arrived, and nothing would ever be the same again. In a way, Isabel's child was as good as her child.

As Pilar was musing over that with a warm smile on her face, she suddenly shuddered and her whole body turned cold. Was she going to love Isabel's baby like Müesser loved Bülent? Like the consolation prize for a renounced life . . .

First they had prepared the funeral helva, then they had prayed. And Pilar had gone downstairs to the living room of her own volition and been present throughout the ceremony. Both because she believed it appropriate, for the family's sake, and because she couldn't think of anything else to do. Should she return to the cemetery to ask whether the person loitering near the graves was Eyüp? Or should she telephone İlhami and confront him with his lie? Had İhami really lied? She was so mixed up that maybe the best thing would be to wait at home without doing anything. The neighbour who had prepared the helva explained that the longer you cooked the helva, and the further its aroma wafted, the greater peace the soul of the deceased would find. Pilar looked first at the helva, then at the woman, and couldn't help wishing, if only I had someone who would cook helva for my wretched soul too. Were the souls of the living any less tormented than the souls of the dead?

It was evening before the prayers were over and the guests eventually left in ones and twos. When the house had quietened down, Müesser went up to Bülent's room to find out how he was, and Perihan took refuge in her kitchen, which she had been trying to keep away from all day. Pilar stuck her head round the kitchen door and asked, "What are you doing, do you need any help?"

"I want to cook something, but I can't."

"Why not?"

"It's the custom. I mustn't cook."

"Why not?"

"Because apparently it will be as though I'm cooking my dead husband's flesh."

Try as Pilar might not to react, she couldn't stop her mouth from grimacing in disgust. Perihan looked so woebegone. She probably wanted to clear her head and thought cooking would be the best way of doing it. But by the look of things, she was fretting over the most bizarre obstacles. Pilar thought for a moment, trying to find a way of telling her what she wanted to hear.

"Well, don't prepare meat then," she said; she had understood what she had just heard, but had also devised a way of twisting the tiny loophole in that strange custom to Perihan's advantage.

"What do you mean?"

"Don't cook meat, cook vegetables. Then it won't be anything like cooking the dead man's flesh."

Perihan's eyes lit up like a child's. Her face radiated genuine pleasure.

"Do you think I could?"

"Yes I do."

Although Pilar couldn't understand what it was about the kitchen that made her so happy, the woman's childlike delight made her feel warm inside. She didn't like Perihan. But Pilar was also certain the woman must have endured a great deal of hardship to make her become so unloveable. Who did people dislike? Those who were too evil to deserve to be liked, or those who didn't like them? And what was it that made some good and others bad? Their nature? Their destiny? Or the people who took one look at them and decided what kind of person they were? The wonder of happiness was that it suited everyone; very few people could be bad while they were smiling.

"In that case, I'll make mixed sautéed vegetables with olive oil. Without meat."

"Good idea. It sounds delicious."

While Perihan was valiantly trying to wipe the broad smile off her face, they heard the sound of the telephone in the living room.

As Perihan ran inside exclaiming, "Uff, this phone won't stop ringing," Pilar scuttled after her, intending to go up to her room. No sooner had she set foot in the living room than she met Perihan's eyes searching for her.

"It's for you," said Perihan. As she was reaching for the phone with embarrassment, thinking her calls had already caused enough offence today, she wondered why her mother was still insisting on calling this number even though she had charged her phone.

"Yes?"

"Pilar, hello."

It wasn't her mother. This voice belonged to a man. A man who spoke Turkish. Even if, for the briefest moment, she entertained the possibility that it might belong to Eyüp and, for a split second, her insides rippled with excitement, the fact that there wasn't the slightest resemblance between the two voices was so indisputable her excitement was rapidly replaced by curiosity.

"Who is it?"

"It's İlhami."

Of course, it was İlhami's voice. Eyüp's likely confidant, his sanctuary, İlhami, who had kept her distracted all day yesterday, who had played games with her as though she were a child. And now he had dialled the number he had got from Eyüp; who knows which scene of his game he was preparing to enact. But he had slipped up in calling this number, he had fallen into his own trap. Pilar wasn't about to be deceived this time.

"Where did you get this number from?"

"You gave it to me."

"*I* gave it to you?"

What a cheek, thought Pilar. Was he trying to suggest she was so wound up lately she couldn't even remember what she had done? No doubt he was getting ready to say, the best thing you can do is go back home as soon as possible, I'll sort everything out.

"I gave you my mobile number, not this number."

"You gave it to me yesterday. For the police, remember?"

"Ah, yes." She cringed with embarrassment; she really wasn't in her right mind. Since yesterday she had lost what little equilibrium she had left; there wasn't a single part of her that wasn't falling apart at the seams.

"What's up, are you all right?"

"Yes, I'm well. I've just had a bad day."

"What's happened?"

Pilar summarised Veysel's death in a few sentences. İlhami couldn't hide his shock when he received the bombshell. Pilar thought her husband would hear the bad news from his friend. He would be upset. But then it might spur him to come home. She felt bad about hoping to benefit from Veysel's death, but she couldn't stop herself from feeding tiny scraps to the hope that was sprouting inside her. After he had offered his condolences for the loss of Veysel, İlhami finally came to the point:

"Actually I phoned to speak to you about Eyüp. I think we should meet, there's something I want to say to you."

When the waiter, who looked as if he had had enough of the heat, and of life, approached her to ask what she wanted to drink, Pilar's heart was racing. She was bursting to know what it was that İlhami hadn't been able to bring himself to say to her on the phone, but had insisted on revealing face to face. "I'll come to you, don't go wearing yourself out travelling across Istanbul," he had said, and arranged to meet her in Emirgân. But what did she care how long the journey took, when Eyüp was at stake? After all, Pilar had come all the way from Spain. Now, 20 minutes before the appointed hour, she was trying to kill the time that was coming between her and Eyüp in this café that İlhami had directed her to, and was only now hearing the question that the waiter had had to repeat.

"What would you like?"

"Tea, please." Pilar was surprised by her order. Actually surprised didn't do it justice; it unnerved her. She didn't like tea. But, as if all those teas she had knocked back one after the other yesterday weren't enough, today she had selected tea again, out of all the choices open to her. How quickly she had conformed to the rules of this city. For some reason, this seemed to be the most logical thing to do in the shade of the plane trees towering above her head.

İlhami eventually showed up when she had almost finished her second glass. His face was flushed the same shade of red as an alcoholic's, and his forehead was covered with large beads of sweat.

"Have you been waiting long?" he said as he sat down. He made no attempt to hug or kiss her, but contented himself with touching Pilar lightly on the shoulder.

"No, I arrived a bit early."

"Did you manage to find it okay?"

"Yes, it's very close to the house."

İlhami, who caught the eye of the waiter standing a few paces away, placed his order by raising his index finger in the air. Pilar knew a raised index finger corresponded to a number, but couldn't work out what that one thing that was coming would be. Although what she really wanted to know wasn't what the man was going to eat or drink, but what he had to say to her about her husband.

"What were you going to tell me?"

"I think we'll be able to find Eyüp."

"Have you decided to tell me where he is?"

İlhami stared at Pilar, uncomprehending.

"What do you mean?"

She wanted to ask what he was playing at. Had he decided to confess what he knew about Eyüp, or was he planning to take her far away from here with a deft new twist of the wheel? Her instinct was to fire her questions at him outright, but she decided it might be advisable to curb her impulses and bite her tongue. Because she wanted to hear what İlhami had to say before she let on that she knew.

"I mean, have you found out where he is?"

"No, I haven't. But there is someone who I suspect does know something about all this."

"And who would that be?"

As he replied, İlhami fidgeted miserably in his seat, as though it hurt him to say it:

"Vehbi."

This time it was Pilar's turn to be astonished.

"Where did you get that from?"

"I made a decision today without consulting you. So I'll start off by apologising. I thought, if Eyüp's missing and we want to find him, then we need to inform someone else, not just the police. In other words, we'll only find him if we look for him. So I thought it would make sense to tell a few people who always keep their eyes and ears open. And of course the first person I thought of was Vehbi. He knows everyone, he can get in touch with anyone. And not just that, he's very fond of Eyüp. I thought, if he knows he's missing, he'll help us."

"And . . .?"

She was both delighted by the possibility of having found a clue that would help her find her husband and wildly curious to know what part the man who behaved like Father Christmas might play in all this.

"I phoned him at his coffee house a few hours ago. There's a young boy he employs as a waiter; you saw him when we were there."

"Yes?"

"He was the one who answered."

"So, what happened?" asked Pilar impatiently. İlhami's method of describing everything slowly and in minute detail was beginning to grate on her nerves. She wanted him to spit out whatever it was he had to say right away. She wanted the result first, the details could come later.

"Well, I asked to speak to his boss and he said he wasn't there. So then I asked where he was."

İlhami paused for several seconds after this last sentence. He may have been trying to build up suspense. Clearing his throat, he continued:

"He said, 'A friend of my abi's from abroad is here. He's gone to meet him.'"

After delivering this statement, he gave Pilar a knowing look. As if to say, you can see what I'm getting at, need I say more? Pilar, excited by the possibility of finally being on the right track, was about to smile with the satisfaction of having made some progress at last. But then her happiness was clouded by the suspicions that rapidly crowded into her mind.

"It might be a different friend from abroad."

"I asked the boy who the friend was and where he had come from."

"What did he say?"

"He didn't know his name, but Vehbi had said the visitor was from Spain."

"Are you being serious?"

İlhami nodded. Pilar perceived that at that moment, somewhere deep inside him, he felt he was betraying his friends and his mind wasn't easy about it. Yes, when you looked at it one way, what he was doing was telling tales, spying, laying a trap for his friend behind his back. But when you looked at it another way, all he was trying to do was help a woman in distress. If Eyüp's absence was a churning river, then which bank İlhami was standing on depended on who was looking, and from where. And Pilar needed to intervene immediately, before he changed his own standpoint.

"In that case, let's get on with it and find him quickly. Let's ask him where Eyüp is."

Pilar was about to get up, when İlhami held her arm.

"Hold on, hold on, calm down. Even if Vehbi does know something about all this, he doesn't seem to be falling over himself to spit it out."

"But why not? And have you spoken to him?"

"Yes, I phoned the coffee house several times. Eventually I managed to catch him. I asked him outright if he had seen Eyüp, he acted surprised and then said he hadn't." Then İlhami swallowed, shook his head, and looked at her as if to say he hadn't fooled him. He obviously couldn't bring himself to call his friend an out-and-out liar.

"But you don't believe him. Why not?"

"How long have we been friends, I know him. His voice changed colour, he started going on and on about how he hadn't seen Eyüp in years, he panicked in other words. A man who has nothing to hide would say I haven't seen him and leave it at that. Or at least want to know why I was asking."

"And then?"

"I asked who the guest from Spain was. He started off by trying to sidestep the issue, saying what guest. And when I told him what his apprentice had told me, he got round it by saying there's no one here from Spain; it's my cousin from Italy, it's him I went to meet."

"And then?"

"There is no then. I was planning to go and see him because it's better to talk face to face, but he told me he was going out and that he wouldn't be back at the coffee house for the rest of the day. So I haven't been able to see him in person."

"Let's suppose he does have news of Eyüp. Why would he hide it?"

"I honestly don't know."

"And why would Eyüp tell him something he hasn't told you? Aren't you and Eyüp closer than he and Eyüp?"

"I thought so too, but it seems I was wrong."

When Pilar detected the hurt in the suddenly childlike voice of the fully grown man in front of her, she couldn't think of what to say for a moment.

"This Vehbi knows you're in touch with me. It's not you they're hiding from, it's me. What do you think we should do now?"

"Don't get me wrong, but I'm really not in the habit of meddling in couples' affairs. And if for any reason I had no choice, I'd prefer to side with my friend. But your case is different. The man upped and went without a single word. And you must have been out of your mind with worry to have come all the way here. First and foremost, he's got no right to put you through all this stress. We'll start off by finding him, to put your mind at rest. And what happens after that is none of my business; that's for you two to sort out. To be honest, I'm not too happy about even interfering this much, but I did promise to help you."

"You think he's run away from me too, don't you?"

"At first I was worried that something terrible might have happened to him. But I realised today that's not the case. To tell you the truth, I don't know exactly why he ran away but, no matter what, I think he owes you an explanation. That's why we have to find him and put our minds at ease before we do anything else."

"But how?"

"The Boss is a discreet man. If he knows something and is hiding it deliberately, you won't have an easy job. But on the other hand, he's got a very kind heart. I don't think he's capable of just sitting back and watching you suffer. He's probably realised how worried you must have been to have come all the way here. The Vehbi I know would never look you in the eye and do that to you. He couldn't do it to anyone. For example, if a woman in your position told him she was going out of her mind with worry because she thought her husband was in some sort of trouble and that just hearing he was all right would be enough, then maybe . . ."

"And you think he'd come clean about everything? Of course, if he really knows that is."

"I don't know. But that's what I want to hope. His values are different. It might only be out of the fear of God, but he does right by people. He can't contemplate knowingly harming anyone."

"And that's what you think?"

"That's what I hope."

On her way home, she felt uneasy about the way everything in her mind had shifted position yet again. Today İlhami, whom she had condemned only yesterday as a number one liar, was her ally again. And Vehbi, who wouldn't have even been last on her list of people who might know something about Eyüp, was now suddenly the top suspect. If you considered all the years they had been writing to each other, there might not be anything strange about Eyüp's having chosen to confide in him, but he was so distracted and chaotic he didn't really seem to be the kind of person to turn to in a crisis. Besides, after yesterday Pilar intended to tread carefully; she wasn't going to trust İlhami blindly anymore. He might still be trying to string her along and divert her attention. There were dozens of loose ends going round and round in her head and Pilar was doing her best to attend to her mind in the midst of so many voices whispering doubts. What she couldn't understand about this equation with so many unknowns was the part of the affair she found most painful. She kept asking herself, why the need for so much intrigue? Wasn't she as close to her husband as Vehbi or İlhami? Even if Eyüp wanted to leave her, couldn't he stand in front of her and discuss it in a civilised manner?

Tomorrow she would go to Vehbi's coffee house by herself. İlhami, who was convinced he had already meddled too much in this affair and that he had somehow wronged his friend, albeit unwittingly, hadn't wanted to be there when Pilar was speaking to Vehbi. If tomorrow's visit didn't bear any fruit either, then maybe she should consider abandoning this game of catch me if you can. Perhaps the time to go back to Barcelona had come long ago. From there she would go to see Isabel and meet her niece. In fact, she could even fly straight to Madrid. All she knew was that her staying here any longer wouldn't do anybody any good.

Mentally and physically exhausted, she returned home with these thoughts racing round her head. Perihan opened the door. Although she didn't seem remotely interested, she half-heartedly asked if she had made any progress.

"No," said Pilar. "I'm going to see another friend of Eyüp's tomorrow. Perhaps he'll be able to tell me something."

"That's good."

Declaring she was tired, Pilar went straight up to her room. She needed to jump into bed and, if possible, stay there for a long, long time. But when the young woman opened the bedroom door, there was a surprise in store for her.

★ ★ ★

I awake to the sound of a piercing scream that slices through the pitch of the night. The voice belongs to my sister. Trembling, I sit up in bed. My sister's bed is empty. I blink several times until my sleepy eyes have grown used to the darkness in the room. Then, with tremulous steps, I head towards the heart of the scream that is coming from the ground floor.

My sleepy legs carry me to the top of the stairwell. Lacking the energy to continue this journey, which I began somewhere between sleep and wakefulness, I slowly sink down right there. Before I drift off once again into the lazy arms of sleep, I watch what is happening downstairs through the wooden banisters, as though I am floating into a scene from a dream. My mother, my father, my sister, my brother are all together. With some soft pillows, to guarantee sound sleep …

There are two pillows. One covers my sister's face. My sister is crying into the pillow that she is pressing into her face.

The other pillow is on the face of my father, who is lying on the three-seater sofa. On one side of the pillow is my father's face, on its other side are my mother's and brother's hands, pressing it down on my father's face. Those hands stop my father's breath with a single pillow. My father's breath mingles with my fitful breathing, which has surrendered to sleep. Together we drift into the deepest sleep …

That was the dream I described to my mother all those years ago. That hazy memory I tried to recall before it vanished completely into oblivion. After she had listened to me, her face distraught, she looked into my eyes that concealed deadly questions and, instead of replying, thought it more fitting to give me advice; my mother stated simply, "You mustn't tell anyone about your dreams." With a single sentence she had locked my father's lifeless body into my child's memory. But that cursed night was as dark as the stuff dreams are made of, and that scream that had made me get out of bed was sharper even than knives.

I think the talk of my sleepwalking coincided with the era after that night when I observed what had happened through the banisters. But for some reason the people who said I walked in my sleep never said a word about when and where I woke up. But no truth can ever stay hidden forever. The things I had made myself forget, hoping they were a dream, have risen from the dead again tonight! I wish I had never . . . remembered these dreams. I wish I had slept once again, poisoned in a darkness I couldn't explain. I seized this murderous notebook without realising forgetting was a prize I had been given. I murdered the innocence of not being able to remember. I haven't just gone and done it by forcing myself to remember this dream, but by writing these lines as well! Because what has happened can be forgotten, but what is written, never! I should never have written this dream down, but abandoned it to its own lost destiny again. But it's much too late now; the more I write the clearer it all becomes. Because that's always the way it is . . . You forget dreams, but you remember sins.

It's obvious that by ordering me not to tell anyone about my dreams, my mother wasn't just protecting herself, she was protecting me too. But as far as I'm concerned, that's still not enough to make her a blameless angel. The same goes for my sister and brother. They joined forces and smothered my father in my sleep. Am I going to spend the rest of my life wondering why? How will I learn to live with the burden of what I saw? From whom will I demand explanations? What am I going to do now?

12

Müesser

A secret swept through the house like a breeze,
The household, uneasy, sensed something was amiss.

Yahya Kemal Beyatlı, "The Evil Eye"

When the bedroom door opened, like a child caught red-handed, Müesser quickly tried to act as though everything was normal. That required getting off the bed, hiding the notebook she was holding and trying to wipe away her tears, all at the same time. Although she couldn't muster the strength to do any of the other things, she did hide the notebook, written like a scream of desperation, behind her back. As she had brought it all the way here, and even left it on her bedside table, Pilar must obviously be aware of its existence. If she had read it all the way through, she would definitely have hidden it, like a sin. The fact that she had left it out could only mean she was still reading it, was planning to read it one of these days, or that she had left it out for Müesser's benefit.

It was already dreadful enough that the notebook had been written in the first place, she couldn't bear the thought that someone else had read it. She was incapable of raising her head and looking Pilar in the eye. She had no way of knowing how much this foreign woman standing in front of her had read, how deeply into this family's dark secrets she had penetrated. Shame, anger, fear ... The grim feelings that had haunted her relentlessly all these years were now attacking all at once, grabbing her by the throat. Like everyone with a secret, whose hidden chests have not been buried, but strewn everywhere, her first instinct was to gather up all the scattered pieces. Then she stopped and thought, once the secret had been whispered, there could be no turning back. It would seep out of every hole it could find and leak endlessly, until it was heard by those who can't hear, and seen by those who can't see ... A secret was like a naked leper, even those who wanted to avert their eyes would stare intensely. It was a sacred chant, sullied on the lips of sinners. Even those who tried to stop their ears heard it. And afterwards, nothing was ever the same again.

The secret was out of the bag now. Eyüp had whispered it, and it had embarked on its forbidden adventure. Eyüp ... Müesser had come up with every imaginable reason to explain all these years of separation. But it had never entered her head that her brother may have woken up on that darkest of nights. To this day it had never occurred to her that Eyüp could have witnessed either that night or the ones preceding it. The idea was so abhorrent she hadn't even considered it within the realms of possibility. Although she knew better than anyone how many reasons existed for a person to leave this house, she had fooled herself for years, pretending to look for an explanation as to why Eyüp had gone.

After the burial, everything had seemed pointless to Müesser. Neither the crowds, nor the prayers recited to ease their souls had alleviated her pain. Nothing could ever fill the gap left by Veysel. She knew there was still one thing that could console her, someone whose face would still bear signs of Veysel, her nephew. This child who had been left without a father at such a young age needed his aunt more than ever now. As his aunt did him, naturally. They were more than just two keepsakes left behind by a dead man, they had to stick together to avoid disappearing.

That's why her eyes followed Bülent the whole day. She kept watch over where he was and what he was doing at every moment. The child was both sad and confused. As someone who had suffered the greatest confusion imaginable after the death of a father, Müesser could understand him better than anyone. And, because he was able to grieve for his dead father, Bülent could be considered a fortunate child. Yes, despite everything, he could be considered fortunate . . .

Everyone bore their grief in their own way. And it was obvious Bülent was in denial, intent on postponing his suffering to a later date. Whereas the truth was, the sooner he accepted it, the quicker his wounds would heal. That's why she had called him today to say goodbye to his father. She had wanted him to say goodbye, to grieve, but then she wanted closure. By the look of things however, the child had not yet faced up to his grief. He didn't mention his father very often. Ever since they had got back from the cemetery, he had been going on and on about tomorrow's solar eclipse, like a scratched record. He kept saying that during the eclipse every secret in the world would spill out one by one, whatever that meant. Yekta's family was taking him to see it and could he go with them, and anyway, his father had already said he could! Then he would stop sadly, as though he had only just remembered his father was dead and, stifled by the crowd, go up to his room and perhaps try and forget all over again.

After the prayers, Müesser went upstairs to be with her nephew. The only thing that could heal her anguish was seeing him. But it was clear that she wasn't the person who could heal Bülent. He had stayed with her for a few minutes and then run downstairs, claiming he wanted to tell his mother something.

After sitting in Bülent's room by herself for a while, she too went downstairs to the living room. When Perihan said Pilar had rushed out straight after receiving a telephone call, she prayed that this time it would be good news. Then she yielded to the devil who was gently goading her and, without really knowing why, climbed up the stairs again, and this time entered the room where Pilar slept. Being close to this woman and her things was somehow like getting closer to Eyüp. If lying on the bed where someone who had recently slept with Eyüp had just been wasn't touching Eyüp, then what was it?

The room was immaculately tidy. Pilar had put the tiny bag she had brought by the door, as though she might leave at any moment. She had made her bed, but she had obviously sat or lain on it afterwards. Involuntarily, Müesser's hand reached out and smoothed the crumpled bed cover. She walked around the room. It was almost like she was hoping to find something impregnated with Eyüp's smell. At one point she even considered rifling through the bag sitting by the door. She didn't mean any harm. All she wanted was to find her brother's smell somewhere. And especially given that she had left Veysel's smell outside in the street this morning, she needed it even more badly.

She had taken his shoes and placed them outside the back door with her own hands. It was the third pair of shoes she had put outside the same door. After her father's and mother's, today it was the turn of Veysel's shoes.

Her father's shoes were huge and jet black. She had felt so crushed under their weight she wanted to put them outside the door and be free of them as soon as possible. When she put them down and turned her back on them, she felt as though she had been liberated from a heavy load pressing down on her. Her mother's shoes were as light as feathers. Her feet were tiny; she wore a size 35. Perhaps that was why she had never been able to tread firmly on the ground. Perhaps that was why it had taken her so long to relieve her children of the burden they carried on their shoulders. Perhaps it had only come to pass, pass, he had passed away, passed because her mother's feet were small . . . This morning, Veysel's shoes hadn't been like any of the others. When she had picked them up it was as though they were still warm inside. Veysel was still there. Because his death had been both untimely and undeserved. And, that being the case, the inside of his shoes had stayed warm; his life had been severed halfway.

It wasn't just his shoes, she had also left her brother's smell outside in the street this morning. In a few days' time, they would pack up all his things and give them away to the needy. You couldn't keep a dead man's clothes in a house full of live people. In a matter of two days she had been stripped, first of her brother, then of his smell. No one could take the place of anyone else, but she needed the consolation of Eyüp's return now more than ever. When she didn't find anything in the room she had circled in the hope of finding something that belonged to him, and sat down wearily on the bed she had just straightened, Müesser once again felt curious about what the bag might contain. As she was telling herself she had no business opening it and foraging inside, the notebook placed on the bedside table caught her eye. It hadn't been there before Pilar arrived, which meant it must be hers. It might be a notebook where she jotted down notes for her work, or an address book. Just as Müesser didn't really dwell on the nature of its contents, neither did she imagine she might find anything in it that would interest her. That notwithstanding, her hand, that was too ashamed to delve into the bag, had no qualms about reaching out for the notebook that was there for all to see.

It was September 1969. The autumn of the year in which Necdet secretly came and waited under her window at night. No matter how much her heart pounded, no matter how red her cheeks flushed, she would not go to the window. She wouldn't give Necdet even the tiniest glimmer of hope. But the young boy wasn't to be dissuaded so easily. He would follow her in the street, telling her he was in love with her, that his intentions were serious, that he wanted to marry her. Despite not having received a single word of encouragement, he twice sent suitors to see her mother. He heard the word no so many times he eventually realised there was no hope and accepted defeat. Although it broke Müesser's heart when he gave up on her, she knew she had done the right thing. She couldn't marry; no good would come to anyone from her. She couldn't look either Necdet, or any other man she would call husband and be intimate with, in the eye. And never mind any other man, even the idea of being intimate with Necdet turned her stomach. Whenever the thought occurred to her she had to go into the bathroom and have a long bath. Her skin would become angry and inflamed, and she would be covered in black scabs.

As if it wasn't already enough that she was a victim of a sin for which no one would take the blame, now she too had declared herself guilty. Her sentence would be to spend the rest of her life alone. She had resigned herself and bowed down to that punishment without a murmur. That year, by rejecting Necdet, vowing to reject every prospective suitor for the rest of her life and to suppress her maternal instinct, she had submitted to her destiny. She had gritted her teeth, endured, obeyed. Of course that wasn't how she had wanted it to be.

It was September of the year in which she had spurned that young man who made her heart quiver, the symbolic mark of her decision to live and die alone. As she was tidying her brothers' things, she came across a notebook from the days in which Eyüp had taught himself to read and write at home. The child had scrawled his name on the first page. Müesser had gazed at his spidery letters enraptured, as though contemplating a magnificent work of art. Like a proud mother, her chest had swelled and tears had pricked her eyes. And then, she didn't know whether what brought it on was the notebook, the past or her long ago renounced future, but she gazed at those spidery letters and cried her heart out. How strange that Eyüp's terrible handwriting, which had once so delighted his sister, had not improved in all these years, but remained crooked and illegible. Müesser couldn't work out why his handwriting was so dreadful, despite all that intelligence and all those academic achievements. She decided his hand couldn't keep up with the speed of his mind, and that he sacrificed the appearance of the letters for the sake of writing them down quickly, finding a virtue even in her brother's unsightly handwriting.

Now, when she opened the notebook Pilar had left behind, she recalled the writing she had gazed upon and wept over that September evening. Her brother's sloppy dashes, his unsteady letters ... For years she had seen Eyüp's ugly handwriting, which was in such stark contrast with the beauty of his face, in so many different notebooks. But now it was as though those rushed, clumsy letters in front of her were a keepsake from that nervously scrawled name from his childhood. They were so similar it was as if the same child had written them on the same day, at the same time. Müesser's eyes shone, like those of a sick woman who has found a cure for her condition. A tiny flower twitched on the edge of her lips. When she realised she was holding a notebook written by her darling little brother, her heart started racing wildly.

Müesser was a timid woman. Foraging in someone else's room, touching their personal belongings without their permission was against her nature. But when she saw that notebook in her brother's handwriting, it didn't enter her head to ask for anyone's permission to read it. She missed Eyüp so much, she had been longing, even for just a hair from his head, for so long, that this notebook belonged more to Müesser now than to anyone else. This notebook, on the pages of which her brother's beautiful hands, with their long, slim fingers, had moved, over which he had leaned and deposited his smell, was hers. What's more, it didn't even matter what he had written in it. Love poems, debt accounts, what difference did it make? This notebook, no matter what was in it, was an unexpected treasure that would be a little balsam to soothe her troubled heart; it was a healing hand. It was from Eyüp.

Which is why, without the slightest feeling of guilt or unease, she started reading:

My doctor, whom I consulted because of irregular sleep and unsettling dreams, believes it will be useful to investigate my nocturnal life, which, in his opinion, must be very convoluted. For that reason he counselled me to record my dreams, which trouble me, as much when they are manifest as when they're not, in writing. So I, convinced the best way of freeing myself of them completely is by bringing them out into the open, reserved this notebook, which I got from the stationery shelves of Mercadona, for my dreams.

. . .

Müesser soon realised something wasn't right. You didn't need to be all that bright; it was there for all to see. What it boiled down to was that that diary was the end result of her brother feeling bad enough to go and see a psychologist. Although Müesser couldn't really understand the benefits of writing down dreams in minute detail, she was still overcome by the bittersweet joy of at least meeting her brother, for whom she had yearned for so many years, in his dreams. Through those lines she opened Eyüp up, examined his grief, tried to touch his pain. As she read, feelings became confused with dreams, and memories with fantasies. Life numbed one against one's own suffering, but what cruel work it was to look at the suffering of those you loved!

It wasn't just Eyüp's writing that was hard to decipher, but the meaning of what he had written too. It was the same when he was little; you couldn't understand what he was saying just by listening to him. The translation of his words required a bit of emotional intelligence and a bit of practice. And now, for all its witticisms, even this notebook was sad. It was just like Eyüp to try and pull the wool over everyone's eyes. To pretend he was laughing when really he was crying, and then drown his laughter in sobs ... That's why Müesser was suspicious of what she read. Of her brother poking fun at the doctor he had consulted to heal him, of his making light of his troubles and their remedy alike, of those facetious games he played, even when he was writing for himself ... It was all so typical of Eyüp. What was clear was that Eyüp didn't just run away from others, but from himself too. In fact, perhaps, like all clowns, it was himself he ran away from the most. He couldn't even open up and pour out his troubles to a tiny notebook.

She had held her breath while she read Eyüp's first dream. She was pleased his brother could still enter his dreams so many years later. But Müesser was afraid of memories. That's why returning to the past, even if it was only in a dream, made her uneasy. The entry about how effortlessly her brother had renounced their blood ties rent her apart. From what he had written, it had not been hard for Eyüp to dismiss his family. He had turned his back and left, without a second thought. But he even remembered that his sister talked to her violets. That meant he hadn't gone as far away as she had thought.

As she turned the pages, Müesser penetrated her brother's heart. She found parallels of her own darkness in his ominous nights. It was strange, but Eyüp's handwriting deteriorated at the point when he remembered his dreams; it was as though he had regressed to the time when he had first learned to write. Most probably out of haste, said Müesser to herself, because he was in a panic to write down everything he remembered before he forgot it. More than the dreams, which she didn't really understand, she was fascinated by his interpretations. In those sections, which were more legible than the dreams, Eyüp became a bit more lucid, and it was possible to touch his wounds. But the notebook was like a leper; it contaminated every place where it shed its ragged, tattered words with its curse, inflicting wounds on its reader too. Had Pilar read the notebook, she wondered. If so, how had she felt about the things her husband had written about her? Had she been jealous of the other women he mentioned? Had the tiny wounds inside her ached too? Suddenly Müesser remembered where Pilar was. The poor woman was still hankering after finding her husband. She was worried and desperate. Had she read all this whilst in the throes of desperation? And what was the notebook doing in her possession anyway?

With each new dream, she added the Eyüps she didn't know to the ones she did. Sometimes she encountered a man she didn't know at all, and sometimes she encountered a child she thought she knew. The more she saw of the consequences of his misunderstanding and being misunderstood, the sadder she felt. He and Veysel had cultivated a sour silence between them since childhood. Each was frightened of the other, each recoiled from the other. Each believed the other didn't think him worthy of his love and inwardly resented him for it. The more they stoked their vat of rage, the quicker any kindness disappeared. One believed his brother looked down on him, the other that he could never get on his brother's good side. Out of fear of not being loved, they pretended not to have loved at all. Now, with one dead and the other missing, there were no brothers left to love. That was what hurt the most.

Müesser noted how, over time, Eyüp's witty lines grew serious. Sorrowful dregs of memories replaced his flippant jokes. When she read the dream in which their late mother had set the table, she was amazed to learn her youngest brother felt so isolated. In fact, they had wrapped him in cotton wool and raised him as the apple of their eye. Müesser in particular hadn't just loved him as a brother, but as though he were her own child. Obviously her inexpert, underage mothering hadn't been enough for Eyüp. So, he had felt excluded; he hadn't run away from his loving home, but from a house where they didn't even set a place for him at the table, which had never been his anyway. Müesser wondered whether they really might have unwittingly excluded him. Could it be possible? They had always doted on him, but maybe ... Just as Eyüp had most probably worked out ... Like a secret society founded on a cursed secret ... They had, perhaps unconsciously, with the aim of protecting him, kept him out of the dark association that united them.

As the notebook evolved from being a dream diary and became more of a journal, a strange fear gripped Müesser. Discovering that her brother, who had gone to a doctor to help him remember his dreams, had recovered unaided, did not put her mind at rest. On the contrary, she preferred to believe that, as darkness conceals sins, his inability to remember his dreams was a miracle. As his mother had said, "You mustn't tell anyone about your dreams," then her brother obviously knew something. And especially when events Eyüp remembered as dreams turned into childhood memories of real experiences ... The seeds of doubt were planted inside Müesser and she panicked. Her brother was remembering the past from behind the shield of dreams. And, no matter how you looked at it, it was better for the past to remain secret.

Nothing in this life had only one standpoint, only one meaning. People were redefined depending on who they were with. Müesser thought that, as she read her brother's dream about his father. What a trustworthy, fearless, magnanimous man the father in Eyüp's memory was. Out of everyone in that whole family whom he believed was excluding him, his father was the only hero willing to invite him in. Whereas that's not at all how the other two children in the family saw him. The Rıfat Bey they knew was someone entirely different.

He kept talking about overcoming misfortunes. He had no idea he had been born in the very heart of misfortune and that those he assumed had excluded him had never done anything but protect him. He didn't know about the misfortunes they had overcome together. He had never known the murderers and the tyrants, the victims and the heroes. If he had, he would have left much sooner. Okay, so what had brought him back to this city? Was he looking for a misfortune to overcome? Going by what his dream diary said, he had obviously missed his country. His longing had intensified with each memory he had recalled. Anyway, perhaps it wasn't his own longing that had brought him back, but his sister's. Perhaps, after all those years of yearning and summoning him, Müesser had finally managed to bring her brother back to her side. And wasn't Adalet always saying people themselves beckoned to whatever befell them? Whether that be good or bad. But Müesser didn't like that idea. She knew some nightmares forced themselves on people, even though they were unwelcome. And that whoever had them spent the rest of her life blaming herself. If people beckoned to whatever befell them themselves, and if she was the one who had summoned her brother, then perhaps the same went for her father ... Müesser bit her lips, crushing them between her teeth.

Not long afterwards, a giant ball of fire smothered her heart. Yes, she was summoning it. But the curse she had summoned had confused its target and was heading for her little brother rather than her. Otherwise, how could a secret that should have remained hidden forever have landed right in the middle of this notebook, spreading its venom in all directions, straight after she had thought of her father? Müesser turned the pages as though in a trance. She felt breathless, she trembled from head to toe. Like an animal in its death throes, she gasped for breath as she read Eyüp's eyewitness account of the night of the murder. She read the next dream too, overcome with anguish, as she sank deep into shame and sin. She read that diary of sins right down to the last sentence. Bitterly lamenting that her life too had not ended beforehand. With Veysel's departure she had presumed she was the only remaining witness to her shame. But her little brother knew everything, right down to the last detail.

To date she had invented dozens of excuses for his leaving. But it had never once crossed her mind that he was trying to escape from the same nightmare as she was. Eyüp had been very young then. Young enough to lose himself in that fine line between reality and dreams ... But even the uneasiness caused by the aftertaste of that line had been enough to drive him away from this house. Then he had got stuck in the slime between dreams and reality, wavering unhappily between peering through the curtain of the past or leaving it be. The events he had buried deep in his memory were being reborn inside him in the guise of dreams. But it was so difficult to accept, that, come morning, the innocent angels of his mind invariably swept away what he had seen and heard during the night as rubbish. But even if he refused to remember the events of the night, he couldn't erase them entirely; he couldn't avoid waking up to mornings heavy with oppression. In the end, when he couldn't decide whether what was bothering him was the dreams he had, the reason why he had them or the fact that he couldn't remember them, he had wanted access to them. And, when he had remembered with so little effort, he had condemned himself to this truth from which there was no return. As for Müesser, she had been imprisoned in it for years.

That night they had found Eyüp upstairs by the banisters. He was lying on the floor asleep, curled up like a tiny snail, and burning with fever. As they carried him to his bed, fraught with worry, they asked themselves whether the small boy had seen anything, but then convinced themselves he hadn't. If he had seen what had happened, would he have been able to just lie down and go to sleep, without a murmur? And when he woke up he hadn't done anything to make them suspect he had witnessed the events of the previous night. He hadn't even learned of his father's death until the morning. His fever had not abated for three days; for three days he hadn't left his bed. Müesser never knew about the dream Eyüp had described to his mother. For some reason her mother had never mentioned it to them. Most probably she hadn't wanted to allow any dangerous ideas to blossom, and assumed she had nipped the problem in the bud by instructing her youngest son, who thought everything was just a dream, to keep his dreams secret. When all was said and done, Eyüp thought it had been a dream. Over the years it would be forgotten, it would be abandoned to the memory's laziest darkness. Like all untold dreams . . .

When the door opened she was in purgatory, oscillating between dreams and reality, past and future, life and death. She was convulsed with tears. When she heard the creak of the door, she suppressed her sobs. She whipped the notebook she was holding behind her back, not because she was ashamed of reading it without permission, but because she had to get rid of it. She looked at Pilar's bewildered face, which she could see clearly from the partially opened door, and tried to ascertain whether she had read all those things. She remained frozen in that pose for several seconds, undecided about what to do. Then, resolving that it was futile, she gave up trying to hide the notebook and let it drop onto her lap, like an offensive obscenity. She asked in a defiant voice, striving to conquer her shame:

"Have you read this notebook?"

Pilar was taken aback. She replied in a near stammer:

"I'm reading it, yes."

"How much have you read? All of it?" The question that had started out imperious ended up like a supplication. She seemed to be saying, please say no, I beg you, say you haven't read it. Finding it hard to understand this odd behaviour of

Müesser's, Pilar said uneasily, "No. I haven't finished it yet. But I'm near the end." Then she asked timidly:

"Why do you want to know?"

Müesser was more interested in satisfying her own curiosity than in answering Pilar's questions. Which is why she replied with a question of her own:

"What was the last dream you read?"

Pilar turned pale and took a step backwards. She found Müesser's manner disturbing, even a bit frightening.

Müesser was worn out. She was exhausted, wretched, grief-stricken. With her hands she covered her face that she couldn't bear to let anyone see now and, ranting hysterically, resumed her sobbing, interrupted by Pilar's entry:

"I beg you, tell me, how much have you read? How much have you read? How much . . .?"

★ ★ ★

We're in the house in Istanbul, in the room I shared with my sister before I started school. I open my eyes in the middle of the night to the sound of the creaking door. My eyes, which have not yet grown used to the dark, see a large shadow looming there. I'm afraid. As the shadow makes its way into the room I realise the huge bulk belongs to my father, and relax. But he doesn't know I'm awake. Dragging his feet slowly, as though afraid of making a noise, my father goes to my sister's bed. Nudging the shoulder of my sister, who is oblivious of our late-night guest, he wakes her up. She sits up with a start. Her hair flows down her shoulders, like a long river. My father walks towards the door, turning to look at my sister, as though checking to see she is following him. My sister's shoulders droop, she places her feet, that she has removed from her warm bed, onto the rug. Then, ghostlike, she glides after my father. When I realise I am alone in the room, I'm afraid. Somewhere between sleep and wakefulness, I whimper, "Abla!" My sister bounds to my side and reassures me in whispers. I'm not placated immediately; she has to get into bed with me before I calm down. My father stands at the door, watching us. But he doesn't remain there for long; I can hear the sound of his feet dragging. His footsteps go to the room immediately beside ours and stop at my brother's door. Before drifting back to sleep I listen to the sound of the creaking door. I cling to my sister tightly.

When I wake up again my sister is sitting on her bed combing her hair. She's crying while she combs it. I can see her thin shoulders trembling. The wind blows its breath in through the open window and, like pregnant women, the curtains swell up, then deflate. The branches of the tree in the garden are beating against the window. My sister is sitting down combing her hair, her shoulders trembling.

I am awake. I wish I'd never woken up at all.

13
Pilar

Hold these cowardly hands of mine endlessly sought
Jump over these houses these houses and these
And let's gaze at the sky.
                    Turgut Uyar, "The Sky Gazing Stop"

Stunned by Müesser's indignant outburst, Pilar remained rooted at the door. The poor woman was obviously having some sort of nervous breakdown brought on by the trauma of her brother's sudden demise. She had been battling to stay strong since yesterday, but in the end it had all been too much for her and she had exploded. Up to that point it made sense, but Pilar couldn't understand the rest. For a start, what was Müesser doing in that room? And what did recent events have to do with Eyüp's notebook? And what was written in it that could have provoked this emotional earthquake? True, from what she had read, Eyüp, bless him, had said things that might have hurt Müesser, just as they had her, but Müesser seemed to be the type who would stab herself with the shards of her own broken heart. She couldn't be kicking up such a fuss just because she was offended.

She advanced fearfully towards the hysterically sobbing woman. Afraid of seeming to undermine her grief, she asked: "What's the matter? Did something happen while I was out?"

"Lots of things," said Müesser through her tears, but did not elaborate, forcing her eyelashes to battle with the relentless downpour once again. People couldn't always be mild and reasonable; Müesser obviously lost her rag from time to time too. She must fill up and up, and then empty herself, like a cracked glass that leaks water. Otherwise she would overflow as she was doing now and get wounded in her own flood. Pilar waited patiently for her to calm down, watching the weary movements of her exhausted body. Now, as Müesser sat before her, crying, her shoulders trembling, the woman who usually looked older than her years looked more like a little girl. Seeing her in that state made Pilar want to comfort her, but they had long gone past the stage where words could bring any solace. With no idea of how Müesser would react, and without really giving it much thought, she reached out for her hair and stroked it gently, as though afraid of hurting her; she stroked her hair and the afflicted head covered by each one of those hairs ... They remained that way for some time in silence, fingers and hair merged together. The two women, unknown to one another, met each other all over again, side by side, knee to knee, wordlessly, without looking. Then, under the effect of the affectionate sympathy she had been craving for so many years, Müesser's lips, tired of being sealed, slowly began to open, like heavily rusted, weighted, double doors:

"He hasn't been running away from us all this time for nothing," said the woman in a strangled voice, trying to suppress her sobs. "He always knew something, but wasn't aware of exactly what. He hid what he saw behind a thick curtain. If only he had never opened it. If only he had stayed far away from us; if that's what would have made him happy ... How will he ever bear what he remembers now?"

"What are you talking about Müesser?" Pilar's voice was like glass, if its pitch rose any higher, it would crack right down the middle. Müesser, for her part, seemed to have a need to first of all wreak havoc and wreck everything around her, and then put it all clean out of her mind.

"See, you want to know too! Why does everyone want to know everything? People are crushed under the weight of what they know. They either surrender to the things they know, or become their victim. How does Eyüp think he'll cope now with all these things he insisted on finding out?"

Pilar tried to make sense of what she was hearing, but could not. She searched Müesser's face for the tiniest clue, but found none. But she understood that the woman was filled to bursting point and needed to offload; she would feel much better if she talked about it. And she understood once again that she had things to learn from Müesser.

"Tell me," she said. Her voice was gentle, soothing, it inspired trust. She was like a hypnotist putting someone into a trance. "Tell me, I might be able to help you."

"Help?" whined Müesser, smiling bitterly. She was like a wounded animal, looking as though she would prefer to die rather than recover. First she wiped the agonised smile off her face, then, with surprising speed, she unwound, like yarn unravelling from its ball. Like bitter water being poured from one glass to another, she spoke, of what she wanted to forget and Pilar wanted to hear . . .

When Müesser left the room, like a corpse searching for its grave, Pilar's face was as white as a sheet, her heartbeat lame. The story she had listened to without saying a single word had rent her soul to pieces and turned her mind into a bombsite. The tale she had heard was so hard to digest that the narrator didn't once look her in the face during her account. She was mortified to have to disgorge her secret, but, convinced that after all this she couldn't keep it hidden any longer, she had related it in blood-curdling detail, as though anxious to purge herself of all the venom inside her.

Müesser had told her everything, without interruption. About the infernal visits her father paid to her bedroom at night . . . About her mother's inability to awake from her deep sleep and her obstinate determination to remain oblivious to those brutal intrusions . . . About how, for years, she had barely made it through the night for her terror of the sound of those slippers approaching to summon her to the living room . . .

She had kept Eyüp in her room until he started school. That's why her father would enter the bedroom, wake his daughter, march her down to the living room and do whatever he was going to do to her there. One night, as she was following him out of the room, Eyüp had woken up and, fearing the dark, called out for his sister. Using him as an excuse, Müesser had run back to her bedroom. As she listened out for the sounds from the hallway, her blood ran cold when she realised that, instead of retreating, her father had entered the adjacent room. She had wanted to go in and save her brother, but hadn't dared. She was young, she was helpless and she was weak. Müesser had no strength to fight her father. No one in the house did. Not even her mother, and in fact, maybe that was why she slept so soundly.

That night, which marked the turning point of her shared destiny with her brother, she wasn't able to do much else other than cower in her bed in fear and misery and pray to God the same thing never happened to Eyüp. During the following nights the footsteps had sometimes stopped at her door, sometimes at her brother's. Müesser faced the hardest test of her life during that period. When she heard the footsteps in the hallway she prayed he wouldn't come to her room, but when the footsteps stopped at the adjacent door she was consumed with guilt for her prayers. Müesser gradually became more and more withdrawn, while Veysel's face became more haggard by the day. From her brother's shamefaced, weary looks, she understood that he too lay awake at night and that he knew what went on in the next room. But still they said nothing to each other; they didn't so much as hint at what was happening. Life continued to flow, and they were growing up in the depths of hell.

The man, who felt free to visit Veysel in his single room, was afraid of waking his noisy youngest son and consequently woke his daughter up and ordered her to the three-seater sofa in the living room. Who knows how many times Müesser had prayed to God on that sofa, asking Him to wake her mother from her sweet dreams. With some tragedy if need be, with a flood that would engulf everything, with a fire that would never be extinguished or an earthquake that would bring the house down on their heads . . . Anything, as long as she woke up. But

Hafize Hanım, who dropped off into the soundest sleep the moment her head hit the pillow and didn't wake up even if a cannon was fired, never once got up, even to go to the toilet. Sometimes Müesser thought about screaming and waking her mother up, getting the entire household up, but she lacked the courage. What if her mother blamed her, what if she said it was all her daughter's fault? Or what if she didn't believe her? That's why Hafize Hanım slept as though she had gone into deep hibernation; she slept through it all. Her soul was oblivious to everything, until once, in the dead of the night, Veysel did what his sister had not dared; plucking up all his courage, he had stolen into his mother's room and tapped her awake with his finger. And after that night she never slept peacefully again. That same night her husband fell into a deep sleep. And after that night he never woke up again.

Everything that had taken place that night and all the nights before it had remained hidden inside the hapless association composed of her mother, her brother and herself, or rather, that's what Müesser had thought. After Rıfat Bey's death, no one had been inclined to discuss the matter ever again. They had hoped that, with time, secrets that were shrouded in silence would fade away and disappear. But every scene of that memory was so thoroughly ingrained in them, that for years, all they could read on one another's faces was that curse. Somehow they had not been able to get away from that heartless story that would persist forever and ever as long as they lived; they had known hell through each other.

As Pilar listened, she watched each and every one of the scenes that unfolded in her mind. She saw the unseeable, she heard the unhearable. Her ears rang, her eyes opened wide in terror. She bit her lips, because she had nothing left to say. How much of all this was Eyüp aware of? Was that why he had run away from his family? Or did all this have any connection with his leaving her? She didn't ask any of those questions. But as Müesser spoke, several of the shadows in her mind began to clear, one by one. Even that cursed three-seater sofa that Eyüp had made such a stand against took on a whole new meaning.

Müesser spoke non-stop, as though compulsively unravelling a defective piece of knitting. She related everything, and for the first time ever in her life ... As she spoke, the seconds that passed between them grew longer, becoming hours, days, months, years and suspending themselves from the walls. But, as the words ricocheted off them, the white walls enclosing the room were completely oblivious of time's altered rhythm. As far as they were concerned, it had all happened in the wink of an eye, before the words were smacked on lips with relish, before they could sell the tickets for the show, before hearts were properly cauterised, the secret had been unravelled. Telling your troubles, making sense of your troubles was arduous, but how easy it was to listen to the troubles of others! The walls wanted to listen to much and understand little; Müesser wanted to relate little and not be understood at all. The walls said, "Is that all? Is that all?" Pilar's distraught ears desired only to be plugged and to turn deaf.

Müesser related all; Pilar wept throughout her narration. Then Müesser gently dropped the notebook on her lap onto Pilar's lap, so she would understand why she was telling her all this now. And, dragging her feet, she left. The venom she had expelled had spread all over the room; an intense smell of putrefaction hung on the air.

Pilar was devastated. Her insides were as dark and shattered as the walls were white and indifferent. But she still didn't know what the things she had discovered had to do with Eyüp's notebook. In the last dreams she had read, Eyüp had remembered his acquaintances and some of his memories. Assuming the dreams that followed had any connection with what Müesser had just told her, was Pilar ready to face it? She didn't want to know any more, but the secret wasn't only upsetting, it was contagious. She opened the notebook and started reading from where she had left off.

When she eventually put the notebook down, her head was spinning, her eyes had turned into two balls of fire that burned with searing flames. While she was on the plane reading the sentences Eyüp had started to write with the facetiousness of an impish child, it hadn't occurred to her that his dream hunt would end up in such a dark tunnel. She had assumed her husband's dreams were like everyone else's and that what he would remember would be run-of-the-mill nightmares such as falling from a height, or no sound coming out of his mouth when he screamed. It wasn't difficult to deduce that he hadn't exactly had the happiest of childhoods, but she had never imagined anything like this. She had thought bad things only happened to strangers; she had trusted in that!

Pilar looked at the notebook again, as though reproaching an old friend who had offended her. She understood now that even the dreams that had started off completely innocently had provided the clues to the tragedy, like an earthquake gradually rising to the surface. But because she had only managed to see the signs she was prepared for, she hadn't noticed those parts, or been capable of putting them together. Although she was interested in her husband's writings, she had used her inability to read Turkish as an excuse and taken her time. Perhaps, subconsciously, she had evaded it. On the other hand, this last part had not just shed light on his dreams, it had elucidated many a black hole in her husband's character too. I'm so ingenuous, thought Pilar. Eventually coming to regard as normal the attitude of a man who didn't once feel the need to see his family in all those years, going on with her life without imagining that beneath that distance lay a truth no one wanted to touch, went beyond mere ingenuousness. In fact, nothing was coincidental. Absolutely everything that happened in this world did so for a reason. Even Eyüp's not taking his notebook with him, or Pilar's finding it and tossing it into her bag. In fact, might Eyüp have felt incapable of telling her what he had discovered and deliberately left it behind for his wife to read? Okay, so why hadn't he told Pilar? Because it wasn't so easy, was it? If something like that had happened to her, would she find it easy to talk about it? What would she do? Even trying to imagine it rent her to pieces. She gave up trying to put herself in Eyüp's shoes. If his coming to Istanbul was connected to what was written in that notebook, then maybe that was why he had left without telling his wife, because he didn't know how to tell her.

Because there were no dates on the dreams, Pilar didn't know when her husband had had them. But she imagined it had been in the past week, when he had been working late in his studio. Most probably the poor man's exhaustion wasn't just down to the panel he was making for the shopping centre. Who knows what had been going through his head as he tried to act as though everything was normal, despite what he had remembered? Under those circumstances, of course someone might wish to be alone. He might well do things that were out of character. Like, for example, follow the trail of the past and come all the way here to settle old scores. But which scores would he settle, and with whom?

Pilar wanted to lie down and sleep. Only then could she retire momentarily from the truths that were shredding her insides. She had discovered it too late, but what bliss it was to be ignorant! However, the moment she closed her eyes, shadows swarmed into the darkness of her mind. Sometimes she visualised Müesser as a little girl, following a man into the living room, and sometimes she saw Eyüp at the foot of a stairwell watching a murder film. Eyüp had run away from this house where they all inflicted such damage on each other, and saved himself. But what about poor Müesser; had she been condemned to sit on the sofa where her father had sweated and panted on top of her for so many years? No matter how many times they had changed the sofas, Müesser was still here. She hadn't managed to escape from this house, where even the sofas had found a way out. She had lain down to die within these four walls. Not just that, but even her grave was ready; she would be laid beside her father! Life shouldn't be like this, thought Pilar; no one should die so many deaths. And with that, her eyes slowly began to close.

That night she dreamt she was in a dark well with Eyüp. They climbed up with great difficulty and scrambled out of the well together. Eyüp said, "Wait for me here, I need to sort out a few things, I'll be right back." Then Pilar found herself in the square behind the San Sebastian Cathedral, with the crowds watching the Aizkolaritza log-chopping competition. Just as she used to do when she was a child, she perched on top of a low roof with other children, watching the game that is the Basques' national sport. As the contestants brought their axes down on the logs they were standing on, she went back to the days of her past and felt the old excitement. Contestants numbers one and five were way ahead of all the others and were heading towards victory neck and neck. Pilar looked at number one – there was lust written all over his face, his mouth foamed as he swung his axe. He filled her with revulsion. Number five on the other hand was resolute and patient. She couldn't see his face because he was bent down over his log, but he was the one she was hedging her bets on. He emanated peace, he even seemed to feel compassion for the logs he was chopping into pieces. He didn't want it to be that way, but somehow, because he had no choice, he was doing his utmost to win the contest. Pilar could sense that and wanted number five to win. In the end, numbers one and five jumped onto their last logs at the same time. The first one to split the log underneath him into two would be the winner; excitement was at its peak. Time stood still, the only audible sound was the axes striking against the logs: thwack, thwack, thwack ... Unable to bear the excitement, Pilar closed her eyes. At the sound of the final whistle there was an almighty burst of applause in the square. That was when she opened her eyes. The first thing she saw was the fuming face of contestant number one. Realising her favourite had won, she let out a squeal of joy. When contestant number five started running towards her, their eyes met for the first time: she couldn't believe it. She knew this man, and she had missed him so badly! She jumped down from the roof so she could reach him more quickly. Contestant number five held out his arms and caught Pilar in the air. And then he hugged her tightly, without putting her down. Pilar threw her arms around his neck with delight. "Uncle Ander," she said "Look at how much I've grown."

When she woke up, it was seven o' clock. She sat up in bed and leaned against the wall. She tried to recall Uncle Ander's face. His catching her in the air, his tight hug . . . The images from her recent dream seemed to be fluttering out of her mind one by one. The square with the lined-up logs, the children sitting on the rooftop with her grew hazy, one by one. Uncle Ander . . . Pilar wanted to protect her dream before it too faded away and disappeared from her mental photograph. It suddenly occurred to her to do as Eyüp had done and immortalise her dream by writing it down. But where would she write it? Eyüp's dream diary still sat on the bedside table, but because she had no wish to open it again, she hastily reached for her bag. As she was rummaging through it, hoping to find a scrap of paper, her fishing line hooked the tiny red notebook Vehbi had given her. She took it out and placed it in front of her. But in that space of time she had become totally alert, the effects of the dream had worn off and she had woken up completely to the stark truth that she had put off during the night by going to sleep. When she remembered what she had discovered last night she no longer felt like writing down her dream, nor doing anything else, the whim stuck in her throat. She wished she hadn't woken up, that she hadn't remembered. As she wearily turned over the notebook she had picked up for the first time since she had received it, a tiny card floated out from between the pages and fell into her lap. Pilar picked it up and looked at it, without much interest. *Razzle Dazzle Palace/Özel Caddesi, Elvan Sokak, N°7 Beyazıt.*

After she had gazed vacantly at the card for a while, imagining it must be a hotel and trying to work out why it sounded familiar, the answer finally hit her. That's right, when Vehbi first came and sat at their table he had talked about that hotel whose proprietor he said he had gone to visit after the mosque, and he had even poked fun at its name. At first she assumed he had tossed the notebook into her bag as a useful gift, without checking what was inside it. After all, he hadn't bought it for Pilar, he had given it to her as an afterthought. In other words, the card being there was a coincidence, a mistake even. But then she paused . . . What had İlhami said yesterday? Hadn't he said Vehbi may know where Eyüp was? Hadn't he mentioned his friend's compassion, his inability to remain indifferent to Pilar's distress? And in fact, wasn't she going to see him in the coffee house today, precisely hoping that would be the case? Okay, so could the fact that a hotel business card fell out of the notebook Vehbi had given her be more than just a coincidence? Pilar tried to recall the moment when he had given her that notebook. Vehbi had presented it to her just as she was about to leave, at the last moment, and after the briefest of hesitations. And before he had given it to her he had reached into his bag and rummaged inside it for a while. Pilar replayed those scenes to herself, as though rewinding a film. Years ago she had read in a book that people store a great many images in their brain without being aware of it. Just as in Eyüp's case, people knew a lot of things they thought they didn't and, with a bit of effort, could pull them out of their hiding place. Pilar strained to remember the moment when Vehbi had taken the red notebook out of his bag. He had reached inside and taken something red out of it. Then he had continued to search in the bag, even though he was holding that red thing in one hand. In other words, if that red thing was the notebook Pilar was now holding, the man had continued to rummage for something even after he had found the gift he was going to give her. The photographs in the archive didn't show the rest, but Pilar now believed Vehbi may well have put the card inside the notebook intentionally. Perhaps he was guiding her to Eyüp's location! Okay, but if he really knew where Eyüp was and wanted to tell Pilar, then why had he been so cloak-and-dagger about it? Most probably he was too loyal to reveal the secret he had been entrusted with, but too compassionate to bear to see Pilar so wretched, when she had come all the way to Istanbul in search of her husband. In fact this behaviour was precisely in fitting with everything she had ever heard about him. Maybe, even though he hadn't been able to bring himself to tell Pilar the truth, he may have devised a way of leaving her a tiny clue that would lead her to the answer. Even if Pilar didn't pick up on that clue, which was far from obvious, Vehbi would at least have eased his conscience by thinking he had tried to help the woman, but without betraying his friend's confidence. Just as she was thinking this was all way too far-fetched, she was suddenly struck by another detail, which hadn't seemed all that significant before. Vehbi had been completely taken aback to see Eyüp's wife in Istanbul, but had been quite nonchalant about his friend's coming to Istanbul and not contacting him. It was as though he already knew Eyüp was here, and the person he wasn't expecting to see was Pilar. She hadn't thought that that day, because there hadn't been any reason to think it. Today she was holding the business card of a hotel in which she suspected her husband might be staying. If her suspicions turned out to be right, then Vehbi had given her a much bigger gift than she had at first thought. Just as her husband had written in his dream diary ... Could it really be true?

When she crept out of the house, fearful of waking everyone up, it was almost eight o' clock. They would be surprised not to find her at home when they woke up; they might even think she had left. Müesser in particular would be distressed, thinking after last night she hadn't wanted to stay in this house a moment longer and had departed without telling anyone. But then she would see her bag and breathe a sigh of relief, before once again exercising her talent for finding things to worry about and fretting about what might have pushed her sister-in-law to take to the streets at the crack of dawn. If she intended to look for the notebook, hoping to read it again, or to destroy it to free herself, she wouldn't find it. Like a newly-appointed payroll clerk, who wants to make sure the money is safe, Pilar patted her bag. She relaxed when she felt the reassuring bump. Its contents were too dark for her to ever allow them to be made public. The notebook must not be presented to inquisitive eyes, the curse of the story it held must not be spread. Which is why, thinking the safest place for it was with her, she had tossed it into her handbag.

She hailed a taxi and handed the card to the driver.

"To this hotel, abla?" The driver hadn't realised she was foreign.

She limited herself to whispering, "Yes." Then, with the resignation of a saint who has learned that silence is the only answer, she remained quiet, not once opening her mouth until they drew up in front of the hotel. She immersed herself in daydreams compiled from memories.

She was intoxicated by the early morning breeze blowing in through the open window and surrendered the right side of her face to a sweet drowsiness. As a child she had loved climbing into the back seat of the car and losing herself in purple daydreams, flowing gently, along with the road . . . Now, on the way to the hotel where she hoped she was about to find her husband, she was once again in a dream world similar to the one from the old days. Because dreaming was a miraculous medicine for coming to terms with life's harsh realities. That's why Pilar fantasised about the waves in Lisbon all the way there. Haunting fados had echoed in the distance. She and Eyüp had walked through narrow streets, climbed up a hill and gazed on the city's red roof tiles. Amalia Rodrigues's breath had blown after them. The fantasy of that first holiday they had had together had brought the smell of iodine with it. When the driver's voice brought her back down to earth, part of her was still floating in her romantic daydream.

"We're here, abla."

She quickly pulled herself together and checked the meter. She took the money out of her bag that was weighing her down as though she were carrying thousands of kilos, handed the money to the man and leapt out of the car.

The moment she entered the modest building, that was more like an apartment block than a hotel, the smell of ammonia assailed her nostrils. Someone had obviously woken up early and cleaned away the dirt and debris left over from the previous day. Although it was old, the building was spick and span inside and inspired wellbeing. As she looked at the large potted plants lined up in the lobby, Pilar wondered whether there were any maggots inside them, and whether everyone had as many maggots inside them as she did.

"Good morning," said the smiling young man at the reception desk. He looked as though he wasn't yet 20. His teeth and shirt collar were white and sparkling.

"Good morning."

"How can I help you?"

How could he help her? So much had happened, she felt incapable of condensing all the thoughts racing around her head into a simple sentence and asking for assistance. She was looking for her husband. A man who, whilst trying to shed light on the dark holes in his past, was now in danger of sending his entire life reeling into darkness. Someone whose shoes no one wanted to be in. Her beloved, whom she feared might harm himself because the horror of what he had remembered was too terrible to endure. And she could sense he was somewhere nearby. Just as they had inhaled the smell of iodine together in Lisbon, she felt as though they had walked through these ammonia flames together too. Right now both their heads needed to be thoroughly cleansed. It was so white in here, so clean. Like a robe designed for a pristine suicide. Pilar shuddered in alarm at the thoughts going through her head. "Eyüp Bahriyeli," she whispered. The young boy merely stared at her out of eyes like two bewildered olive stones embroidered on a canvas. Pilar didn't know whether to attribute his puzzled expression to his not knowing anyone by that name, or to his not having heard her whisper. Clearing her throat and raising her voice, this time she enquired which room Eyüp Bahriyeli was in. She didn't want to ask if he was staying at the hotel, because if she did she risked receiving a negative reply. Pilar was anxious for this hide-and-seek adventure to be over as soon as possible. The fewer the questions, the fewer the answers, the sooner the outcome . . . She was anticipating meeting Eyüp in the flesh very shortly. Impatient to see the effect his name would have on this young boy, she searched for a reassuring sign on his radiant, clean-shaven face.

The receptionist's eyes lit up the moment he heard "Eyüp". He flashed her a broad, confident smile, reflecting his relief at knowing her request was within the realms of his competence. It was obviously good news then. Perhaps her husband was only a matter of minutes away. Perhaps there were just a few stairs separating them. Pilar held her breath so she could hear better what the boy would say to her.

"Eyüp Bey is in room 301, but he's just left."

Pilar was sufficiently level-headed not to despair at having missed him by a hair's breadth, instead her heart leapt with joy at knowing she had finally hit the right target. But then it suddenly occurred to her, what if Eyüp never came back? What would happen then, would he go back on the missing persons list?

"You mean he's left the hotel for good?"

"No madam, he hasn't checked out. He's just gone out."

But Pilar's mind was clouded by shadows now. Flustered by the recollection that finding and losing can mean the same thing, she was preparing to fire more questions at the boy when she realised the metal door that had waved Eyüp off shortly before inviting her in was opening again. The boy at reception greeted the new arrival with a friendly, "Good morning, abi" that was concrete proof of their acquaintance. What's more, Pilar too was acquainted with the owner of those clumsy footsteps stomping on the tiles, making far too much noise. The visitor was none other than the person who had, albeit using the most peculiar method, summoned her to this hotel.

After greeting Pilar with a casual nod, Vehbi, who was making a terrible job of trying to act as if meeting here were the most normal thing in the world, asked the young boy at reception, as if out to confirm what he had heard on the way in, "Isn't Eyüp here?"

"He's just gone out, abi. The lady here was just asking about him too."

Pilar turned her frosty gaze on him, waiting for an explanation, but Vehbi must have been shying away from the moment when he would have to face her, because he carried on talking to the young boy:

"Do you know where he went? Did he say anything when he was going out?"

"No, abi, he didn't."

Pilar wasn't about to wait any longer. Her patience had reached its limit.

"Will you tell me what's going on?"

"When İlhami phoned last night to say Eyüp's brother had passed away, I wanted to come and tell him," replied Vehbi. But he knew full well it wasn't just that precise moment the woman was interested in.

At the end of her tether, Pilar declared impatiently, "That's enough! Don't you think it's time to come clean?" She couldn't bear to know less than others, who had nothing to do with it, about something directly concerning her own life. She didn't want to waste any more time on false questions and answers.

Realising the game was up, Vehbi, his face a picture of meek surrender, said, "Let's go and sit down over there," pointing at the nearby sofas.

Sinking into the sofa, Pilar asked, "Why didn't you tell me? Why did you hide it from me if you knew he was here?"

The young man hung his head, like a guilty child.

"He asked me not to tell anyone. I swore."

"In that case why did you put that card in the notebook?"

When he didn't reply straight away, this time Pilar asked uncertainly:

"It was you who put that card there, wasn't it? Or—"

"Yes, it was me."

"If you're telling me you didn't tell me the truth because you swore, then what was the point of putting the card in the notebook? I might not have seen it, and even if I did, I might not have understood the message you were trying to give me."

The man, who was obviously squirming as he tried to justify his illogical action, whispered, "That's why I put it there. When I saw you were so out of your mind with worry you had come all the way here . . ." And he tried to explain his reasoning.

Because he had vowed he wouldn't say anything to anyone, he couldn't open his mouth and speak, but neither could he just turn his back on Pilar's anguish. He had wanted to find a solution that would make him feel better without breaking his promise, in his haste that was the best idea he had come up with. To be honest, he hadn't thought there was much chance of Pilar picking up on his tiny clue and making it all the way here, but he had wanted her to, very badly.

"Cut out all the nonsense!" snapped Pilar. "I've never heard anything so ridiculous in all my life."

"You're so lucky," replied Vehbi. "Actually, compared with all the strange things that began with Eyüp's coming here, I'd say that is actually quite logical."

He said it so naturally it seemed reasonable to Pilar too. If anyone else had said that to her, she might have taken it as a subtle reproach, but she could see Vehbi had only said what he felt. Besides, what made him so peculiar was probably the way he immediately acted on whatever came into his head. When he saw Pilar looking so crestfallen and miserable he had put that card in the notebook because he couldn't bear to let her leave without doing something. In fact, all he had done was played a childish game to ease his conscience. But even still, he had shown Pilar more consideration than Eyüp.

"So, what is he doing here?"

"I don't know. All he told me was that he was going to chill for a bit, stay a few days and then leave without seeing anyone. He asked me to find him somewhere to stay."

"If he was planning to leave without seeing anyone, then why did he get in touch with you? As if he couldn't find a hotel without you in this huge city . . ."

"I don't know. Maybe he missed me."

Pilar didn't know what to say. After all, sometimes the right answer was so simple it didn't occur to anyone.

"Yes but what did he come here for?"

"He didn't tell me anything. I know as much as you do."

"But I don't know anything," protested Pilar. "He has kept me so far away from him I don't even know if he's alive or dead."

"You're right to worry of course, but I think you were a bit too hasty. The man asked you to give him a few days' breathing space, I wish you'd just stuck it out a bit. If you hadn't upped and come, he would have most probably gone back in a couple of days anyway. I mean, instead of getting all worked up and hitting the road straight away, if you could have been a bit more patie—"

"Just a minute, just a minute," interrupted Pilar. "No one asked me for a breathing space, or anything of the kind. Eyüp took himself off without a single word; he didn't say a thing."

"Okay, of course, it would have been better if he had told you face to face, but he couldn't bring himself to. But he did say, in the note he wrote you . . ."

"What note are you talking about?" exclaimed Pilar, trying to make sense of what was going on.

"The note Eyüp wrote you before he left. I think he left in a bit of a rush. For some reason he didn't speak to you, but he did leave you a note in the house telling you not to worry and stuff, and that he'd be back in a few days."

"I didn't see any note of the kind," grumbled Pilar. "Are you sure he left one?"

"Yes, he told me so himself. When he first arrived, when he was telling me not to tell anyone where he was. He said, "Even my wife doesn't know where I am, I don't want anyone to know." He couldn't believe his ears when he found out you were here. He was miserable about worrying you so much, but also a bit annoyed that you had seen his family and İlhami and got everyone mixed up in all this. Left to his own devices he wouldn't have told anyone he was here. But of course, now things have changed, everyone knows. And what's more, I don't know what made İlhami smell a rat, but he won't stop going on at me to tell him where Eyüp is."

"Did you say, a note?"

"Whatever, when I told him you and İlhami had come to my coffee house, he told me he'd written you a note. He didn't tell you where he was, but he did ask you to give him a few days to think. In other words, he couldn't understand why you were so worried even though he'd left you a note. Oh no, so you didn't see it! So it wasn't for nothing you were frantic with worry and came all the way here! I think he said he left it on his desk or something. If you didn't look around . . ."

"Of course I did!" said Pilar.

The instant she said it, she remembered the moment when she went into the study to get the address book, when all the papers on Eyüp's desk had flown up into the air as soon as she opened the door. The way she had quickly gathered up all the papers that had scattered in all directions and put them back on the desk, and then her rummaging in the drawers in case she found anything. The way she had searched far away for the answer that was right under her nose . . . Just then Eyüp's image came to life before her eyes. The man, who had woken up from his darkest dreams, was pacing up and down in the house, desperate to bury what he had learned and be free. Then, for some mysterious reason, he was deciding to come to Istanbul. To that hell, where everything had taken place, and from which he had run away for years without knowing the reason why, or had pretended not to know why. He was searching inside himself; he couldn't find the strength to tell his wife what was on his mind. Rather than fabricating some lie explaining his trip, he preferred to postpone the conversation he needed to have. He was going into the study, writing her a tiny note and leaving it on the desk, in a place where she would easily see it. Then Pilar thought of herself. She had returned from work, waited for her husband . . . Had she gone into the study prior to needing the address book? She had most probably just nipped in and out quickly. But she had seen no need to go in and sit down, or rummage around. In her mind, that was Eyüp's territory. Besides, even if she had thought her husband might leave her a note, she wouldn't have looked for it in the study, but on the living room table, or the fridge, or maybe even on the bed.

Pilar tried to re-enact her entry into the study to find the address book, her parting of the thick velvet curtains and her opening of the window. The papers on top of the desk that flew into the air, her gathering them up, her abandoning them on the desk like dead birds that have given up the fight on their very first migration. That note that she had dumped there to rot in the midst of all the other birds . . . The lost proof that her husband hadn't completely passed her over . . .

"So he left me a note," she murmured to herself.

"Do you know what it is that's upset him so much?"

"Yes," said Pilar wearily. "I think I do."

"Is it something that can't be put right? Is it really that bad?" It was clear that this man, who was trying to contain his curiosity out of respect for their privacy, was concerned about his friend. But Pilar didn't know the answer to that question either. She had never woken up from any nightmare to a truth as horrific as Eyüp's. She couldn't predict what happened when you picked at the thick scabs of old wounds. But still she said, "No, it isn't," to lighten the mildewed load in this kind man's heart. Trying to lighten the load of others was good for one's own self too. The time had come now to find Eyüp and try to soothe the paper cuts in his child's soul. Even if there was nothing she could do, she needed to be with him. Especially now she had told everyone he was missing and complicated things so much for him, and multiplied the number of people he would have to explain to . . . Ah, if only she had seen that note, would things have turned out this way? Pilar knew only too well that yes, they would have. She still would have hit the road, this time under the pretext of finding out what had affected her husband so badly as to drive him to leave home. She admitted now that she hadn't made this journey for Eyüp, but for herself. That when she set out she had been more anxious about the future of their relationship than about her husband . . . But here, once she had opened it up and looked inside, it was as though she had realised that love needed to be different, and she had felt ashamed of her selfishness. For the first time in her life she had experienced heartfelt grief for an affliction that didn't directly affect her. For the first time ever, someone else's wound had seared her flesh. She had had a whole new experience of compassion and love . . . She knew now that, no matter how this story was written, this was how they had to act it. Pilar would look for him and find him. And, if she was lucky, she would complete what was missing in him. She wasn't in the least bit angry with Eyüp anymore for not having chosen to tell her everything right from the start, instead of running away. It wasn't easy to say things you can't bear to whisper, even to yourself, out loud. But last night, Pilar realised as she was listening to Müesser that, just like unmourned deaths, unspoken words were painful. Sometimes, in order to be able to go on living, it was necessary to talk at great length, to cry your heart out and to try and cleanse yourself of the pitch of the past. Bottled up words must be liberated, built up tears must be shed freely, ungrieved deaths must be mourned one by one, so that the soul, which grows heavier as it withdraws into itself, weighing its owner down, can find joy at last. Because some burdens were much too heavy to carry alone throughout an entire lifetime.

Why was Eyüp here? she thought, for the umpteenth time, In this city, where everything had started . . . If all he wanted was to put his memory in order, he could have done that perfectly well in Barcelona. If he insisted on being alone, he could always have gone to a hotel or something. But no, he had come to Istanbul. Even if he wanted to confirm the truth of what he had remembered, wouldn't he have wanted to speak to his brother and sister? But no, he hadn't wanted to do that either. In that case why had he come here, what did he want? I wonder, thought Pilar, could he have come here to confront his demons at last?

Fixing her gaze on the large plant pots in the lobby, she asked Vehbi:

"Do you know what he's been doing here?"

"No, I don't. Several times when I've come to the hotel he's been out. He would nip out somewhere from time to time, but never mentioned where he went. And anyway, I never asked him."

"I think I know," murmured Pilar, without taking her eyes off the soil in the pots. Her mind had started to work like a butterfly struggling to emerge from its cocoon.

Standing up, she said to Vehbi, who was staring at her in bewilderment, "But please don't ask me, okay?" It was time she and Eyüp both became someone different.

"Stop here," she said to the taxi driver. She had found the green light that would lead her to her husband. Perhaps in a few minutes she would be standing face to face with Eyüp. She dreaded his eyes, demanding an explanation. His were eyes that had seen everything; would they not see Pilar's egotism? A self-centred European who couldn't see anything beyond herself, who couldn't bear to be excluded and was kicking and screaming to claim her place in her husband's and the world's centre ... Yes, because she lived in mortal terror of being abandoned and ending up alone, she had set out on this journey under the pretext that something terrible may have happened to her husband; she too knew that very well. She even liked the idea of being able to confess it. When all was said and done, she could have an honest relationship with herself. Yes, she had set out on this journey because she was afraid Eyüp might abandon her. But on that journey she had met people who had been abandoned by their own lives. And the dreams of a child who remained trapped in his past ... Now it was time to make a fresh start in getting to know herself and that child. They would do something they had never tried before and touch one another's wounds. That would turn them into genuine people, true lovers. Now it was time to build new hopes, have new dreams. Pilar didn't know how she would go about it yet. She hadn't even thought about what she would say to him. What could she say to the 37-year-old version of the child who had fallen asleep by the banisters? What could one taciturn person, who had subjected his shoulders to the yoke of a heavy secret, say to someone else?

Given that everyone was finally naked, the time had come for them to snuggle up together to protect themselves from the cold. They would not kiss their most attractive parts anymore, but each other's wounds, and slowly, heal them. Most probably in the beginning, like a child's first steps, they would be fearful and unsteady. Like birds venturing to take their first flight, the flapping of their wings would be fragile. Perhaps a little timorous, retiring, reserved and bashful ... But there was no doubt they would succeed in emerging triumphant from the obscurity together, in taking a deep breath. In breathing in each other's lungs and climbing with each other's nails ... With these thoughts in her head, Pilar stood on the ground more firmly. She embarked on the path that would lead her to Eyüp, with conviction.

She imagined she would find him beside Rıfat Bahriyeli's grave weeping, or furiously demanding explanations. She imagined she would find him standing beside the aged marble, preparing words that would attempt to penetrate its rigidity ... In fact, he was neither at the graveside of his father, whose memory had dragged him all the way here, nor was he snorting through the nose, enveloped in a cloud of rage ... He was crouched down in silence beside the newest grave in the family plot, staring at the pigeon walking timidly up and down in front of it. He was a small child crouched down before the banisters. He was looking for someone who could explain the notes he had written in his arithmetic book, but clearly couldn't find anyone. Seeing her husband in that state filled Pilar with tenderness. She wanted to run to him, hug him tightly, save his soul from every fire. But because she wasn't sure how to go about penetrating a silence to which she was not invited, instead of flinging herself into his arms, she stood there, waiting for him to notice her.

Eyüp didn't seem overly surprised when he became aware of his wife. He simply raised his eyes from the ground and, with the long suffering affection he would show a naughty child, said, "So, you found me in the end?"

Pilar, who had spent the entire journey there trying to think of ways of confessing that she had read his notebook, realised, when her eyes met Eyüp's, that there was no need to say anything. Her husband already knew that she knew everything ...

"I found you. I came," she replied, with the brittle syllables of a nervous child. But then she paused, one by one she shooed away the pigeons that had landed on her voice and added, in her most obstinate, most compassionate, most belligerent, most loving tone, "Whenever you call, I'll be there. Even if you don't call, I'll be there."

The face of Eyüp, whose gaze was fixed on something in the distance, as though struggling to remember an old song, lit up, if only for a few seconds. His eyelashes flickered, a delicate spring nestled on the corner of his lips, the pigeon on the ground departed hastily. First of all, Eyüp blossomed in an unexpected season, then, awakening from the spring outside to the autumn inside, he shed his leaves. Indicating the grave in front of him he whispered, as though revealing a secret he had guarded for years:

"Do you know what? Until yesterday I could have said so many things to him."

"Perhaps you still can."

"To hell with it," said Eyüp to his wife, letting the soil fall through his fingers. "It doesn't do the living any good to try to talk to the dead. They're not interested in the words that call them. You should say whatever you have to say to the living. You should say it while you still have time."

Pilar gazed at her husband's childlike eyes lovingly.

"Stand up in that case," she said, holding her hand out to him. Eyüp eyed the friendly hand willing to pull him out of dark wells and blinked. He asked in his most innocent, defenceless voice:

"Where are we going?"

"Somewhere where there are people who are still living."

As he was standing up supported by the hand his wife was holding out to him, Eyüp pointed to the family plot and said, "Don't let them put me here one day, okay?"

Swallowing the lump in her throat, she nodded to her husband. The seal had been broken. Even if it was too late for the dead, the destiny of the living would change. And naturally, when the time came to change his abode, Eyüp's lifeless body would not be buried in that autumn garden that had been withered by that cursed memory. She squeezed her husband's hand, as though to reassure him of that. A gentle breeze blew, the trees rustled above their heads. Leaning against one another, they started walking. The soil too walked in their wake. As did the sky and the clouds. A few hours later the Moon would come between the World and the Sun, like a giant curtain; there would be a total eclipse of the Sun and secrets would come out into the open. And, once there had been an eclipse, nothing would ever be the same again.

"Last night I had a dream," Pilar started explaining. "I was with you. In a pitch black well . . ."

As each of them dragged their weary footsteps after the other's, the cruel carnival of hearts that constrict with pain on this earth continued. The season was summer, the month was August. It was the last year of the 1990s. Each household, each closed door embroidered its own ill-fated secret on the lacerated, dilapidated embroidery frame of affliction. The first ones who would be saved in a fire were the first to be sentenced to die by the death committees. Women and children were the first to be carved on the white marble of the gravestones. The victims' dates were written over and over again, along with their vows of silence. But alas, hope was so indispensable, the taste of living so strong, that after every unrest, life-saving blood was sought out urgently, for a story that was yet to be written . . .

As all of this was occurring on land, the earth's crust, grown heavy with the load it carried, unable to bear the heaving inside it a moment longer, prepared to crack at any minute. Because, in the absence of friends with whom it could fill up and overflow, sooner or later it would have to disgorge. To avoid rotting inside and being destroyed completely . . .

Glossary and Translator's Notes

Abi: A respectful but affectionate term for an older man, usually, but not always, an elder brother

Abla: A respectful but affectionate term for an older woman, usually, but not always, an elder sister

Acemkebabı: A thick stew made from lamb, pulses and vegetables

Acıka: Spicy breakfast dip made from tomato puree, walnuts, garlic, chilli and spices

Adile Naşit: One of Turkey's best-known and best-loved actresses, an icon of classic Turkish cinema, who usually, but not always, plays comic roles

Allâhümme bârik: Namaz prayers beseeching God to grant prosperity and abundance on the Prophet and his people

Allâhümme salli: Namaz prayers beseeching God to grant mercy and grace to the Prophet and his family

As-Sirāt Bridge: The bridge, as narrow as a hair strand, which everyone must cross on the day of judgement in order to enter paradise

Bayram: One of two Muslim festivals, the first being at the end of Ramadan and the second the Feast of the Sacrifice, whereby an animal, usually but not always, a lamb, is sacrificed and the meat distributed to relatives, neighbours and the poor

Bismillahirahmanirrahim: In the name of God, most Gracious, most Compassionate – repeated by Muslims when embarking on any significant endeavour

Börek: Pastry parcels filled with meat, cheese or vegetables

***Canım Kardeşim* (My Beloved Brother)**: The tragic film that Eyüp describes in his dream on pp. 275–77

Dolma: Vine or cabbage leaves (or vegetables such as peppers, onions or potatoes) stuffed with rice, onions, tomatoes, mint, olive oil and lemon juice, or meat

Fatiha: The opening chapter of the Quran

Halit Akçatepe: Very well-known Turkish actor, who usually plays comic roles

Hanım: Respectful title used to address a woman; more formal than "abla"

Helva: Halva – sweetmeat, mostly made with semolina or flour, sugar syrup and almonds; often distributed at funerals in honour of the soul of the deceased

Kahraman: The name Kahraman means "hero" in Turkish

Kimse Şah Değil Padişah Değil: Song by Sibel Can

Köfte: Patties or balls usually made with meat, onions and spices, but sometimes with lentils

Kuru fasulye: A stew made with white kidney beans and tomato sauce, typically eaten by the poor, but extremely popular amongst all social classes

Mashallah: (Arabic) Praise be to God!

Metin Akpınar: Highly acclaimed Turkish actor

Mevlit: Islamic memorial service consisting of the recital of a long poem in Arabic about the life of Muhammed

Namaz: Islamic ritual prayers, performed five times a day at prescribed times

Placing the shoes of a dead person outside the door: According to some beliefs, the custom of placing a dead person's shoes outside the door, facing away from the entrance, is in order to keep death away from the house

Slapping girls who menstruate for the first time: In Turkey and in several other cultures it is customary to slap the cheeks of a girl when she menstruates for the first time. The official reason is "so that roses will bloom there"; however, it can seem like a punishment

Sübhâneke: Islamic prayer recited at the beginning of the namaz

Tarık Akan: A beau and icon of Turkish cinema.

Vallahi: Originally Arabic term meaning "I swear to God," often used as emphasis

Ve Celle Senâüke: A prayer recited exclusively by men at the funeral namaz

"Wait. Let's get it set up and working and *then* we'll wake him up": In the film that Eyüp describes in his dream on pp. 275–77 (*Canım Kardeşim*) Tarık Akan steals a television in the middle of the night to make the dying wishes of his younger brother (Kahraman) come true. His friend (Halit Akçatepe) wants to wake Kahraman up immediately, but Tarık Akan says they have to get the television up and working first. But when they eventually go into his room to tell the child he has his television, it is too late

Yenge: Name given to a brother's wife

Yeşilçam: Turkish cinema production company, representing the heart of Turkish cinema for many years

References

Melih Cevdet Anday, "Bu Kırlangıçlar Gitmemişler miydi?" ("Hadn't These Swallows Left?") *Sözcükler*, (*Words*), İş Kültür Yayınları, 1st edition, 2007.

Ece Ayhan, "Anahtarlar" ("Keys"), *Şiirimiz Mor Külhanidir Abiler* (*Our Poem is a Livid Furnace Brothers*), YKY, 3rd edition, February 2011.

Yahya Kemal Beyatlı, "Nazar" ("The Evil Eye"), *Kendi Kök Kubbemiz* (*Our Own Base Dome*) Gençlik ve Spor Bakanlığı Yayınları, Türk Klasikleri, 1988.

Faruk Nafiz Çamlıbel, "Alçıdan Heykel ("The Chalk Statue"), *Han Duvarları / Toplu Şiirler* (*The Inn's Walls / Collected Poems*), YKY, 16th edition, October 2011.

Edip Cansever, "Ben Ruhi Bey Nasılım" (I'm Ruhi Bey How Am I) *Adam Yayınları*, 12th edition, 2001.

Şeyh Galip, "Gizli Sırların Ortaya Çıkışı" "The Coming Out of Hidden Secrets", *Hüsn ü Aşk (Güzellik ve Aşk) (Love and Beauty)*, intralinguistic translation: Ahmet Necdet, Adam Yayınları, 1st edition, April 2003.

Ahmet Haşim, "Bir Günün Sonunda Arzu" ("Wish at a Day's End"), *Complete Poems*, Can Yayınları, 1983.

Bilge Karasu, "Çeşitlemeli Korku," ("Variations of Fear"), *Kısmet Büfesi* (*Destiny's Kiosk*), Metis, 5th edition, December 2009.

Birhan Keskin "Salyangoz," ("Snail") *Yeryüzü Halleri (States of the Earth)*, YKY, 1st edition, January 2002.

Cemal Süreya, "Sizin Hiç Babanız Öldü Mü?" ("Has Your Father Ever Died?"), *Sevda Sözleri*, (*Words of Love*), YKY, 45th edition, January 2012.

Ahmet Hamdi Tanpınar, "Kış Bahçesinden" ("From the Winter Garden"), *Complete Poems*, Dergâh Yayınları, 2nd edition, 1982.

Turgut Uyar, "Göğe Bakma Durağı" ("The Sky Gazing Stop") *Büyük Saat/Bütün Şiirleri (The Large Clock/Complete Poems),* YKY, 11th edition, October 2011.

Cahit Zarifoğlu, "Savaştığımız Günler Kendimizle" ("The Era of Battle with Ourselves"), *Poems, Complete Works,* Beyan Yayınları, November 2000.